SING ME HOME TO CAROLINA

Also available by Joy Callaway

The Star of Camp Greene

What the Mountains Remember

All the Pretty Places

The Grand Design

Secret Sisters

The Fifth Avenue Artists Society

SING ME HOME TO CAROLINA

A Novel

JOY CALLAWAY

alcove press

Books should be disposed of and recycled according to local requirements. All paper materials used are FSC compliant.

This is a work of fiction. All of the names, characters, organizations, places and events portrayed in this novel are either products of the author's imagination or are used fictitiously. Any resemblance to real or actual events, locales, or persons, living or dead, is entirely coincidental.

Copyright © 2025 by Joy Callaway

All rights reserved.

Published in the United States by Alcove Press, an imprint of The Quick Brown Fox & Company LLC.

Alcove Press and its logo are trademarks of The Quick Brown Fox & Company LLC.

Library of Congress Catalog-in-Publication data available upon request.

ISBN (paperback): 979-8-89242-111-9
ISBN (hardcover): 979-8-89242-247-5
ISBN (ebook): 979-8-89242-112-6

Cover design by Heather VenHuizen

Printed in the United States.

www.alcovepress.com

Alcove Press
34 West 27th St., 10th Floor
New York, NY 10001

First Edition: June 2025

The authorized representative in the EU for product safety and compliance is eucomply OÜ Pärnu mnt 139b-14, 11317 Tallinn, Estonia, hello@eucompliancepartner.com, +33757690241

10 9 8 7 6 5 4 3 2 1

For my BFF, Maggie (Peg) Tardy—if you hadn't agreed to wear the matching pleather glow-in-the-dark pants, participate in my childhood plays, or made me laugh so much, there's a good chance Mountain View would've been a normal, boring town.

CHAPTER ONE

Mountain View, South Carolina was a staticky AM radio station. I barely turned the dial on Daddy's 1952 Chevy 3100 pickup, hoping that on a night this clear the satellites could help the signal over the hill in the distance and that Sam Cooke's "Twisting the Night Away" might override the white noise, the dying sigh of this town.

Sam had visited Mountain View once in 1958, back when his second cousin Ronald Robinson—a renowned songwriter and Nat King Cole's former guitar player who accidentally founded the town—was still sure Mountain View would become a sort of Camp David for musicians who wanted to get away from the limelight. Sam had played "You Send Me" in town square while the facades of the new downtown buildings, etched along their borders with music notes, were unveiled. Ronald had stood at a podium in front of town hall after and waxed poetic about how he and his wife Elita had been on their way to a new life in Georgia when their truck had been swallowed in mud so deep they were stuck for days and finally decided to stay. He'd said back then that Mountain View was a special place, a place that would thrive for centuries to come.

I'd always thought that his getting stuck was a trap. Mr. Robinson had been one of the most prolific musicians of his time. Instead of taking a break and then continuing to grace the world with his talents, he got marooned in nowhere South Carolina and became a peanut farmer. After tonight, I knew without a doubt that founding Mountain View had been a mistake. His former land, land that had been given to my parents twenty-two years ago as a fertile peanut farm, had now been deemed so minerally depleted that it was unfarmable by three different experts. My parents were so devastated they'd gone to bed immediately after they'd heard the news. When I suggested they could move to Charlotte with me, they'd only shaken their heads and retired to their room, insisting that the results were wrong and that they'd be okay after all. When I'd gone out to get in the truck tonight, I'd tried to envision my parents in Charlotte working ordinary city jobs and cried when I couldn't see them there. Their lives were crumbling beneath their feet. On the way down the driveway, I'd looked at Mr. Robinson's truck, still stuck in the dirt in the middle of our farm and thought that maybe getting stuck was the fate of the whole town.

I flipped the staticky radio off and cranked the window down. I breathed in the sweet smell of earth and green. Maybe it was the sound of burbling river water and crickets, the peace, the aroma of nature, that intoxicated everybody, making them cling to the belief that Mountain View was thriving. Back home in Charlotte, there was no such intoxication. The air smelled like asphalt and exhaust and my Citizen app constantly reminded me that those sharp pops in the night were, in fact, gunshots and not fireworks. The truth slapped you across the face in cities. In the country, it wore the mask of beauty and pretended to be your friend before it stabbed you in the back.

My phone sounded loudly from the passenger seat, startling me. I glanced over at a text from my high school friend Annie, who'd invited me to meet her for a drink at the bar. Or rather, at Fox's Hardware Store, which turned into a bar on Friday nights.

Where are you? Sterling's brought his disco lights again. You know what that means. Can't listen to his story about winning the breakdancing competition at the Hampton Inn in Myrtle Beach one more time.

I laughed. Sterling Manacusco was a hippie goat farmer who made his own fruit wine. You always knew he'd been leaning into a bottle of what he called his peach jubilee when he materialized at Fox's Hardware with his strobe lights.

Up ahead, the one stoplight at the corner of Route 2 and downtown blinked yellow. In the seconds of stagnant light, you could barely make out a group of bulldozers and backhoes in the distance at the Pine Summit-Mountain View border. Construction had started last week in Pine Summit to clear the sides of Route 2 for imminent expansion. The larger highway would provide easier access from I-85 to the proposed new Carolina Panthers stadium in either Mountain View or Cardinal River, the town just east of ours. The news that one of our towns would be chosen for the site had just been announced last month, sending the whole community into a tailspin. Columbia's *The State* newspaper had said that Mountain View and Cardinal River were perfect for the stadium because they happened to sit exactly between Charlotte and Greenville, making the Panthers a team truly shared by both Carolinas, and there was an Amtrak station nearby and enough open acreage that the state could swipe from farms.

Being selected would be Mountain View's worst nightmare, but I saw it as a saving grace. If Mountain View got the stadium, it might actually have a chance of surviving like Mr. Robinson had always hoped.

I turned on to Main Street. All of the streetlights had been extinguished at eight—the same lights-out policy had been in place since the forties—but even darkness couldn't mask the town's decay. Old Cheerwine advertisements from the seventies lined the windows in the shuttered general store, and rotting plywood boards patched broken windows from fallen debris or storms at Simpkins's Theater and the arcade and the coffee shop. The music notes carved in the limestone crumbled along the top border of all of the stores and some even appeared to be crying. I couldn't blame them. Living in this town would make me cry too. The only storefronts still in business were the Mountain View Bank, Paradise by the Dashboard Light Diner, the Cut & Curl—ladies still got their hair set once a week around here—and Fox's Hardware.

The hardware store was at the very end of town. Light poured from the expansive glass windows in alternating shades of yellows, pinks, and greens indicating Sterling was now flailing in circles at the back of the store, his limbs barely avoiding jars of local honey and bins of nails.

I turned the corner to pull in a parking spot and my body froze. My ex-boyfriend Leland Lockhardt's palomino quarter horse, Slugger, stood hitched to a railing bordering the sidewalk. Surely Lee wasn't home. He was starting shortstop for the Atlanta Braves, and they were in San Diego playing the Padres this week. Maybe his dad or brother had taken to riding his horse to town as a sort of tribute to Lee when he left. Daddy and Mama hadn't said he was back home either—but then again, they'd barely mentioned his name since our breakup.

Sing Me Home to Carolina

I pulled into a parking spot between Slugger and Fox's electric Ford F-150 that the whole town was buzzing about and got out of the car. The progression from horse to 1950s truck to 2024 electric truck appeared like a sort of transportation museum display.

I eyed Slugger one more time, patted his neck, and then squinted toward the store's windows, trying to figure if I needed to steel myself for the first in-person sighting of Lee in eleven years. The last time I'd seen him, we were in Mr. Robinson's truck, making out the night before I left for college, when he'd stopped kissing me to say that we should take a break instead of staying together long-distance, that Wake Forest and South Carolina were too far apart. I'd unraveled in that moment, saying I regretted our four years together and hated him. Hours later, he was hooking up with my friend Willow.

Although we'd followed each other on Instagram for a few years—until he'd deleted his account to focus more on the game—and I was *mostly* over what happened, the truth was that I wasn't entirely. I knew it was childish to be hung up on a high school breakup, but my heart didn't care. If I was honest, I'd never loved anyone else and that was probably the problem.

It wasn't like I hadn't moved on. I'd dated Austin, a Sigma Nu I'd met sophomore year of college at a frat party, for almost two years but had never been able to tell him I loved him back. Then, after college, I'd casually dated a few guys my friends called "The Jocks"—former running back turned nurse Kenny, and former point guard turned investor Harris. Although they were both fun, they weren't relationship material. Then there was Hunter, a sweet attorney I met at a networking event and stayed with for almost a year before realizing, when he told me he loved me, that our relationship was Austin all over again.

Something crashed inside the store. I could hear the distant sound of glass shattering and then a collective groan. Fox would be in a mood. Despite having only met him a handful of times since he took over after the old Fox's passing a few years back, it seemed he was always in a mood. Then again, he hadn't initiated the whole your-store-turns-into-a-bar-on-Fridays thing and I guess it was probably annoying to have to babysit the town on your off hours. I walked down the sidewalk toward the entrance. I caught my reflection in the swirly original glass windows and balked. I'd forgotten the state I was in—hair upswept for earlier farmwork, just-cried under eye bags accentuating my makeup-free face. I was wearing cutoff jeans—not the sort from a trendy boutique, but actual jeans I'd cut the legs off earlier that day—and a twenty-year-old T-shirt from my fifth-grade softball season.

I paused outside the entrance, staring at the patinaed copper double doors and the hammered tin sign reading Fox's Hardware, desperately trying to recall if I'd seen Lee playing on TV earlier. The game had been on when I left the house, but I hadn't paid it much mind in the wake of the latest soil expert's sentence. Surely, Lee was with the Braves out in California and I was working myself up for no reason. Then again, on days like today, when the world seemed to spin off its axis, running into your ex while looking like a cave dweller instead of making him weak in the knees as the hot sophisticated event planner you were made sense.

I took a breath, freed my hair from the elastic, and attempted to tousle the flat shoulder-length mess. I still wasn't used to the length. Then again, the nine inches I'd had chopped at the SaveCuts instead of the two I'd wanted were my own fault. Twelve-dollar haircuts were like roulette. You sat in the chair and took your chances.

The door flung open, nearly knocking me over, and Sterling stumbled out, his arm wrapped around his portable disco light console.

"Ain't nobody appreciate art no more, Hattie," he said, his eyes shaded by round Ringo Starr sunglasses. "I came by tonight to pep the place up. Even drove to Columbia and got me this Jheri curl 'cause I thought I'd sing a little Lionel after my breakdancing. Had to be ready for what the people wanted, but apparently they don't want a piece of Sterling tonight. Guess I'll settle for entertaining Vern when he gets home from the junkyard."

I grinned. "Vern's gain, everybody else's loss."

"They think crying into their drinks and listening to country music is going to fix the stitch we're in right now with the stadium, but it ain't," he said. "Might as well get funky today because being sore isn't gonna do nothing."

"That's right. In fact, I'm going to march in there and tell them they're a bunch of whiners," I said. The truth was that I was going to do no such thing. I had no right to. I'd be back home in Charlotte on Sunday. If the town wanted to lament the stadium potentially coming in and forever changing the sad state of Mountain View, that was their prerogative.

I opened the door and was immediately struck by the noise, the crowd, and the unchanging smell of earth and oil and new lumber. People stood or sat in every available space—on top of old bulb crates and behind the rows of barstools Fox set up in front of the glass display cases. Lee was nowhere to be found. The sound of an acoustic guitar barely sounded above the voices from the back of the store near the old Coke iceboxes. It was probably Tosha Foster playing through her songs again about the McDonald's closing. I was surprised people listened to her play about the magic of the golden arches. The town had boycotted the restaurant, because it was a chain, so effectively that it had shut down exactly a year after it opened, taking Tosha's hope of becoming Mountain View's guitar-playing Ronald McDonald with it. Rumor had it that she'd almost quit music altogether after it closed, even considering forfeiting her long-standing gig as dinner entertainer at the retirement home in Pine Summit, but her boss had given her a raise and she'd reconsidered. Still, it was clear she wasn't over the sting of losing the McDonald's. Sometimes Tosha was seen camping under the arches that were still firmly planted in the ground outside of town just to pay tribute to the dream she'd lost.

"Hattie!" I turned to see Annie sitting on Fox's cashier's stool tucked between the old oak counter and the windows. She held up her mason jar filled with what appeared to be Jack and Coke and gestured at me to take a seat beside her on the windowsill. I started over, pushing past Gene and Rascal Conrad to get there. In contrast to my farmhand couture, Annie was wearing a chic white feather-hemmed shirt dress that made her mahogany skin and black hair glow. I envied her hair. It cascaded in perfect waves nearly down to her waist. Then again, Annie was the mayor now. She probably thought she had to look perfect at all times.

Annie stood when I neared and gave me a hug.

"Gosh, you look exactly the same," she yelled over the voices. "How long has it been?"

"Maybe eight years? When Dolly threw Rocky that party to celebrate the Oscar Mayer job?" I said, letting her go and taking my seat on the uncomfortable windowsill. Dolly was my best friend since diapers.

"Oh, right," Annie said. She sat down, then extracted a pitcher from behind her as well as an empty mason jar. "Want some? Jack and cherry Coke." She didn't wait for me to answer before starting to pour.

"Sure," I said unnecessarily.

"Well, either way, it's ridiculous that it's been this long. Me, you, Dolly, Willow, Linds, Jess—us cheer girls used to be so close. But then I guess we all have jobs or families or both now and life is busy." She took a long sip. "I actually heard from Linds yesterday. She texted to see if I still had my old white choir robe. She got a new job at the Pine Summit Visitors Center as that fake ghost, Lavinia Astrid, and apparently the sheet she's been using keeps tripping her up when she runs through the camp site spooking visitors."

"Putting her theater skills to good use," I said. Linds had always been the lead in the annual Mountain View High musical. Annie laughed and I did too.

"Yeah, I guess she is."

Of the six of us, only half of us had conventional careers. Linds, Dolly, and Jess had gone the eccentric Mountain View way. Dolly and Rocky and their two kids were gone every weekend driving the Oscar Mayer Weinermobile all over the southeast, and Jess and her husband, Sawyer, were sign holders with the rodeo. The rodeo made me remember Slugger parked outside.

"Who's been riding Slu—"

My question died at the sound of a deep raspy voice singing the opening notes of Tom Petty's "Won't Back Down." I hunched over, my whole body seized by the implication of the sound. Lee *was* here. I yanked Annie toward me, nearly toppling her glass with the motion.

"Why isn't he playing baseball right now?" I whispered, as though there was a chance he could hear me over the noise. I lowered myself further until I was almost atop my knees. I couldn't see Lee from here, and I knew he couldn't see me. But still, I couldn't risk it. I always told myself I'd be poised and distantly friendly if I ever ran into him again, that he'd leave thinking he had absolutely no effect on me anymore, but judging by the way my heart was hammering and my cheeks were burning, I doubted I'd come off the way I hoped.

"He tore his rotator cuff super severely a few months ago. His baseball career is over," Annie said, looking at me like I'd asked the dumbest question in the world. "How did you not know this? It was all over ESPN, socials too."

I had to leave.

"The Leland Lockhardt Band—all of them—have been playing every Friday night. That's why it's been so crowded these past weeks," she continued. "Woody even quit his Nickelback cover band to come back."

"Wow," I said. "That's something. I guess that run in with Chad Kroeger at the state fair finally lost its luster?" I glanced around the packed room. "Remember when the guys tried to play that special concert for the town on the Fourth of July that year and only our group showed up?" Lee and his friends would bring out their guitars and sing at practically every party we threw, but the greater community never lined up to see them.

Annie laughed.

"Well, that was before Lee was an all-star baseball player." She paused and glanced at Duke who was funneling a glass of wine in front of us. "There's also a record amount of loan applications now that Lee's taken over his daddy's position at the bank."

"I wish everyone would get out," Fox grumbled to no one in particular, materializing from the only clear area in the store—behind his cash register.

"Oh, Foxy, don't be such a sour Susie," Annie said, her hand brushing his arm as he passed. He stopped and looked at her.

"I didn't sign up for this." He glanced at me. "Hey, Hattie."

"Always read the fine print," Annie said, and winked at him.

"Yeah, yeah. I'll be right back," he said, his eyes fixed on JT and Danny who were getting a little too loud and a little too heated in front of his glass display case. He started toward them.

"Don't you think he's hot?" Annie asked when he was out of earshot. Fox was at least six foot four and broad shouldered with thick brown hair that he wore a little too long and curled around his ears. His facial hair was a little too long also.

"Yeah, who wouldn't? It's also kind of weird how much he looks like the original Fox when he was young," I said.

"I know. And to think this version is fine with everyone calling him Fox too, even though we all know it's not his real name. Think he's Mr. Fox's son none of us ever knew about?"

"Y'all still don't know his real name?" I asked.

"Nope. Then again, I haven't asked." She shrugged. "When Loraine accidentally introduced him by Mr. Fox's name after she sold him the store, that was that. Old habits die hard. I guess Mountain View is just used to calling the hardware store owner Fox after all these years."

In the momentary silence, Lee's voice was clear, haunting, in more ways than one.

"I'm sorry, Annie, but I've got to go. I didn't realize Lee was going to be here and I haven't seen him in eleven years. I look—"

"Like you've been hiking the Appalachian trail for the last month without a shower."

"For the last *month*?" I asked. "I look that bad? Last I checked I don't have any ticks or a pocket full of cast-off trail mix raisins in my pockets."

"We always promised not to lie to each other," Annie said, grinning. "Anyway, as long as you stay right here, he won't be able to see you and I promise I'll sneak you out before the set is over. They always close with 'Mountain View Royals Getting Rowdy Tonight.'"

"Really?" I asked. "They're still playing that song?"

"It's a hit. Everyone loves it."

I was almost as shocked at the town's acceptance of the song as I was the town's acceptance of Tosha's McDonald's ballads. The mayor had outlawed the song being played in public our senior year of high school after much of the town complained that it celebrated carousing. Maybe Mountain View could change after all.

"Listen, since I know you're trying to bail on me early, I'm going to admit something. I asked you out for a drink to catch up, but I also wanted to ask you a favor—mayor business." She took a drink and I did the same, trying to ignore the way Lee's voice broke through the noise of the crowd now and then. The band was playing Boyz II Men's "End of the Road" with a country twist that made it even more heartbreaking than it already was. In front of Annie and me, Jozelle Hunter was weeping.

"Shoot," I said. I tipped the mason jar to my lips and gulped half of the contents so I wouldn't join Jozelle in her hysterics. What Annie wouldn't know was that Lee used to have horrible insomnia and on the few nights we were able to sneak out and spend together, I'd wake up in the middle of the night to him playing his guitar and singing quietly in a darkened corner of the room to songs just like this one. The sound of his voice now brought me right back to the feel of soft sheets on my skin and the smell of his cologne.

"You've established quite the name for yourself over there in Charlotte and I know just how popular your events have become. What did you raise the other week for Make-A-Wish? Thirty million? It was all over socials."

"Yeah," I said, setting the jar down on the sill beside me. "But that was easy. Make-A-Wish is a worthy cause, and lots of people are excited to pitch in. Not all events are like that."

"It still wasn't a cake walk. All those flowers and Barbra Streisand and the three-hundred-person banquet table was impressive."

I laughed.

"I guess you did see it online."

"And on the news," Annie said. "Listen, I'm not asking you to do something that crazy. For one, we don't have the funds, and for two, you know Mountain View doesn't do glamor well. But we need to bring some awareness here to make sure the stadium doesn't land in this town." She paused and rifled through her clutch for some lipstick. This move wasn't because she needed lipstick; it was diplomatic. Annie always left room for uncomfortable silence on purpose to get others talking. It was too bad that I already knew this strategy. I sat there and finished the last of my drink while she slowly colored her already painted lips a cherry red.

"You know what all is happening now, right?" Annie asked.

"Yeah. The state's deliberating on Mountain View and Cardinal River, trying to decide which one gets the stadium. I've heard it all from Mama and Daddy," I said.

In fact, after the failure of our farm, the stadium was the only thing they'd talked about.

"Well, what you probably haven't heard is that we've hired an attorney out of Atlanta to help us fight this build," she said. She took a drink. "She said our best bet is to show the state that we're resisting from the start and that choosing Cardinal River would be less of a hassle than dealing with the hornet's nest here. We started a petition on change

.org on her recommendation and got everybody in town to sign it, but word got out somehow and now Cardinal River has one too. Thankfully, Mayor Scoggin over there is neutral on the stadium, so they don't have leadership support, and a couple other residents want the stadium to come—lord knows why." Annie's nose scrunched and she shrugged.

"But that will all hopefully work to our advantage. Our attorney says the state plays into divisions on stuff like this, but since we're united, we're strong, sending a signal that this town won't back down without a fight." She pounded the table with her fist like she was giving a political speech, then smiled at me. "We do need more signatures, though. As many as we can get outside of Mountain View. She suggested highlighting the town's history and creating a public outcry to get more signatures. An event would help with both of those things." She reached for her purse. "Speaking of the petition, let me get your signature real quick. Yours is the only one we don't have yet. I know you don't live here anymore, but you're considered a citizen since your name is on the farm deed with your parents." She grabbed her phone.

I couldn't sign that petition.

She set her phone in front of me on the table, and I stared at it.

"Are y'all sure you don't want to fight *for* the stadium?" I asked, instead of picking her phone up and signing the petition. "I know it might change things a bit around here, but a stadium would make the town's profitability skyrocket."

I paused, and Annie's eyes flickered with anger.

I held up my hands. "Just playing devil's advocate."

I didn't agree with stopping the stadium—and progress with it. Towns that fought against advancement and won mostly stumbled along until they died. I'd seen it firsthand when I'd driven across country with my college roommate after graduation. There were towns that had folded because a factory closed or because they protested a highway or because the land dried up. When it boiled down to it, most towns were left to ghosts because they didn't have an opportunity like the stadium to revive it. This development would bring thousands of visitors to town and their money with them.

"We are proud of our town as it is," Annie said coldly. "And our attorney told us that just last year, plans for a new soccer stadium on St. Louis's North Riverfront were moved inland to preserve the industrial historic district there. The city got enough names on their petition for it to mean something. I know we need more people to join us in resisting the build here. That's why I'm asking for your help. We need to spread awareness outside of town." She ran her finger around the rim of her jar.

"Sorry about running off. Last week, JT and Darryl threw some punches and I wasn't about to let JT get so red he'd swing again," Fox interrupted, edging around Jozelle who was still crying although the band had moved on to an upbeat song they'd written, "Where Football Was King." He popped the top on a Miller Lite and smiled at me. Annie wasn't wrong about him being hot. He looked like one of those rugged guys on *Yellowstone*. "Annie tells me you might help us push this stadium project out of town, Hattie."

I didn't know what to say. Even back home, I was only required to take on projects that I was passionate about. I had never planned an event attached to an initiative I was against.

"A big event to catch the attention of the state would be amazing," Fox went on.

"Initially, I thought about a Battle of the Bands or something, but our attorney thinks the state is in a hurry to decide and might reach a resolution within the month." Annie turned to me. "I thought we'd pivot and focus on bringing people to town for Founder's Day." She turned back to the room to address Fox and me both. "I know it's only a week away and festivities really start Monday, but if we had the right contacts, Hattie's contacts, and her events acumen, I know we could get some press here on the big day and a decent amount of buzz ahead of it on socials too. It might be our last chance."

I didn't say anything. Her request had taken me entirely off guard.

"Why don't you ask Lee? He probably has better contacts than me and he's a celebrity himself, he would—"

Fox choked on a sip of his beer and lifted his hand to me.

"Not after that last press conference in Atlanta. He kind of ruined his connections when he flipped that table over on those reporters," he said, glancing toward the back of the store as if Lee might suddenly materialize. "I can't imagine he's not blackballed after that."

I was shocked. I couldn't imagine Lee doing anything like that. He was passionate, definitely, and his temper was quick, but he'd never been a violent person.

"I know he is," Annie said. "But I've always thought it was shitty of that reporter to tell the world about his MRI results before he had a chance to speak about it himself. It was clear he was still in denial."

What he'd done wasn't excusable, but I couldn't imagine someone else ending my career on my behalf.

"Anyway, back to Founder's Day," she went on. "The event is already pretty much fully baked, but of course, you're welcome to polish anything. We're planning to start at 4 PM, 1940s theme, as always. We'll do the reenactment of the Robinsons coming to town. I'm playing Mrs. Robinson—I think we sort of look alike anyway—and Loraine talked Rudy into playing the mister again whether he wants to or not. Foxy here is the narrator this year."

She elbowed Fox in the ribs, and he rolled his eyes.

"Chester was supposed to do it again, but he got the mumps somewhere and still ain't right," Fox said to me.

"That doesn't surprise me," I said.

Chester's parents, Cletus and Charlene, were conspiracy theorists and they'd passed their suspicions down to their sons. None of them had had a vaccine in their lives because they believed shots injected people with microchips. They proudly told everybody on a regular basis that when the government started controlling us like robots, they'd be the last real people standing. They didn't consider that when the rest of us turned bionic, it'd be billions against the four of them.

"When Annie asked me, I warned her that I wasn't the right one for the job. I tried out for my elementary school's reader's theater program once and was told I delivered lines like the Terminator. Should be a year to remember," he said.

"It'll be fine. Chester isn't exactly Ryan Gosling." Annie laughed. "Anyway, after the reenactment, we'll do the Mountain View and Robinson Family trivia. Then I'll get up on stage and talk about why we need to stop the stadium. After I'm through, we'll be on to the pie walk and the swing dance tutorial followed by the big Mountain View family potluck. The night will end with the Leland Lockhardt Band for a few hours and then Sterling and his disco light 'til midnight, for any stragglers."

I smiled and took a sip of my drink.

"Sounds fun," I said.

"So, could you help us? We'd just need you to make a few calls to any press you know—in Charlotte, Greenville, Atlanta, anywhere, really—and reach out to as many influencers as you can. People would be fascinated to learn about the Robinsons, I think."

In the background I could hear Lee singing the first few lines of "Mountain View Royals Getting Rowdy Tonight," and my heart started to race. I stood up.

"I've got to go. Let's talk about this later," I said. "I'm in events, not public relations, and a lot of our press comes from our partners' outreach, not ours'."

I wasn't lying. Not entirely, anyway. Charlotte Luxury Events focused primarily on events and left the publicity to our clients. That said, I did have a significant amount of relationships with press and influencers by happenstance, just because I'd been in the business for so long. But I couldn't in good faith use those connections here, when I didn't believe in the initiative.

"Plus, I'm only in town until tomorrow evening and I'm overcommitted right now. I've got a lot to do ahead of my library benefit with the Panthers in a few weeks," I said, dropping the bomb nonchalantly. "Just reach out to the press yourselves. They're always looking for a good story."

"You have an in with the Panthers too? Of course we need you, Hattie. Now more than ever. We don't have reach outside town like you do." Annie grasped my hand and tried to pull me back down to my seat.

"Yes, you do. The internet is a great resource," I attempted. I took a step away, but Fox stopped me.

"This is your hometown, Hattie. It could all disappear. You may not have as many connections as some, but you surely have more than we do."

Lee was singing the final chorus. My veins buzzed with nerves.

"Your family legacy—four generations if I recall correctly—would all be gone in a blink. If this place means anything to you—"

"Fox, you're new here. Surely you've been somewhere else where the community is thriving and you know the difference," I said, suddenly unable to stop myself from telling them the truth. "This town will be sentenced to a swift death if something isn't done quickly to bring commerce in. Look around, your store is one of four in business in a stretch of thirty storefronts."

"What are you saying, Hattie?" Annie asked, suddenly rising. "Are you saying you're not with us on this?"

"I tried to keep my opinion to myself, and I hate to admit it, but the stadium is a good idea." I hadn't meant for the statement to come out in a shout, but it coincided with the final strum of Woody's guitar and the final breath of Lee's voice and ricocheted through the store. The entire place silenced, and everyone's attention snapped to me, the turncoat of Mountain View. Annie sighed and moved away from her position in front of me, and then there he was, directly down the center aisle. His old ball cap was pulled over his baseball mullet and his blue eyes seared me through, even in the dim.

"How could you?" Jozelle breathed. I barely heard her. Instead, I couldn't look away from Lee's gaze, but wanted, with everything in me, to turn and run before he could truly see me.

Lee handed his guitar to Woody and started walking up the aisle toward me.

"She ain't wrong," Lee said loudly to the room as the voices started to rise. "She ain't right either. Let's give her a minute to think on it, okay?"

He reached my side, tucked his arm around my waist, and swept me out the door into the still night.

"You always knew how to make an entrance." Lee laughed when the door clicked shut behind us. He didn't let me go but led me around the side of the building to the place where I'd parked instead. I thought to step away from him, to treat him with the distant friendliness I'd always planned but couldn't somehow. It was like the moment I heard his voice and saw his face, the last eleven years disappeared and any awkwardness with them. Just like that.

"As did you," I said, when his hand lifted from my hip. He smiled as he walked around Slugger and slung his tall frame into the saddle.

"I guess that's why we made such a good team," Lee said. "Want a ride home?"

I was sober. Any buzz that the drink might have given me was good as dead in the wake of the town's disdain and the shock of seeing Lee again. I could have driven home without issue. Instead, I took Lee's hand, settled behind him, and wrapped my arms around his waist.

CHAPTER TWO

Letting Lee take me home was a mistake. I knew that from the second Slugger started off down Main Street. Riding a horse with someone was intimate, and despite Slugger's smooth gait, my body kept jostling against Lee's, forcing me to hold him tighter. His body felt the same as it always had beneath my hands. I tried to distract myself by thinking of the consequences of my actions back at Fox's. There would be hell to pay with Mountain View tomorrow, but even the threat of being snubbed couldn't hold my attention. A decade later, here we were, riding the same stretch of dark road we'd ridden along every weekend for four years. If I closed my eyes, it felt as though no time had passed at all, like we were eighteen again. And that was the root of why this was such a problem. Being near him stirred up old emotions, a bone-deep desire I knew I shouldn't feel so quickly after this many years apart, especially after I'd tried so hard to feel it with other men who'd loved me.

"Alright, buddy. Good run," Lee whispered to Slugger as he slowed at our rusted mailbox.

The stars were bright and the moon was nearly full. The light illuminated our little ranch farmhouse down the drive and the near one-hundred-year-old oaks surrounding it.

Colt stopped Slugger a distance from the house, and I removed my arms from Lee's waist. I half expected him to stop me, to grasp my forearms and pull me close like he always used to, but of course, he didn't. He'd left me and hadn't come back for me since. He didn't regret it. His offer to take me home was just him being friendly, like I'd hoped it to be.

"Thanks for the ride," I said. I held on to the saddle's cantle and dismounted. "Have a great night, Lee."

I started walking toward the door, but then I heard his low chuckle.

"That's all you want to say to me after eleven years? Damn. Too bad. I was kind of hoping you'd at least have the decency to cuss me out," he said.

I whirled around and smiled.

"You weren't talking either, cowboy," I said. "Maybe there's too much to say?"

"Got some time?" he asked. He adjusted his hat and gestured down to the field. "We could take a walk?"

"Not sleeping again, I see," I said. I knew I shouldn't, but I started back toward him against my better judgment. "Come on. Let's take Slugger down to the barn and get him some water."

We walked down the back acreage in silence. The overgrown grass tickled my feet atop my flip-flops.

"I sleep sometimes," Lee said finally. "After big wins, mostly, and whenever my mind is clear, but lately it ain't been."

"Why's that?" I glanced over the fields, forty acres, that had once grown enough peanuts to keep our family fed and clothed for a year. I truly didn't know what my parents were going to do.

"I guess because my career is over," he said. "I got that degree in finance because people told me baseball wasn't going to be forever, but I didn't really believe them. You know baseball's all I've cared about since I was five."

I did. We'd been on the same T-ball team. He was the only one who knew what he was doing. I still remembered us all gawking at his fancy baseball bag equipped with a brand-new Easton bat he'd earned from his daddy by spending hours in their yard passing and doing hitting drills, while the rest of us shared a dented bat Coach picked up from the Goodwill in Clover.

Lee and I had circulated around each other like that our whole lives—playing on the same teams when we were little, sitting across the classroom from each other in middle school, but until high school, we'd never really noticed each other that way. The Lockhardts had always been part of a small white-collar crowd, different from us farm kids. Lee's daddy was a banker.

"All good things come to an end," he went on.

"I'm sorry. I only found out tonight. If I would have known, I would have—" I stopped myself. "I was going to say that I would have reached out, but that's not true."

"Yeah. I understand," he said.

Up ahead, the barn was dark except for a single light bulb in the loft Daddy always left on. I glanced at Lee. I'd only seen him in a suit twice—once for prom and once when he was televised signing his commitment to Wake Forest. Somebody—Shakespeare maybe—said that the clothes make the man, and the clothes that had made Lee were dry fit, not dry clean. Thinking about him suiting up every day, uncomfortable and unhappy, made me sad.

"You don't have to work at the bank, do you? Couldn't you take some time and figure something else out? Maybe coaching?"

Lee laughed and the noise echoed over us.

"Coaching? I haven't changed much, Hat. I'd get fired the first game. You and I—and I guess the rest of the world after my press conference—know my temper is too quick for coaching." He shook his head. "And, no. I don't have to work at the bank, but I also can't just sit around. I'm too restless. Thought about staying in Atlanta, but it was hard to even go to the grocery store without getting stopped for an autograph or picture. I love talking to fans, but everything took so much longer. And outside of the Braves, I didn't really have a life there anyway. I was dating this girl off and on when I was in town, but I think she liked the idea of being with me more than actually being with me." He shrugged. "It just made sense to come home for a little while."

For some reason hearing him talk about his life in Atlanta was jarring. Here, tonight, he'd felt like normal Lee, not the Leland Lockhardt whose face was on billboards, whose line of shoes was near as collectable as Jordan's, whose last name graced kids' jerseys.

"Shit. I'm sorry. I sounded like a jackass just now. I know I'm not Cal Ripken Jr. or anything, obviously, but—"

"No, you're definitely a big deal. Didn't that Nike ad say that you were the best infielder since Chipper Jones?"

We got to the barn and he looped Slugger's reins around a hitching post while I flipped on the light, grabbed a bucket, and went for the hose.

"Were," he said quietly. I didn't know if he expected me to hear him or not, so I didn't reply.

I filled the bucket, and Lee put it in front of Slugger, who immediately began to drink.

"You know, Hattie, I didn't think to ask, but—there ain't some guy waiting for you up there, is there?" He nodded toward the house.

I glanced at him for a second. He had his arm resting on Slugger's neck and the other hand in his pocket. He looked so good.

"Nope. No boyfriend right now." I smiled. "I mean, I was dating this one guy off and on, but he was only dating me because of my not-to-miss celebrity events. I was just too famous." I laughed, and Lee swirled his hand in the water and flicked the droplets at me.

"Come on. Let's walk down to the river and see if the moonflowers along the Armstrongs' bank are blooming. I haven't taken the time to see those since I went off to college."

"I haven't either," I said, at once wondering why I hadn't. The Cardinal River ran down the mountain and under Route 2 in Pine Summit before paralleling the road in Mountain View from Main Street. Then it ran past every farm on the west side of town, including ours. The Armstrong family had over five hundred acres of river frontage on the opposite side of the water in the town of Cardinal River, and Mrs. Armstrong always planted thousands of moonflowers each year. The contrast of the white flowers in the moonlight, their reflection like stars on the water, was something truly special to behold. I'd barely gone down to the riverbank since I moved away.

Lee strode toward me and looped his arm over my shoulder. He smelled the same as he always had—like leather and Tide—and I leaned into him to breathe more of it.

We started walking across the lower field. In the distance, the rusted top of Mr. Robinson's truck protruded from the ground, and beyond, the grove of pines that masked the view of the riverbank.

"Heard about your parents and the farm," he said as our shoes sank into the soft dirt. "Sorry about all that."

I shrugged, and he patted my shoulder, then drew me a little closer as we walked. The late summer wind swept across the flat plane of the farm, cooling the sticky humidity.

"I'm sorry about it too, especially because I don't know what they're going to do. Without the farming income, they won't be able to afford to keep this place and no one's going to want unproductive land around here, except for maybe the state."

"If it's happening to your parents, it's got to be happening to others too. Or at least it'll start happening," Lee said. "Mountain View should see y'all's farm as a wakeup call that this town's going to have to change to survive. You're right about the stadium that way." He let me go and shoved his hands into the pockets of his jeans. "But you know this town. Everybody wants things to stay like they are. They cling to this town like a tick."

"Are you?" I asked, glancing at him. "Clinging to this town? You have a job you don't even need here now."

He laughed. "Nah. I'm fine being here for a while, just to figure out what the hell I'm doing next, but the minute it dawns on me, I'm out. Probably about the same time my parents and Tim get back from the chateau. I love them, but I can't live under the same roof with Tim anymore. My contract was the worst thing that ever happened to him."

When Lee first signed with the Braves, he'd gifted his parents a million dollars. They'd immediately bought a tumbledown chateau in the south of France that they'd only seen on Facebook. Thankfully, the house did exist when they got there, but it was basically a lean-to. They'd spent half of a year each year for nearly a decade in France trying to fix it up, and Lee's younger brother, Tim, tagged along under the guise that he was handy, when in actuality he was only handy with the ladies and booze.

"Do you think you would've been happy playing baseball for the next decade if you hadn't been injured?" I asked.

I breathed deep. The wind had turned away from us, and now the scent of earth and grass and flowers was pronounced, almost overpowering.

"Yeah, of course. I love the game. It was everything. How about you? You happy these days?"

He was staring at me so I kept my eyes fixed ahead, on Mr. Robinson's truck bed and the Queen Anne's lace that was growing all around it. I still hadn't forgotten what Annie said—that I looked like a hiker who'd been living outside for a month. Lee was probably reciprocating the question to figure out if it was dissatisfaction that had turned me into one of the hobbits from *Lord of the Rings*.

"I think so," I said. "I love my job. My boss has offered me a third of the company interest and partnership if I nail this next event, and I feel like we're making a difference. We're working on a gala for the Panthers' grants that will benefit the Charlotte libraries in a couple of weeks. The whole convention center uptown is going to be transformed into Narnia, and we're bringing in the cast of the Narnia movies too. I can't wait." I smiled, imagining it, and Lee whistled under his breath.

"That smile," he said. "It still takes my breath away."

I laughed. I didn't know what else to do or say.

"I guess I'm like you, though. I don't really have much going on outside of work. I'm friends with my coworkers and my neighbors. My sorority twin from South Carolina lives two blocks over, but she has a baby so I only see her every other week or so." I sighed. "I don't know."

At first, my life in Charlotte had been an extension of college. My big sis from Alpha Xi Delta had interned with me at the NASCAR Hall of Fame, and we'd both snagged jobs in town after. When my boss, Merry, told me that she was going to rent out her uptown townhouse and move to the suburbs and wondered if I wanted it, I'd jumped at the chance. Maggie moved in too, and we'd had a year of working by day and partying by night—until Maggie met Rob and got engaged four months later. Now she lived in Lexington and had two kids. Most of my friends had followed similar tracks, and my partying had slowly dwindled to a happy hour once a week with my boss.

In the distance, an owl hooted, and we were close enough to the river to hear the water burbling over the rocks.

"Think we should've both stayed here in Mountain View? It seems like Dolly and Rocky and Annie are all happy enough," Lee said.

It was funny. Lee had always wanted to move away—professional baseball required it—but I didn't remember exactly when I'd sworn off the town. It had been more of a gradual thing. After high school graduation, I'd never really considered where I'd end up, only who I'd end up with, but after Lee broke up with me, I hadn't wanted to come home to a town full of our memories. And then the years passed and I fell in love with planning events and living in a city. Mountain View seemed more and more backward and boring the longer I was gone. Now I couldn't fathom ending up here.

"Definitely. Driving the Oscar Mayer Weinermobile would've been a better choice for you than playing in the MLB. Especially given your track record with large vehicles." I laughed, remembering the time he'd moved the athletics bus for his coach. He'd sideswiped an entire row of cars. Lee chuckled. "And I could've auditioned to be Linds's ghostly understudy at the Pine Summit campground." I suddenly couldn't stop laughing imagining Linds dolled up in Annie's old choir robe running through the campground, moaning and howling in the middle of the night. In the midst of my hilarity, I slapped Lee's chest with the back of my hand. He clutched it and pulled me close at the exact time the sky opened up.

"Robinson's truck still open?" Lee yelled over the downpour. I nodded and we ran for the cab. Lee opened the passenger door. I threw myself onto the cracked leather seat as the door screeched and slammed shut. Seconds later, Lee was beside me, his shoulder against mine, skin to skin, breathing the same old car smell of leather and glues and musty carpet.

"Feels exactly the same." His eyes searched mine and my heart quickened. This was the place we hid the years we dated—from our parents, from our friends, from disappointments, from change. Mr. Robinson's truck was the site of so many firsts.

"I'm just glad we killed all the yellowjackets that were in here yesterday," I said. I rubbed the goosebumps on my arms. Lee stared out the driver's side window, watching the rain soak the barren land.

"Remember that time you stepped into that nest on our way to the dance at Limelight Farm?"

"Yeah, but I'm not sure which was worse—the eight stings or watching you try and Dougie," I said.

"I don't know what you're talking about. For one, I perfected the Dougie, and for two, watching me dance couldn't have been that painful because that was the night that—"

"I almost broke up with you over it—the Dougie," I said quickly, interrupting his mention of the first night we spent together. I didn't want to reminisce about us, about our relationship. I didn't want to recount the way I'd fumbled with the buttons on his flannel shirt or the way his fingers had trembled unclasping my bra or the way lying in bed with him, hearing him whisper he loved me, had forfeited my heart to him forever. It had been perfect. We had been perfect, solid, unsinkable—or so I thought. But much like the *Titanic*, we sank quickly. "Dolly talked me out of it."

Lee cleared his throat. "You know Limelight closed last month?"

"No. Why?" I asked. The place was an institution. A huge old barn with a beautiful dance floor and sparkling chandeliers, it was three miles away in Cardinal River and had been the site of proms and weddings, baby showers and funeral services. Mama had told me a while back that people were annoyed because the original owners had sold it to a family who didn't believe in dancing or alcohol. I hadn't figured it would really hinder business, though, since it was the only decent venue around.

"The contracts kept getting violated because the allowed activities—cake walks and dunking booths—are about the dumbest things you could do at a wedding reception, so they decided to shut down the whole operation."

"Dunking booths?" I started laughing.

"Yep. In the last couple months I've seen a bride, a groom, and the pastor get dunked. I went to Suzie Anne and Blade's wedding the weekend before they closed, and after they tapped the Mountain Dew keg, Bernie snuck a Bose speaker from his car and started playing some 2000s rap. I guess that was it for the owners. They announced the shutdown the next day."

Lee grinned, and I suddenly realized I was staring. His thin shirt had been plastered to his chest in the downpour, accentuating the ripple of muscles along his torso. I recalled the hours upon hours he'd worked each day on the baseball field and in the weight room to build the body he needed to make his dream come true.

"You can't stay here." I blurted the words and his nose scrunched.

"You want me to get out of the truck?" he asked, turning to look out the window at the still driving rain.

"No. I mean, you can't get stuck in Mountain View. You've worked too hard to make your own way apart from this place. I know you said you can't coach, but there's got to be something else."

"Don't worry. I ain't at risk of becoming a lifer. I told you I'm just here for a little while, Hat." He slung off his ballcap and tossed it into my lap. "Should the mullet stay or go? Some of the old ladies at the bank don't approve."

"Up to—" I started to say that the way he wore his hair was up to him, but he cut me off, his eyes lighting.

"I've got it. Listen, your parents' farm and I are basically the same thing. We both need to be repurposed, and I think I know exactly the thing for this farm. Y'all should become the new Limelight. You've already got the barn and your events background."

The excitement in his voice was contagious. He was right. It would be a long shot, but if we could transform our farm into a new Limelight, Mama and Daddy could afford to stay here too.

"The boys and I have loved playing again. We could be the house band. Remember when the Limelights had that family band that played for their events? It was the best." He grinned at me. "Hattie, y'all would be booked solid the minute you opened. You could host all the town's events and Pine Summit's and Cardinal River's too. Shoot, Cameron and Hunter had to go all the way to Greenville to get married when if y'all had a venue here, they could've just driven down the road."

I squinted through the rain to the barn across the field. It was an old barn, built by the Robinsons, and the wood was gray and worn. It was a building meant for working, not entertaining. It would cost a lot of money and take a lot of time—and we didn't have either of those things.

"I think it's a genius idea, Lee, but I can't stay here and run a business for my parents. Plus, we don't have the money to renovate the barn," I said.

"You could train your parents and let me take care of the money part," he said.

"No way. I mean, of course I could train my parents, but no, we're not letting you pay to renovate our barn. It would cost tens of thousands. My first internship in college was working events at this crappy old amusement park outside of town, and the owners were renovating this little dining building. It was a thirty-thousand-dollar job." I nodded toward the barn. "That's triple the size, and construction supplies are ridiculous right now."

"So? I have the money to . . . I mean, I can afford it, and it would benefit the town."

I knew Lee had what most would consider bottomless pockets. Right before he'd deleted his Instagram five or so years ago, he'd reposted an article about signing a contract extension. The article said the extension awarded him $35 million. Renovating our barn would barely *touch* his fortune. Even so, he was my ex, and I couldn't feel like I owed him something, even if it meant my parents could stay on the land they loved.

"I can't let you do that."

"Hattie." He cut me off, and his eyes met mine and stayed. "Let me. Please."

"I can't." For some reason, whether it was his tone or the way he drew close to me, it triggered the emotions of our last night, the night before I left for South Carolina, sitting just like this in Mr. Robinson's truck. "You can't do something like that for us."

Lee took my face between his palms. His thumb swept my cheek, and I barely stopped myself from shuddering beneath his touch. How quickly my body recalled the way it had always wanted him.

"Yes, I can. I'd do anything for you," he said softly. He leaned in, and I closed my eyes and reached for him, threading my fingers in his hair. I could feel his breath on my face, the whisper of his lips on mine.

"I've missed you," he said against my mouth, but the moment his lips met mine, I jerked back. The last thing he said before he left me in the car that night eleven years ago was that he would miss me—and then he went and hooked up with Willow hours later.

"I'm sorry," Lee said, his face painted with shock.

"We can't pick up right where we left off. Even if tonight feels like you never broke up with me and we never left Mountain View, we did. I . . . I can't." I took a breath, my heart still hammering from the almost-kiss that I desperately wanted despite it all. "I didn't want to bring it up. I know we've been over for more than a decade, but you shattered my heart and I still haven't forgotten the way that felt."

"Neither have I." Lee looked down at his lap. "That night is one of the biggest regrets of my life."

Out the window, the rain slowed. When I didn't respond, he opened the door.

"I'm sorry," he said. "Can I walk you to the house?"

"No," I whispered, my head full of memories and regrets. "I think I'll stay here a while longer."

CHAPTER THREE

I woke to the sun streaming through the lace drapes. My feet were freezing, poking out between the metal rails of Mrs. Robinson's antique bed that had been made special for her, a woman of four-foot-eleven. Mama had transformed my bedroom into her crafting room when I'd gone to college and had gifted my queen bed to Dolly and Rocky for their wedding gift. I rolled over, blinking at the blue shag carpet piled with dusty old yarn and cast-off Styrofoam wreath forms from when Mama had a mind to sell yarn wreaths by the roadside, a bunch of bags of Mr. Peanut Head appendages Mama had used at the Cardinal River farmers' market one year in an attempt to make peanuts fun for the next generation, and at least a decade's worth of *Farm Living* magazine stacked beside the door. You never knew when you were going to need that apron pattern from the February 2012 edition.

I rubbed my eyes and eyed the clock—ten twenty. It was late, but I hadn't been able to sleep. I couldn't get Lee or my parents' fate off my mind.

I sniffed. No bacon, no coffee. My room was situated right next to the kitchen. There had only been a couple times in my life I'd woken up at home without the smell of breakfast—always coffee, bacon, and fried eggs—urging me out of bed. One was when Mama had been initiated into the Mountain View Melodies and she'd been kidnapped in the middle of the night. The other was when Mrs. Robinson passed.

Since there were no other crazy country sororities for Mama to be initiated into, I figured something was wrong. Daddy always woke at six thirty sharp every morning to start on chores and Mama with him. They never went without coffee. My head started spinning. Surely I was wrong. Surely we weren't being kicked when we were already down.

I threw MawMaw's old mothball-smelling quilt off, walked around Mama's yarn to the closet and opened the door. I tugged an old Mountain View High sweatshirt off of a hanger and was struck by my photos still taped to the interior closet doors. There was Dolly and me at church camp, our faces slick with sweat from playing Capture the Flag, and then there was my first picture with Lee after his championship game freshman year. Lee was caked in dirt and my face was painted blue and green, but he'd kissed me anyway. Maybe I should've kissed him last night after all. Then again, the earth-shattering feeling of his lips on mine wasn't worth the heart shattering that would likely follow.

I walked out of my room to an empty kitchen. The coffee pot was empty beside the sink, and the window above it boasted a vacant porch swing.

"Mama? Daddy?" I yelled, running my hand down the old green laminate countertops as I went, but got no response.

I walked over to their bedroom, knocked on the door, then opened it. The bed was done up as it usually was—the whole of it covered in an antique quilt of pink and white made by Mama's grandmother.

I closed their door and walked out to the porch. Mama and Daddy sat on the steps, silent, looking out at the sun bathing the fields and the barn in misty morning gold. A few birds swooped to perch on the top of Mr. Robinson's truck and took off as quickly. I pulled my sweatshirt sleeves down into my palms to counter the slight chill and sat down on the top stair above my parents.

"Penny for your thoughts?" I asked.

Daddy didn't look at me, and I noticed he was wearing jeans instead of the Carhartt overalls he'd worn every day for his whole life.

"That's the problem, Hattie, there ain't a productive one to share," he said finally. Mama put her hand on his shoulder.

"We've been talking it over all morning, and we don't have a way out of this. Not this time," Mama said. She glanced at me and nervously palmed the perfect curls she'd had wet-set at the Cut & Curl last week.

"I went down to the lumberyard over in Pine Summit this morning to see if they could use a man, but they're full up. Don't need help at the Amtrak station over there either, and ain't none of our friends hiring hands," Daddy said. He shrugged. He'd always been a thin man, strong, though, but this morning, he looked nearly frail.

"I know it's not what you want, but there are plenty of jobs in Charlotte. You could sell the farm and live with me until you get settled."

"We're not leaving," Mama said. "And nobody's going to buy this land. What would they do with it?"

I balled my hands, pushing my nails into my palms. Mama and Daddy were exactly like everybody else in Mountain View—stubborn as a mule wearing blinders.

"What if you can't eat? What if there's no money coming in and you can't afford the AC or the water? Sometimes circumstances require us to do things we don't want to. The bank won't come for the farm, y'all own it, but this land and these bricks won't feed you."

I stood as my irritation rose to a boil.

Daddy looked at me and snapped his fingers.

"That's one place I haven't checked this morning. I'll get gussied up and head down to the bank to see if Lee knows of a job for this old farmer," he said.

I looked at him as if he'd just sprouted wings. Daddy didn't own khakis let alone a suit. His idea of getting gussied up likely meant what he had on and adding the imitation turquoise bolo he'd won from Mountain View Presbyterian's silent auction.

"Lee isn't giving out jobs, Daddy. He only works there. You'd need to speak with Mr. McCorkle . . . wait," I said. I'd been so discombobulated without the coffee and breakfast and with my parents in such a bad state that I hadn't thought to bring up Lee's suggestion. "I ran into Lee last night and—"

Mama and Daddy shared a look, a look that meant they already knew about my riding off down Route 2 with Lee and causing a stir at Fox's because the town's rumor mill was churning. I chose to ignore it.

"We know. Fox brought the truck by this morning. You left the keys in the ignition," Daddy said.

"Anyway, Lee and I were talking, and he mentioned that we should open an event space. With Limelight closed and all, a new space is needed and what better place than our farm?"

Daddy slapped the stair.

"That's plumb genius. The land would still be useful and we could stay right here. And with you in events, it's a natural fit. Limelight charged upwards of two thousand for a wedding. We could make near as much as we did farming if we do it right."

"You'll help us run it, won't you?" Mama asked.

The way her face softened when she asked the question made me angry. They'd never understood why I hadn't made my life here. Though they'd never made it an issue, it was clear they were disappointed. Hardly anyone left Mountain View. Only nine of my classmates had gone on to college, and of those, seven, now eight if you counted Lee, had returned to either run their family farms or work to better the town, like Annie.

"I'll teach you what I know from Charlotte, but I can't run a business here. I already have a job I love, and there's a lot on the line with this event I have coming up," I said.

"Oh, well, I'm not sure it'll work then," Mama said. "You know what they say about teaching old dogs new tricks, and we haven't the foggiest about running events."

"I told you I could teach you from Charlotte. We could Zoom."

Mama cocked her head. "What's Zoom?"

"Tell you what, Hattie. Stay 'til Founder's Day and help us sort this thing out. Then you're welcome to go back to that traffic you love so much." Daddy laughed and stood as though we had been negotiating and the matter had been settled.

"Like I said, I have a huge event in two weeks, and Merry said if it goes well, she'll make me partner. I could finally buy my own townhouse and possibly get a car too.

I'm sorry things are out of sorts, but I need to head back home later today as planned," I said firmly.

"Can't you tell Merry your family is in crisis? You'll be back well ahead of your benefit," Mama said. "I don't trust those Panthers anyway, trying to threaten Mountain View."

"We need you to help us right here if we're going to consider this, Hattie," Daddy said. He tipped his head down at the barn. "I'm no expert, but I don't think anybody's going to pay to get married in the barn as it stands and if it was up to me to fix it, I'd likely put new straw down, wheel the icebox into the corner, and call it a day."

There was so much to do ahead of the benefit. Triple-checking the catering, finalizing the guest list, developing the seating chart, confirming my decorating team, confirming travel for the celebrity guests, double-checking the floral arrangements with the florist, touching base with Park Road Books for book sales, sending final communication to guests, and the list went on. I couldn't afford to stay for the week they were demanding, but I didn't have much choice. Daddy was right. Neither of them knew what they were doing, but they also wouldn't take the initiative to figure it out themselves. That part irritated me. If I didn't help them, they'd lose the land and the house and they'd end up in my townhouse in Charlotte—miserable and out of sorts. Life required quick pivots sometimes, but around here it seemed your destiny sunk your feet in cement the moment you were born. Mama and Daddy had had their boots buried in dirt for decades, and they weren't keen to kick it off, even if it meant keeping their farm.

"I guess I'll email Merry and ask, but if I can't spare the time, I can't, and you'll need to either decide to learn event planning yourselves or consider selling."

Both of them just stared at me. I expected an apology for the inconvenience and a thanks for the idea, but none would come. In Mountain View, family came first. Period.

"I told you we ain't selling," Daddy said. It suddenly felt like the porch was about to crumble beneath me and I couldn't stand the sight of their faces anymore.

"Are we out of coffee?" I asked hurriedly, before I blew a gasket and said something I'd regret.

Mama shook her head, but I held my hand out to Daddy anyway.

"I'm going into town," I said. "I need the keys."

When I was growing up, it was hard to find a parking spot downtown on a Saturday morning. Not so now. As it stood, there were a couple cars parked up at the Cut & Curl and a handful in front of Paradise by the Dashboard Light Diner. The southern stretch of Main was a ghost town. Even the gazebo, Mr. Robinson's pride and joy he'd built large enough for a choir to fit beneath its roof, was vacant and weathered.

I pulled into my parking spot in front of Simpkins's Theater, the same exact spot where I'd parked as a teenager when strolling down Main was what you did on the weekends. Cruising was popular in other larger towns, but here, a cruise down Main would take all of two minutes.

In front of me, faded posters from the theater's last stand in 2011—*Water for Elephants* and *Pirates of the Caribbean: On Stranger Tides*—were still displayed in the windows. Closing night seemed like yesterday and a century ago.

I yanked the hem of my cropped white shirt down, smoothed my wide-leg linen pants, and climbed out of the truck. I'd been in such a hurry to get away from my parents that I'd nearly driven away in my ratty high school sweatshirt and pajama shorts. I might run into Lee, and I wasn't about to face him again in the state I was in the night before. Sure, he'd tried to kiss me, but that only meant he'd been as swept up in memories as I'd been, not that he necessarily found me attractive. If I saw him today, I wanted him to think about me later. I wanted him to feel the way he'd felt when he'd accidentally hit me with that football freshman year because he was staring at me in my leather shorts instead of focusing on Woody, his intended target. Those shorts had been the start of it all. He'd written me a note in English class the next day saying he was sorry if I caught him staring, that he'd had a crush on me for months and wondered if I'd go on a date with him.

I shut the door, locked it this time, and glanced at my phone. I'd sent a quick email to Merry explaining my family's crisis and asking to work from here for the week. I didn't expect her to reply quickly—it was Saturday after all—but even asking her for the time off made me nervous this close to an event.

I tucked the phone in my purse and stepped up on the sidewalk. As I did, I caught a reflection of myself in the window of the theater. For a moment, the girl in couture clothes was a stranger, and I was the little girl with pigtails marching into the theater behind my daddy on a crowded Saturday morning. Back then, Simpkins's Theater offered double features starting at ten—usually an old Bugs Bunny cartoon followed by a Western—and the whole town would line up outside Paradise to grab some grits and gravy biscuits before the ladies retreated to the Cut & Curl and the men and kids went to the shows. On certain occasions like Founder's Day or Christmas, the Mountain View Melodies ladies' show choir would arrange themselves at the town square gazebo and serenade the townspeople under Mr. Robinson's direction.

A few days after the Christmas show in 1998, Mr. Robinson suffered a stroke, and Mama and Daddy began to help Mrs. Robinson take care of him along with their farmhand duties. A year later, Mrs. Robinson made the decision to move them both into Pine Summit Retirement Home and gifted my family their house and farm. I still remember the day we moved out of PawPaw Norwood's house. My Uncle Jasper had been thrilled. PawPaw had passed away four months before, and Uncle Jasper had officially inherited the farm and house as planned since he was the oldest. He was a bachelor, and I knew he'd never really enjoyed sharing the house with my Barbies and crayons, but later I thought maybe we'd kept him on the straight and narrow, because when I was in high school, he sold the farm to the Mainerts for gambling money and moved to Atlantic City.

I turned away from my reflection and started walking down the sidewalk toward the Cut & Curl. Tammy's wetsets weren't exactly my style, but the mini donuts she made every Saturday in the back of her store were to die for. She made a decent pot of coffee too. My stomach growled, and I crossed the street at the gazebo. I startled when I came across Tosha sitting on the sagging step beneath the chipping white paint. She was wearing a floral muumuu similar to the one she'd been wearing last night and held a chipped ceramic coffee mug stamped with the McDonald's logo between her knees. She strummed her guitar.

"If they won't go for a McD's, why would you think they'd like a stadium? Please," she sang.

"You make a good point," I called out to her. Rumor had it that it wasn't only the McDonald's food that had made Tosha such a fan. She'd also been sweet on the manager from out of town. Apparently, he'd promised her the world—including a world tour as a singing Ronald McDonald.

I kept on toward the bright pink awning of the Cut & Curl, passing the old ice cream shop as I went. The windows had been broken when a tree fell during a freak tornado, but dusty Cheerwine bottles still lined the walls and if you looked through the broken glass panes, past the barstools, you could see the jukebox. My MawMaw had helped manage the store when she first moved to town, after her divorce from my cheating granddaddy. She and Mama had lived on the second floor in a little storeroom turned apartment until Mama married Daddy. The state of the shop made me sad. It was just like Mountain View to leave a place everyone once loved broken. It was as if when the founders of this town died, the ingenuity and excitement and interest in progress died with them.

"You're mighty brave to be wandering around town after last night." Fox leaned out of his truck window and pulled into a space in front of me. He grinned and quieted the ignition, though you couldn't hear it anyway. It was a peculiar thing, the silence of electric trucks, when you were used to a roar.

I pushed my sunglasses to the top of my head and rolled my eyes. He got out of the truck in his plaid shirt and Carhartt overalls. I wanted to ask him if he'd brought any of his own clothes when he moved to town or if he'd just gone through Mr. Fox's old trunks at the back of the store and decided to wear those. I was guessing the latter.

"What do you mean? Is there some sort of criminal on the loose?" I asked, laughing.

Fox stepped onto the sidewalk in front of me, pushed his hands in his pockets, and shrugged. "Some would say your take on the stadium is criminal enough," he said.

His lips turned up. "You seemed awfully keen to hightail it out of my store after you let the town know what you thought."

"I didn't hightail it out of anywhere. I only left because Lee wanted to talk to me," I lied. "And just because I have a different opinion than everyone else doesn't make me a villain. Why should I be afraid of the town anyway? What are they going to do? Kick me out? Fine. I'll go."

He balled one hand and clapped the other over it, making a popping sound. "If I got excommunicated from this town, I don't know what I'd do. This place is as close to paradise as I can imagine."

I waited for him to laugh, but he didn't. He only stared down at me with those dark green eyes and pushed his toothpick to the corner of his mouth. Annie was right to say he was hot. I wondered if he'd ever kissed her.

His stare unnerved me, so I looked down Main at the destruction of time and dwindling funds, then turned back to him.

"You're joking, right? You think this broken-down little town is paradise?"

"Yeah, I do. I know the buildings need some updating and all, but the people here are the kindest I've ever known. I just spent the morning delivering bags of mulch, but I wasn't only working. I was seeing my friends. Mrs. Mainert asked my advice on her flower garden, Mr. Turney invited me in for a country ham biscuit, and little Elvira Brown asked me to come to her fifth birthday party—it has a hunting theme. Phil's going to dress up like a deer and run around and they're giving all the kids paintball guns. Whoever shoots Phil first wins a mounted deer head."

My eyebrows rose at that, and we both started laughing.

"Phil's chocolate-dipped venison jerky is the party favor," he said, then sobered. "I know it's weird as hell around here, but our people don't deserve to lose their farms so the NFL can build a stadium they don't really need."

"They might not need it, but Mountain View does," I said. "You're not from here, and since you've chosen that electric F-150 I'm going to assume you hail from a city." I paused, thinking he'd tell me where he came from, but he didn't. "Look behind me. Fifteen years ago, all of these businesses were open. Fifteen years is recent history. Now there are only four left. If the stadium is built, fans will need places to buy goods, food, sportswear. This downtown would come alive again and Mountain View might wind up being a place people actually want to live."

"At the expense of everybody already living here who like it just the way it is," he said, then plucked his toothpick from his mouth.

I started to tell him that there wouldn't be a town to like if nothing changed, but he spoke first.

"We're not going to agree on this. Let's just drop it, okay?"

"Sure," I said.

He grinned.

"See you next time you're in, then. Sorry for holding you up. If you're meeting Lee and Willow for breakfast, you won't be that late. They only just walked into Paradise as I was pulling in." My heart seized as Fox nodded behind him to where the diner's ripped rainbow canopy fluttered in the breeze.

"What?" I asked. "What did you say?"

"*Hattie, I . . . I don't know how to tell you this.*" I could still hear Dolly's hesitant voice. "*I was on my way to meet Rocky for our morning walk when I saw Slugger outside of Willow's house.*"

Lee and I had only been broken up for four hours at that point, and I'd been crying the whole time. To think he'd spent the night with another girl, especially one of my friends, was unfathomable. In fact, I hadn't quite believed it at first, so I'd tried to ask Willow or Lee myself. Neither of them answered their phones, and they were nowhere to be found. But information spreads fast in a small town. It was said he'd told her he'd wanted her for months. It was said that afterward, she slept in his shirt. The next day, I left for college, and the day after that, he left too. He hadn't seen me off as he'd sworn he was going to do after he broke up with me. Willow never reached out to apologize for hooking up with my ex-boyfriend so quickly after our split that my ChapStick was still on his lips.

A few weeks into school at South Carolina, I'd received a text from Lee saying he was sorry for going to her so quickly. I hadn't responded. I hadn't known how to. On the one hand, he didn't have anything to apologize for. We were broken up. But on the other, he had to know without a doubt that what he'd done had killed me.

"You alright?" Fox's fingers grazed my arm and I nodded.

"You said Lee and Willow just walked into Paradise? Together?" I asked. I recalled the way Lee and I had reached for each other in Mr. Robinson's truck last night. I could still feel the whisper of his lips on mine.

Fox's eyes crinkled.

"Yeah. They have breakfast there every morning," he said. "They're seeing each other. Have been for, I don't know, two months? They moved back to town around the same time. He took his daddy's job at the bank, and she came back to fill in at the clinic in Cardinal River while Chantelle's out on maternity leave. She's a travel nurse."

"Oh," I managed to say, suddenly horrified. I couldn't stand Willow, but I'd nearly been like her all the same. *Worse* than her, actually, if they were together like Fox said. If I hadn't pulled away, Lee would have kissed me last night.

I stared across the street at the diner. I'd always hoped Lee thought hooking up with Willow all those years ago had been a mistake, that he'd only been reeling from our breakup. In fact, he'd pretty much told me that was the case last night. But now knowing they were seeing each other, I wondered if the rumors had been right back then after all, if he'd fallen for her while he was with me and still wanted her now. If so, to reach for me the way he did last night wasn't the result of love he'd never been able to get over, but the work of a cheater. Anger prickled my skin.

"Did I say something to upset you?" Fox stepped closer and touched my arm again. I shook my head and met Fox's gaze.

"No. Of course not," I said. He was probably the only person in town that didn't know about my history with Lee. I was glad for the expressionless way Fox had told me the news, rather than the look of pity I'd receive from everyone else. It didn't matter that our breakup had happened ages ago. Mountain View remembered everything. "It's only that I was heading for donuts at the Cut & Curl, not for breakfast at the diner."

"You better get going then. Tammy's been running out by eleven most Saturdays. She came up with this one topping—a peanut butter chocolate drizzle." He closed his eyes for a moment and did a chef's kiss.

"That sounds amazing," I said. I took one more glance across the street, but still didn't see Lee or Willow in the window. "Well, good talking to you, Fox." I smiled at him. "And I promise I'll keep my opinions to myself the next Friday I find myself in town."

He grinned. "I'd appreciate it."

I started to walk away.

"Oh, Hattie. One more thing." He jogged a few feet to catch up with me. "Completely forgot. When I was over at the Browns' this morning, they mentioned that your family wanted to host Founder's Day at your farm? It makes sense given the land was the Robinsons' and all, but I also know that you said you didn't want to help Annie with any sort of event last night, so I wasn't sure what the deal was. Doesn't really matter to me, but if the party isn't downtown, I bet I'll get out of hosting the afterparty this year, which would be nice. Last year, Chester and Billy got into it over Tosha and broke two of my display cases."

I didn't quite know what to say. Clearly Lee had been talking, though he'd said nothing last night about us hosting Founder's Day. I wanted to tell Fox that the rumor wasn't true, but I also knew that Lee's event venue idea was a good one. I'm sure he thought Founder's Day would be a perfect time to showcase the place for events—though he clearly knew nothing about the time it would take to get our barn in shape. It would take significant effort to even clean the place up, and Founder's Day was only a week away. Plus, our farm hosting Founder's Day meant I'd be a party to Annie's last-ditch effort to keep Mountain View as it was.

"I . . . It's the first I've heard of this."

"Well, damn," Fox said. "Guess I'll be ordering some gym floor mats to tie to the glass this year."

I laughed. "Let me talk it over with my parents. If we can somehow get the barn fixed up, hosting at our place might be okay as long as everybody understands that just because we're hosting doesn't mean I've changed my mind on the stadium. My parents are hoping to open the barn for events anyway since the land isn't yielding anymore, and this might be the right time to share the news. I'll have one of them call you, okay?"

"Sounds great."

He started to cross the street to the diner and the hardware store next door. Ahead of me, my mama's best friend Belinda emerged from the Cut & Curl looking like Aretha Franklin from the '60s with a beehive that reached heaven.

The mouthwatering scent of fresh donuts wafted into the street and over me. I quickened my pace.

"Is Tammy out of donuts yet?" I asked her.

Belinda stared me down, something I'd seen her do to unruly children, her husband, and the nurse tending her the one time her Melodies skirt got caught in her electric scooter, but never to me.

"No, but she's probably not going to sell them to you anyway. I can't believe this is how you repay our town for your wonderful childhood—by hoping for our demise."

She pointed her finger at my chest and appraised my outfit.

"Turncoat." Belinda turned on her heel and walked toward her car.

"Oh, and Hattie," Fox called, now from across the street. "You might want to grab your donuts and get on the early train back to Charlotte."

"Why?" I yelled back.

"Annie's planning to come by your place with a crowd to protest your position on the stadium and try to convince you to sign the petition." He held up his phone. "Just got the text."

"Really? With signs and bullhorns and all that?" I asked.

"Seems like it's a full-on protest," he said, looking at his phone. "Of course I'd like for you to change your mind. Our attorney said that even one missing signature gives the state an inch. They'll hope your sentiments will spread and take a whole damn mile. Like Annie said, if we're united, it'll give us an advantage over Cardinal River." He paused. "Still, I told her I doubt it'll work." He waved at me and disappeared into his store. I stood on the sidewalk for a moment, steeling myself for the scolding I knew I'd face if I walked into the Cut & Curl. I considered turning back to the truck, but my stomach growled and the memory of

Tammy's heavenly donuts urged my hand to the doorknob. I opened the door and stepped inside, finding myself immediately enveloped in sudden silence and the smell of frying dough as every woman in the Cut & Curl turned to stare at me.

CHAPTER FOUR

I should've heeded Fox's warning. I shoved the last bite of burnt donut in my mouth as I walked back toward Daddy's truck, then mopped my forehead with the back of my hand. In the half hour I'd been in the Cut & Curl getting berated by all of Mama's friends for supporting the stadium and refusing to stay for a few months until Mama and Daddy were on their feet, the sun had cleared the three-story limestone buildings. I felt like an ant under a microscope.

My breath came in short gasps, and I pressed a hand to my damp chest to stop it. First there was the news about Lee and Willow. Then there was the town's anger. Plus everything I had to get done for the benefit back in Charlotte. It was too much.

Tammy had started in on me the moment I stepped inside the store. She'd said I was born and bred in Mountain View and to speak against the people that had raised me, regardless of whether I agreed with their wishes, was betrayal, pure and simple. Then Bobby Jo, who lived across Route 2 from us, turned off her dryer and started crying.

She asked me what had happened to me, why I'd forgotten the meaning of family and what it meant to put others first.

I'd teared up then and started to explain why I thought Mountain View needed the change when Cricket interrupted. She'd whirled around in her salon chair, her hand pinched on a donut, her hair covered in foil, and asked the room full of women if they'd considered that I could've been the one behind the stadium proposal to begin with. She'd said that I rubbed elbows with all the decision makers attached to the Panthers because of my job. I tried to tell her that I wasn't that influential, but then Tammy interrupted.

At that point, the whole place began to smell like something was burning, and it was. With my entrance, Tammy had forgotten to pull the latest batch of donuts from the oil.

The moment Tammy started toward the back, my anger erupted. I told them they should be ashamed, I told them that I believed in the stadium because otherwise the town would die, and I told them that of course I was going to help my parents, but I also had a life of my own. Then I walked to the donut fryer, snatched a paper bag from the wall, and elbowed Tammy out of the way while I fished the two burnt donuts out of the oil. I slapped a five down on her counter and marched out of the Cut & Curl.

My phone dinged in my purse, signaling a new email. I attempted a deep breath as I passed the ice cream parlor, but it was no use. I was on the verge of a panic attack and prayed Merry's reply was a good one.

Hi Hattie—

I understand how difficult is it when your family is in crisis. I will grant the week of work away, but I'll tell you honestly that I need you back as quickly as you're able. I'm juggling PNC Bank's literacy initiative at the schools as well as the North Carolina Governor's Luncheon and now having to run point on the benefit for the week.

Speaking of the benefit, I was hoping you'd be able to join me for dinner Wednesday evening. Eliott Walker has asked us to go over the particulars of the Narnia event with him and I thought it would be nice if you could talk a little about your hometown. I know they'll need a contracted events company attached to the new stadium and if your town is selected, we could be a shoe-in.

I stopped on the sidewalk. Eliott Walker was the Panthers' owner. Most of the time, we worked with the marketing staff of the company we'd been hired to help, and the executives just showed up.

Eliott and I worked together years before when he was minority owner of the Colts. He has always respected the way I do business and is a man who greatly values connections. I know you can't be there, but perhaps you can tell me a few things about Mountain View and Cardinal River that might help him see we're the best choice. Maybe we could tell him that your local connections would help with hiring, for instance?

I shoved my phone in my purse. Cricket was right, sort of. I hadn't had a hand in any of the planning, but I guess I did have access to the powers that be. And Merry wanted me to convince this man that Mountain View was the right place, that I was the right person to talk the local people into working at the stadium they believed would ruin their lives.

My skin prickled. My whole body felt like it would burst into flame. I thought of Bobby Jo. She was nearing eighty. She wasn't going to work at a stadium in any capacity, not even as a greeter. And then I thought of the Harolds who had the farm beyond hers. Like my parents, they'd spent their whole lives growing one crop and they wouldn't know what to do if their farm was taken from them. There weren't apartments here in Mountain View for people to move into if they wanted to downsize or consider their next move. If the stadium came, some families would have to leave town. The money the state would give them wouldn't cover the purchase of another farm and the material needed to start over again.

I reached Daddy's truck. The leather burned my legs through my linen pants, and the hot air in the cab nearly stole my breath. It was true that everybody could lose their homes, but if our farm was any indication of the land's health, they were on their way to losing them anyway.

I ran a hand across my face once again, mopping the streaming sweat. My mind spun. There wasn't a best option. If the stadium came, it would reinvigorate this town at the expense of some. If the stadium didn't come, Cardinal River would thrive and this place would become a ghost town or a sea of parking lots in a decade or less. But there was no way to convince anyone of this. No one wanted to believe it, so they didn't.

At once, the heat was so stifling I couldn't take it. I got back out of the truck and walked down Main toward Route 2. I passed quaint little Mountain View Presbyterian Church sitting next to the one stoplight at the interchange where Main Street turned into Possum. The road here was dirt and it led to Dolly's house and the river.

Old Mrs. Muffet—yes, that was actually her name—was sitting and knitting on the front porch of her small clapboard house. I waved at her and she pretended she didn't see me. If my nerves had been less tense, I would've greeted the hundreds of ceramic Mother Goose figurines adorning her front yard, but I wasn't in the mood today. My hands had been shaking ever since the Cut & Curl and I needed a way to calm them, to make my mind stop reeling.

Up ahead, past the twin dollhouses—really she-sheds from Lowe's adorned with fancy molding—owned by Tammy's sisters, was Dolly and Rocky's house. My heart slowed and I pushed the metal gate open. Dolly wasn't home. Oscar Mayer had contracted Rocky to drive the Weinermobile to Gatlinburg for the weekend. But even the sight of their little brick house, a house that had been Dolly's childhood home and one of mine too, made me feel better.

I kicked my wedges off and padded around the side of their house to the backyard in my bare feet. The water swirled in their above-ground swimming pool, pushing the kids' swan and giraffe floats and a generous amount of bugs and sprouting algae around and around. Just beyond the pool, their yard dipped to the riverbank. The dock Rocky had built Dolly for their first anniversary jutted out into the rushing water.

I grabbed a swan float from the pool and walked down to the dock. I stood at the edge for a moment. Upstream were a few farms in the town of Pine Summit, then the railroad tracks, then the mountain, Pine Summit itself. The Cardinal River ran around it, fed by the streams, some originating at 1,700 feet. It cooled the water significantly by the time it ran past Mountain View.

I took a breath, lowered the swan into the water, and jumped aboard. I screamed when the swan tipped and my body submerged in the frigid chill. I hoisted my soaking body, see-through shirt and pants and all, onto the swan's back as the rapids took me west, toward home. I hugged the swan's neck and closed my eyes, listening to the burbling, feeling the cold of the water and the heat of the sun through the breaks in the branches over me. This was peace. It had always been. Ever since Dolly and I took our maiden voyage from her house to mine at age ten until now, riding the river was solace from anything.

I pushed my sopping hair back from my shoulders, twisted it, and let it go. On the Cardinal River township's side of the river, the land was wild, the whole stretch owned by the Armstrongs. But on the Mountain View side, there were thirteen farms between Dolly's house and mine.

First up was the Sedgewicks'. Back when Mr. Herbert was living, the little brick farmhouse Mr. Robinson had built for him was always tidy, but now that his boys lived there, bricks were tumbling in and the fields were overgrown.

My anxiety burbled up at the sight of it. More evidence of this town's disrepair. As the river planed and slowed, I wrapped my legs around the swan's neck and lay down against its back. I shut my eyes to the canopy of green and light above me and hoped I'd drift off to sleep. It would take at least half an hour to get home and if I missed my stop, I'd undoubtedly catch myself when the river curved, before Bobby Jo's passed me by.

My body went limp and my mind stilled.

"Watch out for gators!"

I jerked up at the sound, just in time to see Lee running down his dock fully clothed, a goofy grin on his face.

"Lee—"

I tried to tell him to stop, to leave me alone, but he catapulted into the river, his backward cap flying from his head, his arms wrapping around the swan and me as he met the water. The raft tipped and I fell into the river, but he pulled me up, righted the swan and flung me back on the raft before I could do it myself.

"What the hell?" I sputtered, glaring at him. He swam next to me, his head dipped close to the water, laughing.

"Sorry," he said. "I was mowing the grass and saw you going by dead asleep. I was bored and you were an easy target." He started laughing again. I tugged my shirt away from my skin, regretting the lace bra I'd worn beneath it.

"You better pray you never fall asleep in my company," I said.

"What would you to do to me? Draw on my face? Cover me in honey?" He glanced at me and winked before his gaze fell from my eyes to my lips to my body and his smile disappeared.

"I'm partial to the wet the bed trick," I said. I covered my breasts with my arms, at once keenly aware that Lee had noticed my see-through outfit. I was basically wearing lingerie with sheer pajamas over top. "All it takes is a little warm water." I laughed to encourage him to do the same, but he didn't. He only swam closer.

I inhaled and jumped off the swan into the water. Like the first time, the shock of cold took my breath, but at least now my body wasn't on display. I swam forward, faster, hoping to outpace Lee, but he matched my stroke.

"Hattie." He said my name, but I ignored him. "Hattie," he said again, and this time, his fingers caught my wrist and stopped me.

"What?" I asked. My legs churned in the water. I could feel his too, and his eyes on my face, but I pretended to study the side of his house through the trees in the distance, the way the windows of their sizeable A-frame caught the sunshine.

"Hattie. You're driving me damn near crazy. Look at me."

My gaze settled on his, on the blue that had always stopped me in my tracks. Surely he was about to tell me he was seeing Willow so I could tell him to leave me alone.

He reached for my shoulders and I let him touch me.

He leaned into my ear.

"The hand in water trick doesn't work," he whispered, and then he dunked me. When I emerged from the water, I could hear him laughing and it struck me too. I lunged for him, threw myself onto his back, and wrapped my legs around him.

"I think you've forgotten. I was always the chicken fighting champ." I felt him laugh as he struggled beneath me, and I shoved my hand under his arm and wiggled my fingers before throwing my body weight toward the water. He howled and we fell together.

When we came back up, his hands found my hips.

"You win," he said, grinning. He lifted me as high as he could while treading water. We'd done this all the time in his parents' pool in high school. We'd wrestle and he'd help me with cheer stunts and then we'd kiss . . . a lot.

"Ready? Okay!" I said, laughing, then clapped. I knew how dumb it was to be almost thirty years old acting like a teen, but it felt good, it felt light to forget the baggage of the past decade, the past day.

When Lee didn't throw me into the air, I looked down at him. There was a chance he couldn't manage to throw me when he was treading water at the same time. But his eyes met mine and there was a heaviness to his gaze. He lowered me until my body was against his. I could feel his fingers on my waist, the way they'd constricted in the last seconds. I could feel the ripple of the muscles along his chest and the bulge of his arms beneath my hands. He leaned in. And then I remembered.

I pushed him. Hard. And then I pushed him again. Lee's nose crinkled with confusion and he tried to grab my arms, but I swam away.

"Hattie, what—"

"I forgot," I yelled. My veins seethed with anger. It was one thing for us to play around as friends. It was another thing for him to keep pulling me close, to keep trying to kiss me when he was with Willow.

"Forgot about what?" By the time he reached me, he was out of breath.

"Oh, let's see. About you dating Willow and trying to kiss me anyway, about you volunteering our barn for

Founder's Day when you know good and well it's not going to be ready in a week and I'm for the stadium."

I swam to the bank of the river, where a few planks of our old dock still hung out of the clay.

I hoisted myself onto the bank and pulled the linen out from my legs and the cotton from my chest. Lee followed me.

"It's not like that with Willow and me," he said. I paced up the hill through the long grass.

"Just go home."

"Hattie. Come on. I'm not lying to you. Sure, Willow and I see each other, but we're not exclusive."

I glared at him and it only made me angrier. I wanted to find him hideous, repulsive, but I didn't.

The lawn planed toward the barn, acres of overturned dirt and dead peanut plants.

"She's never been you and you know it," he said finally.

I whirled toward him. "What the hell does that mean?"

He looked down at his feet.

"Actually, don't even bother answering that," I said. "I know who I am. I'm the idiot who loved you and she's the one you wanted. She's the one you still want as evidenced by whatever y'all are doing now. I don't really know why you're here. Leave me alone like you have for the last eleven years."

I quickened my pace. Water dripped from my hair and pebbles dug into my bare feet. My face felt hot. I wanted nothing more than to get on the train and go back to Charlotte, to forget I'd ever seen him again.

I walked around the edge of the barn.

"I can't do that. I can't leave you alone," he said. "If you'd just stop, I could explain."

"I'm not interested," I said.

He tried to grab my hand and I avoided his touch. In a way, I knew what he meant. I gravitated toward him naturally. It had taken incredible effort to push him away in the river. We hadn't been in town at the same time since the day we both left for college, and before that, we hadn't been apart for even a day for four years. He was as home to me as my house, my family, Main Street, this town.

"Lee, Hattie." Fox stood in the driveway in front of the barn, a bag of grass seed slung over his shoulder. He looked from me to Lee and back again. I held my arms against my chest. "Nice day for a swim, I guess."

"Yeah. It was supposed to be," I said.

"Y'all have history." Fox cracked a grin and lugged the bag into the barn. "Should've known. I heard Tammy tell Willow she saw y'all riding through town together last night when I was getting in my truck this afternoon. Willow about took me out in that little convertible of hers she was so heated." I was thankful he hadn't mentioned my reaction to his telling me Lee was dating Willow. I know he'd connected the dots now.

Lee didn't react to the news that Willow had been upset at all.

"We have history, but it's history," I said. "The only business we have now is Lee sticking his nose where it doesn't belong. Actually, Lee, why don't you tell us why you thought it was a good idea to offer up this shitty barn to the town for Founder's Day? Take a look, Fox, do you think it looks ready for a party?"

Fox snatched another bag of grass seed out of the truck like it was a feather and carried it to the growing stack in the barn. He laughed.

"Not really."

"I only mentioned it to a few people, and word got around. I thought it'd be a way for your parents to test things out before they committed to the events business," Lee said. "Of course we'd planned to ask them if they wanted to first, but a test run makes sense. If they hate hosting the event, people crawling all over the farm, they move on and do something else. If they love it, they have an event under their belts and they know how to do it the next time. Look, it doesn't have to be perfect. It's just us Mountain View folks. I told you last night that I'd help get things in order around here and I meant it. And my band is up for playing no matter where it is."

"Well, good luck to all of you," I said evenly. "If Mama and Daddy agree to the idea."

"What do you mean?" Fox asked. He picked up the next bag. "Your mama said you were staying through the week when she called the store to order this seed. She'd heard about Lee suggesting the farm for Founder's Day and was excited about it. You'll help out, won't you?"

"I don't hodgepodge events together, and there's not enough time to make this one a success."

I looked out at the field. Dead peanut plants in the overturned earth. Weeds sprouted around Mr. Robinson's truck. Part of the barn's roof sagged.

Lee stood beside me, silent, as Fox kept unloading the seed bags without responding to my ridiculous statement. I'd crafted luxurious events in less than a week before, so I knew that wasn't really the reason for my resistance.

"I don't like to be blindsided," I said quietly.

"I know," Lee said. "I'm sorry."

"I hope you change your mind," Fox said to me. He came out of the barn and wiped his dirty hands on his pant legs. "If you do, this Founder's Day might be the best yet." He smiled at me. "I know I said this place ain't ready for a party, but with the right help, it could be. I'm pretty free this next week. I'm happy to lend a hand too."

"Thank you, and I know," I said. "It's not that I don't want to do it, it's that I should have been told before anything happened. Not knowing made me feel foolish."

My eyes teared suddenly, catching me off guard. I blinked and looked toward the house. Out of the corner of my eye, I could see the confusion on Fox's face. Of course, my statement had nothing to do with Founder's Day. I was angry with Lee. He'd confused me. He was confusing me now.

"I didn't mean to make you feel that way," Lee said. He stepped toward me and I backed up.

"Go home." I couldn't stand to look at him. Not after he'd admitted to seeing Willow while coming on to me. I didn't care if they weren't exclusive. She clearly had feelings for him and him her.

"I've got to go change," I said. "See you around, Fox."

I tipped my head at him and left both men standing in front of the barn.

CHAPTER FIVE

"Leave it, Hattie. Fox said he'll bring that sod cutter later," Daddy called out from across the field as I wiggled the shovel with all of my might under a patch of weeds.

I flung the shovel down and reached for my water bottle. Exhaustion was setting in. I'd been up since four emailing my decorating team for the gala, making sure they were ready to set up at the convention center starting Monday and that they had all of the supplies I'd ordered—the uplighting, the five hundred birch twig trees, the electric lampposts, the white drop curtains, the tabletop candelabras. Then I'd filled out all the paperwork for a liquor license to give to Cletus, Mountain View's ABC rep, in case Mama and Daddy ended up wanting to make a go of this events business.

At five, I'd closed my computer and went outside to try to get the field in order. I took a sip of my water. Buying grass in the middle of August in the South was a dumb idea. They'd spent a few thousand on the seed, thousands they didn't really have, and the grass would be scorched the moment it came up despite Daddy swearing he was going to irrigate it so well it wouldn't.

The piles of old peanut sprouts and shriveled casings that never took stood next to the riverbank, both near as tall as I was. That had been my first order of business. We'd burn them in a few days. I rubbed my biceps and lifted the hem of my shirt to my face to clear the sweat. I wasn't used to farmwork anymore.

Daddy stood in front of the barn holding a two-by-four, appraising the structure like he'd never really noticed the way it leaned to the right or the soffit and rafter tails that had pretty much rotted away. Inside, the floorboards in the loft were hit or miss and the rafters had spread a bit with age. It would take a lot of work, a lot of manpower, to get the barn back to plumb again. I couldn't figure out why Mama's first thought was grass seed and not the barn. I guess the barn would be alright for Founder's Day—the town knew the state it was in, after all—but you definitely couldn't charge a soul to host a wedding or party in it looking like it did. I'd seen pictures of it after it was first built, Mr. Robinson and a small group of men standing in the open doors. It had been a good-looking barn. Now it looked like the rest of Mountain View.

"Hattie, Helen Sue," Daddy hollered to me and Mama, who was lounging on the porch swing in her curlers and polyester rooster print nightgown. "I'm going to need y'all's help 'til Fox gets here. I'm going to sister up some rotten spots in the rafters, and I need the both of you to make sure I don't fall through."

"When's Fox coming?" I yelled back. "And how much are we going to have to pay him?"

"He's coming by when he's done with the morning rounds. He said he's doing this pro bono." Daddy threw up his hands. "Or whatever that word is that means free, because it's for the town." He adjusted his trucker hat just barely atop his thick gray hair. It still looked like it could blow off given the right breeze.

Mama walked down from the porch in her slippers, nightgown, and curlers, not bothering to change into something suitable for work. I couldn't help but laugh looking at them. I'd seen an article in the *Charlotte Observer* about how grandparents as we knew them were disappearing, replaced by youthful, fit, fashionable elders who'd given up their La-Z-Boys and Christmas sweaters for Pelotons and Lululemon. My parents were basically an endangered species.

I ran my hand over the top of Mr. Robinson's cab. It was rusty, of course. That was part of its charm, part of the memories that called it home, memories of me and Lee.

Daddy called for me again, and I picked up my pace. Last night, after a frustrating day of nothing but TV church and rain—Mountain View took Sundays seriously— I'd gotten an Instagram DM from Lee. At first I thought maybe it was a spam account, but then noticed the handle @LelandLockhardtBand and figured the guys must have decided they needed to start one. Most of the pictures focused on Lee. I couldn't help but replay how it had felt to be near him in the river—the laughter, the way his hands had felt on my body, the way his body had felt under my fingertips, the familiar churning in my stomach when his eyes met mine. I'd wondered what would have happened if I hadn't pushed him away, but I already knew.

And I'd been glad, looking at the band's Instagram, that it hadn't happened. Before, we'd belonged to each other and we'd both been here, our whole lives ahead of us. He'd loved me and I'd loved him and life had been simple. Now we'd lived a whole decade apart. We knew the teenage version of each other, not the people we were now. Now there were careers and Willow and whoever else he'd talked into a non-exclusive piece of Leland Lockhardt standing between us, and we couldn't exactly pick up where we left off.

When I finally decided to read his message, that's what I'd thought he was talking about at first. He'd started off by saying that he didn't have my phone number, but that he was sorry about everything. I'd assumed the "everything" was him coming on to me when he was seeing Willow, no matter how casually. But then he'd said he shouldn't have suggested the barn for Founder's Day without consulting me first and he'd only done it because he thought it would draw attention to the business if we decided to do it. He'd told me he'd ordered some things for the barn after our fight yesterday—a dance floor, a chandelier, a small stage, and a dozen tables—since it was his fault we were hosting, and that they would likely be delivered today. He mentioned he'd asked Fox to help install them and that he was going to Atlanta for the day to see his chiropractor for his shoulder. Apparently, he'd tweaked it when he'd jumped in the river after me. Then he said he'd be back later today and would love to see me. He said we had a lot to talk about.

I'd thanked him for his help with the barn, but said we were going to pay him back. I didn't want to owe him. I also didn't reply to his hang out request, so he'd asked again after telling me he knew we'd accepted Fox's free labor on behalf of the town and accepting the things he'd ordered was the same. I could see his point, and I knew we couldn't afford either labor or materials otherwise, so I'd said okay but hadn't responded to seeing him later. We did have a lot to talk about, but talking was pointless. He'd explain and we'd reminisce and he'd try to kiss me again—just like the last two times—and maybe I'd give in and we'd wind up in his bed.

As hot as that would be, as much as I wanted Lee one last time—or a few last times—it would only be a hookup.

Maybe he thought I would be fine with that, that I'd evolved to enjoy a good time and leave it alone, but that wasn't exactly me. Especially not with Lee, with the man a part of me would love forever. Not when I knew for certain that we wouldn't get back together and he wouldn't follow me to Charlotte.

Lee's next stop would be wherever was best for him. I'd learned that from our college decisions. We'd applied to the same four schools—Wake Forest, Furman, South Carolina, and NC State—because those were the schools recruiting Lee. I was accepted to all of them except for Wake. And suddenly, after my rejection, Wake was *the* school for him. To be fair, they had the best baseball record, but I'd always wondered if he'd been relieved when I didn't get in. Maybe he thought I'd muddle his devotion to baseball, or maybe he wondered what it would be like to be with someone new. Regardless, we hadn't worked outside of Mountain View then, and I was certain we wouldn't now.

"Daddy, are you sure that's a good idea?" I stepped into the barn, forcing my mind away from Lee.

Daddy was standing in the hayloft toward the back of the barn, his steel-toed boots settled on two beams that looked a little too splintered for my liking. Between the beams were gaps and rotten wood. He tapped around on the thicker exterior planks, then extracted a hammer from the loop of his overalls, nails from his pocket, and a little metal thing that looked like a hinge.

"This ain't gonna work long term," he said.

Mama stood in the open doorway of the barn behind us, shaking her head. The sun illuminated her silhouette, making the finest polyester Walmart had to offer shine like silk.

"I told him to wait for Fox to get here," she said. "He has no idea what he's doing. Being an expert in farming doesn't make him an expert in remediation."

"Damn it, Helen Sue. This ain't rocket science, and I don't need that young man's help. I just told him he could come to be nice," Daddy said.

I grinned at Mama, and she laughed under her breath. I wandered around the empty space, thinking of how we could arrange something suitable for Founder's Day. It was pretty much a blank slate, nearly five thousand square feet. Mr. Robinson had had a bunch of horses at first and had built the barn large enough for twelve stalls. After he sold the horses, the stalls had been in disrepair, so he'd had them removed to create one big room.

My phone pinged and I took it out of my pocket.

Party Rental Plus is saying we only need 45 tables. I see on your sheet you indicated 145.

Merry wasn't happy. Usually, she finished her texts with a *Thanks!* Or a smiley face. It killed me that I was leaving her in the lurch.

Sorry. I'll call them.

I dialed Party Rental Plus and left a message, then followed it up with an email.

Someone was coming down the drive. I could hear the crunch of tires on the gravel outside.

"Did you order something from that company that's using robots now?" Mama screeched and ran into the barn.

"What are you talking about?" I passed her and walked out into the sunlight.

A sizable Amazon delivery truck was backed up in the driveway, and a guy in jeans and a blue and black Amazon shirt got out.

"Watch out!" Mama yelled as if she could no longer tell the difference between a normal thirtysomething man and a bionic one.

"Stay back, Hattie. Let me get my pocket knife out," Daddy hollered behind her. Then something crashed. I turned to find Daddy dusting himself off after jumping down from the loft like Spider-Man. Maybe country folk turned into grandmas and grandpas faster than city folk, but it didn't mean they were feeble. Most sixty-five-year-old men weren't keen to launch themselves off a two-story hay loft to save their daughter from an android.

"Y'all can stand down," I said, laughing. "You're thinking of drone delivery. Nobody has robots yet. Not even Amazon." Clearly Mama and Daddy had never ordered a thing online, and I bet most of Mountain View hadn't either. Shopping at Walmart had just become acceptable about five years back, after Mrs. Muffet shut the doors to her clothing store, the Barnyard Boutique. To make the name super relevant, Mrs. Muffet brought chickens in to wander around the store with the shoppers. She didn't seem to notice the barnyard smell that came with the clothes, and everybody else just endured it because there was nowhere else to go.

The Amazon driver saw me at the bottom of the drive. "Miss Hattie Norwood?" he called out. "I've got quite a bit in here. Where do you want it all?"

"If you could back down here, it's all for the barn," I said.

"Hattie. What in the world?" Mama whispered as the driver got back in the truck.

"It's a dance floor, a stage, some tables, a chandelier. Just a few things Lee ordered since he's the one who volunteered our barn," I said.

"Now we're going to have to pay him back. We can't take free from everybody," Daddy said when he finally ambled over to Mama's side. I noticed he was limping a little from his jump.

"He's insisting we take it as a gift," I said when the truck reached us. "It's for the town. Same as Fox's help."

That seemed to satisfy them, and they let the driver begin to unload the boxes.

Just then, the Mountain View school bus, the one that had been sitting behind the high school baseball field since the 1970s, pulled into our driveway. People hung out the windows and Gotye's "Somebody That I Used to Know" poured from speakers somewhere inside.

I froze.

"What in all of tarnation," Mama said. "Vern got the bus started." She smiled really big, like Vern Trisdale, town tinkerer, had just rounded everybody up for a ride around Mountain View and had come to pick us up too.

But I knew what this was.

Vern pulled the bus across our driveway and shut off the ignition. People poured onto our lawn. Tosha with her guitar, Chester, Charline, Bobby Jo, Tammy, old Mr. Carpenter, who they'd clearly broken out of the clinic in Cardinal River because he was still wearing his hospital gown, Lee's band, Annie carrying a megaphone, and everybody else too.

I followed Mama and Daddy up the driveway, but not before the Amazon driver pulled me aside.

"Am . . . am I going to be able to get out? It's not like I own the company, ma'am. I know some people loathe us, but I just need to get on with my deliveries."

"They're not here for you," I said. "They're here for me. And you can get out around the other side of the house. Just pull through the field."

He opened his mouth as though he didn't quite think he could manage driving through grass and then shrugged.

I caught up to Mama and Daddy. Even though we were less than half a football field from the crowd, both of them still seemed to believe the town had descended on our farm because Vern had finally started the bus.

"Well, I'll be," Daddy said. "This bus used to take me to school when I was a youngster."

"They're not here to show y'all the bus. They're here to protest me refusing to sign the petition," I said.

Mama and Daddy stopped in their tracks. The mob started chanting, led by Annie's megaphone. It was one of our cheer chants she'd transformed for the occasion.

"We want a what? Yeah, we want you to sign, you gotta sign," they yelled.

Mama grabbed my arm. "Why in the world won't you sign it? I know you think the stadium is a good idea, but you don't live here anymore. Our town could be torn apart if you don't."

Mama's eyes teared, and I started to tear up myself.

"Mama," I said quietly. "Can't you see? Mountain View is going to disappear if something doesn't change."

The crowd moved on to the next chant, and their voices got louder.

"No, no, we won't go. Not 'til Hattie signs real slow."

It was the dumbest chant I'd ever heard.

Daddy shook his head and took his hat off. Of course I'd told my parents that I thought the stadium was a good idea for Mountain View several times over the phone, but I guess they didn't think I'd stand in opposition to the town's desires if it came to it. I figured over the past few days that someone had told them about my scuffle at Fox's, but then again my parents hadn't left the farm besides Daddy's early Saturday morning jaunt to the lumberyard.

"Now a few of us are going to tell Hattie why we signed the petition," Annie said into a megaphone while the rest of the group kept yelling.

"Mountain View means everything to me." The crowd's chanting died out as a soft voice took over. Willow. I hadn't seen her slither out of the bus, but I suppose her speaking first made sense. She was doubly mad at me, I was sure. First because of Lee and second because of the stadium.

She was standing behind Tammy and Bobby Jo, but Vern pushed her forward. She looked like a young JLo, with perfect makeup and perfectly curled hair and a pink chiffon skirt with a high slit to show off her sculpted legs. Her mama had started her on the beauty pageant circuit young and she'd racked up titles—Miss Turnip Green to Miss Cardinal River—all the way through high school. People in cities sometimes gave beauty pageant girls a hard time, but the truth was that every pageant girl I knew always looked flawless.

I, on the other hand, had always been a minimalist when it came to self-care, and as I stomped toward the angry crowd in my work boots and cutoff jean shorts, my ponytail lopsided and tired, I wished Mama had had the decency to let me compete for Tiny Miss Pine Summit all those years ago.

"As y'all know, I was employed in San Diego for several years after college. I loved my job. I worked in the ER and really felt like I was making good on those promises I'd made on pageant stages all those years ago."

She had the pageants to thank for her stellar public speaking too.

Out of the corner of my eye, I noticed my parents walking toward the crowd. They were joining the town, abandoning me, their only child, their own flesh and blood.

Sterling kept patting Daddy's arm, and Tammy had her arm wrapped around Mama's shoulders.

"Several months ago, I was talking with Mama when she told me that Chantelle was having her baby soon and they were having a hard time finding somebody to cover the nursing vacancy at the clinic. Now I know Cardinal River's our rival right now, but y'all know we claim it as our own when we're sick. Taking over for Chantelle gave me an opportunity to come back home to Mountain View." She paused. Her eyes met mine, and then, I swear, her nostrils flared.

In high school, I knew exactly why Lee had chosen me over Willow—even though she'd had a crush on him since the sixth grade like the rest of us. I was pretty, but I wasn't a dainty flower. I was a girl who could throw a baseball, who didn't mind getting dirty. I was a girl who would wrestle with him and give it all I had. I was a girl who was comfortable around his friends and didn't mind their jokes.

But now, I wasn't sure he'd choose me again. All of the reasons he'd liked to be around me then didn't matter so much anymore. Willow was gorgeous, articulate, and smart.

"I realized I was miserable in San Diego, really," Willow went on. "I had friends, but not any great ones. My community was still here, in Mountain View, in the South. All of my best friends were here."

She tilted her head, and her face softened as she looked at me, as though I was supposed to consider that I was one of the friends. Maybe she wasn't as smart as I assumed. Nobody kept on being friends with a person who screwed their longtime boyfriend hours after they broke up. I'd forgiven Lee because he'd apologized—whether my heart had actually ever reconciled what he'd done, I didn't really know—but Willow hadn't even said she was sorry.

I glared back at her, and the Pollyanna façade dropped away.

"We all love Mountain View because it's a family. Family cares about each other. If this stadium comes in, it'll change this town forever. Nothing will be left."

Suddenly, my nerves snapped. "Don't y'all get it? I didn't take any of you to be idiots, but now I'm questioning that," I shouted. My face was burning, and a collective gasp came from the group in front of me. "I'm not refusing to sign the petition because I hate this place. It's not the place I choose to live anymore, but I don't wish it, or y'all, ill will. The thing is, I've been out of here. I've seen what happens to small towns like Mountain View when the businesses start closing and the land starts to dry up and everybody digs their heels in and refuses to change. They die."

My voice rose louder on the last word. Behind me, I could hear the Amazon truck's tires spinning and lurching in the tilled dirt.

The crowd was silent. I noticed several people weeping. My parents included.

"I know it's hard to hear. But there's another way out. The stadium is going to bring new life to one of two towns, and I hope that town is Mountain View. It'll bring new restaurants and shops and tons of new people."

"I don't want to curse at you, but hell, Hattie, you're getting it all wrong," Vern said. He ran a hand through his permed mullet and then pushed his hands into the pockets of his tight Wranglers. "We've heard about all the so-called advantages. Our attorney was kind enough to walk us through it. She said we might even become the next Gaffney. But that's the problem, see? Because all of the advantages she mentioned were disadvantages to us. If my parents lose their farm and other families too, and we have to move out of town, well, this place ain't Mountain View anymore."

"I understand," I said, my tone soft. "But there are two options, Vern. Let Cardinal River win the stadium and sentence this town to death in a decade or earlier or say okay and figure a way to get excited about the future of this place, even if it'll look a little different."

"Our town won't die if the stadium doesn't come in. None of our families are leaving," Willow said. "Just sign the petition, Hattie. This isn't your fight anyway." She smoothed her red lipstick. "Even Lee signed it."

I froze. It had never really occurred to me that he had, or that he would. He'd claimed to agree with me.

"I don't believe you. Show me." I paced toward her.

"The signatures are all online. Hold on, Hattie, let me get my tablet out," Annie said. She dug in her Tumi briefcase, pulled the iPad out, and tapped on it while I pretended that Willow didn't exist.

"See here," Annie said and pointed at Lee's name. The signature was dated August 13, the day before he'd told me he felt the same way I did about the stadium.

Surely there'd been some error. Maybe Willow had signed his name without him knowing. He wasn't here to ask. And the signature was just a typed name on a page, not a real signature that someone could easily dispute as a forgery if it wasn't right. Then again, if the town was in the business of forging names, they would've made it easy on themselves and forged mine already.

"How did you get him to sign this?" I asked Willow. My palms were sweating and my heart raced.

"What do you mean?" She laughed. "He was happy to do it. We were laying there one morning and—"

"What the hell are y'all doing?"

Fox's truck appeared around the edge of the school bus with the sod cutter Daddy had requested, interrupting our conversation. Fox's eyes flitted to mine and then scanned down the line of protestors.

"Annie," he said, a disapproving edge to his deep voice.

Annie held up her hand.

"I know what you said. Which is why I didn't text you this time." Her face clouded.

Fox killed the engine on the truck and stepped out. He extracted his sunglasses from his shirt pocket and put them on, then walked over and stood next to me.

"She'll be here until Founder's Day. Y'all have six more days to change your tune. You think you're going to make her see our way by bullying and protesting? I *know* your mamas taught you that you catch more flies with honey than vinegar." He turned to me. "Not saying you're a fly." Fox grinned at me and I smiled back.

"Yolanda told us all of Mountain View needed to sign the petition ASAP," Annie whispered, walking over to him.

"I know that. And I'm obviously on y'all's side. But I'm telling you. Cornering Hattie like this ain't going to get you what you want."

He touched Annie's shoulder, and she lifted her hand to his. Something was definitely going on there.

"Plus, shouldn't most of y'all be resting up for the Coconut Pie 5K tonight?" Fox glanced over at Sterling who had a stomach of steel and had been Mountain View's self-proclaimed Forrest Gump in his younger years. He glared at Fox and scuffed his old white Reeboks in the dirt. He'd won the annual contest, which served as a kickoff to Founder's Week festivities, twenty-seven years in a row because he could stomach sprinting a mile and a half, eating an entire coconut pie, and then sprinting another mile and a half to the finish in the town square. But apparently, for the last two years, Fox had bested him. "I'd hate to be the one crowned the victor again because y'all were out here using up all your energy to harass Hattie."

Annie sighed.

"Alright, y'all. I think Fox is right, but any of the rest of you are welcome to say your piece to Hattie," she said to the group.

Sterling shook his head, curled his arm around Vern's waist, and started toward the bus. The rest followed.

"Fox is right. I'm not going to convince you to oppose the stadium by being nasty. I'm ashamed of how I acted

Saturday morning," Bobby Jo said, coming to my side. She looked at her shoes—bedazzled Keds. "I think everybody's just in a panic."

"Thank you," I said. She patted my hand and joined the others as they filed onto the bus.

I watched the crowd depart and at once thought maybe I should just give in and sign the petition. Willow was right. I wasn't going to live here and the fate of the town wouldn't impact my daily life. Maybe that's how she'd convinced Lee to sign.

But if I signed the petition and the town shut down, if every farm turned out barren like my parents', an event space at our farm wouldn't matter and my parents would truly lose everything. Surely there was a way to figure out a new place for the families that would lose their farms with the stadium. Then again, there was nowhere else for them to work, to go. Daddy had struck out in a matter of an hour because the only employers were other farms, Amtrak, and the lumberyard in Pine Summit.

When the school bus pulled out, leaving Mama, Daddy, Fox, and me standing in the driveway, Mama sighed.

"I guess I should go put my face on. And some clothes too."

"Mama." I caught her arm. "I'm sorry I disappointed you. But I can't let the town die."

"I know you think you're doing what's best, but I pray you'll come around," she said.

"Let's start on the barn. That should help," Fox said. "Want a ride down the drive?" he asked Daddy and me.

Daddy shook his head.

"I'm going to have a word with Helen Sue and then I'll meet y'all down there."

I followed Fox to the truck and climbed inside. Besides the engine's silence, the cab was exactly the same as a normal F-150. The truck was immaculately clean and smelled like leather. Chuck Berry's "Johnny B. Goode" was playing staticky and low.

Fox settled in the driver's seat beside me.

"Thanks," I said.

He glanced at me.

"For getting them to leave me alone."

"You're welcome. I know you're probably right about this town needing change, but like I said before, an NFL stadium ain't it. Mountain View could reinvent itself another way. Maybe we could work to emphasize its history or simply look at the skills of the people here and lean into those. That's what the Robinsons did when they founded this town, and I think if we could stoke that spirit, it could make a difference."

I didn't say anything. Mainly because I doubted anybody would do anything different than what they'd always done.

"People that live here do so because it's small. Even Mr. Robinson, after all of his fame, figured maybe this little place was where he belonged. That really resonated with me when I visited for the first time. It was freeing to realize that maybe he felt like I did, that a big place wasn't meant for me. I don't think I fit in in cities."

I laughed.

"Really? You seem pretty normal to me, and normal fits about anywhere. You don't hold a candle to Sterling or Mrs. Muffet or Cletus."

He smiled and put the truck in gear.

"Let's think about that again, Hattie," he said. "I love this place so much I adopted another name to be a part of it. You don't find that strange?"

We drove down the drive and I stared at him. He was handsome and generous, kind and a good businessman.

But maybe he was hiding something ominous. The idea startled me.

"Yeah. I guess that is pretty weird. Why'd you do it? What's your real name anyway?"

He rolled the window down as we caught up to Daddy making his way to the barn.

"Sure you don't want a ride?"

Daddy shook his head, and Fox turned to me.

"Everybody just started calling me Fox and I went with it. I didn't mind leaving my old self behind. I don't have a record, I'm not in witness protection, and I'm not a criminal if that's what you're wondering. Just starting fresh."

"I wasn't thinking that."

"Yeah, you were," he said. He grinned and pulled the truck in front of the open barn doors. "Listen, you can pay me back for warding off the mob and fixing up your barn by just mulling over the possibility that Mountain View could survive a different way, that volunteering the town to the state ain't the only path forward."

"Okay," I said, mainly to appease him.

"Alright then. Let's get this barn ready for Founder's Day."

He got out of the truck and as he was coming around to my door, I realized he still hadn't answered my question about his real name.

"It's something embarrassing like Coot, isn't it?"

He laughed.

"You don't need to hide it if so. In fact, you'd be in perfect company," I said as I walked past him.

"Maybe."

"Okay, so let me guess. Doberman? Jaws? Knuckles?"

He shook his head, then opened the back of the truck and hoisted the machine out.

"If you're thinking of some list like Best Pet Names of the late '90s, you ain't going to get it. My parents weren't into pets. Well, except for the hermit crab they caved and got my brother and me at Myrtle when I was eleven. It died a few days later."

Fox pushed the stamper toward the barn.

"Okay, so Pincher? Shelly?" I asked, laughing, as he disappeared into the barn after Daddy.

CHAPTER SIX

I could still hear Cletus in the distance, wailing Mr. Robinson's song "Mountain View Ballad" on the karaoke machine from the town square as I jogged past the mile mark on Route 2 by the Mainerts'. Nothing primed the muscles for a race more than a slow, sad song. He could've chosen Mr. Robinson's "Get Up and Dance," but no.

I smiled at the Mainerts' cows as if they would return the favor, and then passed Tosha. She was wearing a pair of leather pants and a fringe vest. Most people weren't running in athletic wear. I'd passed Lee's friend Woody early on. He was hobbling along in his tight rock and roll jeans, a cigarette burning from the side of his mouth. I couldn't imagine how terrible snug jeans would feel after downing a whole pie at the midpoint and running back to town.

Up ahead, I could see Lee at the pie table eating his last slice, shirtless, his abs and arms glistening with sweat—well, besides the lower portion of his right arm that was covered in a sling. Ordinarily, the sight of his body on display would make me weak in the knees, but right now, I wanted nothing more than to shove the pie in his face. I couldn't believe he'd signed that petition.

I picked up my pace. I'd been late to the start because we'd lost track of time. Mama and I had cleared the barn floor and installed the dance floor over the dirt while Fox and Daddy sistered the rafters—whatever that meant. When we were through, I thought we'd head to the house and collapse in front of the old rear-projection TV in the living room, but the minute we'd gotten back Mama and Daddy started preparing for the race. Mama put on her coconut hat—Chiquita Banana but with coconuts—and Daddy dug his *Watch Our Coconuts Run* T-shirt from ten years ago out of his armoire. I'd decided not to fight it. I'd already given them enough heartache for the day. So I'd swapped my farmwear for Lulu and Nike running shoes. We'd pulled onto Main Street just as Darius, Loraine's brother, who was dressed as Mr. Robinson, and his wife, Sugar, who was dressed as Mrs. Robinson, kissed passionately to signal the start of the race.

I reached the pie table in the driveway of the Smiths' farm just as Lee started running away. Little Gin Smith held a pie my way.

"I'm sorry, but I have to go," I said, suddenly furious. "Don't worry, I'm not going to win!" I hollered as I took off, in case she thought I'd somehow catch up with Fox or Sterling who were so far ahead I couldn't see them.

Ordinarily Lee would be in the lead too, but it was surprisingly difficult to run quickly when you couldn't move one arm. I sprinted as fast as I could and caught him as he was passing Bobby Jo's mailbox.

She was sitting on the porch of her small brick house holding a posterboard that said, "GO!" The color looked familiar. The other side likely read, "SIGN THE PETITION, HATTIE!"

I waved at her anyway, then stared at the back of Lee's head. My muscles tensed and my heart pounded so hard I felt faint.

"You signed the petition," I said when I caught up to him.

He glanced at me, startled, then wiped the sweat away from his face with the palm of his hand.

"How could you do that? You said you agreed with me," I said.

"I didn't really know what I was signing," he said. "It was still dark and I was half asleep. Willow just said she needed my autograph and held up her phone."

He didn't look at me. Instead his gaze was fixed on the long stretch of road ahead, toward the break in the buildings on Main Street that led to the gazebo and the finish line. His response only made me angrier. It was dismissive. When we were together, he'd been thoughtful. He'd been a man who loved me well and owned his mistakes—until the night he broke my heart. After that, things were different.

"It wasn't something I thought about, alright? It's not worth discussing."

"Yes, it is. The whole town hates me. I thought you were the one person with me on this." My breath was coming in short gasps. "You know what? Never mind. I guess you're still pushing things under the rug like you did eleven years ago. What happened to you? You used to care about people, about me," I said. My side began to cramp, but I kept his pace.

He looked at me.

"What the hell are you talking about, Hattie? I've always cared about you. I will always care about you," he growled.

"Always? Maybe you believe that, but you don't. We were just kids when you broke up with me and hooked up with one of my friends the same night, then ignored me for weeks after knowing I knew. But we're not kids anymore, Lee. We've spent time together. You've tried to kiss me—*twice*—yet you're acting like I shouldn't care that you signed a petition *you don't agree with* just to appease that same ex-friend who you're *sleeping with again*."

My head ached, the heat and the anger burdening my body to the point I thought I might pass out. I wasn't even sure I made sense.

"I know we were young, but I made a mistake back then. I thought you understood that when I apologized." His voice was low, and his jaw was tight. "I don't know why I did it. And I should've paid more attention to what I was signing, I do agree with you, but—"

"That's bullshit. You know exactly why you did both things. Willow's your siren. There's something about her you can't resist."

I clenched my hands into fists. I wanted him to admit it, to say that he thought he should be with someone like me but couldn't resist her. Maybe then I could leave him behind once and for all.

"This is why I wanted to talk to you," he said. "There were things I never told you and maybe it doesn't matter anymore, but I still thought you should know."

We waved at the Brown family gathered in their front yard. Elvira, the youngest, was sitting in a mud puddle wearing goggles and a snorkel.

"Remember when I went to Wake for that immersion weekend to check out the team?"

I didn't respond. Of course I did.

"Well, they took me to a party. There were girls all over us," he said. "I told the guy I was shadowing, Mojo, that I had a girlfriend and the other guys overheard. They told me I'd never make it to the pros if I was in a relationship. They said I'd prioritize you over the game. Coach basically told me the same thing."

My heart was in my throat. I had never asked Lee to choose between me and baseball; I'd always assumed we could both be in his life.

"That's why you were relieved when I didn't get in to Wake," I murmured. I didn't even know if he'd heard me.

"Mojo and the guys told me they'd all broken up with their girls before coming to school. I told them I didn't know if I could do that. I said I loved you and didn't think I could get over you. They said I was crazy and told me to hook up with someone else after I ended things, to get you out of my system."

"You did exactly what they said to do. As though you had no mind of your own," I said. My voice shook. "Still. Why her? Why not Jozelle or Vi or Sarah? Someone I wasn't friends with."

"Because she'd been coming on to me for years. I knew she'd agree to it. And you're right. I did exactly what they told me to do, but they were wrong. That hookup, every hookup . . . it didn't get you out of my system."

I could feel his eyes on my face, but I couldn't look. If I did, I'd cry.

"But it got me out of your way."

"Maybe. I don't know what would've happened if I would've ignored them. I can't change what I did. But I'll always be sorry that I hurt you. I hurt myself too."

I was equal parts furious and sad. I wanted to hit him and hug him. At least now I could get some closure.

We were half a mile from downtown now. Behind us, someone vomited. The sound turned my stomach, and I was suddenly more than thankful that I'd bypassed the coconut pie.

"Thank you for telling me," I said finally.

"Should've told you a long time ago. We've just been apart for so long." He cleared his throat. "I guess if all of that taught me anything besides what an idiot I am, it taught me that I shouldn't give out advice like Mojo did. People should make their own decisions and mistakes. And that includes this town. Maybe that's why I didn't make Willow delete my name once I realized I'd signed. I wasn't lying when we were talking the other night. I do agree with you, but we also weren't talking about the petition."

We passed LeeRoy Johnston, who'd run track in high school. He was wearing the same split leg running shorts he'd worn since then.

"Like you, I get that if something doesn't change, this town is going to die. But I shouldn't be the one deciding whether people keep their farms. Because at the end of the day, the fate of this town won't really matter to me or you. We ain't staying. We might have to help our parents out down the road if things go south, but that's as far as it goes for us. Whereas for these people," he said, nodding down the road at the farmland, "this place is their whole world."

Ahead of us, in the distance, the sun was setting over the mountain, washing the town and our farms in pinks and golds. The sight calmed me somehow.

"Remember when we hiked up there?" Lee asked.

"I can't believe in all of the years we lived here, we only hiked to the top once," I said.

"That's because there was no need to repeat it. That day was perfect."

We'd decided to hike Pine Summit one Saturday our junior year because Lee had had a random day off from baseball and the weather was heavenly—a seventy-degree cloudless spring day. Lee had packed lunch for us, and when we reached the top, we'd come face to face with the most beautiful meadow tucked into the rock. It was surrounded by boulders on all sides but one, and you could see the patchwork farms below and the buildings of downtown Spartanburg if you squinted. After we'd eaten our sandwiches, Lee opened a bottle of champagne he'd smuggled from his house and we took turns drinking it until we were thoroughly buzzed. Then we'd kissed until our bodies found each other and the grass prickled my skin and the cool breeze whispered all around us.

"Yeah. It was," I said quietly. That was the day I told myself I was going to marry him someday.

A few feet in front of us as the road narrowed between the buildings, race spectators twirled noisemakers and yelled encouragements.

"Almost done," Lee said. "Let's finish strong."

He grinned at me and started to sprint. I matched him. The cheering was deafening as it echoed between the buildings. We cleared them, and the finish line drew near, right in front of the gazebo. Fox and a group of others who'd already finished clapped for us.

I glanced at Lee. He was struggling, and I edged ahead as I crossed the finish line.

I raised my hands and turned to gloat, just as Willow emerged from the line of spectators and launched herself into Lee's arms. He caught her with his good arm as her legs wrapped around his waist.

My heart shriveled. He'd just said he'd never gotten over me. He'd just told me that hooking up with her that night was a mistake. I'd assumed it meant he felt the same about being with her now—but that's not what he'd said. Then again, I hadn't said much about my current feelings either.

I turned and walked toward the gazebo where my parents stood next to Fox.

"It bothers you, doesn't it?" Fox asked. He stepped into the gazebo, toward the table filled with coconut pies. Most races gave out Gatorades and granola bars after races. Not Mountain View.

"Here." He handed me my pie and a fork. "It ain't as good as the winner's pie with the whipped cream and fresh coconut shavings and all that, but I guess it's decent." He was wearing a Dri-FIT shirt and athletic shorts, looking more the picture of an athlete than Lee did at the moment. I'd never seen him in anything but plaid and work pants.

"You're not wearing Carhartt," I said.

Fox looked down at his clothes.

"Nope." He grinned. "It pains me to say it, but Carhartt's inferior in the athletic wear area."

"Guess that's why you beat out Sterling," I said, watching him trudge across the finish line in his overalls.

Fox grit his teeth. "Hope he lubed up or he's gonna be hurting. That canvas in this heat would chafe the shit out of your thighs."

I laughed as Sterling walked away from the finish line, his legs spread like he'd just gotten off a horse, then dug my fork into my pie and took a large bite. Out of the corner of my eye, I saw Willow talking with Lee behind the wall of townspeople on the other side of the street.

Fox looked at me.

"No," I said, belatedly answering his first question. "It doesn't bother me at all."

CHAPTER SEVEN

I'd never been very good at Canva. I could make any space look beautiful in a matter of a few days. I could organize a complicated seating chart—in fact, I'd been working on the 1,000-seat arrangement for the gala earlier today. I'd also arranged the exact sorts of cars the celebrities requested to pick them up at the airport at eight different times and from seven different car services. But I was horrible at graphic design.

"Hey, Fox. When you take a breather, will you look at this graphic?" I called.

I was sitting on one of two carved walnut church pews Mama and Daddy had excavated from the old five and dime downtown. I'd told my parents that old church pews would be perfect for the perimeter of the barn and they'd asked Annie if we could have them. Pews were great because they held a lot of people while adding a lot of character. That's why the Lincolns, who had owned the five and dime, had bought them from an old church in Clover in the first place. They looked good and held a lot of weary men while their wives shopped.

"Yeah, sure. I have a couple more panels and then I'll need to come down for more lacquer," Fox said.

He was standing on Daddy's rickety ladder across the barn, treating the top half of the wall that led to the hayloft with shine that made the old wood sparkle and the room smell like it was about to catch fire. I didn't bat an eye at almost anybody on a ladder, but watching Fox perched up there made me nervous. I knew the ladder claimed to be able to hold his weight, but he was tall and solid, and I couldn't help but worry it would buckle. The metal squealed every time he moved.

He'd been on a ladder all day yesterday too, when he'd tackled the exterior. He'd volunteered to paint the top sections in red while Daddy and his friends Harry and Gerald, whose lithe frames could've scaled the ladder no problem, took the bottom. It had ended up looking perfect, but I'd retreated into the house before it was finished to touch base with my gala vendors. I'd also called the couples displaced by Limelight's closing to gauge interest in our barn once it was done, mainly because I couldn't stomach wondering if Fox was going to fall.

I swiped through the photos I'd taken on my phone yesterday evening. With the barn freshly painted and the sunset on the horizon, it actually looked like a place somebody might want to get married. Originally, I'd been on the fence about painting the barn. By the time I was born, most of the red the Robinsons had painted had chipped off, so the natural wood was all I knew. But Fox and Daddy agreed that paint was needed. It would help prevent rot and red was iconic.

I zoomed in on the last picture I'd taken—a horizontal shot of the barn, Mr. Robinson's truck, the sunset and the trees hiding the river beyond. I stared at the photo, envisioning couples posing against the barn, next to the truck with a crowd of their friends.

A few days ago, I'd thought this dingy barn only suitable for livestock sales or hoedowns, but now, with lots of help from our friends, this place was shaping up to be a plausible event space.

My email pinged and I rolled my eyes at the subject line: *Plastic or Glass?* We'd contracted Squeeze of Lime Bartenders for the gala, a new company who'd given us a major discount, but it had been a mistake. They had clearly never done an event this big. I tapped on my email and responded to their owner, Drake, that no, guests paying $150 for a ticket didn't want plastic coupe glasses.

I closed my email and opened the Instagram account I'd created yesterday in case Founder's Day went well and Mama and Daddy wanted to move forward with the event business. @RobinsonsEvents—*Built in 1943. Given new life in 2024. Book your celebration with us in beautiful Mountain View, SC.* I uploaded my favorite photo of the barn as our profile picture and saved it.

"What's up?" Fox appeared, startling me, though I should have heard him creaking down the ladder. He ran a hand over his beard, removed his hat and stared up at the wall he'd just finished. "Looks decent." He dragged his hands through his sweaty black hair, then put his hat back on.

"Have you ever thought about shaving your beard and getting a haircut?" I asked.

He grinned. "Is that what you called me over here to say?"

"No," I said, laughing. "And I don't mean for looks. You look fine. I mean, you look normal." I stumbled over my words and his eyebrows rose.

"Okay."

"I only meant that you might feel cooler in the heat if you didn't have so much hair." I started laughing again and he chuckled.

"That's probably true, but I'm keeping it. I look normal now, and that's a win. Think about it like this—nobody's ever seen Chewbacca without hair. He might look appalling. Same goes for me."

I studied his face, and then my eyes drifted to his body. I suddenly realized what I was doing and forced my gaze to his, but it was too late.

"Since you ain't disagreeing on the matter, I guess the beard and hair stays," he said graciously.

"Anyway." I stood. "I'm going to have to bounce out of here right after Founder's Day so I'm thinking ahead about what Mama and Daddy may need in case they end up wanting to go through with this events business. I've taken some exterior photos and videos, and I've overlaid them with text for socials, but I'm not sure it looks right."

I tapped on my photos and chose the first, a video of my parents walking toward the barn hand in hand. I'd made Daddy put on his nice jeans and forced Mama into wearing her only dress that had a shape to it. Over top of the video, I had text scrolling about the Robinsons and then about Mama and Daddy. At the end, I encouraged viewers to join the tradition of true love.

"I love it," Fox said when it was over. He stared at the stilled screen.

"Do you like the font I used? I could pick a sans serif instead of the cursive."

"It's good like it is."

I tapped on a couple of other graphics, one that was just the barn with a call to action *Book Now* beneath it. And then a carousel reel with photos of the Robinsons on the farm leading up to the barn as it looked today with the text: *Their love stood the test of time. Now it's time for your forever.*

Fox's eyes met mine.

"How can you do all this and not want to stay?"

"I told you, I—" My chest tightened. I was tired of defending myself.

He held up his hand.

"It wasn't really a question. I know why you want to go back," he said. "I guess I should've said that being a part of this project, renovating the family homestead of one of my heroes is unreal to me."

I thought back to what Lee said during the run, that Mountain View was paradise for some. It had been hard for me to fathom, but seeing Fox's face when he'd watched the video of my parents and the Robinsons, I understood. It was one thing to love the only place you'd ever known, but to love a place you'd chosen was different.

"My daddy was an alcoholic for half of his life," Fox went on. "He wasn't abusive or anything, but he couldn't stop drinking. Then he got picked up for a DUI when I was around three or four. He got in an AA program and had a sponsor that changed his life, but every now and then when he'd feel the urge to pick up the bottle, he'd turn on his old Nat King Cole and Ronald Robinson records and sing instead. Ronald Robinson was the soundtrack to my childhood, my life, really. I wish I could've met him."

"You have," I said, sliding my phone into the back pocket of my jean shorts. "He was his music. He had an unbridled joy about life but was grounded enough to know about its sorrows too. Elita was the same way."

"Think he'd like what we've done with his barn?"

I started laughing.

"I can hear him plain as day. 'Now this sure is pretty, Hattie, but you ain't gonna be able to bring your horses in here.' He had an old southern accent, straight from Georgia. The kind that you don't hear much anymore unless you're from the deep South. Know what I mean?"

His eyes met mine, and then it occurred to me that I'd asked a question that skirted close to "Where you from?" I hadn't meant to. Still, I wanted to know.

"Yeah." He looked at the unvarnished ceiling. "Sure you don't want me to put some gloss on that?"

I eyed the twenty-five-foot ceiling above us.

"Yep. If it's glossy it'll radiate the light from the Edison bulbs and the chandelier light, and we want the ceiling to mute it, to create a warmer ambiance."

Edison bulbs and twinkle lights would drip in undulating strands from the hayloft to the doors, and a crystal chandelier that Lee had ordered would hang over the stage. The chandelier wasn't exactly my taste. In fact, I would have opted for something more rustic elegant if I had been the one to choose it, but the fixture had been free, and it was a quality piece.

"Speaking of lighting, should we go ahead and hang the chandelier? I have to wait around until the varnish dries to make sure it's even anyway," Fox said.

I hesitated. Hanging the chandelier would involve Fox getting back on the ladder.

"If you think Lee wants to handle that, by all means," he went on.

I smiled. "Lee is good at a lot of things, but construction, electrical work, painting . . . basically all manual labor is out."

"How do you avoid learning that stuff growing up in a place like this? I mean, I have my job for a reason. There are plenty of people in town that just don't want to do handyman work or can't anymore, but most know how to wire a light."

"You have to have a banker as a daddy and get good at baseball." While most boys I grew up with were required to help around the farm on the weekends, Lee was always at the field or in the school's weight room.

Fox laughed. "I guess I could see that." He paced toward the ladder, then stopped. "I might need your help, actually," he said. "The chandelier's up in the loft. Your dad put it up there yesterday, and he said, and I quote, 'I'm putting the light up here 'til we're ready to hang it, Fox, but don't you go after it unless you want to fall through the roof. You're too big.'"

"I'll get it," I said.

I walked across the new dance floor, skirted the modular stage still folded where the laminate parquet ended, opened the skinny door and went up the steps. I was glad Daddy had told Fox to avoid the loft. Even though Daddy had tried to repair the floorboards, some were still missing and a few were beginning to rot through.

I stepped carefully around the perimeter to where the chandelier box sat in the first gable. Daddy had placed it next to his collection of long forgotten but important items—an old computer, three or four monitors, a boom box, and a carton of old CDs.

"You up for some music?" I yelled. "I just found my old boom box and a bunch of burned CDs."

"Depends on if you have good taste," Fox yelled back.

I grabbed the chandelier box and stepped gingerly across the loft to where it opened to the barn below. Fox looked up at me and smiled. At once, I couldn't look away from his face. His dark green eyes lightened to moss with the beams streaming in from the windows, and he had one dimple above his beard in his left cheek I hadn't noticed before. My stomach flipped, and I glanced down at the ground to squash it. This reaction was ridiculous. Back home, I'd all but written men off after Hunter, sure I couldn't find my way to feeling again, to loving again. But here, I'd run into Lee. Maybe facing the man I'd loved for so long had nudged my heart awake.

I set the box on the loft floor, laid on the iffy beams, and handed the chandelier down to Fox. He took it from my hands.

"I'll have you know I had—and still have—exceptional taste in music," I said.

"Then bring the boom box down and prove it."

I walked back toward the gable, grabbed the boom box and carton of CDs, and made my way back down the stairs.

When I reached the bottom, I plugged the CD player in and thumbed through the cases. Most people my age would think it was strange that I had old CDs at all. Even though smartphones had been out for years by the time we reached our senior year, nobody in Mountain View had them. Cletus and Charlene had rented out the theater when the iPhone launched to show what I now knew to be a conspiracy theory video about how smartphones were bugged by China to take over America. Somehow all of Mountain View became convinced that our town's abstinence would save the country.

I glanced down at the CD case in my hand. *Graduation Party.* Dolly had written the words in her signature pink sharpie and then drawn little party balloons all over the front. I tossed the rest of the cases back in the carton. The student body had put Dolly and me in charge of the graduation night celebration, and we'd talked Principal Gaston into letting us use the baseball field. I'd had Paradise make up twelve different types of sliders, and I'd displayed them on a big plywood banquet table on the infield. We'd had a photo booth and carnival games rented from Party Supplies Plus in Spartanburg and superlative trophies. But every time I thought of the party, I thought of the music. Dolly's playlist had been gold, set to motion by Sterling's strobe lights. Looking back, it was my first foray into event planning.

"Whoever drew on that CD should be an artist," Fox said, standing over me with the chandelier box.

"She is, or was, I guess. She hasn't painted in years. You know my best friend, Dolly."

"Oh, right. I always forget about y'all since I don't think I've ever seen you together. I didn't know she was an artist."

"Oscar Mayer books them out of town a lot on the weekends, which is really the only time I'm in town," I said. "And yeah. She was planning on majoring in visual art, but then Rocky proposed after graduation and he already had the job doing farm irrigation work for the town, so Dolly let her acceptance lapse." I shrugged. "Back then, I was really upset with her for letting her talent go, but she doesn't regret it, so I guess it worked out."

"Sometimes dreams change." Fox knelt down behind me and took the chandelier frame out of the box along with the crystals and instructions.

I popped the CD in and pressed play.

Macklemore's "Thrift Shop" blared from the speakers, and Fox groaned.

"What? That's a banger and you know it." I skipped it anyway and Miranda Lambert's "Mama's Broken Heart" came on.

"Alright, you've redeemed yourself with this one." Fox opened a pack of what looked like a thousand gold wires and then glared at the instruction manual. "Just let it play and come help me. Seems like Lee ordered the most frustrating fixture on the market."

I sat down in front of him and opened a dozen bubble wrapped crystals.

"If you could just loop this wire through the top of each of those and pinch it closed, I can start assembling." He handed me the wires.

I plucked the first crystal from the wrap and attempted to extract a little wire from the bundle but stabbed my hand instead.

"Damn," I whispered, waving my finger in the air.

Fox glanced at me. "You need a Band-Aid?"

He got up and walked to his toolbox before I could answer. The song switched to George Strait's "I Can Still Make Cheyenne" as he rummaged around for my Band-Aid. A deep voice dripping in soul quietly joined George's. It was so moving it nearly made my spine quake. Lee had a beautiful voice, but his was baritone, a versatile sound that could adapt to any genre. This voice, Fox's voice, was something unique.

When Fox retrieved the Band-Aid, he turned around, and stopped singing.

"You were singing," I said.

He laughed. "Yeah, people do that sometimes when they like a song. This one's kinda complicated for me, but I can't hate George for it."

"You should join Lee's band," I said.

He rolled his eyes.

"I mean it, Fox. Your voice almost gave me the shivers."

"Thanks, but I'm not a natural performer." He sat back down in front of me. "In fact, that's always been the thing with me. I don't have that kind of charisma."

I grinned, assuming he was joking, but he was studying the instruction manual, his face sincere.

"How do you figure? If you haven't noticed, you're kind of popular around this town."

"This might seem hard to believe, but my last job was pretty high-profile," he said, deciding not to respond to my last statement. "I worked my ass off to prove myself. More than anybody else. But then, when it came time to promote somebody to a leadership role, I was told I didn't have the magnetism. And then, a few months later, I was blamed for something the new CEO did and was subsequently fired." He laughed under his breath. "When I got in the car to leave that day, this song was playing. I've had a love-hate relationship with it ever since. It used to be my favorite. Aaron Barker wrote it. He's a damn genius. It's relatable and earnest and doesn't try to be anything it's not."

"Those people at your last company are idiots," I said.

He shrugged.

"You're beyond valuable to this town. I'm pretty sure we'd go under without you." I hoped the compliments would cheer him up. "Did you come here after you were fired?"

"Yep."

"Why? I mean, how long did it take you?"

His face clouded. He knew what I was doing. He knew I was prying, and I couldn't bear the weight of his glare, so I stood up and played the song over.

The fiddle started, and at once, randomly, I could see a bride and groom dancing to a song like this in our barn, under the glittering chandelier light. I closed my eyes.

"Dance with me," I said, completely without thought. My body rushed with nerves. I didn't know why I'd suggested it or how it had come out of my mouth. I wanted to take the statement back, but I couldn't.

"What?"

"Dance with me," I forced out again, opening my eyes. "You said this was once your favorite song and now, well, you said you can't love it completely anymore, but maybe a better memory would help you get it back."

"Okay," he said. He stood and paced toward me. His hand clasped mine, his arm wrapped around my waist, and he held me close. I'd never felt so small, so entirely consumed by a man. Fox's gaze found mine. I knew I should say something, but I couldn't. Instead, I let my head fall against his chest. For some reason doing so felt easier than speaking. I listened to the song and breathed him in. He smelled like his store, like lumber and gardens.

When the song ended, I forced myself to look at him. I smiled. I hoped it looked friendly, like his arms around me hadn't had me feeling any sort of way.

"Maybe it'll be my favorite again after all," he said.

"I'm glad I could help." I stepped away the moment the last note sounded.

I sat down in front of the crystals and busied myself rearranging them. "This is going to take forever and it's past lunchtime already. I could call up to Mama and see if she could bring us some sandwiches."

Just then I noticed Fox was still standing. His face was ashen, and he was staring at the boom box.

"What is it?"

"Where the Statue Crumbled" by Dirt Road was playing over the speakers now, the bass and the quick Appalachian fiddle a contrast to the melodic song before.

"Will you . . . will you turn it off? Please."

"Of course."

I practically ran across the barn. I couldn't figure if he was reacting to the song or if he was about to be sick.

"I can't do this," he said, before I could switch the song.

"What's wrong?" I asked when I reached the boom box, but he turned and walked out of the barn, leaving me with questions and the echo of the fiddle's wail.

CHAPTER EIGHT

It was one of those evenings that promised cooler weather but lied about it. A few hours ago, a thunderstorm had come through, bringing downed limbs and hail along with lower temperatures. I'd even walked outside in my white sundress and thought I might need a jacket. But as soon as I got out of the truck on Main, I realized my error. Even though the temperature was cooler, the humidity was so thick you could cut it with a knife. The moisture clung to my linen dress, dampening the fabric and making my skin feel sticky.

Everyone was in a bad mood. The annual Robinson Walk Around, a twelve-hour event done in shifts in a loop around Mountain View to commemorate the twelve days the Robinsons had spent living in their truck before they decided to stay and establish the town, was on a delayed finish due to the storm. That meant that the Wild Ramp Dinner, a celebration of Mrs. Robinson's first meal made in Mountain View—a wild ramp wilderness stew made from pickled ramps she'd bought when they'd passed through West Virginia—was also delayed. Lee, who'd volunteered for the last shift of the walk around after work at the bank, was finally on the last lap.

"Mayor should've called Lee in after he came through town this last time rather than letting all of our food sit out. Mr. Robinson wouldn't have minded," Mama said, as Billy Bobby Brown tooted Mr. Robinson's song "Golden Sky" on his recorder from the gazebo. Little Zuzu Mainert, who had the misfortune of sitting on the curb closest to the gazebo, covered her ears. Annie, who has on her other side with Willow, patted Zuzu's head and tried not to laugh.

"I know he wouldn't have. He and Elita appreciated a good meal. Unlike this new generation." Pam jabbed a fluorescent yellow manicured finger toward Annie.

A group of the Melodies were gathered in front of me in lawn chairs on the sidewalk outside of the Cut & Curl. It was closest spot to the buffet laid out on a series of sawhorses and plywood sheets stretching from the gazebo to where we stood. The rest of town lined the path that Lee would take to the gazebo as though waiting on the king of England to pass through. I eyed the platters of now-cold shrimp rampy, fried ramps with ranch, ramp fritters, wilderness stew, spaghetti with ramps, ramp and buttermilk biscuits, pickled ramps, and pasta with ramp pesto wondering how anyone could find the spread appealing. I didn't like ramps to begin with, but the food looked even worse than it had when it was first set out, like the forgotten vat of carrots at the Golden Corral. The cheesy pasta sauces were hardened and the oil in the fritters had cooled, creating a film on the breading.

"It's a shame about the meal. My shrimp rampy ain't as good chilled," Loraine lamented. "And we all spent a pretty penny on getting our pickled ramps shipped in for this. I feel it's a waste now." She pursed her lips and smoothed her sunshine yellow shift dress that complemented her floral scarf and ebony skin tone perfectly. Unlike the rest of the Melodies, she refused to wear the matching pink T-shirt that Belinda had made a decade ago that said, "Get Your Stink On" with a wild ramp pictured beneath it. Loraine claimed she couldn't wear it because she was the town's realtor and had to maintain her professionalism at all times. It was a good excuse.

"Do you want me to go out and find Lee and ask him to run the final lap?" I offered, but no one responded. It had been like this since we arrived. I'd been pleasant, greeting everyone with a smile, but it seemed that the town had made a pact not to speak to me. I guess they'd decided not to take Fox's advice to kill me with kindness after all.

I glanced up the street at the hardware store. I hadn't seen Fox since his sudden departure yesterday, and it was odd that he wasn't out here charming the town while we waited on Lee to finish up. Fox seemed to love stuff like this.

"You know," Tammy said to the Melodies, her fluffy blonde curls shaking as she spoke, "The walk around will take even longer if that awful stadium comes in. There will be so much traffic it'll be near impossible for someone to keep walking through their whole shift. They'll have to stop for traffic lights."

I rolled my eyes. I knew the comment was directed at me.

"I'm feeling a little lightheaded, Helen Sue," Belinda said to Mama, who was sitting beside Tammy, acting like I didn't exist to fit in with her friends. "I normally eat right at 6 and it's already 6:23. I think my sugar might be low." She paused. "Or maybe it's all the stress. I just don't want to lose our town." She pinched her eyes closed and leaned into Mama's shoulder dramatically.

I didn't know why I was still standing there. I didn't have to listen to these comments. I had calls to make anyway.

I skirted the table at the end of the buffet displaying Vern's signature ramp moonshine and walked across the street to the hardware store. I glanced in the windows, finding it empty, before sitting down on the concrete sill. I called Park Road Books in Charlotte and spoke with Sally and Sherri to confirm they had everything set for the gala, then hung up just as the town started to cheer.

The families that had been wilting on the alley's curb only moments before now jumped to their feet and yelled when they spotted Lee. I couldn't see him from my vantage point, but when the Melodies all stood and began to clap too, and Annie took the microphone from Billy Bobby's recorder and tapped it, I knew he was getting close.

"The moment we've all been waiting for is finally here! The walk around has concluded! Welcome to the annual Wild Ramp Dinner!" Annie announced. "Before you dig in, I wanted to remind y'all to invite anybody you know to Founder's Day. It's important this year. Our attorney said the state's due to make a decision on the stadium location likely within the week, and we need all the support we can get." She paused. Somebody had brought cowbells and the earsplitting rattle of a group of them took over the moment she stopped talking. "Now without further ado, the buffet is open!"

Lee appeared by Annie's side at the gazebo. She grabbed his hand and lifted it into the air as the townspeople scrambled toward the tables. Lee pulled off his hat with his other free hand and waved it around. Then his gaze swept down Main, over the town ravaging the cold buffet like a wake of vultures, before finally settling on me. He smiled and I grinned back. Letting go of Annie's hand, he stepped out of the gazebo still looking my way as though he was planning to walk toward me. But then Willow appeared. She looped her arm around his waist and pulled him close before drawing back to unscrew the top of her signature bread and butter ramps she'd come up with in high school. Even though they were awful and barely touched on the buffet each year, she kept making them. She held one up to Lee's mouth. He grimaced, but opened his mouth anyway and let her feed it to him.

Lee chewed, clearly attempting to hide his disgust, and then tried to edge around her, but she clutched his waist again and drew him to her, initiating a long open-mouthed kiss that made my stomach turn. I thought he'd push her away, but he didn't. Instead, his hands gathered on the small of her back. The way he touched her made me sick. The way I imagined the kiss tasted made me sicker. Ramps were pungent. Horrifically so. You wouldn't want to breathe the same air as anybody who'd recently had one, let alone explore their mouths with your tongue.

"Gross." Fox emerged from his store behind me at that moment, his nose scrunched at the sight.

"I know," I said as Lee and Willow finally separated.

Fox stood next to me, watching Mountain View continue to swarm the tables.

"Are you going to get a plate?" I asked.

"No. I'm not into ramps." He kept his eyes fixed on the buffet line. "Hey, about the other day . . ."

"It's fine," I said. "You don't need to explain yourself." People were complicated and I didn't need Fox to detail why he'd left. "I mean, you did leave me to assemble that chandelier by myself, which took me four more hours, but Daddy hung it up yesterday and it looks great." I laughed. Fox didn't. Instead he exhaled through his teeth and shook his head.

"Sorry." He glanced down at me and readjusted his trucker hat, a vintage red with a puffy crown that read *Fox's Hardware* and then *est. 1963* in smaller letters.

"You're wearing that wrong," I said. "Mr. Fox wore his hats like Daddy does, like a strong wind could blow it off."

He adjusted the hat, then gestured to the new style.

I squinted at him.

"Eh. I don't know. Mr. Fox had white hair. You look like him—like the pictures when he was young, I mean—but I can't picture you old."

He laughed and put the hat back on his way.

"I know you said you don't care, but I'm going to explain anyway," he said. "It was rude for me to bail when you needed my help."

The town seemed to withdraw from the buffet tables all at once. Most of the serving dishes were completely empty and the north end of Main was quiet again as the town congregated to eat in the gazebo and on the little green around it where some chairs and a few tables were set up.

"There's not much to say. It's just . . . that song's a bad memory. Maybe the worst I have. You don't hear it that often anymore so I guess when it came on right after 'Cheyenne,' it caught me off guard. I was right back there, in that shitty place I try to forget about." He'd palmed his face. "You probably think I'm crazy. It ain't like I've got an album's worth of bad memories or anything. Just those two. And when they played back-to-back . . ."

"No, I understand. I have those too."

"You do?"

I thought for a second about my serious answers. "What If I Never Get Over You" by Lady A had been playing after I broke up with Hunter. And then there was Dolly Parton's "I Will Always Love You." Lee had played it for me on the edge of his pool deck the night he told me he loved me. I glanced across the street at the Cut & Curl and started laughing.

"'Any Man of Mine' was playing when I got this haircut the other week," I said. I ran a hand through my lopsided shoulder-length hair, and Fox reached out and touched it.

"It looks pretty good to me, and Shania wouldn't steer you wrong," he said, a smile on his face.

"Maybe not, but Cherry, the hairdresser at SaveCuts did. My hair was long, mid-back length, and I asked her to trim it to the base of my ribcage. She thought I said shoulder blades."

Fox laughed. "It could be worse," he said, tipping his head at Mama's friend Cricket who was pouring herself another glass of ramp moonshine. I knew she'd had foil on when I'd gone into the Cut & Curl for a donut, but I guess I hadn't seen her for the finished result. Undulating racing stripes in red, pink, and green wiggled down the strands of her permed hair. "Word is that Tammy told Cricket if she let Deanna apply her dye, she'd get a discount. I guess Deanna has been thinking about going to beauty school."

"Deanna's color blind," I said, unable to look away from Cricket's hair.

"Yep," he said. "Guess she thought those were the highlight colors Cricket usually gets. And speaking of color blind, I told your dad I'd come by and finish wiring that chandelier tomorrow morning. He didn't wire it in himself, did he?"

"No, thankfully. He tried to talk me into it, but I told him that setting fire to himself and the barn wasn't the explosive kickoff we were thinking of for Robinson's Events."

Fox laughed.

"Good call."

"Foxy!" Annie yelled from the gazebo. Her eyes swept mine, but then she pursed her lips and focused on Fox. "Got any bug spray? The mosquitos are having a feast of their own over here."

"Yeah," he yelled back. He turned and disappeared into the store, emerging moments later with a citronella candle and a bug spray. "Be right back," he said to me before walking down the street to join the rest of the town. He stopped next to the tables and turned toward me. "Thanks."

I looked at him, confused.

"For understanding me, I guess, and for letting me help out with the barn."

"Yeah, of course," I said. "But we should be thanking you. You're the one helping us."

He shrugged.

"Maybe, but I still can't believe I'm working on Ronald Robinson's barn." He smiled. "We'll make him proud."

I stared at the dark chandelier, then plugged the Edison strands in to the outlet and watched the barn glitter. Outside, the sun was setting, and the ambiance in the barn was warm and perfect. We had two more days until Founder's Day, and there were still a lot of things to do—replacing outlets, touching up the external paint, clearing a decent space for cars—but the barn looked completely transformed. I remembered what Fox said earlier this evening; I did hope the Robinsons would be proud of what we were doing.

My phone sounded in my sundress pocket and I pulled it out.

Hope things are going better at home . . . I'm going to need you back here as soon as you can Monday morning, Merry emailed. *The good news is that the meeting with Eliott went well last week and he wants to meet you and talk more about Mountain View and the possibilities there. I think we have a great chance at the events contract if things go well, but the bad news is that I got a call from Liam Neeson's manager today and the airport delayed his arrival time for his jet to an hour before the event. They're trying to work it out, but if not, you'll have to call Concord Airport and see if they can accommodate and then rearrange the car service to pick him up there. And then, three of the sponsors want to change their signage, never mind that we've already gone to print.*

My mind began to race, and I could feel the urge to turn and run to the train station burning in my veins. Merry was juggling too many things and she was getting frustrated. If I didn't get back soon, the event would be a flop and I could kiss that partnership and the raise that came with it goodbye.

I'll be back as soon as I can, I wrote. *I'm sorry I've put you in this spot.*

"Wow. If this isn't lipstick on an opossum, I don't know what is."

I whirled around as Blaze, Lee's friend and former pitcher for the Mountain View Royals, a man who looked no older than fifteen but who had a beard that rivaled ZZ Tops's, wheeled his drum set through the barn doors.

"Uh, thanks?"

I couldn't figure if he was impressed or assuming the dance floor, stage, paint, structural security, and lighting were just a façade covering a dump heap. Then again, Blaze wasn't exactly the smartest cookie in the box and had no idea about rehabbing anything except for old Gameboys. That was his supposed job, after all.

"You look surprised to see me. Your mama and daddy told us we could come rehearse tonight when we saw them at dinner," he said as he pushed the drums across the dance floor.

"They didn't tell me, but yeah, sure, y'all can." My heart started to race, and I turned back toward the open barn doors to find Lee, his guitar strapped to his chest, carrying a microphone under one arm and an amp under the other. "Will you pick that up and carry it so you don't scratch the floor?" I asked Blaze, mainly in an attempt to pull my attention from Lee.

"Hey, Hat." Lee grinned when he saw me and his gaze lingered on mine. "It's okay if we're here, right? Your parents—"

"Yeah, of course," I said. I noticed he wasn't wearing the sling. Come to think of it, he hadn't been wearing it earlier either. "Guess your shoulder's better?" The vision of Willow's kiss pushed into my mind, and I looked toward the stage. Blaze hoisted the drums atop the platform and then flung himself beside them as though the simple movement had rendered him lifeless.

I heard Lee's footsteps stop beside me and then the soft thud of the amp as he set it down.

"I only had to wear it that one day since my shoulder had been adjusted the day before," he said. "Can we go for a walk after this?"

I could smell the ramps beneath the Tide laundry detergent on his clothes.

"Why?" I waved at Woody and Clay, who walked in wearing full leather—pants and sleeveless vests—carrying only their electric and bass guitars, respectively. Woody and Clay had thought themselves the stars of the band ever since they did an interview on the Cardinal River radio show before graduation. Never mind that the only reason they were asked to do the show was because Lee had been out of town on a baseball recruiting trip.

"Hello!" Woody yelled and then nodded his head. "Acoustics are good. Nothing like that shitty Hinterwood Arena my old band played at last year."

Woody's former band was Nickelby, a Nickelback cover band. The reason he was knocking Hinterwood Arena was because they'd been ranked in last place at Nickelback Battle of the Bands.

"You know why," Lee said to me. "We got into some things on our run and I know you. You think I'm lying about me and—"

"Babe, where do you want me to put these power strips?" Willow appeared behind Cassidy, who was wearing his violin case like a belt bag and lugging his keyboard toward the stage. She was wearing bell-bottoms and a fringed shirt with a plunging neckline to accentuate her sizeable boobs. I was always envious of those boobs in high school. They'd filled out our cheer uniform nicely while my top always hung limply over my tiny breasts.

"What the hell," Lee muttered, but then he pivoted toward her, and I watched his eyes settle on her body. He'd always sworn he was a butt guy and that large boobs weren't really his thing, but honestly, guys were drawn to both and Willow knew it.

"Hi, Hattie," she said and smiled a little too enthusiastically at me.

She said it as though she hadn't seen me in years, as though she hadn't been protesting me on my own farm days ago.

I ignored Willow and started walking toward the stage where Cassidy's keyboard's cord hung down the side.

"I'll get some extension cords from the loft," I said.

"Thanks," Cassidy said. He'd always been soft-spoken, a foil to his looks. He was huge, practically the Raiders' Marquan McCall's twin. He was the only one in the band who hadn't played baseball. Football had been his thing. Now he was farming.

I started up the stairs to the loft. The boom box I'd pulled out was back in its spot, ready to collect new dust, the CD crate too. I edged past them to grab the pile of extension cords, started back down the stairs, and nearly ran into Lee. He caught my arms.

"I didn't know she was coming here." His fingers remained on my skin. "She rode with Cassidy. I guess she saw him walking out to his truck next door and said she'd come along. I would've asked her to stay home."

Here, in the shadows of the tight stairwell, I wanted to lean into him, to kiss him hard, to prove that I was the better match for him. But despite Willow's intrusion, he hadn't pushed her away after the 5K, and he hadn't pushed her away at dinner tonight. And anyway, I was leaving in a few days, and he would leave eventually, and none of this would matter anymore.

I pulled my arms gently away from his grasp.

"You could've asked her to go when she got here, but you didn't. Clearly a part of you enjoys her company and that's none of my business. But you can't keep coming after me like this. I know it's been a while, but I haven't changed. She might be okay to share men with her friends, but I'm not," I said.

I could tell he wanted to say more, but he moved just slightly, and I pushed past him and out into the barn before he could. If he was going to disagree with having feelings for Willow, he'd had the chance. Maybe it was only guilt that compelled him to keep coming after me, to keep trying to make things right.

"Here," I said, handing the extension cords to Cassidy. Willow was standing in the middle of the stage next to Lee's microphone. I wondered if maybe she'd tried to talk him into letting her sing with the band. She'd been in choir with me in high school, though singing had never been her passion.

I walked toward the back of the barn, thinking I'd go to the house and work while the band rehearsed. If it had just been the guys, I would have stayed, but now with Willow lingering, it was uncomfortable.

Woody's guitar wailed from the amp, an ear-piercing riff that made my body rattle. But beneath it, Lee began to play. I could hear the simple chords, and then he started to sing the opening verse of "I Will Always Love You".

I couldn't help it. I turned around despite the symphony of emotions. Unlike Fox's reaction, the sound of this memory made me want to hear it forever.

Lee's eyes met mine. Willow, who was sitting on the edge of the stage staring at Lee, noticed his attention on me and her face pinched. I wanted to confront him. I wanted to ask if this was his way of confessing his love for me or if he was just confused and hoping to reel me in to figure it out. Either way, it wasn't fair. This wasn't us at our start fifteen years ago, innocent and in love. This was us after our end, jaded and unsure.

Lee kept singing.

"This ain't on our set list," Blaze said, pushing a hand through his hair.

"Yeah. We start out with our new one, 'Cardinal River Ain't Runnin Like Me,' remember?" Cassidy asked.

"He's warming up his voice," Woody commented, his gaze shifting from me to Lee. He'd been Lee's best friend in high school. I knew he probably understood what this song meant.

"I think you're warmed up, babe," Willow attempted, standing up on the stage next to Lee, but his eyes didn't stray from mine. Even when Willow brushed up against him.

Cassidy started in with accompaniment, stalling the next line. I thought I might throw up. I wondered if Lee had somehow overheard my conversation with Fox earlier. Why else would he be singing this song right now?

Before Lee could get to the line about always loving you, Willow unplugged the microphone.

"Lee, sweetheart," she said, her voice low. She reached for his chin and directed his gaze to hers. "You only have a little time to rehearse."

I turned away, deciding to head back to the house as I'd planned. It wouldn't do for me to stand here, watching Willow with Lee. Eventually, her perfect body would win out and Lee would realize she was the object of his affection after all, just like he had two times before within a matter of a couple days.

"How's it going down here?" Mama materialized around the side of the barn holding a tray of plastic wine glasses I was pretty sure she'd dug out of storage from my twenty-first birthday, filled to the brim with a light-yellow liquid and a lemon garnish.

"Fine. I think they're about to start practice, and I'm heading in to catch up on some work. What's this?" I asked, as the band started "Cardinal River Ain't Runnin Like Me." It was catchy, something like Florida Georgia Line would've come up with.

At the bridge, the instruments faded, leaving only Lee's voice. His tone was perfect for this song, smooth like Darius Rucker's with a bit of Morgan Wallen's grit. Then the band picked up at the chorus as though they'd been playing the song for years instead of a few weeks. I honestly couldn't believe how good they were.

"I wanted y'all to try out the signature cocktail I'm thinking we'll make for Founder's Day," Mama said. "Have one." She angled the flimsy plastic tray toward me, and I took a glass.

"Since when do you know about signature cocktails?" Mountain View didn't do things like this. Mountain View did punch, kegs, and maybe some moonshine if

Cletus or Vern had a batch ready or Sterling's peach jubilee fruit wine.

She grinned. "You left your laptop open, and I saw that you were having the bartenders do something called a mocktail and also a cocktail for your Narnia benefit. The recipe looked pretty good."

"Yeah. The White Witch," I said, grinning. "Basically a white Russian with Turkish delight for a garnish. So you decided to make one yourself? What's this one called?"

"The Robinson, I suppose."

I lifted the glass to my lips. I braced myself for something awful, mainly because I wasn't sure if Mama had ever had a cocktail herself. On the occasions she did have a drink, it was a Zima or a Boone's Farm. I took a sip. It was light and sweet and spicy all at the same time.

"Do you even have a shaker?" I asked. "How did you do this?"

"What's a shaker? I just threw it in the blender. I thought that's how you did it," Mama said. "I put in some of your daddy's vodka, some chili pepper from my container gardens, honey, lemon juice, and mint."

"Well, it's an unconventional way to mix, but this is delicious."

Behind us, I could hear the crunch of tires over gravel, and I whirled around to find an old Ford Taurus parking on the side of our driveway, its headlights swinging over the barn and toward our house.

An older gentleman in pressed khaki pants and a starched white shirt got out. He clearly wasn't from here. A few people in town wore suits on occasion, like Lee at the bank and Pastor Matthews for weddings and funerals, but nobody wore khakis. Nobody in town knew what business casual meant, and there wasn't a golf course for thirty miles.

"I'll be back," I said to Mama and walked up the driveway. The only thing I could figure was that this was one of the soil experts we'd called who hadn't returned our messages. The second guy we'd called had just shown up like this. I couldn't have him getting to the door before me, to speak with Daddy and give him false hope like those other three had before they realized they were wrong and the land was barren after all.

"Sir?" I called. He didn't hear me and started walking toward the porch. I lifted the wine glass to my lips and downed the rest of Mama's cocktail, then began to run. "Sir! Excuse me!"

I was breathing hard by the time I reached the man at the foot of our steps.

"Can I help you?" I asked, my hands on my knees.

"Oh, yes. I know it's terribly late. I got turned around back here, I'm afraid. But I'm with the state of South Carolina. I've been asked to come down here and look at some land possibilities for the stadium project, and I need to be back to Columbia tonight," he said. "I wondered if I could park here?" He pushed his glasses up higher on the bridge of his nose and squared his hips. He probably thought he was about to be chewed out.

"And before you tell me to shove the stadium up my ass," he went on, "I want you to know I don't have a say over where they tell me to look or what they'll decide. I'm just gathering metrics and data. I'm just a surveyor."

"I understand. And if you had to park on any property in this town, you came to the right place. I happen to be for the stadium." I smiled and he relaxed.

"That is quite unusual," he said.

"If this town doesn't progress, it will die." As I said it, I looked at him, standing on our farm and felt a strange twinge of sadness. I knew full well that the stadium could require our land, yet deep down it seemed I'd assumed the build would circumvent us. Still, I stood by what I believed. I had to. It was the best thing for the town.

"Indeed. It's a shame, but it's the truth." He paused. "Well, I'm much obliged. I'll take a quick look around down Route 2 here, and I'll be out of your hair in the next half hour or so. The western side over there looks promising, almost as good as that tract in Cardinal River," he said, mostly to himself. "Wouldn't have to deal with the river." He squinted across the road, then stuck his hand out. I took it, that feeling of unease disappearing with the words that indicated he wasn't interested in our land. "Richard Brantley."

"Hattie Norwood," I said. "Nice to meet you."

I started back to the barn as Mr. Brantley wandered toward Route 2.

Outside, the music from the barn sounded softly, quieted by the summer night air and joined by the cicadas. Cassidy was playing an interlude on the keyboard, a sweeping sort of tune I'd never heard before.

Lee emerged from the barn and jogged up to meet me.

"You okay?" he asked. "Your mama stopped us to give us those drinks and told us you were going to speak to some stranger who'd come by. Sounded kind of shady."

Lee's eyes met mine, and I looked away.

"Yeah, of course. It's just a surveyor from the state wanting to look at tracts for the stadium if it ends up here. He said he's interested in the land on the other side of the street."

"I'd hate that for Bobby Jo," Lee said. "The Harolds and Mainerts and Starns too."

Guilt rippled through me at the relief I'd felt when I'd realized Mr. Brantley wasn't interested in our land. I pushed it away and reminded myself of the town's inevitable demise if the stadium didn't come.

"He indicated there was a good tract they were considering in Cardinal River too," I said.

"Your mama down at the barn?" Daddy hollered from the back porch. His lanky six-foot-three frame was washed in the yellow of the porch light, and when his eyes leveled on Lee and me standing in the drive, he grinned.

"Yeah, Daddy," I yelled back. "She's down there boozing the band up with her signature cocktail."

"Well, I'll be." He paused. "You know, seeing the two of you together makes me think I've traveled back in time. It was practically yesterday I was seeing y'all off to prom," Daddy said, his voice echoing across the farm.

A hush fell over us, and I stared at the light coming from the barn, at the shadow falling over Mr. Robinson's truck, anything but Lee.

"Feels like yesterday to me too, sir," Lee finally shouted back.

"But it's not." I glanced at Lee. "And maybe that's what's confusing us. You aren't the same person you were and I'm—"

"Yes, I am," he barked, his face suddenly drawn. "I made some mistakes. But I'm the same damn person I've always been and you're the same girl . . . the same woman, I mean."

"Babe!" Willow's voice ricocheted over us. "Can you come back? The guys can't exactly rehearse without you."

He waved a hand at her.

"We've said a lot over the last week, Hat, but mostly we've been tiptoeing around each other. And the bottom line is that I ain't said all I need to say to you. We've been talking in fits and starts, and we keep getting interrupted or you won't listen or I hold back." He paused. "Before you go, promise me we'll take the time."

"Alright," I said. "But it's not going to be tonight. She's clearly not going anywhere." I gestured toward Willow who was standing right in front of the open barn doors. I thought he might say he'd ask her to leave, but he didn't.

"Maybe tomorrow, then," he said, and left me standing in the drive wondering if I'd just handed him over to Willow yet again.

CHAPTER NINE

"Why didn't we do this before?" Dolly yelled over Lee's band playing Mr. Robinson's "Sunrise on the Farm" at a speedy tempo that kept everybody dancing.

The barn was jammed full for Founder's Day. So full, in fact, that I could hardly wiggle my hips without bumping into Tammy twerking or Sterling twirling in a small circle on the floor. Outside, the crowd spilled out over the farm, past Mr. Robinson's truck. Some were waiting in line for a hot dog from Rocky—he'd brought the Wienermobile after Oscar Mayer approved his request to donate hundreds of hot dogs at the last minute—but most were dancing under the stars.

"This is much better than crummy downtown," Dolly went on. She swayed to the music, beads of sweat dampening the vintage 1940s gown she'd found at Salvation Army in Pine Summit fifteen years ago. It was a gorgeous white dotted-Swiss dress with a tiered skirt, puffed sleeves, red polka dots, and red ruching. She wore it every year. Almost everybody dressed in '40s attire to celebrate the 1943 founding of Mountain View.

"I'm just glad y'all made it back," I yelled. I tugged at the spaghetti strap of the Ava Gardner–inspired gown I'd ordered in high school. It was undeniably sexy—a gold silk that hugged my body with a slit that began midthigh—but it didn't quite fit the same now and I was pretty sure that despite my dousing it with perfume, I smelled like mothballs.

Dolly laughed and tilted her head back, letting her pin-curled blonde hair cascade down her back.

"I know you are. You needed saving, sugar, and I've always been the one to throw you a life raft."

Dolly and Rocky had rolled back to town last night, and I'd gone over to her house and told her everything. Even though she already knew about my stance on the stadium and disagreed with me, she hadn't thrown me out when I told her I hadn't signed the petition either. She'd always been levelheaded that way. She told me I needed to think long and hard about Mountain View and whether or not I could deny my people. She said I was right, that Mountain View could die without the stadium, but wouldn't it die with the addition of the stadium too?

"I'm glad you wore the dress," she said. She tipped the last of her Robinson into her mouth and leaned over to the cocktail table we just happened to be dancing beside to snatch two more.

"I'm not so sure."

"Well, I am, and my opinion is the one that matters."

She pressed a drink into my hand and discarded my empty one. Then she cheered as Woody fell to his knees at the front of the stage and threw himself into a riff that absolutely hadn't been in Mr. Robinson's original version.

"He keeps looking at you," she said, tipping her head toward Lee.

At the moment, his head was bent low over his guitar, but the sight of him made my heart trip. The band all wore vintage '40s black suits Lee had found on eBay, though they'd all discarded their dress coats in the heat and now played in T-shirts tucked into the high waisted pleated pants. Lee's shirt was nearly soaked through.

I took a sip of my drink. Dolly had been clear last night, when we'd talked about Lee's strange behavior, that he was telling me the truth about Willow. She said everybody knew they were having a little fun together, but no one thought they were a true item. She'd said she figured Willow had tried to make it appear that way to me so I'd back off because she'd probably always loved him. That part made me feel bad for a moment, until it didn't.

"I wish he wasn't so hot," I said. I stared at his chest and then at his face, at the square jaw and the full lips. He looked like a young Elvis, really, except for the mullet.

"I've never seen the appeal." Dolly grinned. Any woman with eyes would see the appeal. But Dolly had always been into men she could dominate, both in stature and personality. Rocky was perfect for her. He was short and a bit stocky, loyal, and altogether happy to go along with whatever Dolly wanted.

The band transitioned into "Cruise" by Florida Georgia Line, and Lee looked up, across the crowd on the other side of the stage and smiled. I followed his gaze and immediately wished I hadn't. Willow was attempting a line dance with Annie. Both of them wore sheer dresses with tulle skirts, though Willow's was black and Annie's was blue. Beside them, a group of out-of-towners who had undoubtedly read about Founder's Day in *Billboard* or Nashville's *The Tennessean* tried to join in. Those two publications had been advertising Founder's Day for decades at the request of Michael Sumner, a classical vocalist who hadn't been back to Mountain View since he got discovered by

Mr. Robinson's manager during a choir concert in the '80s. I guess Michael considered it his contribution to the town who'd raised him. Regardless of the publications' dedication, they never brought many outsiders to town. You could always pick out the couple dozen strangers easily though, because they didn't know about the 1940s dress code.

"Want to go skinny-dipping in the river after this?" Dolly asked, going for yet another drink.

"Yeah, sure." I took a sip of mine, thinking I should slow down. The lights above me were starting to blur, and I had that warm contented feeling in my chest. I loved being tipsy. Being drunk, not so much.

"Really?" Dolly clutched my hands and jumped up and down. "It'll be just like high school. We could float down to the Turneys' and steal their cow blankets for cover, then run through town."

"Okay, but let's watch where we're stepping this time. Do you remember when—"

"No. I've forgotten that time I submerged myself in cow shit." Dolly rolled her eyes, then she noticed something over my shoulder. "Lee might have his appeal, but he ain't the only hottie in town these days."

"Hey, Hattie." Fox's voice boomed over the music, and I turned, barely avoiding Tammy's elbow to face him. He wore a tan tailored suit fitted perfectly to his tall frame and he'd slicked his hair back with pomade. "Have you seen your mama? Or Annie maybe?" He looked over the crowd, but I suddenly didn't want him to see Annie. I wanted him to look at me.

"No," I said quickly. "Do you need something?"

"Maybe it's you. Out with the old, in with the new," Dolly whispered in my ear and then giggled. "Well, hi there, Fox."

"Dolly."

His green eyes met mine, but he didn't answer my question.

"I keep meaning to tell you. You did a great job today as Mr. Robinson." I burst into laughter. He shook his head.

"It was awful. I told you I was going to sound like a robot."

The play that always kicked off Founder's Day in town square had been hilarious for a change. Normally, it was boring and then gross at the end with Rudy's Mr. Robinson trying to smooch Annie's Mrs. Robinson, but today it was Annie overacting and Fox stammering through the narrator's part. At the end, the town had booed, and I'd laughed so hard I thought I might never stop.

"You do know how to read, don't you?" Dolly interjected. She grinned at him sweetly.

"Guess not. But I did win Mrs. Mainert's peanut butter chocolate pie in the pie walk *and* the Mountain View trivia, so go ahead and sit up there on your high horse."

I was pretty sure Annie had rigged the Mountain View trivia contest so he'd win. The prize was dinner with her, and I had a feeling she wanted him.

"Anyway. I'm working at the petition table and I need to charge the iPad. Your mama said she had a charger and I know Annie always has one in her briefcase." He paused. "I'd ask you, but I don't know if getting me a charger would be like pinch-hitting for the other team, so . . ." He grinned and I laughed.

"Considering you're going to get it one way or another, I guess I can help you," I said. "If you want to follow me up to the house, I can grab Mama's from the living room."

I wondered how many signatures they'd added. There weren't many out-of-towners in the barn, maybe twelve, tops. But I knew there were more outside. I could tell through the window that there were some foreign cars in the side yard—Toyotas, Kias, Mercedes, and the like. Mountain View residents only considered Ford or Chevy.

"Thanks," Fox said.

"I'll be right back, Dolly."

She threw her empty cup into the trash can and reached for another. By my count, she'd had at least five drinks in an hour. It was by design. She could stop if she wanted to, but I knew Dolly well enough to know she took full advantage of a night out without kids, and the more she drank the more fun she insisted she had.

"Don't drink any more of those 'til I get back," I instructed, starting to follow Fox down the side of the crowded barn. Dolly glared at me. "You don't want a repeat of prom 2011."

"The hell I don't." She lifted another drink to her lips. "Rocky proposed that night. I was naked as a jaybird standing in front of the Cut & Curl."

"I know," I called back to her. "I was there."

"I'll streak if I want to! I'm still hot and the life of the party!" she yelled, encouraging a series of whoops from Tammy, Bobby Jo, and Sterling.

"Is she for real?" Fox laughed as he looked back at me. "Is that really how Rocky proposed?"

My eyes got big, and I pointed behind me to where Dolly had climbed atop one of the pews and was throwing her hair around like the band was playing heavy metal.

"What do you think?"

"I guess I haven't seen her drinking much. She's never come into the store on Fridays. I just assumed she was a sweet little country girl."

I started laughing. "I mean, she is sweet, but no one can out-party Dolly."

"This is lovely, Hattie." Cricket grabbed my hand as I walked past her. "I know we have our differences of opinion, but we've all come together tonight, haven't we? And I'm going to have my second cousin's daughter, Delinda, reach out to y'all about her wedding. It was supposed to be in a couple weeks at Limelight. If your parents have the date free, I bet they'd want to get hitched here the same weekend." She let my hand go and smoothed the bodice of her powder blue shirtwaist dress. All the Mountain View Melodies ladies, including Mama, had made their own '40s cocktail dresses back in the '90s that they still wore today. The fact that most of them were still wearable was a testament to the quality of handmade fashion.

"That sounds great. You can have her call Mama to check." This was the fifth person who'd talked to me about booking a wedding tonight. I was interested to see how Mama and Daddy took to having a bunch of people here. I looked around the room, at the sparkling lights and the varnished walls and the people dressed in beautiful costumes. Sure, it was hot. Sure, some people were getting super drunk. But for the most part, this was a night most people dreamed about, and I knew that's why we'd had so many people interested in events here.

Cricket smiled and turned away from me, back to the stage where Cassidy was taking his turn showing off his skills on the piano while the other guys chugged bottles of water. I watched as Lee emptied a bottle on his head. The water drizzled down his already saturated T-shirt. I forced my gaze away.

"Alright. To the charger," I said to Fox.

He glanced at the stage, then back at me.

"They're good," he said, but I could tell he'd wanted to say something else.

"Yep. Always have been."

Fox pushed through the crowd, clearing a path for me. "Do me a favor before the night is over?" he yelled over his shoulder.

"Okay, what?" I asked.

"Save me a dance?"

I stared at the back of his head, remembering what it had felt like to be in his arms.

"The last one was nice," he went on.

"It was. I'll save you one," I yelled.

Up ahead, a group of visitors edged into the barn. Two of the men wore Ronald Robinson tour shirts, and another wore a cowboy hat and looked like Garth Brooks.

"Well, howdy, Jake," one of the T-shirt guys said to another visitor in cut-off flannel and Wranglers who'd been here for quite some time. Cowboy Hat bumped into Fox, and he muttered a quick "Excuse me."

Fox picked up his pace, and when we reached the threshold, he eluded the light beaming from beside the doors and stood in the shadows next to the wall. He looked panicked, like he'd seen a ghost.

"Are you alright?"

"Yeah . . . yeah. I need to run back to the store."

I listened, wondering if the band had begun to play the song that had turned his mood the last time, but Lee had given Woody the mic and he was singing a horrible rendition of Nat King Cole's "L-O-V-E."

"I just remembered that I made lunch in the kitchenette, and I don't think I turned the burner off."

He ran a hand across his face. I didn't believe him.

"Are you sure nothing's bothering you?"

He glanced through the doorway and stepped into the light.

"Yeah, like I said, I just need to run back and make sure my place isn't going up in flames. You know that whole block of buildings in Magnolia got swallowed up a few weeks ago because somebody left their coffee pot on. That's the last thing Mountain View needs with this stadium project lingering." Fox smiled, but it seemed forced. "I'll be right back."

Just beyond him, the line at the Wienermobile had died down some, though there were still about fifty people waiting for a hot dog. Across the drive from Rocky, Annie had abandoned the dance floor and was sitting with the presumed dead iPad, a charger attached to a power strip hanging from one end of it.

"It looks like Annie found a charger," I said.

"Yeah. I guess so."

He turned to go up to his truck parked in our driveway, removing his jacket as he went. He slung the coat over his shoulder, then stopped.

"Save me that dance," he said. "Even if everybody's gone by the time I get back."

I looked around at the crush of people milling around on our land and the packed barn. Unless he wasn't planning to return until morning, there'd be people.

"I think you mean even if Sterling's broken out his disco lights and the only suitable dancing is break," I called out.

He laughed, and I noticed Annie watching us. I smiled at her despite my irritation at the way she'd pivoted from my friend to frenemy in the matter of a week, but she didn't return the grin, only held up the iPad.

"Thirty-four more signatures," she yelled. "Thirty more than Cardinal River. You might have refused to help us spread the word, but we're getting there anyway."

"You're using my barn for this event," I called back. "I'm helping plenty."

I whirled around and walked back toward the barn, pushing past a group of Mountain View High kids who had all just received their loaded hot dogs from Rocky.

I missed those days. I missed how easy my life had been. There were no expectations back then. Not really, anyway. And any ambitions I had were dreams, far away from the here and now.

By the time I made it back into the barn, Cassidy had abandoned the piano bench and had taken up his fiddle. Lee pulled a stool from the side of the stage to the front and sat down.

"We sure appreciate y'all being here tonight," he said into the mic.

The barn erupted in cheers.

"Shut up and play!" Vern yelled and launched a discarded hot dog bun at the stage. "Ronald Robinson didn't take no breaks, and Chester was just about to have him a dance with this lady here."

Lee looked down at the bun and then over at Chester and his lady—a visitor with a Joan Jett haircut who scooted away from him—and laughed.

"We'll get back to playing in a second, Vern," Lee said. "But first, it's only right to let you visitors know something really special—this barn, this farm, was Ronald Robinson's. He built this place with his own two hands, and he and his wife, Elita, made this town a home for over fifty years."

A hush fell over the crowd.

"The Robinsons are the reason Mountain View exists," Lee went on.

I pushed my way down the side of the barn toward Dolly, who was swaying without music, occupying a place directly in front of Blaze. He was holding his bass and staring at her, nearly unblinking, as though he'd forgotten she was married to one of his friends.

"We owe a lot to the Robinsons," Lee went on. "And all of us in Mountain View have borrowed a piece of their legacy at one time or another."

He strummed his guitar, then pushed his hair out of his face and squinted over the crowd until he found me. His gaze pierced through me, and I stopped where I was, pressed between the window and a group of bearded bikers. It wasn't a flirty glance or a quick acknowledgement. His blue eyes held me where I was with a weight I felt acutely but couldn't understand.

"As for me, one of the things I borrowed pretty often was his truck out there." Lee nodded past the wall where I stood. He was speaking to the crowd, but his attention didn't shift from me. My chest tightened and my stomach lurched with nerves. Everything in me wanted to break eye contact, to turn and run from the barn, but I couldn't. "Those hours in the cab of that truck." He paused.

My face flushed. At once, I felt the echo of his hands on my body, the tacky old leather on my bare back, his tight muscles and soft skin brushing my own, the warmth of his mouth, the hours we lay together, swearing we'd be in love forever.

"They were the best of my life. And I want to play y'all a song I wrote about it."

I held on to the windowsill and thought my knees might give out.

"It's called 'I Borrowed His Truck.'" Lee smiled. "Cass," he said, and Cassidy started playing. The fiddle was haunting and beautiful, and it seemed that it commanded the barn to silence. Then Lee started to sing.

> He knew where he was going when he got
> in that Chevy,
> with his guitar and his lady beside.
> That truck would take him to Georgia
> and he'd leave the bright lights behind.

Sing Me Home to Carolina

Blaze's guitar joined Cassidy's fiddle, and Woody's voice fell in behind Lee's in a harmony I had no idea he was capable of. This wasn't about me after all. It was about the Robinsons. I smiled at Lee and my heart settled.

But that truck knew where it was going
and it decided on another fate.
They landed soft in the Carolina mud,
and unlike us, those lovers stayed.

Woody's electric guitar swelled the melody, and I balled my fingers into my hands to stop their sudden shaking. I was wrong. It *was* about us. For a time everything in our lives had been about us.

He never threw me the keys,
he never let me drive,
but I borrowed his truck anyway,
I found me a girl,
the light of my world,
and I kissed her in the cab that day.
I didn't know what the hell I was doing,
what spell I'd wandered into,
but in that old borrowed truck, girl,
I swore there'd be none but you.

He stopped singing and Cassidy started playing that wailing melody again and my eyes teared.

I knew where I was going when I got in that Chevy,
with my glove and my lady beside,
I thought that truck would steer us right,
but it had other plans in mind.
Should've realized that truck had its own way,

that it broke down where you didn't want to,
that its tires were stuck, that the keys were long gone,
and its magic wouldn't stop me losing you.

A tear ran down my face. Even from this distance, I could see Lee's eyes well too. A part of me wanted to crumple on the floor and sob, to let the heartache I'd held for a decade break free and heal me, but I couldn't, not with all these people watching.

Still I think of those nights in that old borrowed truck,
stolen kisses and promises too.
Maybe if we'd followed after those lovers before us,
landed soft in this Carolina mud,
I wouldn't still be missing you.

Cassidy took up the music. I watched his bow move slow on the fiddle, and suddenly, with my gaze away from Lee's, something snapped in my heart.

I pushed through the crowd to the exit, my body quaking.

I should've known I would go nowhere
when I let that old Chevy steer.

The reverberation of his voice ended, and the crowd erupted as I cleared the barn lights and shrouded myself in the inky black of night. I stopped for a moment. My breath came in short gasps, and I pressed my hand to my chest, then kept walking down the side of the barn toward the river. Nobody would be back there, on the river's edge, and I could sit down among the trees and settle my heart, my mind.

"Where the hell are you going?"

I turned at the sound of Lee's voice breaking, but before I could reply, he took my face in his hands and kissed me. It was a soft peck, a whisper of lips, but when I didn't pull away his mouth found mine again, and I closed my eyes and let his lips lead. I leaned into him and deepened the kiss, reveling in the warmth of his mouth and the feel of his tongue, of the way he took his time. I was home.

His mouth broke from mine, and he pushed a strand of pin-curled hair back from my forehead.

"I'm sorry," he whispered. His face was shadowed by the moonlight behind him, but I could still see his eyes fill with tears.

"For what? I . . . I liked the new song."

His heart raced against my chest, and I knew mine matched.

"It ain't new." Lee's thumb drifted across my cheek, and his fingers tangled deeper in my hair. "I wrote it on the drive to college. I just never sang it because I couldn't get through it. I didn't know if I could tonight either, but I told the guys I wanted to try." He leaned down to kiss my forehead. "It's been the only song in my heart since the minute I left you, and I ain't never stopped singing it. I've never stopped loving you."

His eyes searched mine, and I suddenly began to cry.

He pulled me closer, and I sobbed into his chest.

"I'm sorry," he said as I cried. "I should have left it alone. I tried to. I've known for years that I put you through hell and I don't have a right to your heart, so I've tried to move on. But these past days . . . I kept almost telling you I love you and forcing myself to stop. Tonight, I just couldn't."

I heard him swallow.

"I won't say it again if you don't want me to, but it ain't ever going to change and now you know."

I looked up at him. His face was a reflection of my heart in spite of it all.

"You know how I feel."

He shook his head.

"I've always loved you. I'm always going to love you."

He grinned that stupid goofy grin that meant he was insanely happy and leaned down to kiss me again, but beside us, in the barn, the wail of Woody's guitar reminded me of reality, and I stepped back.

"What about Willow? Lee, I love you, but you kept on with her even when we were getting closer."

"Being with her was a mistake. Then and now. I told her when she asked me to take her home at Fox's the first night I was back that I didn't want a relationship. She asked me why, and I told her I still loved you. She said she didn't care, that she wasn't looking for anything serious either." He reached for my hand and drew me toward his chest. I let him.

"This is how I've lived since we broke up," he went on. "I guess I thought if I had someone else, I wouldn't want you so bad. It worked back in college and in Atlanta and here too, any place you were far away. I'd distract myself enough with someone else to stop me from breaking my promise to your mama, but when you turned up here—"

"What promise to my mama?"

He froze. His breathing stilled against my chest.

"Lee."

"Shit." He sighed. "When I got home summer after freshman year, I came by to see you. I was hoping you'd forgive me and we could try again. I wanted you back so bad." Lee lifted his hand to my cheek. "But you weren't home yet, and when I told your mama why I'd come, she made me promise I wouldn't try to get you back after all. She said she'd heard what I'd done when we broke up and that though it wasn't cheating, it was damn near close and she wasn't about to have her daughter end up with a man who'd go out on her. She said her daddy had been a cheater and it had ruined her mama's life. She said she'd seen an echo of that heartache in you when I left and said if things went wrong a second time that you'd never be the same. She said you were healing." He paused. "I knew I couldn't live with myself if I ruined your life, so I left you alone. Maybe I should've this time too, but I couldn't."

"She had no right," I said. Fury burned through me. I couldn't believe it. We'd been apart for a decade because she'd decided to interfere.

"Yeah, she did. I hurt both of us, and for what? I've carried the guilt of that for a long time, convinced myself I was probably a cheater like she said. Up until the other day, I thought I was right to make that promise, that I was just a heartless son of a bitch who didn't deserve a second chance." His face tightened. "But then when we went swimming in the river the other day, I realized something. I might have messed up and I might have kept on living a life I wasn't proud of, but all this time, I've only loved one woman and that woman is you. And even though I've made mistakes, I didn't cheat."

I reached up and pulled his face to mine. I kissed him again, tasting the familiar sweet warmth of his mouth.

"She shouldn't have made you promise to stay away. It wasn't fair to either of us and it's wasted our time, Lee."

He took my hands in his.

"Don't be mad at your mama. She only meant to protect you." He paused again. "I told you me and Willow ain't in a relationship, and we're not, but I'm going tell her whatever we're doing is over." He squeezed my hand. "I know I'm asking a lot, but would you give me another chance, Hat? I know we live in different places right now, and we'll have to figure that out, but I promise I'll never leave you again."

I smiled and suddenly all of the tension and the anger and the nerves and the fear went away.

"Well," I said. "It's a lot to consider, but—"

"Leland Lockhardt?"

The Garth Brooks lookalike I'd seen come into the barn walked up, hat pressed against his chest.

"Yeah?" Lee's eyes flitted from me to the man as though if he looked away from me, I'd disappear.

"Well, I'll be. I thought that was you. You really turned tail after that press conference, didn't you?"

"Not really," Lee said. I could tell he was annoyed that this random man had cornered him to remind him of one of his worst days. "I'm through with baseball, so I came home."

"I hear you. Same thing happened to me. Believe it or not, I was a bull rider when I was younger. Heralded as the best in Texas, maybe in the country. And then I broke my spine."

"Damn," Lee said, then whistled. "But you're still standing."

"Yeah. And I found something I love more than the rodeo." He reached into the pocket of his jeans. "Can I get your autograph for my grandson? He's a big fan."

Lee reached for the scrap of paper and pen the guy was holding out, then glanced at me.

"Oh. This is Hattie, my . . ." He hesitated, looking to me to fill in the blank of what we were, but then I heard screaming coming from the barn.

I ran toward the entrance. When I got to the drive, Annie was coming out of the barn and stopped me.

"I called an ambulance, Hattie. We think your daddy's had a heart attack."

CHAPTER TEN

The sun was barely rising as Vern helped us out of his van.

"Now, you lean on me, Helen Sue," he said to Mama as he opened her door.

Mama made a dismissive sound and climbed out of the passenger seat on her own, still dressed in her Mountain View Melodies gown, lugging her purse filled with Uno playing cards and Tic Tacs with her. The car smelled like the hospital, like stale antiseptic. I guess that made sense since we'd been sitting in the Cardinal River Clinic waiting room for the last ten hours.

"I'm not the one who had a heart attack," she said. "But I thank you for caring, Vern. You're a good friend."

I got out of the back seat and followed Mama and Vern toward the house. The dewy yellow sun washed me in warmth. I glanced across the field to the barn and Mr. Robinson's truck, expecting the farm to be riddled with discarded cocktail glasses and plastic cups, but it wasn't. Lee had texted to say that he and Fox and the others would take care of the place, but I guess I didn't understand that meant they'd clean it up too.

"You alright, honey?" Mama lingered in the doorway.

"Yeah." I said as I made my way slowly toward the porch. My feet ached in my kitten heels, and my swollen eyes started to tear.

Daddy would be home in a couple days. His heart attack was minor, they said, caused by plaque buildup related to prolonged stress. Dr. Gerard said the new business venture and the death of the farm and the stadium possibly looming likely pushed him over the edge. I'd always thought that blaming a heart attack on stress was an old wives' tale, but apparently it wasn't. The doctor said that when you're mired by fear, your amygdala reduces the flow of blood to the heart, which deprives it of oxygen, over time leading to inflammation that promotes plaque.

I hadn't noticed Daddy was panicked. I guess I hadn't wanted to see it—the tension on their faces when the peanut plants were dug up last year shriveled and tiny, the quiet way they'd disappeared into their bedroom after the first soil expert came back with the results, the way they'd smiled and nodded last week when the final sentence was executed, while the light extinguished in their eyes.

Mama and Daddy had always been quiet optimists. Our family motto was unofficially something like "it'll work out" or "it's not the end yet." I'd been trained to look for the silver lining in every disappointment, to step back into thought instead of forward into panic with each setback.

There was only one time it hadn't worked and that was when Lee broke up with me. It had felt like the world was ending. I guess that's how Mama and Daddy had felt for the past year, that everything they knew was about to be taken away and there was nothing they could do about it.

"Take care of your mama," Vern said as he passed me. But then he stopped and tugged at his vintage Rusty Wallace T-shirt.

"I will. What is it, Vern?"

"I know you city folk are used to change. A new building over there, a new restaurant replacing that old one over here." He gestured around like he was actually standing in front of a block of buildings. "But remember for a minute how us people here think. You know I drove that 1983 Cadillac Deville for near twenty-three years. And when she died and I went to pick up this here Previa van from the Discount Car over in Spartanburg, I felt almost like I was replacing a person. I was almost despondent. Even Sterling couldn't pull me out of my funk. I didn't want a new car. But I had to get one anyway. And then I had to learn how to work all the gears and fancy features that come with driving such a luxurious automobile. It's a 1999, you know."

I glanced over at the maroon Previa and tried not to laugh. It wasn't that I was making fun of Vern for appreciating his car. It was only that I was pretty sure the van, even brand new, wasn't considered luxurious.

"I understand," I said.

"But do you really?" His bushy eyebrows rose and he leaned in closer. I could tell him that I heard his analogy loud and clear—that country folk like my parents weren't used to change, didn't want change, and that any sort of change would have to be eased into slowly, but he was going to bring this lesson home whether I needed him to or not.

"Cause what I'm saying is that your parents have been through an awful lot this past year. First their farm is barren, then they're havin' to start up a new business, and, on top of that, they're worried about the town being stamped out altogether while their own flesh and blood stands in opposition to them."

I stood there and nodded.

"If you don't want your mama to go down the same way as your daddy, you better take care of them, Hattie. Of course, we'll be here, but we ain't their daughter."

"I've got it, Vern."

Ordinarily, I'd take offense at someone insinuating I wasn't up to snuff as a daughter, but Daddy's heart attack had already accused me plenty.

"Alright then."

I patted him on the arm and shuffled toward the porch. I stepped over the threshold, kicked off my shoes and took a big breath. It smelled like home—like decades of morning coffee and bacon and Mama's pineapple candle she ordered special from *Candle Emporium* magazine.

"Mama?" I called out.

"I'm going to recharge for a little bit, Hattie. Just for an hour or so. And then I'm going to drive back to the hospital when visiting hours open up at noon and stay until they kick me out at five." Her voice was muffled, coming from her bedroom.

"Why don't you sleep as long as you want? I'll change and head over there at noon if you're still resting. We can swap out after a while."

I wandered toward my room. My suitcase, half-packed for Charlotte, lay on the floor beside the closet. Dr. Gerard had told us in the waiting room that Daddy would need help getting around for a while, at least a few weeks, that he'd need as many hands as he could at home. He hadn't told me to stay. Not directly anyway, but his pointed stare had.

I didn't know what to do. Even though the doctor had assured Mama and me that Daddy would fully recover, I couldn't help but worry he'd missed something or that Daddy might have another, larger, heart attack in the future.

I walked over to my closet and opened the door to look at the picture I'd taped there of Daddy and me at my high school graduation. He wasn't a man of many words, but he didn't need them. He'd always been a solid, unwavering force in my life, the personification of unconditional love. My eyes teared, and I thought for a moment that I should just quit my job, that nothing was worth more than the health of my family. But then what would happen if things went south here and they needed help with health care or living arrangements? Maybe if Mama could handle things in Mountain View, just for a week or so, I could come back and help after the gala, after Merry gave me the partnership and promotion. That way, if Mama and Daddy needed a place to stay down the road, they could live with me. Then again, Mama had scheduled Cricket's second cousin's daughter's wedding last night for the Saturday after next, and though the barn had been spruced up enough for Founder's Day, it wasn't suitable for a wedding. The temporary dance floor, that had been scratched beyond repair from nearly the first hour of Mountain View men clacking across it in their cowboy boots, would have to be replaced with the permanent hardwood floors we'd ordered along with three more chandeliers we'd install down the center of the ceiling. We also needed to start and finish the bridal suite we'd planned in the hayloft. Even though the supplies were paid for—thankfully Mama and Daddy had just enough room on their home equity line—we couldn't afford to outsource all the labor to Fox and his men. He'd refused payment for the zillion hours he'd put in ahead of Founder's Day, saying he was happy to do it for the town. But this next bout of work was for our new venture, and I knew how much a temporary crew charged CLE for event setup. Fox had saved us thousands last week. We'd still have to hire him, but if I helped, I knew we'd cut the bill in half.

"No, Hattie." Mama's voice came from down the hall. "You're needing to head out of town today. I figure you'll lose your job if you don't since Merry's counting on you and the gala's in six days. Plus, I can't get used to having another hand around when it's going to be just me and your daddy here."

I grabbed my phone from my purse and sat down on my bed. I studied my wrinkled silk skirt, and then the room, not having any idea what I was going to say to Merry. I opened my notes app and scanned my checklist. The seating chart was done, the decorating crew was set to begin tomorrow morning, I'd rerouted Liam Neeson's car service, Park Road Books was all set to sell books. All that was left was to touch base with catering, double-check the floral delivery, and send a final communication out to the guests on Wednesday morning.

I took a breath and locked my phone. The closet was still slightly ajar and the photo of Lee and me was washed in the window light. At once, I felt the rush of elation, the freefall in the pit of my stomach, his lips on mine, his hands in my hair. Last night's kiss had felt exactly the same as that night on the field. I knew it always would.

I opened my phone to his last text.

Your daddy's going to be okay and so are you. I love you.

I stared at the last three words. I couldn't quite believe any of this—Lee's love for me, Daddy's heart attack. Maybe I'd had too much of Mama's cocktail and had passed out.

I pinched my arm as hard as I could.

Nothing.

I tapped my email and then Merry's address and started typing.

My daddy had a heart attack last night. He's going to recover, but I can't leave my parents alone right now. I'm so sorry. Elizabeth and the rest of our temp crew are set to start tomorrow so that will help, and I can call Elizabeth and ask her to take the temporary lead on the vendors as they arrive. I promise you I'll be back on Thursday at the latest and will be on the ground for the event.

I pressed send and sighed, then stood and slipped out of my gown and pulled on my jean shorts. I eyed the T-shirts in my suitcase and grabbed a white one, then reached in the back of the closet for the blue plastic bin behind Mama's baskets of yarn. When I found it, I pried the lid open, dug my hand to the very bottom, and pulled out the threadbare sweatshirt.

Mountain View Royals Baseball it read on the front, with the logo, a roaring lion, beneath the print. I turned it over and read: *Lockhardt*

I pulled it over my head. I hadn't been able to get rid of it when we broke up. For one, it was the most comfortable sweatshirt I owned. It had been perfectly broken in from years of wear and washing, and for two, it was a gold mine. I knew, even back then, that if I held on to it for long enough, it would be worth something. I figured I could sell it if I ever decided on revenge. Word would undoubtedly get back to Lee that his ex-girlfriend was selling his high school baseball sweatshirt for thousands on eBay, and he'd know then that I was really and truly done with him.

But, of course, that would have been a lie.

I snuggled into the thin coziness and walked into the kitchen. Mama was snoring in her bedroom. I grabbed the Folger's from the cabinet and made some coffee.

Ordinarily, I'd be staring at my phone, terrified that Merry would write back that she was letting me go, but this time I wasn't. Getting fired was still my nightmare. I loved my job and knew I'd tripped into something I was underqualified for when I snagged it. I wouldn't get another job like it if I lost this one. But there was nothing I could do about it. I wasn't going to leave my parents when they needed me most.

I pulled my hair into a ponytail while I watched the coffee drizzle into the carafe and the morning haze burn away atop the mountain out the window. Across Route 2, Bobby Jo was getting settled on her riding mower in her church dress. Even though nobody lifted a finger on Sundays in Mountain View, Bobby Jo reasoned that it wasn't really Sunday until after worship, so she always got her mowing done in the early morning before church.

When the coffee was done, I grabbed one of MawMaw's vintage Corelle spring blossom coffee cups, poured myself some coffee, and headed for the porch swing.

The cicadas were loud today. When I was little, Mama always told me they were saying "Ho-t, ho-t" and she might as well have been right. The louder they yelled, the hotter it would be later.

I took a sip of the coffee and rolled the sweatshirt sleeves up to my elbows. I'd give Mountain View one thing—it was picturesque here. Peaceful too.

A wolf whistle sounded behind me, and then there was the deep roar of an engine and tires crunching over gravel. I turned on the swing to find Lee pulling onto the drive in a midnight blue Lamborghini. He leaned out the window, his eyes shaded in Ray-Bans, his ball cap backwards, and smiled at me. I grinned back as he drove the car closer.

"Don't move," he called out. He pulled his glasses off and stared at me. "You're the prettiest picture I've ever seen."

I laughed.

"You're still the worst at pickup lines."

He angled the tires around Daddy's truck, turned off the engine and got out, holding a shopping bag and two coffee cups.

"What happened to Slugger?" I asked, nodding to the car.

Lee laughed.

"Oh. That's him. A few years back, he got bit by a radioactive bug of some kind. Now he's a transformer."

"It's an impressive suit," I said.

"Custom."

Lee set the coffee cups and the bag down on the top step when he reached me. I stood and he wrapped me in his arms.

"You kept that old thing?" He glanced down at his sweatshirt.

"Yeah, barely. It was one bad night away from eBay."

I smiled, and he leaned down and kissed me. I deepened the kiss, letting my fingers skim the space between the top of his jeans and the hem of his shirt.

"Hat," he said when our lips parted. "I love you so damn much I can hardly bear it."

I reached up and held his face in my palms. He was perfect. We were perfect. Just like we were before.

"I love you too."

"And I'm sorry about your daddy. I've been praying for him all night. I'm glad to know he'll pull through."

"Thanks. I appreciate y'all holding down the fort here. There's not a plastic cup in sight."

Lee kissed me on the forehead and laughed. "Yeah, well. There were. I think Fox and I filled something like twelve trash bags of litter." He shook his head. "People are slobs."

"I guess they are. It was a fun night, though, until Daddy . . ." For some reason I couldn't say it, that he'd had a heart attack. I'd thought my daddy was invincible and, somehow, I figured articulating what had happened to him would make it sink in. When I really just wanted to hold on to the belief that nothing could take him down.

"I'm still going to remember it—the way you held my eyes across that crowded barn. You have no idea how hard it was for me to finish that song. And then when you let me kiss you . . ." Lee paused. "I'm not sure how you felt about it, but for me it was like you gave me my heart back."

"Kissing you again felt like coming home."

"Yeah."

Tears blurred my eyes, and he leaned in and kissed me gently. When he pulled away, I looked down at the cups at his feet.

"What'd you bring me?"

"Coffee and your favorite scone." He grabbed a cup stamped with Pine Summit Coffee Co. and held it toward me.

The coffee smelled like coconut. I grinned at him. "I might've changed my order in a decade, Lee."

He laughed under his breath, grabbed the other cup and the bag and sat down on the swing. I sat down beside him.

"You might've, but you didn't. I don't know about you, but sometimes I like it when things stay the same."

He winked at me and took a sip of his coffee. I was suddenly reminded of what Vern had said earlier about country folk resisting change. Maybe I still had a little Mountain View in me after all.

Lee took my hand, and we drank our coffees looking over the field in silence. You could only do such a thing with somebody you knew like your own soul. With someone like that, silence meant comfort, it meant peace.

"Here," he said sometime later and let go of my hand to give me the blueberry scone. It was still warm, made with fresh blueberries from Mrs. Sunshine's patch in Pine Summit.

I closed my eyes when I took the first bite.

"Want some?" I held the pastry out to Lee.

"Nah. I already ate one on the way over," he said. "It was so good that honestly, if I didn't love you so much, I would've eaten yours too."

I broke a piece of the scone off and handed it to him.

"I can't eat it all," I said. The truth was, I most certainly could, but we used to share everything, and I'd missed this.

"I talked to Willow last night." He glanced at me.

I stopped eating. I'd forgotten all about her. Sitting here with Lee, things felt so simple. But they weren't. Not like they used to be. Willow hadn't been working at the clinic when Daddy had been admitted the night before, but she'd be working at some point when I'd go visit and I'd have to see her.

"She knew it before I said anything. She said that she figured I'd come around to telling you how I felt," Lee said. "I don't think you'll run into her much at the clinic either. Chantelle's coming back Wednesday, so Willow will be on to her next position, wherever that is."

I turned the scone over in my hand. Lee took my free hand in his.

"All I can keep saying is that I'm sorry," he said. "I know that it bothers you and you can't just forget it. But, Hat, I swear. Being with you was—" He stopped midsentence and looked at me. I thought of what my life had been like without him. I thought of the way my heart broke every time I saw his face on socials or on TV, how I couldn't seem to give my heart to anyone else. And now, he was here. We were together again. And he was saying he loved me. I could trust him or I could turn my back because of what he'd done. My heart wouldn't allow the latter. "When I asked you to give me a second chance last night, you never answered because of that guy cutting in."

"Yes."

I drew his face to mine and kissed him. As his mouth opened, as his lips made my stomach flutter, I remembered how many nights I'd fallen asleep praying that we'd find our way back to each other someday.

"And if that crazy baseball fan hadn't interrupted us last night, I would've said the same thing and I would've kissed you the same way," I said when the kiss faded.

Lee laughed and squeezed my hand. "He was weird." He set the empty scone bag down on the ground beside us. "I guess it shouldn't really surprise me that there are weird people turning up in Mountain View, but that dude. Something's wrong with him."

"What do you mean?"

"Well, first off, he comes up and basically accuses me of being so damn embarrassed at myself I ran away, and then he asks for my autograph and then—here's the kicker—after I was done signing he tells me he's a scout for Hot Rod Records and that he wants the band to consider coming to Nashville . . . to meet him and discuss recording a demo."

Lee started laughing and couldn't stop. It was catching, and I started laughing too.

"He said he liked our sound and our look. Our look? Like we're supposed to believe a record executive glanced at us and thought, hell yeah, they're perfect. Let's get this colorful group of rednecks up on the Opry stage."

"Plus, did you see what he was wearing?" I was laughing so hard I could barely speak. "He looked like he googled 'country music outfits' and dropped by the closest Goodwill on the way."

"No shit. No one who's anyone randomly comes to Mountain View for Founder's Day."

"Don't tell the guys," I said. "You know Woody would do it even if it was a scam."

"I love him, but he's an idiot. I can hear him now, 'Everybody has to get their start somewhere, Lee.'" His impression sounded just like Woody's lopping southern accent.

Lee sighed and took my hand. "You think this is what heaven's like?" he asked, looking out across the field. "Sitting on the porch swing in the sunshine with the smell of fresh cut grass on the breeze, holding your best girl's hand?"

"I hope so." I squeezed his hand, but nerves suddenly balled in my stomach. We were perfect sitting right here, but my mind thought of his song, of the way he'd insinuated that leaving had ruined us.

I leaned into Lee's chest and closed my eyes. He put his arms around me and suddenly, the sound of his heart, the feel of his touch, filled me with a peace I hadn't felt in years. He'd been right to say we held a piece of each other. We weren't whole unless we were here, together.

"Did you mean what you said in that song?" I opened my eyes and tipped my chin toward his face. "That you regret leaving Mountain View?"

He looked down at me. "I don't know," he said. "But we work here, Hattie, and I'm not happy without you." Lee kissed the top of my head. "I guess sometimes I think that if we'd never gone off to bigger places, maybe we wouldn't have ever known any different. And maybe we would've ended up married and happy like the rest of the people here in town." His eyes met mine. "But speaking of leaving, you've got to go back to Charlotte tomorrow, don't you? Ain't your benefit in less than a week?"

I sat up a little and looked at our empty coffee cups sitting side by side on the ground. I looked at our hands tangled together. I didn't want to say yes in case my leaving would shatter us again.

Lee squeezed my hand and smiled. "I can hear you thinking," he said. "And I'm not going anywhere. I'll be right here. You can call me when you're away and when you're done with your event, you'll come back and we'll talk this through."

"I don't actually know if I am leaving. I mean, as far as work goes, I need to. But I just texted my boss before you showed up to see if I could stay a few more days. She might say no. I might get fired. But Mama's going to need help with Daddy when he gets out of the hospital in a couple days, and then we have the first wedding here coming up in a couple weeks, and we can't just count on Fox to do all the labor."

"I know you love your parents and they're in a tough place right now, but your daddy's going to be okay and you need to go," he said. "I'm here. I can help. I can even stay over if that's what I need to do. Richard ain't going to fire me for missing a few days at the bank."

"I can't ask you to do that, Lee."

"You didn't ask. But I can't let you lose your job. You made me stick with baseball on my worst days, remember? I probably would've quit if it wasn't for you. You helped me win my dreams. Now you're going to let me help with yours." He squeezed my hand again. "I've got to drive to Atlanta today to have my chiropractor recheck my shoulder and do some kind of scan. It ain't a big deal, but I've got to stay down there overnight. He'll read the results tomorrow morning, and then I'll come right back to help your parents with whatever they need. I'm guessing I'll be home around one. You gotta promise you'll get out of here as soon as my tires hit your driveway."

"I wish I could come with you."

Suddenly the thought of his hand lifting from mine, of me being away from him filled me with dread.

"I'd love nothing more. I'd take you to my favorite restaurant for the best fried chicken you've ever had and then we could get drinks with some of my friends." He grinned. "They've heard all about you, you know." He took his hand from mine and glanced at his car.

"They have?"

"Yeah," he said simply. "And then we'd get a room at the St. Regis because it matches you. It's the most beautiful place."

I leaned in and kissed him. "What would we do at the St. Regis?" I whispered in his ear and he laughed, a low rumbling in his chest.

"Anything you damn well please, but I have some ideas." He kissed me again and then stood, palmed his face, and shook his head. "I don't want to, but I've gotta go. I'm going to be late. Even so, if your mama wasn't home right now . . ."

Lee glanced down at the field, toward the barn and Mr. Robinson's truck, and I knew what he was thinking.

"The sun is bright as a spotlight, it's a million degrees, and she'll come looking for me." I smacked his chest with the back of my hand and then put my arms around his waist. "And anyway, I don't want to rush things. Not after all this time."

He sighed. "Me either." Lee pecked my mouth and let me go. "I'll miss you," he said. "Pack your bags tonight. I'll come here right away to help your mama so you can go back to Charlotte."

I watched him get into his car. I watched him pull his Ray-Bans back over his beautiful eyes, and then he turned the ignition. The car roared to life, and he backed it out and started down the drive.

"I love you, Hat," he said, stopping the car in front of the porch.

"I love you too."

I grinned at him and waved as he pointed the car toward Atlanta and sped down Route 2.

CHAPTER ELEVEN

Everything could be made into a casserole. You realized that pretty quickly when somebody was sick or had a baby or died in Mountain View. I eyed the rows of Pyrex dishes lined up on the kitchen counter and watched Mama staring at them, trying to figure which ones deserved refrigerator space. We'd returned home from the clinic to the crowd of them occupying the porch. We hadn't even been able to get to the door without sidestepping Vern's vegetable soup casserole and Agnes's chicken chest. Agnes thought it was poor form to say "breast," even when it came to meat.

"Why don't you go on back to your room and finish packing?" Mama asked me, without looking my way. She opened the plastic lid of the middle casserole and her nose scrunched. "That's Crystal Fawn's imitation tuna." She slid the dish toward the sink. I didn't know what imitation tuna was, but I was imagining sardines or worse—the leftover remnants from sardine packaging plants.

I hesitated.

"Mama, I'll be back in a few days, you know. I'm not leaving you and Daddy high and dry." After Lee had volunteered to stand in for me, I'd emailed Merry back to tell her I'd be in town tomorrow after all.

My mother whirled around and shook her head. Her curls looked wilted, and standing there in her house dress and mismatched fuzzy slippers, she seemed entirely disoriented. It reminded me of the way Willow had looked earlier at the clinic. She'd been professionally pleasant with us as she'd taken Daddy's vitals, but I could tell she'd been crying and she hadn't been wearing lipstick. If she'd ever tried to make amends for what had happened all those years ago, even once, I would have felt horrible for her heartbreak over Lee. I thought there was a chance she'd say something. We'd even been alone in the hallway together earlier in the evening as Mama told Daddy good night, but she'd only told me she was glad Daddy was getting better and then busied herself at the computer.

"Lee said he'll even stay over if you'd like him to," I went on, turning my mind from Willow. "And I'll be back home the minute the gala's over. I'm sure Merry will be fine with me taking some time off after this event, and we'll get everything done for Timmy and Delinda's wedding."

"Do you really think we're going to be able to get this events thing up and running? It's going to take a long time for your daddy to get back to where he was, Hattie, and I don't know that I have the energy to do it all."

Mama turned back to the line of casserole dishes. She hated any sort of conflict and didn't want to see my reaction. She peeled another casserole lid off and made an agreeable little sound.

"Bobby Jo made Spam Brittany, your daddy's favorite."

Spam Brittany was sliced Spam layered with apples in orange marmalade. It was disgusting. But it was the cover model for the last Mountain View Presbyterian church cookbook in 1965, and because of that, it was a staple dish in town.

"We're going to *have* to get this events thing up and running, Mama," I said. "We're going to have to make it work. Thankfully, we'll have plenty of help. We're going to need to pay him this time, but I know Fox will be here and like I said, Lee will lend a hand with Daddy until—"

"I heard you the first time, and that's awful sweet of Lee, but he isn't family anymore."

"We're back together."

She looked at me. "When did that happen?"

"Last night," I said. "Well, I guess it's been tiptoeing that direction since we saw each other at Fox's, but he sang me that song—were you there?—and then he followed me outside and told me he'd never stopped loving me."

"And you just told him okay? After all that parading around town with Willow Hibberts?"

I was stunned at her reaction even knowing what I now did. She'd always seemed like she loved Lee.

"He told me about you making him promise to stay away from me. I know you were looking out for me, Mama, but you had no right to do that," I said. "Even though he went and had a fling with Willow—then and now—he never cheated on me. He's got his flaws and I've got mine, but he's not Granddaddy."

Her eyes teared, and she opened the refrigerator door and busied herself with loading casseroles into the empty space.

"I took him back because I love him, I always have, and we think we belong together," I said quietly. "And yeah. In spite of Willow."

She shut the refrigerator and turned to look out the window, at the light dwindling in the distance.

"I'm sorry," she said finally. "I know it was wrong for me to ask him to stay away from you, but put yourself in my shoes. You're my baby girl. You had your future all planned, and he pulled the rug out from under you. I knew how much he'd hurt you, and I wanted you to find somebody who would never make you feel that way again. MawMaw never got over Granddaddy's infidelity and I saw the same scars on you. Lee might not have cheated, but you felt that way in your heart. I could tell."

"He might have been the one to break my heart, but he broke his own too when he left me those years ago," I said. "He made a mistake."

She smiled.

"Alright. You're a grown woman. If you want to try again, I'll accept him. I know he made you happy for years when you were younger, and I think he's a good man. But be careful."

"I will, Mama."

I nodded toward a large Tupperware bowl next to Tammy's ham and bananas hollandaise—another revolting recipe from the church's cookbook.

"Hand me Dolly's banana pudding, please. And a spoon."

Mama took a spoon from the drawer and gave me the bowl. I opened the Barbie-pink lid, extracted a huge scoop of pudding, and deposited it into my mouth.

Dolly was a horrendous cook, but she'd somehow figured out how to make her grandmama's banana pudding and it was heavenly.

A sharp rap on the glass door beside me startled my blissful moment, and I opened my eyes to find Fox standing there with an insulated bag.

He grinned at my mouth stuffed full. I probably looked like a squirrel.

"Can I come in?" he asked.

"Depends," I said, after I'd swallowed. "What's in that bag? If it's congealed or casseroled you might as well turn around now."

"Oh, don't be silly," Mama said, coming around the peninsula to swat me with a towel. "We'll take whatever you've brought, dear. It's so kind of you to think of us."

She pushed around me and unlatched the door, holding it open for Fox.

"Thank you, Helen Sue. At least someone around here knows how to accept a token of care from a neighbor." He leaned down and wrapped her in a hug. I swear Mama blushed. "I'm glad to hear Junior's better. I was in town checking on something at the store when he collapsed. Annie called me in a panic because she was worried the ambulance wouldn't be able to get around the construction trucks in Pine Summit."

"I couldn't believe how fast they got here," I said. "Or that Sterling was certified in CPR. He kept Daddy going until the ambulance pulled up. It's all a miracle, really."

"Yeah, it is. My daddy wasn't so lucky. He was alone at work when it happened to him." His eyes met mine as he walked toward the kitchen and set his bag down on the peninsula beside me.

"Oh, dear. You must have been devastated," Mama said. She patted his shoulder as she scooted around him.

"I'm sorry to hear that, Fox," I said softly. The news made sense. Fox was probably only a few years older than me, but if you really looked at him, you could tell he'd weathered more than most.

"It's alright. It was a long time ago. I was eleven." He paused. "We were the recipients of a bunch of food too." He gestured to the array of Pyrex across the counter. "We were so poor Mama made us eat it all. One lady brought a can of pineapple that she'd just poured lime Jell-O into. That was lunch one day. I haven't been able to eat pineapple since."

He laughed, and I did too.

"That sounds about as bad as the ham and bananas hollandaise," I said, pointing my spoon at the dish.

His nose scrunched. "Gross."

I dug my spoon back into the banana pudding and took another bite.

"That Dolly's pudding?" Fox asked. He leaned over the peninsula to extract a spoon from our silverware drawer.

"Help yourself, dear," Mama said, not at all offended that he'd beat her to the punch. "We've got a little of everything. In fact, why don't you stay for dinner?"

"Damn," he whispered and then his eyes widened. "I mean, darn. I'm sorry, Helen Sue. But that's the best banana pudding in the world. And I'd love to stay for dinner. I brought burgers and homemade onion rings. After my experience with sympathy food, I decided I'd bring people what I would've wanted."

"You better be telling the truth." I reached for the clasp on the bag that had always sat under the cash register at the hardware store with the coolers.

"Guess you'll see. Maybe I'm pulling your leg and it's a jelly bouillon ring with hot dogs and boiled eggs. Our pastor brought us that one."

"Your town must have had the same cookbook as ours," I said.

I pried my fingers between the plastic pieces on the clasp, but it wouldn't open.

"It's the thought that counts," Mama said.

Fox reached for the bag and opened it. The smell of fried onions and grilled burgers immediately made my stomach growl.

"I could kiss you right now," I said, grinning. His gaze steadied on mine and at once, I wished I could take it back. Of course, I'd said it as a joke, but it didn't matter. Everything seemed to still.

He laughed under his breath and reached into the cooler.

"Better not. I doubt your new old boyfriend would take too kindly to you kissing me for your dinner." His tone sounded strange.

Nothing had ever gone on between Fox and me, and yet the news about my getting back together with Lee felt uncomfortable. I couldn't quite figure out why. Of course, Fox and I had danced together—would've last night too, if he hadn't left to go check on his store—but friends danced all the time.

"Probably not, although if he was in this spot, he'd probably kiss you for a burger and rings too."

"Would you like a drink, Fox? I'm afraid we don't have much, but we've got milk, water, and sweet tea," Mama said, getting the glasses out of the cabinet beside me.

"Sweet tea would be great, ma'am. I have toppings, but I can just bring them to the table," he said.

"Did you make all this? I thought you meant you just ordered some stuff from the diner. But the onion rings over there definitely come frozen," I said.

"Yeah, I made it. You know how Dolly can only make the banana pudding? Well, that's kind of like me. I can make one meal." He tipped his head toward my plate. "Go on."

I snatched an onion ring off the top of my stack and took a bite. It was amazing.

"Here you go, Helen Sue," Fox said. He carried his plate and Mama's to the small table.

Mama brought the drinks over and sat down. Fox folded himself onto the ladderback chair between us.

In the midst of our eating, we fell silent, and Fox eventually spoke up.

"Besides Junior's scare, how did you feel about the party, Helen Sue?"

Mama set her burger down.

"I thought it went pretty well, but I don't have much to compare it to besides other Founder's Days past. Seemed like people had a good time."

"They had a great time," Fox said. "So good, in fact, that Annie said we added sixty-four names to the petition. We're really blowing Cardinal River's out of the water now. Our attorney's pleased and will take it to state officials on Friday." He didn't look at me when he said it, and instead, cleared his throat and went on. "And the acoustics in the barn were actually great. I didn't know how it would be since there are a few sizeable spaces in the walls, but it worked out well. The band sounded amazing."

I laughed.

"Yeah. So amazing, in fact, that some random visitor claiming to be a label executive cornered Lee and asked him to consider bringing the band to Nashville to record a demo." I took a bite of my burger. "We thought that was pretty hilarious. There's no way he's legit. He's probably just hoping Lee's an idiot and he can talk him into giving him some crazy fee to record some music. Sorta like those modeling agencies that make you pay thousands for headshots when the real scouts pay *you*."

Mama chuckled. "I can't imagine any of those boys on the radio. Especially that Woody."

Fox kept his eyes fixed down at his plate.

"You never know what kind of folks the Robinsons are going to attract on Founder's Day," he said finally. "But it was a great night nonetheless, and I didn't have to host the afterparty."

"You act like you don't like babysitting Mountain View every Friday night," I said.

"Actually, speaking of that, I wondered about something. I know y'all will need floor installation and some build-out in the loft ahead of the wedding. Is there any chance you'd be up for me doing the labor for free in exchange for hosting the town here on Friday nights? More people are showing up now because of Lee's band, and every Friday somebody breaks something—a display case, a window—or damages the merchandise. I could be here to help make sure the Cavendish boys don't set the barn on fire or something, but since it's about ten times larger than my store, it might be a better fit." He glanced at Mama, whose face was blank, and then at me. "I'd fix anything they might mess up too. Free of charge."

"This is a generous offer, Fox, but you can't work for free," I said.

"Yeah, I can. But, in my opinion, it's an even exchange anyway."

"Mama, what do you think?" I asked.

My phone sounded loudly from my shorts and I edged it out of my pocket.

Hey Hat. Shoulder seems to be all good. Apt took forever.

Then:

Out getting drinks with the guys now, but all I can think about is you.

Then:

Doc's reading the scan at eight. I'll be back right after. Also, check this out:

The typing dots came and went until a photo of the man who'd interrupted our reunion last night popped up on the screen.

Alan Brownell, Chairman and CEO, Hot Rod Records

Manager forwarded me an email from him about our conversation last night.

Then:

Guess he's legit. Said he was always a big fan of Mr. Robinson's and wanted to make it to a Founder's Day someday. See the pickup and all that.

Then:

Still pretty sure he was just drunk or something. Don't tell Woody or any of them if you see them around. Not worth bringing it up to let them down.

I read Lee's messages over again and at once, sitting there at that table, my world stopped. Lee said point-blank he wasn't interested in Alan's offer, but the way he told me the news reminded me of his acceptance to Wake, of the way he'd acted like it wasn't a big deal at first, like he was still considering other places so he wouldn't have to hurt me yet.

If you change your mind, I need to know.
I can't take you up and leaving again.

I sent the texts and received an immediate response.

I don't give a damn about anything but you.
Promised you I'm never leaving again, and I'm not.
I love you.

I typed, *I love you too.*

"Everything okay?" Fox asked.

"Yeah." I put the phone back in my pocket. "That was just Lee. Apparently the guy who claimed to be a record executive really is." I wanted to tell them that he'd asked the guys to come record again, but Lee had asked me not to mention it.

Fox took a bite of an onion ring and then a swig of sweet tea.

"Oh, okay." He cleared his throat. "So, Helen Sue, Hattie, what do you say about my proposal?"

I stared at Fox. It was as if I'd told him that Lee said that the grass was green, not that a big-time record executive had just visited our little tiny town.

"I . . . uh . . . I think it's a great idea, but Mama, that's your call. I'm leaving tomorrow to go back to Charlotte for my gala and although I'll be back and forth for a while, I doubt I'll be around on Friday nights long term—or even during the weddings much once Mama and Daddy get the hang of it."

Fox scooted back from the table, and his eyes narrowed. "What? Are you serious? Hattie, what about—"

"I'm sorry to interrupt, but I think that's a fine idea, Fox. And I don't mean to be rude, but I'm going to excuse myself from the table." Mama forced a smile at Fox, and I noticed her hands shaking as she pushed her plate back. "Dr. Gerard said I could stay overnight if I wanted and I'm going to do that. I'm off to pack a bag."

She shuffled toward her bedroom in her slippers. Her posture was bowed, and I couldn't figure why. She knew I was planning to leave for Charlotte in the morning. She knew I'd arranged for Lee to help. And she knew I'd be back in a matter of days.

I got up from the table and started clearing it. I could feel Fox's stare, but he said nothing, only stood and tossed what remained of his dinner into the trashcan. At once, it was too much—Daddy's heart attack, Lee's text about the music guy and the worry that he'd leave me, Mama and Fox's clear disappointment, the laundry list of gala needs that I couldn't take care of remotely.

"Will you take me to Dolly's please?" I asked Fox. He had just grabbed his bag and was about to walk out the door without saying goodbye.

"Yeah, sure."

He stood there in the doorway waiting, examining the molding, the patina on the brass knob, anything to avoid me. I'd sold my car when I moved to Charlotte. My townhouse was located in a great spot and I could walk everywhere I needed to go. When I wanted to come home, I took the train. But in times like these, I missed my Accord.

"I'm going to Dolly's, Mama. I love you. Tell Daddy I love him too," I called out.

"I will," she hollered from the back room. "I can take you to the station tomorrow afternoon."

The first train to Charlotte came at two. I'd arrive in Charlotte by four-thirty and could be downtown at the convention center by five. The thought of standing in the event space steadied me. I could work twelve hours if I needed to and get everything done so I could get back to Mountain View as soon as the gala wrapped. It would all be alright.

Fox pushed his way out of the house and into the night. The humidity was sticky and the crickets hollered for the stars. He didn't wait for me, but paced to his truck, flung the bag in the bed, and opened the passenger door.

I got in and he didn't look at me. He closed the door and stared at the steering wheel.

When he started the truck without a word, I spoke up. "What's wrong with you?"

"Nothing," he said. His tone was icy. "But your dad just had a heart attack and you're leaving. Why?"

"Of course I'm leaving. Everybody knew I was leaving. I have the most important event of my career this week," I said evenly, unwilling to give him the courtesy of my anger. "Lee's going to help out with my parents while I'm gone."

"Is that so? Well, then, where the hell is he?"

"He's in Atlanta. He had a follow-up with his chiropractor and he'll be back in the morning."

Fox made a dismissive sound, like he thought Lee going away was ridiculous, but said nothing else.

I stared out the window at the farms as we passed. It was only 8:45, but already almost all the lights were out.

"Maybe you don't understand how important this gala is to me. I've worked so hard to get where I am. And if I nail this event, I make partner. I get a massive raise, ownership in the company, and I'll finally have enough to buy a place of my own, somewhere my parents can go too if they ever need to. I'll only be gone for four days, and the doctor says Daddy's going to be fine."

"I get it. And I'm sorry for blowing up like this, but Hattie. Shit." He stopped as though he'd decided he wasn't going to say something he was thinking. He glanced at me. Up ahead, the one stoplight blinked. "Believe it or not, I've been where you are right now and I took the same road you're about to take. I walked away from what mattered most for a weekend, for a feather in my cap that doesn't matter anymore, and Mama—"

"I'm not you." The sentence hissed from my lips. "I love my family, but I want a life away from this place. I *have* a life away from this place, and I can't throw it all away because Mama and Daddy won't leave. Lee understands and he'll help. I'm not leaving them alone."

"I'm not talking about the events business. I'm talking about you leaving right now with your dad's health the way it is. If your company can't understand that, then what kind of devil are you working for?"

Fox jerked the wheel down Possum Drive and the tires bumped over the potholes.

My body prickled with rage. It wasn't okay for him to speak to me like this. My parents would be in perfectly good hands with Lee while I was away.

Fox pulled into Dolly's driveway next to the Wienermobile bathed in the motion light and turned off the ignition.

"Here." He handed me the keys. "You're going to need a way back home. I can walk home, and I'll come get the truck from your parents' in the morning."

I wanted to throw the keys at him, but he was right.

We both sat there for a moment, staring at the old clay brick façade of Dolly's house.

"I'm sorry," he said finally. "I overstepped in a big way." He sighed and ran his hands along the steering wheel. "And you're right. You're not me and you're not going to experience what I did. But sometimes something hits so close to home that it scratches an old wound open again. That's what happened tonight."

My shoulders relaxed and my heart slowed.

"Are you alright?"

"Yeah. I guess I just wish I could have one more day with either of them, you know? My mama and daddy, they're both gone. They were like your parents. Wholesome, hardworking, loved me with all they had. I knew Mama was sick, but she told me to go that day." He swallowed hard. "And I'm not telling you this so you'll worry about your dad. It's a different thing altogether, and he's got good care and I'm sure Lee will watch out for them. I'm just explaining why your leaving struck such a nerve."

"I'm sorry it's been hard."

His brow furrowed.

"Life," I said.

"Ah, well. It's hard sometimes, and then other times you feel like you're walking on a cloud."

Fox opened his truck door and got out. "Good luck with the gala. The barn will look great when you get back." He smiled at me, and I returned the grin. He started to close the door but stopped. "I've liked having you around."

"You sure about that?" I asked, getting out of the passenger side.

He laughed. "Nah."

He started walking away from me, up the dark dirt road.

"Get Aslan's autograph for me, will you?" he called out before he disappeared into the shadow of Mrs. Muffet's house.

"He's a lion. He can't write," I yelled back.

His deep laughter echoed over me, and I walked toward Dolly's front door, throwing and catching his keys in my hand.

Dolly and Rocky had transformed their little sunroom into a beach bar. Never mind that Dolly had never really liked the beach. She hated sand.

I stared at the fishing net hanging in the corner, then at the blinking *Ahoy!* sign above the little plywood bar with a plastic parrot on top. I'd been talking for over an hour, about Lee and my new relationship, about my argument with Fox, about Daddy's health, and about the gala, my leaving, and Lee's run-in with a legitimate music executive, but Dolly hadn't said a word. She'd just sat there on her upholstered chaise longue by the windows in her floral pajamas and sipped the painkiller Rocky had mixed up for us before he'd disappeared to put the kids to bed.

I took a few sips of my drink, thankful Rocky was always heavy-handed with the rum.

"Go ahead and say it," I said finally.

Dolly pulled her hot pink scrunchy from her blonde hair and tousled the perfect mess with her fingers.

Beyond her, in the moonlight, I could see that somehow the swan float I'd borrowed from Judi had returned. It circled around the pool with Clay's giraffe, its smile never revealing that it had been on a grand adventure down Cardinal River.

"This time, I really don't know what to say." She set the drink down on the table beside her, the edge of it adorned with a faux grass skirt. "That's why I've been so quiet. I'm glad you got it all out, but whew." Dolly sighed. "I guess I don't know what you want from me. Do you want my opinion? Like, what I'd do? Or do you want me to just listen?"

"Both?" I adjusted my weight on the vintage metal lounge that, unfortunately, didn't come with a cushion.

Dolly waved her arm around the room.

"Hattie, I chose simple."

I laughed.

"You think this beach bar sunroom is simple?" I asked. "Joanna Gaines would beg to differ."

Dolly rolled her eyes.

"I'm talking about my life. We went opposite directions, you and me. I walked through Door A—Rocky and this town. And you chose Door B—a fancy career in a big city. Sometimes I've thought about what would've happened if I would have gone your way, but I always end up knowing I chose the right thing for me. I guess you feel the same, even with all the stress you're carrying."

She ran her fingers through her hair.

"You're going to have to let something go. I know you get that. I know that's the problem you're asking me to help you solve, but in your heart of hearts I think you want me to help you find a way to have it all—to be the daughter you need to be to your parents, to be the employee your boss can count on, to be a friend to a man who loves this town, and to be a girlfriend to a man you're terrified will leave." She picked up her drink and downed the rest of it. "And he will.

I don't mean he'll leave you, but I do mean he'll leave this town. He'll take that chance. Y'all are ambitious that way. It's the same reason you're going back for the gala. On the good side, it means you understand each other. Maybe this time, you'll make it work for real."

Dolly always told me straight. She'd never backed away from hard truths. But hearing aloud what my heart was already telling me brought tears to my eyes.

"Maybe," I said. "He promised he wouldn't leave me again, but if we go separate ways, to different cities or something, I don't know if we'll survive it." I swallowed the emotion. "It's not that he'd break his promise intentionally. Like you said, we think we can have it all." I took a sip of my drink.

I thought about my conversation with Lee my first night back. We'd asked each other if we were happy, and outside of our professional aspirations, we couldn't answer. Now, it seemed, we were happy personally, while our professional lives were in shambles.

"If you had to choose right now. Lee and Mountain View or Charlotte and your job, which would you pick?" Dolly bit her fingernail and snapped at Rocky who was passing by the door. "Can I have another drink, honey?"

Rocky emerged from the shag carpeted living room in a worn Mountain View High T-shirt and plaid pajama pants.

"Sure thing, sweetie."

He grinned at us both and walked to the bar.

"Just need Lee and then it's the four horsemen once again," he said.

I laughed, but Dolly's question hung in the air. My heart said the right answer was Lee, but saying it felt wrong. So did saying Charlotte and my job.

Rocky started pouring.

"Some guys get all the gifts, you know," he said, chuckling. "Dude's about as good at music as he is at baseball."

Dolly's gaze leveled on me. I'd told her she wasn't allowed to tell anybody about Lee being approached by Alan. Not even Rocky because he let things slip. There was a chance he'd overheard our conversation.

"Then again, it makes sense. He played guitar on rainy days and ball when it was nice, while I just sat around and played Nintendo."

"Babe, you have—" Dolly started to reassure him, but he waved his hand.

"Hey, I ain't complaining. *Mario Kart* prepared me for my job. Who would've ever figured I'd be driving a giant Hot Wheel for a living? And they send us all over tarnation too. We're driving up to Bristol tomorrow for a NASCAR thing. They'll put us up at the Best Western for free."

He poured Dolly's drink and crossed the room to hand it to her.

"It was nice of Oscar Mayer to donate the hot dogs for Founder's Day," I said.

"Hell yeah, it was. They're a good company to work for. You need more to drink, Hattie?"

I shook my head.

"I think we have the best life," Dolly said to Rocky.

"Oh, we do. Even if Kyle Busch showed up at my door with a check for a million dollars and an offer to be on the circuit, I'd shut him down. This right here is paradise."

Rocky kissed Dolly's head and wandered out of the room.

"You didn't answer my question," Dolly said.

I could feel my heart racing, and I forced my body back against the metal lounge.

"Right now, I'm choosing him and he's choosing me no matter where we are," I said. "One of my college professors said that thinking more than one day ahead is the root of all evil."

"Pretty sure he got that sentiment from the Bible, but okay. Maybe that's your answer," Dolly said, lifting her drink toward me. "To one day at a time and a life well lived."

CHAPTER TWELVE

The house phone rang again. I pushed the pillow over my head and tried to ignore it. Nobody used house phones anymore except for criminals phishing for money from the elderly. That's why my parents kept the line live. Daddy loved messing with scammers.

My head ached. Rocky's painkillers only worked when you were drinking them. I had to blame the rum. He claimed it was Bacardi, but I knew he'd bought it from the gas station ABC store between Pine Summit and Clover whose manager had been caught trying to pass his homemade liquors for name brand.

The phone screamed from the hallway once more, and I groaned and pushed myself out of bed, stumbling over a collection of Styrofoam wreath forms I forgot I'd knocked over in the middle of the night on my way to the bathroom.

I snatched the teal receiver off the wall.

"Hello."

"Hattie." Mama's voice wobbled and then she started crying. I froze. I'd only seen Mama sob one time in my life and that was at MawMaw's funeral.

"What is it?" I didn't want to know the answer. My skin went cold and the kitchen walls felt like they were closing in. I sank down on the floor and hugged my knees as my Mama sobbed. "Mama."

"Your daddy."

"Is he—" I started, but Mama interrupted.

"Your daddy had a rough night." She sniffed. "At first they thought it was a mini heart attack, but it wasn't. He's stable now."

"Why wouldn't you just say that? I thought he was . . . I thought the worst," I said, rising to my feet.

"I'm sorry, but I guess everything just built up, Hattie. My cellular ran out of charge, and I couldn't remember your phone number, so I've been trying to call for the past hour. I'm at my breaking point, baby girl." Her voice was soft at the end, and it startled me. "We both are. Now Dr. Gerard is suggesting we hire extra help when Junior gets discharged day after tomorrow, since he had the other episode, and we don't have the money. And then we have to get the barn up and running in time for those folks' wedding in a couple weeks or we'll have no income at all. And then, I went into the lobby to pick up a paper this morning—they get *The State* here—and there's a big article on the front page with two sketches of the new stadium, one sitting right in the middle of our town, the other sitting right in the middle of Cardinal River." She started to cry again. "The article said the state's decision is imminent, and last night I saw those dozers clearing road right at the town line."

I fitted the loops of curly phone cord over my fingertips. If Daddy hadn't been sick, I would've suggested they consider Charlotte again, but even mentioning it would send Mama into a tailspin.

"We'll figure this out together."

"No, we won't. You're leaving." Suddenly, her tone was sharp and even, void of the sadness I'd heard earlier. "I need to ask if you'd give Fox a call since I don't have my numbers. I need you to ask if he still has Mr. Fox's handrail and shower chair up in his apartment somewhere or if he got rid of it. Junior's going to need one until he gets his strength back."

"Alright, Mama."

I walked over to the kitchen window, the long phone cord trailing behind on the linoleum. Fox's truck was gone from the driveway. Granted, it was going on nine-thirty, and I knew he opened the store at seven.

"Can I talk to Daddy? I want to come see him, but I can't exactly drive over to Cardinal River right now." Even though Cardinal River was the next town over, the clinic was on the far side fifteen miles away, by "the Development" as everyone called it—the Dollar General and the Pizza Inn.

"No. He's resting." She sighed. "But he knows you love him. By the way, I hate that I've got to do this, but I'm not going to be able to see you off today. I'm not going to leave Junior again until he's home day after tomorrow. I'll be worried sick. I've called Bobby Jo. She'll take you to the station later unless Lee's going to do it."

"Okay."

"Love you, bye." She seemed to sob the last word and hung up before I could reply. I put the receiver back on the wall and rubbed my eyes. I could feel the weight on my shoulders. I could feel the tension in my chest. One more thing. Only one more thing and my dam would burst, same as Mama's.

A Lowe's truck pulled onto our drive. I walked out to the porch, and an older man in a trucker hat got out.

"I'm here to deliver some hardwood flooring y'all ordered and to do some wiring. The gentleman I talked to from Fox's Hardware said you need power to a hayloft?" the man called out.

"Yeah, that's right. Down at the barn." I pointed toward the end of the drive. "I'll get some shoes on and meet you down there."

"If it's open, there's no need. That is, if you trust your local guy. He sent me a layout of the space." The man waved a paper at me. I couldn't believe Fox had gone to the trouble to draw it out. Granted, if it wasn't this guy, it'd be Fox putting the power in and I knew he had other jobs he was getting paid for that he'd need to spend time on.

"Sounds great then. Just holler if you need me."

I walked back into the house and into my room to change and grabbed my cell. I pressed the number for Fox's Hardware and pushed the speaker button as I pulled on my Lululemon shorts, a sports bra, and a cutoff T-shirt I'd made in college boasting my sorority letters in puffy paint. It smelled like mothballs thanks to Mama's packing.

The phone rang and rang and finally I ended the call and tried Fox's personal number instead. He didn't pick up.

I folded my pajamas and put them in my suitcase, then zipped it up. Only a few more hours and the to-do list that had been staring me down every time I unlocked my phone would be on its way to completion. But not before I kissed Lee goodbye. My stomach flipped at the thought of his mouth on mine, then the feeling deadened with a wave of guilt. I remembered Fox's words and thought that maybe he was right. Maybe I was selfish to be thinking of work and Lee at all while Daddy was still recovering.

I rolled my suitcase into the living room, wiggled my feet into my running shoes, then threw my hair into a ponytail. I'd run the three miles into town and see if I could find Fox at the store.

I walked toward Route 2, then pushed my body to a jog. It was a good day for a run, and the breeze broke the humidity just slightly. The Turneys were watering their soybeans up ahead and I ran faster, hoping for a bit of the spray, but when I reached their property, the wind turned.

I mopped my forehead with the back of my hand and focused on downtown ahead. Maybe I could snag a cold Coke from the old icebox in the back of the hardware store.

The Mainerts' cows were out, mooing in the heat while they ate what little grass they could find on the horribly maintained front lawn. The lawn had looked bad when Uncle Jasper owned it, but somehow the Mainerts had made it look worse. Across their farm, in the distance, I could barely make out the line of road where Main Street ended abruptly in a small clearing right before the high school and the start of the Harolds' farm. The old McDonald's arches shuddered in the breeze, and beneath I could barely make out Tosha with her guitar. Tuesdays were her day off from the retirement home and she usually spent her free time with the arches.

I slowed when I reached the alleyway that would lead me to the gazebo. My head throbbed. That was never a good sign.

My phone rang and I fished it out of the pocket against my back. It was Merry. I took a breath and answered.

"Hey, Merry. I'll be on the train shortly," I said before she could ask.

"When did you schedule the food to be delivered to the venue?" she asked, her voice clipped.

I sat down on the gazebo steps.

"Wednesday," I said. "You know I always schedule it two days before the event."

"It was delivered last night. All of it. Five hundred pounds of steak, the ice cream for the sundaes, the cheese for the puff pastries, the puff pastry dough, the coffee creamer, all of it was left out for eight hours on the delivery ramp at the convention center."

My head spun and my heart pounded in my ears.

"There must have been a mistake." Tears sprang to my eyes. "I . . . I know I scheduled it for the right day. I did it before I left for here." I put her on speaker and started to open my email to confirm I'd done the right thing. I always did the right thing.

"Maybe so, but we're responsible regardless and now I'm out thirty thousand dollars." She was livid. I didn't blame her. "I'm going to have to pray I can find replacement food at this short notice. I'm not sure I can. And if I can't, any hope we have at securing that events deal with the Panthers is gone."

"I'm sorry," I said, wiping my eyes. The service was terrible, and my email wouldn't load. "I'll call down to Wholesale Food and work this out. They delivered it early, I know it."

Merry laughed, a short bark in the back of her throat.

"And what happened the last time we had an issue like this? It happened at the Gaston County Historical Society event four years ago too, remember?"

"No, it didn't. It almost did, but it didn't. When Susan called to tell me the trucks were loaded and ready, I told them that it wasn't time to come yet."

"That's right," Merry said. "Susan calls every time, doesn't she? I bet she tried calling you this time too." She paused. "I know you've been distracted and rightfully so. But we're a small business, Hattie. I count on you, and this event is make it or break it for me. You and I both know this company can't keep limping along doing one-off events."

"I know, Merry. I'm sorry," I said. "I'll be back later today and I'll make it right."

"You can't this time, Hattie. The food is spoiled. I'll have to pay for it. It's our whole commission." She sighed. "I guess you got my voicemail last week and contacted the Blossom Shoppe, though, right? We can have no roses at the event. Absolutely zero. Eliott's CEO is allergic."

I said nothing. I hadn't received such a message.

"Hattie?"

"Yeah."

"Did you take care of the flowers?"

The pitch in her voice rose, the stress strangling her. It was strangling me.

"No." I cleared my throat. "I never got that message, Merry."

I heard a muffled noise and then a scream from somewhere in the distance.

"Hattie, I have counted on you for years," she said. "And you have counted on me. I let you rent my townhouse when you moved to Charlotte. I have lent you my car when you needed one. I have always made sure you were paid well and on time. I was considering making you partner." She sounded strange, matter-of-fact, and my fingers gripped hard around my phone.

"You can still count on me, Merry."

"I know you have a lot going on personally right now, but this event, my business, is in shambles because of you. I need someone who can focus to take the reins and the only person who can do that is me. Send me your files. I'm going to handle this event by myself."

"I can be there tonight, Merry."

"No. You're going to stay out of my way," she snapped. "When the event is over, if I pull this off, we'll talk again. If this thing goes south and I lose my reputation and the contract over your blunders, I'll cancel your lease, have movers pack up your things, and I never want to speak to you again."

"But . . ." I started to cry.

"I know it seems harsh, but you have your family. My company *is* my family. It's all I have. Go help your family. I've got to save mine."

"Merry, please."

She hung up on me.

I stared at the phone in my hand. I was done. It was gone. Everything I'd worked for was being ripped away from me.

Lee texted: *Back on the road. Shoulder's fine. Waze says 1:38. Can't wait to kiss you. Just checked Amtrak too. Your train is on time.*

No rush. I just got fired. I'm stuck here, I texted back.

I began to sob. The sound echoed off of the buildings, but there was no one around to notice.

No, you're not. We'll fix this, Lee wrote. *Just hang in there 'til I get back.*

I read his words while tears rushed down my face. I wanted to believe him. After all, everything Lee touched turned to gold, but I wasn't sure if that magic included me. I'd been the one thing that had shriveled to dust in his life.

I called the clinic and asked for Mama. I told her I was staying and forced myself to be calm when I heard the relief in her voice, when she immediately asked me again if I'd gotten ahold of Fox about the handrail and shower seat. Daddy's heart attack was nobody's fault, but to my grieving mind, it felt like it had trapped me in this measly, dying town.

Up the street, I watched Tammy park the Kia Soul she'd only bought because she liked the commercial with the hamsters and unlock the Cut & Curl. I suddenly had an urge to walk into the salon and ask her to shave my head or to steal her car and drive off toward Charlotte as fast as I could go. But of course I wouldn't do either of those things.

Instead, I walked toward the hardware store, past Fox's truck parked out front. I opened the plate glass door and stepped inside. I breathed deep, hoping the smells of potting soil and antique wood and fertilizer would smother my fury, but they didn't. They only reminded me of the fact that it had smelled the same since I was a kid. It reminded me that for now, this never-changing town was my home again.

There was always the chance that Merry would come through this somehow and I'd get my job back, but I knew how deeply my mistakes had buried CLE.

"Fox?"

My voice sounded dull over the hardwood floor and the wooden shelving lining the walls. I ran my hands down the glass display cases. My fingers shook. I wondered how it would feel to punch the glass in, if it would give me any relief, but of course I wouldn't do that either.

When I reached the iceboxes, I reached inside, letting the ice burn my fingers as I searched for a glass bottleneck. I found one, pulled it out, and twisted the lid off. The bubbles hissed and sparkled from the lip, and I took a long sip.

I leaned into the office doorway behind the wall of nails at the end of the room, but no one was there. I glanced at the door across from his office, the door that I knew led to a flight of stairs and his apartment above the store. I'd never been up there. Not even when I was little and Mr. Fox had been laid up for weeks from some illness and the whole town took turns pitching in to bring him dinner and do his laundry until he recovered.

I knocked on the door, but there was no answer, so I tried the knob.

"Fox?"

I heard his voice upstairs. Maybe he was on the phone. At first, I figured I should turn around and close the door, but if I didn't get an answer about the shower supplies, Mama would pester me until I lost it—and that wouldn't take much today.

I started up the narrow stairwell. Dusty photos lined the whitewashed walls—Mr. Fox as a young man standing outside of the store, Mr. Fox with the Robinsons, Mr. Fox with the rest of the town in front of Mountain View Presbyterian for Easter. There wasn't one picture of new Fox. I wondered about Annie's suspicions she'd shared with me my first night back. Maybe Mr. Fox was somehow Fox's daddy after all. Maybe that's why he'd changed nothing.

"Fox?"

When I reached the top stair, I found myself in a sizeable living room. The couch and rug were 1970s matching plaid, clearly left over from Mr. Fox before him, but there was a leather armchair and a large TV I knew Fox had contributed. The kitchen adjoined the living room, but it was tiny, a small L-shaped space with barely enough counter area for the Nespresso and the air frier he'd added.

I could still hear Fox's muffled tone, but not much else, so I wandered into the room and glanced down a short hall to my left. I startled. Annie was standing in Fox's bedroom. She was fully clothed in her normal mayoral costume of dress slacks and a matching blazer, but that didn't matter. Fox was sitting in a chair facing away from the doorway, and though I couldn't see much, I could definitely tell that at the very least he didn't have a shirt on. She laughed at something and leaned toward him flirtatiously and I heard his voice again. I couldn't move. For one, though I hadn't noticed the floorboards squeaking, I knew they likely did, and for two, I was literally paralyzed by the sight of them. My brain screamed for me to move, but the direction I wanted to move was toward Annie, not down the stairs. I suddenly wanted to punch her.

I whirled on my heel before I could give in to the crazy in my mind and the floor wailed. I ran, hearing my name called behind me, first by Annie and then by Fox.

I threw myself into the store and shut the door to the apartment behind me, but not before Fox caught up.

"What are you doing?"

He stood in the doorway in running shorts. That was it. I stared and tried to catch my breath. Where Lee's body had always been rippled with lean muscle, Fox's abs were bulky and cut, matching his arms. I forced my gaze to his.

"Nothing." Embarrassment singed my cheeks. "I saw your truck out front, and Mama wanted me to see if you still happened to have the shower chair and the handrail Mr. Fox left behind. She wanted to borrow it for Daddy."

He nodded. "Yeah. I think I do. I'll look around in storage and drop it off later if I find it."

"Thanks." I backed toward the iceboxes. "Sorry to have interrupted." I said, gesturing behind him where Annie appeared on the stairs. She smiled. Fox didn't.

"Interrupted what? I just got back from a run. Looks like you did too," he said.

"You about scared me to death," Annie said. "Did you come to sign the petition now? Finally? That's what Fox and I were just discussing, you know—how to get more support for our cause in the next few days. We want to be able to say we're unanimously against the build and our attorney says we can't use that phrase unless you sign. You're hurting our case."

I looked from Annie to Fox and back again. I'd never had a meeting in a person's bedroom. And I was sick of

Annie making me out to be a villain. As of today, I was trapped here. I'd lost everything I'd worked for all because I'd spent the last week stuck in this town.

"No. No, I didn't come to sign the petition. I'm never going to. I haven't changed my mind. This town is a waste of space, a dying breath."

I fisted my hands and turned and paced down the center aisle toward the door. The Coke I'd opened and abandoned sat on the display case, the condensation dampening the glass. I plucked it up, and when I got to the cash register, reached behind the counter for one of the abandoned liquor bottles I knew Fox stashed back there after everyone left on Friday night.

"Jack. Great," I mumbled when I'd retrieved the half empty bottle of whisky. I screwed the top off, took a long draw, and chased it with the Coke, then started toward the door with both bottles in hand.

"Hattie, wait." Fox walked up the aisle toward me. "What's going on? What's wrong?"

I laughed when I stepped outside. I glanced back at him.

"Everything. But nothing this old guy can't fix."

I tipped the whisky into my mouth once again and started walking down the street without looking back.

"Let's finish our discussion," I heard Annie say from the doorway, and I kept on toward the gazebo, having no clue at all where I was going.

CHAPTER THIRTEEN

I'd been talking to Slugger—the horse—for at least a half hour before I realized I was thoroughly sloshed. Alternating as many shots of whisky as I wanted with Coke wasn't diluting the alcohol like I'd once thought it had in college. Or maybe I was just a lightweight now or probably dehydrated. Either way, when I started crying about my job and being stuck in Mountain View and wondering why Slugger wasn't talking back to me, I knew I had a problem.

"You're a horse," I remembered slurring, and then I'd given Slugger a nice pat on the neck and walked down the Lockhardts' manicured drive toward the house, thinking how glad I was that Lee's parents were away in France.

The Lockhardts' house was the sort of A-frame you'd find in the mountains. Mr. and Mrs. Lockhardt had built it before Lee struck it big. Before the baseball money came in, it had looked nicer than the rest of our farmhouses, but nothing you'd stop your car to stare at. A sunflower field had occupied most of the side yard except for an acre for Slugger and his sister, Shorty. The barn was falling in, and the house had been landscaped by whatever weeds decided to grow around the foundation. But then, in ninth grade, Mr. Lockhardt's daddy passed away, leaving them eighty thousand dollars. They'd put in the pool that year—an in-ground pool, not the above-ground type everybody else had. People started to talk about the Lockhardts being super rich, which was appropriate foreshadowing for what was to come. Because now the thirty acres that had once been used for flowers was manicured grass, maintained by Vern, and the house had undergone a major renovation our freshman year of college and doubled in size.

Everything looked like a polished version of the same thing except for the pool. The pool hadn't been touched. It was already nice.

Maybe it was that sentiment, the idea that it was the one spot at Lee's place that still held our memories, that made me climb over the wrought iron fence, grab a pool float from the shiny new pool house, jump in the water, and subsequently fall asleep.

I rubbed my eyes and sat up. My face was hot and likely fried. There was no shade here. I dipped into the pool, submerging my dry clothes once again. At least I wasn't still drunk. I eyed the clock attached to the pool house. It was 4:25. I couldn't believe how long I'd been asleep. Then again, drunk hours tended to blur together. Lee was probably looking for me.

My phone, the spent bottle of Coke, and the mostly exhausted bottle of Jack were baking in the sun on one of the fancy lounge chairs beside the pool. It was so hot I had no doubt my phone had long since shut down to preserve itself.

I held my breath and plunged under the water, swimming from the shallow end where the little fountain jets sprinkled, to the deep end where the water was usually a little cooler. I came up and pulled my scrunchie from my hair, tossing it on to the chair with my other stuff, then leaned back and floated. My life was in shambles, but right here, right now, I felt a strange sense of peace. This was Lee's pool, the place where I'd always felt treasured, always felt wanted and loved. He'd said it would be okay, that he'd help me out of this, and I believed him.

Suddenly, my outburst at Fox's seemed stupid. I remembered the fury I'd felt at Annie, Fox too. Now, floating here, I knew why. I was mad that they were where they wanted to be and I was not. I guess in my anger over my job, I'd forgotten that in one huge way, I *was* happy. I was in love with the man I'd always been in love with, and he'd loved me all this time too.

I glanced at the pool gate. Surely, Lee would wind up here eventually. My body tingled at the thought of us making out in the pool again like we used to. I knew exactly how his wet skin would feel beneath my hands. I knew that after our longest kiss, right when his fingertips would start inching under my clothes, I'd squirm away and dunk him. We'd wrestle and fight until, eventually, he'd corner me and we'd start kissing again.

I craved him. Desperately. If I'd gone to Charlotte today, I wouldn't be here, where he was, and something about that made my career ambitions temporarily disappearing seem okay for now.

Voices sounded from the driveway, beyond the gate, and I swam to the side, reaching the edge at the same time Woody appeared with his guitar, followed by Cassidy, Clay, and Blaze.

Woody grinned when he saw me, but then he shook his head.

"We should've known," he said, setting his guitar down on a chintz ottoman that matched the rest of the lounge chairs.

"What do you mean?" I asked, but I knew exactly what he meant. In high school we'd always ended up here. Old habits die hard, I guess.

"You know the whole town's been looking for you, right?" Cassidy said. He deposited his keyboard and fiddle cases on the pool deck.

"No," I said. "I fell asleep on that float over there, and I'm pretty sure my phone shut down in the heat."

"Tammy sounded the alarm when she saw you walking down Main with a bottle of Jack at ten in the morning," Blaze said. He tried to be serious, but laughter burst through his closed lips.

"Fox and Annie went down to Dolly's, but you weren't there," Cassidy said.

"Dolly and Rocky are out of town." I'd considered floating down the river again. In fact, that had been my first choice, but I was worried the rocks would wind up breaking the two glass bottles I was holding, and that wouldn't do.

I had a vague recollection of deciding to walk back home down Route 2, and I'd started to, but then I'd been sidetracked by Slugger who was standing right at the top of the Lockhardts' farm, waiting for me.

"We need to call Lee." Woody dug his phone out of his Wrangler's, pressed a button, and held the phone to his ear.

"Where is he?"

"Where isn't he?" Cassidy said. "He's been everywhere looking for you—your house, all around your farm, the river, the town. He even went to the clinic thinking you might have gone to see your daddy."

I felt terrible.

"I'm sorry I scared y'all. I just had a hard day."

"Yeah. Lee said you got fired for staying to get your parents on their feet. Your boss sucks," Blaze said helpfully.

"I did screw up her largest event of the year, arguably her career."

"Hey, man," I heard Woody say. "We found her." He paused. "Yeah. She's in your pool." Woody looked at me. "Lee's going to let your mama know. Visiting hours are almost over, but Dr. Gerard is going to let her stay with your daddy again overnight."

"Thanks," I said.

The guys just stood there, staring at me.

"Y'all have a practice planned?"

"Not really," Blaze said. He lifted his shirt to wipe the sweat from his face, revealing a sizeable belly covered in a blanket of curly black hair. "We just show up every day around evening and play with whoever's here. It's important to keep the hinges greased in case we're asked to play—like maybe at that wedding y'all are hosting coming up?" He looked at me like I had the answer to the question. I wasn't the bride or the groom, and I had no idea what their tastes were. "We figured Lee might not be here tonight since y'all are an item again and all." He winked at me.

"Are there towels in there?" I asked, nodding toward the pool house and ignoring his statement, though it made me happy to know Lee had told his friends about us.

"Yeah, why?" Woody asked. He noticed the bottles, my phone, and discarded scrunchie on the lounge chair and pointed at the scrunchie. "Can I borrow that?"

"Sure," I said and watched as he pulled his hair into a man bun. "I'm asking if there are towels because I want to get out."

They all stared at me instead of catching my drift and fetching me a towel.

"Never mind. Just go ahead with whatever you usually do."

I swam toward the shallow end, thankful that I was wearing workout clothes and not my typical fare for this time of year—either a sundress or shorts and a thin T-shirt.

Behind me, the gate whined on its hinge and I turned around to find Lee grinning at me. He was wearing a gray T-shirt, jeans, and his baseball cap—basically the ingredients for my own personal kryptonite. I smiled when our eyes met, and then he started laughing and tossed his hat on the lounge next to my stuff. I couldn't believe he was mine again. Most guys would be livid, annoyed at minimum, with my antics today but not Lee.

"I'm sorry," I said as he walked toward me and knelt down at the edge of the pool.

"I thought I told you to hang in there 'til I got back." He smiled, and I waded toward him, pulled his face to mine, and kissed him. The guys whistled behind us, and when his lips broke from mine he chuckled. "You ain't drunk right now. I can tell that 'cause you're not out there conversing with Slugger anymore—"

"People saw that?" I whispered.

"And your eyes don't have that sexy sleepy look they get," he went on, ignoring my question, "but you taste like you've been washing your mouth out with whisky."

"Sorry."

He dropped a kiss on the top of my head.

"I don't mind it. I'm friends with Jack."

"Is Mama okay? Daddy too? I didn't mean to scare everybody. I was just . . ."

"Angry? Disappointed? Feeling a decade of work crumbling away?" Lee ran a hand across his face. "At least you didn't throw a table at a group of press and then spend the next ten minutes losing your shit." He sighed. "I get it. You've worked hard and you didn't deserve to be let go like that. Especially with everything going on. And your parents don't know you went AWOL. Everybody decided it was best to try and find you first. If we couldn't, we'd tell them then." He placed his hand over the back of mine sitting on the edge of the pool. "When I went to see them and you weren't there, I told your mama I must have missed you at the house, but that I'd let her know when I caught up with you. Your daddy's doing well. Gave me a pretty stern talking-to about my intentions with you, actually."

"And what are your intentions, Mr. Lockhardt?" I asked.

He glanced at the guys behind us, then lowered his lips to my ear. "Why don't you stick around and find out?"

"But you have all the guys here. You could meet me at my house later?"

"Or you could hang out and listen to our songs. You didn't get to hear them all on Founder's Day. You could let us know if we're good enough to be the house band for some of the weddings maybe and on Fridays. Fox told us he's kicking us out." Lee grinned.

Thinking about Fox made me want to crawl into a hole. He and Annie had seen me at my most hysterical. It wasn't a good look. I'd have to text them both later and apologize.

"Okay."

"Alright, fellas," Lee said, rising to his feet. "Let's set up. Hattie's going to stick around and tell us whether we should keep it up or toss our instruments in the river."

"I think it's been established that y'all are good. That guy even—" I stopped midsentence.

Lee's eyes widened, and he shook his head quickly.

"A lot of visitors at Founder's Day mentioned they loved listening to y'all," I amended. "Can I get a towel?"

Lee nodded and disappeared into the pool house while the rest of the guys set their instruments up on the deck. I got out of the water and pulled my old college T-shirt out from my stomach, noticing the old puffy paint didn't hold up well in chlorine. The three horizontal lines that made up the *Xi* were all peeling off.

"Hey, Hattie," Woody said. He met me at the edge of the pool, his eyes darting over my shoulder for Lee.

"Yeah?"

"You're going to hear some things when we play that might resonate," he whispered. "We don't really practice the covers. We've played those since high school. We practice the originals. And I need you to act like every damn song is the best one you've ever heard."

I looked at him like he was crazy.

"I *do* think y'all are good," I said. "No pretending here."

"Okay, but you haven't heard them all. We only played five at Founder's Day and only play a couple Friday nights."

"Still. I doubt they're bad."

"They're not bad. They're great. At least we think they are. It's just . . . Lee's our songwriter and . . ." He waved at Lee coming out of the pool house. "It's clear that every word he writes is about you—about him missing you, about him loving you, about y'all's memories." He shuffled his feet in the water. "So just keep that in mind if you think one of them sucks. He might not hear that it's the song you don't like, I guess is what I mean."

"Here you go, Hat," Lee said, appearing over Woody's shoulder. "You can change in the pool house if you want." He handed me a fluffy towel, a pair of his sweats and a dry T-shirt, then clapped Woody on the back. "Get moving, man. It's time to show our audience a good time."

Lee stepped toward me, pulled me to his chest, and kissed me. I leaned into him, the echo of Woody's words in my mind.

"I love you," I said when I finally let him go. "And I'm still pissed about my job, but I'm glad to be here."

"I wanted you to go because it was the right thing, but I can't pretend I'm upset that you're here tonight." He smoothed my damp hair back from my forehead and kissed it. "After you change, sit over there, will you?" He nodded to a stone fire pit area right beyond the pool with a kidney-shaped wicker couch around it. That part was new. "The acoustics are better. And I can turn the fire on later if you're cold."

"Sounds good." I pulled the towel around me and shuffled toward the pool house.

"I'd offer you a glass of wine, but—"

"No," I said, more forcefully than I meant. I started laughing. "Whisky's one thing, but a few glasses of wine in and I'd start singing with you."

"Yeah, I know," Lee said, as he walked into his house and emerged a minute later with his guitar case. "Why do you think I rescinded the offer?" He winked at me. I rolled my eyes and walked into the pool house with his clothes that smelled like him, listening to the sound of the guys tuning their instruments outside, realizing I was suddenly at peace.

"Y'all better watch out. You especially, Hattie," Cassidy said from the back of the diving board. "I'm going to win. Y'all understand you can't beat this hunk of man, right?" He flexed his arms, which weren't that impressive and took a step forward. His bulky frame was washed in moonglow that dappled across the rippling pool water.

"I don't know." I swam to the other side of the pool to join Lee and Woody. Lee's sweatpants encouraged considerable drag. I felt like I was moving in slow motion. "My splash reached the edge of the fountains."

"Yeah. But we're going to have to bet on Cassidy this time," Woody said. "He's been practically clearing the pool since he was six. Remember the way those kids screamed and swam away at church camp that year?" Woody asked Cassidy.

Cassidy laughed. "I've only perfected my form since."

He paced back down the diving board and stepped off to stretch. Clay yawned. It was contagious and I did the same. The clock on the pool house read eleven thirty. It was the latest I'd stayed up in a year at least outside of a work event.

I pushed my elbows up on the edge of the drain and leaned back, listening to Lee and Woody argue about who had really won the smallest splash. It had been Woody by a mile. He had absolutely no body fat and generally looked like a pencil.

Swimming around like this made me feel like a kid again. It was just what I needed. Because only an hour before, I'd been snuggled onto the couch with the fire blazing, listening to the band play their final song, crying. Nobody had been able to tell. I was all the way across the pool from them and I hadn't been sobbing. The last song they'd played, "Strike Out," hadn't even been a sad one. It was a party song about a guy who kept trying to get a girl's attention, and on the last attempt he finally struck out. But the whole lineup of songs had been the sort of music you'd hear on country radio, and I'd been crying because I knew I had to tell Lee to take Alan's offer.

I'd tried to envision Lee staying, singing at the barn and working at the bank, but I couldn't. He'd told me that first night that his being back in Mountain View was only a pause until he could figure out his next act. Well, his next act had been dropped in his lap, but for some reason, despite telling me to go, he wouldn't do the same. I knew he understood how good the band was. I knew he understood that passing this by was wasting his talent and the talents of his friends. There was no way he didn't when I could see it so clearly. But maybe it had caught him off guard. Maybe he'd figured his next move would be a normal job, like a sportscaster or a banker in a bigger city, some steady role that would allow him greater control over where he was, some role that wasn't dictated by the winds of fame, some role that would allow for us.

My eyes teared again, thinking of it. But I couldn't be the reason he stayed here. Just like he didn't want to be the reason I gave up my dream.

"Here I come!" Cassidy propelled himself into the air and crashed into the water. The waves hurtled over us, completely dousing the pool deck and my phone that had only recently revived itself enough for me to call Mama.

"You win," Blaze shouted. "I ain't even going to try."

I wiped the water from my face as the guys started arguing over the next contest.

"You alright over here? You got the worst of it," Lee said, swimming around Woody.

"Yeah. He did warn me."

Lee put his hands on the edge of the pool on either side of my elbows and leaned in to kiss me. He'd stripped off everything but his boxer briefs—all the guys had—and I sat up from my slouch and pulled him closer, feeling the tight muscles along his back under my fingertips, wrapping my legs around his waist.

He stopped kissing me, and his mouth drifted to my ear.

"Stay with me tonight," he whispered.

I hesitated. All the thoughts I'd had about him leaving swirled in my mind.

"We don't have to do anything," he said softly. "I just want you near me."

At once, I realized I didn't care about tomorrow. What mattered was what I wanted right now.

"Okay," I whispered.

I leaned away and dug my fingers into his side where I knew he was the most ticklish.

"Hattie," he growled through his laughter and caught my arms. "You're coming with me."

Before I could reply, he plucked me from the side of the pool, threw me over his good shoulder, and waded out of the water and up the walk toward the house.

"Put me down," I said, laughing as he reached over with his other hand and started tickling the sides of my back with his fingertips. "Lee," I howled, kicking my feet in the air.

"Let yourselves out when you're done, boys," Lee hollered over his shoulder.

He opened the glass door with this free hand and stepped inside the house, still holding me upside down.

The place smelled exactly the same, like Mrs. Lockhardt's spaghetti sauce and vanilla candles.

Lee walked through the living room and into the kitchen. My hair and shirt dripped on the hardwood floor.

"Grab our snacks since you're down there," he said to me when the cabinets came into view. They were the same ones they'd had before, only Mrs. Lockhardt had painted them white.

I reached for the knob and was surprised to find the cabinet stocked with our favorites. Bags of Sour Patch Kids and containers of vanilla Oreos sat next to the rest of the family's snacks of choice—chips and crackers and chocolate bars. This had been our ritual every time we'd stayed together. We'd bring everything we'd want into the room with us so we wouldn't have to leave.

"What's taking you so long?" he asked. "Do you see them?"

"You still want the same thing?" I eyed the other snacks. There was always a chance he'd changed his preference over the years.

He chuckled, a low rumble in his chest that made my skin flush with heat.

"Yeah. I'd say I do."

I grabbed a bag of candy and the carton of cookies and clapped my hand to the back of his calf a few times like I was smacking the top of a cab.

Lee started walking toward the back of the house, toward the stairs. We passed the hallway to the addition I'd never seen, and I was strangely relieved to find that we were going to his room, to a place that had known us before.

The clock on the hall wall upstairs chimed midnight, the Westminster tolling evenly and stoically. We passed Tim's room, then his parents'. Lee edged his door open, leaned over, and set me down.

"Wow." It was like I'd traveled back in time. His medals hung beside his door on the hook I'd made him for his sixteenth birthday, and the bookshelf beside the door to his bathroom held the same trophies and books that had been there the last time—*The Greatest Baseball Stories Ever Told, Ball Four, Our Team.*

I set the snacks down on his black nightstand with the same metal lamp adorned with the same cockeyed lampshade. I could feel Lee watching me but reveled in the silence. Something about this moment felt sacred and necessary, this reacquaintance with the man I'd known and loved my whole life.

I walked around the edge of his sleigh bed. It was barely made, the maroon quilt flung haphazardly across the sheets, but even the sight of that was comforting somehow. He hadn't really changed. I glanced at the matching nightstand on the other side. Before, both nightstands had held photos of me. Now, of course, they were gone. It made sense, and yet the reality of it made my heart ache. Maybe he'd put them away because of Willow. I tried to focus on the big photograph of his final play for Mountain View his mama had blown up. It was between the windows, a picture of him with his teeth gripped to his bottom lip, the ball flying through the air toward home from shortstop. And then I kept on walking, pausing in the far corner where his first guitar sat on a stand.

I heard a drawer open, and I looked toward Lee, who was standing in front of his dresser across the room. He extracted a frame I recognized, wiped the dust from it with his palm, then walked across the room and put it on his bedside table. It was a photo of me floating in the river.

"I wasn't hiding them," he said. "I've never . . . I've never brought anybody up here but you. I put them away because I couldn't look at them. I didn't think I'd ever be able to tell you I loved you again."

My eyes filled with tears. I looked away from him and down at his old guitar to distract myself. Suddenly, the reminder of his music pressed into my mind. I knew what I needed to say. If I didn't now, I would never have the strength, and it was only right.

"You have to take Alan up on his offer, Lee," I said quietly. Our eyes met. "You have to go to Nashville. You know you do."

He swallowed.

"I don't want to talk about it. Not right now. Not tonight. If that's okay?"

"Okay."

I shivered and pulled my arms around me as the air conditioner kicked on overhead.

"Let me get you some dry clothes."

He walked back over to his dresser. I watched the way his body moved, the way his abs constricted with each step. I didn't want to think about Nashville either, or anything tomorrow might bring.

Lee opened the middle drawer and got a T-shirt out, then a pair of boxers from the top one. I took the clothes from his hands, but then he pulled me into his arms and kissed me.

"I love you," I said against his mouth. I touched his chest, then drew my hands down the length of his stomach and he kissed me hard. His fingertips skimmed the hem of my shirt, then pushed the damp fabric up my bare back.

"Lee," I whispered as his lips found my neck, as his teeth grazed my earlobe, as his hands found my breasts. I could hardly breathe. I could hardly keep from begging for him.

"We're going to take this real slow," he murmured in my ear. "I'm going to show you just how much I love you, how long I've dreamed of being with you again."

CHAPTER FOURTEEN

A phone kept ringing somewhere. I ignored it and reached for Lee, but my hand grazed cotton sheets instead of the man who'd held me all night. I opened my eyes and squinted at the light beaming in from the windows highlighting the picture of me floating in the river he'd put back on his bedside table. I smiled at our clothes dotted across his floor like a trail to the bed—first the shirt he'd lent me beside his dresser, then his boxers in the middle of the rug, then my borrowed sweatpants at the edge of the mattress. I burrowed into his quilt and closed my eyes, remembering every stroke of his fingertips, every kiss, every sensation of us together, the way the elation of us had poured out of our hearts and rippled through our bodies. He hadn't let go of me since, not once all night until now, and I'd fallen asleep with him whispering promises in my ear—that he'd never leave me, that he'd always love me, that he'd always loved me. We were us again. Finally. After all this time.

The phone rang again. I pushed the pillows aside and found Lee's phone just as the last tone sounded. From the looks of it Woody had called five times in a row. I picked it up and he started calling again, so I answered.

"Hey, Woody. Lee—"

"Who the hell do you think you are?" he shouted.

"What?"

"I just got a call from a man named Alan Brownell, the damn CEO of Hot Rod Records who claims he can't get in touch with you after he spoke with you at Founder's Day about having us meet him to talk about recording a demo. He said he's reached out to your manager, he's reached out to your agent, and you haven't returned his call. What the hell, Lee?" Woody was screaming into the receiver, his voice shaking. "I know you talk to both of those guys on the daily so I know good and well you planned to hide this from us for some reason or another, and I bet that reason is Hattie."

"Woody." I said his name, but it was like he couldn't hear me. Maybe he thought he was leaving Lee a message.

"It ain't fair to throw our dreams out with yours just so you can shack up with the love of your life. I've wanted this for so long. I've worked toward this forever. You ain't taking this from me."

"Woody," I tried again, but he kept on.

"I'm in Clover picking up a carburetor for my Camaro, but the minute I get it I'm coming straight for you, man, and we're calling Alan back together. You ain't getting out of this."

"I'll have Lee call you back," I said, but he hung up on me.

I tossed the phone back onto the mattress and fell back against the pillows, my heart hammering. I pinched my eyes closed and tried to stay calm, but I knew what his call meant. We hadn't wanted to talk about it last night, but today Lee and I would have to talk about Nashville.

"Hey, Hat." Lee's voice came from the doorway, and I pushed up in bed to find him standing there in his boxers carrying a tray with coffee and pancakes. He grinned at me, the sort of look that meant he was about to set the tray on his dresser and come for me. My body flushed with heat.

"Come here," I said.

He put the tray down, then lifted the quilt and lay down beside me, his arms automatically encircling my body, pulling me to him.

"Hat," he said into my hair. "This doesn't feel real."

"I know, but it is," I said. "I'm yours and you're mine."

He leaned in to kiss me slow as his hands explored my body, each touch the seasoned flip of a switch. Lee rolled on top of me, and I pulled his face to mine and kissed his ear.

Just then, his phone rang again and I jerked at the sound. I'd forgotten about Woody. Or maybe I'd intentionally blocked him out.

Lee didn't move to silence his phone, just covered me with his body again and kissed me. I wanted to keep on, to ignore the ringing and Nashville, everything except for Lee, but I couldn't. Not when Woody was on his way here in a fury.

I placed my palm on Lee's chest as he continued his pursuit of me, his knees nudging mine, his lips on my neck.

The phone kept ringing.

"Lee," I whispered.

"I'll get there soon enough," he said, his voice rough.

"No," I said. "Your phone."

"Let it ring." His mouth dropped to my collarbone, and I closed my eyes, tempted once again to let it go. But I couldn't. Each time his phone sounded, my heart lurched out of my chest.

"We can't. It's Woody."

"Woody can wait."

His gaze met mine, and at once, my eyes filled with tears.

"No, he can't."

He stilled.

"What's wrong?" Lee's hands framed my face, brushing the hair above my ears back toward the pillow.

"When you were downstairs, Woody kept calling over and over, so I answered. He must have thought he was leaving a message for you because he started yelling about how Alan had reached out to him this morning about the meeting since he couldn't get ahold of you. He's mad you didn't tell him about it. He's on his way here." I swallowed hard. "We need to talk about Nashville, Lee."

Lee nodded and looked away from me, his thumb stroking back and forth across my cheek. I wrapped my arms around his back, relishing the weight of him, the feel of his skin against mine.

"I'm not going," he said finally. "I ain't leaving you."

"If I wasn't here, would you?"

His eyes met mine and he shrugged. "I don't know. I guess. I mean, I love playing, and the guys have always talked about what it would be like to hear one of our songs on the radio, stuff like that." Lee leaned down and kissed me. "But you are here. And I don't care about anything but you."

I pushed his hair back from his face. "I know. But you can't stay here because of me. This isn't our home anymore. You're too talented. The band is too talented, and they can't do it without you."

He traced my collarbone with his fingertips. "Maybe so," he said, "but I ain't going if it's going to cost you. I finally got my heart back."

I sat up on my elbows and kissed him. "Mine too." I sighed. "I can't make the decision for you. I want nothing more than to stay right here in this bed with you and beg you not to leave, but I know you. If you don't take the meeting, you'll always wonder. There will always be that 'what if' lingering. Maybe you'd regret it. I can't be the reason you pass this dream by."

He picked up my hand and studied it, then drew the lines across my palm.

"Reading palms these days?" I asked.

Lee laughed. "Yep. It says here that you're destined to marry a handsome baseball player," he said, pretending to examine my hand.

"I like that prediction," I said.

My heart felt like it could burst. He was right—this didn't feel real. My thoughts snapped back to Nashville. If I was being honest with how I felt, I'd ask him to stay, to never leave my side again. But I knew that wouldn't work. Years from now he'd remember that he always thought he'd get out of Mountain View and he'd wish he'd seen this opportunity through—even if he loved me.

"Maybe the right thing to do is take the meeting. It's just a meeting anyway," he said. He glanced at me and I nodded. "If Alan ends up wanting to sign us, we'll figure it out then. But I'm thinking that's a long shot after he talks to the rest of the guys." Lee laughed under his breath.

"I think that's a good plan," I said.

Outside, I could hear the roar of Woody's muffler racing down Lee's driveway. Lee groaned at the sound and kissed my forehead.

"If for some reason Alan finds the guys eccentric rather than weird and we wind up with a deal, maybe you could move to Nashville with me? You could start an events business there."

"Yeah, I could."

I kissed him.

"We're going to be okay," I said when our lips parted, mostly to reassure myself.

A pounding came from the front door, followed by Woody yelling. "Open up, Lee. I got a bone to pick with you."

Lee buried his head in the crook of my neck.

Woody kept pounding on the door.

"He's not going to go away," he murmured into my hair.

"I don't think he is." I ran my hands down his back, and he raised his face and kissed me quickly.

"Let me go take care of him, but will you stay here?"

"There's nowhere else I'd rather be."

He lifted off of me, then got out of bed and snatched a pair of sweatpants from his drawer.

"Sorry if it's cold now," he said, depositing the tray of breakfast in my lap. He kissed my head and walked out of the room. "Be right back."

I took a sip of coffee and tried my best to stop the fear of losing him from swallowing me whole.

CHAPTER FIFTEEN

"It's incredible to think that just a few days ago I could've fallen through the floor up here." Fox stood in the middle of the quaint bridal suite, the old hayloft, his Carhardtt pants and dirt-smudged T-shirt looking completely out of place in the elegant space.

"Yeah. Let's hope the new floor holds," I said, bouncing a little on the LVP planks. "Can you imagine? Delinda falling through to the altar? That'd be an entrance."

I laughed. I didn't know who I was imagining. I'd never laid eyes on the bride or the groom, and when I'd called to ask them if they had any last-minute needs the day before yesterday, Delinda had told me that they didn't need to see the space, that their decorations were versatile, and they were fine with "that band or whatever" for the reception. I didn't know what that meant, really, besides that Delinda was not a bridezilla. That was a great thing, at least for this first wedding.

"This floor is solid as steel. Everything's brand new," Fox said. "You like the way I hung the clothing racks, or do you want them somewhere else?" He pointed his hammer to the far corner of the room where two white poles stuck out from the wall beside the tufted white couch. The space was on the smaller side, only three hundred square feet, so I'd ordered racks that took up the least amount of room.

"It looks great." I glanced around. The new walnut floors were covered with a fluffy white rug. The walls had been whitewashed while the ceiling had been painted haint blue. "I can't believe how quickly this came together. Y'all have worked so many hours. I don't know how I'll ever thank you."

My eyes filled, and I glanced at the white vanity with the old Hollywood big bulb mirror over it to avoid him noticing my tears. I turned to examine the enormous trifold gilded mirror behind me in the corner. Fox, Vern, and a crew of five other guys had been working twenty-four-hour shifts for three days to get this place ready for the wedding—and Fox had refused payment, saying he'd take care of Vern and the others. I didn't know how he could afford to cover us. Even with us buying the supplies, there was no way his hardware store was so profitable it allowed him the option to work for free, but there was no convincing him. He kept saying that we were doing him a favor by hosting the town on Friday nights and that was payment enough. That meant we could use all of the six thousand dollars we'd collected in wedding rental fees from four different couples to pay back what we'd taken from my parents' home equity line.

"Like I said, you don't owe me, us, anything. This is a special place and it's an honor to help fix it up." Fox was over by the clothing racks, jostling the poles even though I'd told him they were fine.

"Daddy was nearly in tears when Mama and I brought him down to see it," I said. "He said Mr. Robinson would have been so proud." Daddy had gotten home last night, an hour after I'd seen Lee and the band off to Nashville. My eyes blurred again, remembering the way my heart had plunged into my stomach watching the caravan of their cars drive away down Route 2.

"I'm glad he's home and on his way to recovery," Fox said, jolting me out of my thoughts. He hammered a nail into the bottom of the rack, then stepped back and appraised it. Next to him, the dainty grandmother's clock we'd poached from the old coffee shop read 11:55. The band had been in their meeting with Alan for almost an hour now.

"I am too. It's the best gift." My voice sounded strange and I swallowed the lump in my throat. I wanted the meeting to go well for the sake of the guys. I'd figured I'd move to Nashville with Lee if things went well. I could start my events business there like we'd discussed. But the minute Daddy arrived home, I knew that wasn't going to be possible. Daddy was weak, much weaker than he'd seemed in the hospital the day before, and though he'd never been a loud man, the fire in his eyes had dulled. Mama said that Dr. Gerard said his recovery would take some time, two or three months, maybe longer. I couldn't leave them to follow Lee anywhere. Not anytime soon at least. Even thinking about my relationship seemed selfish when Daddy was so far from himself.

"You alright?" Fox's eyes steadied on mine, and it was only then that I realized mine had filled again. He wiped his hands on his pants and paced toward me. "Is it your dad? I know seeing him like that is startling, but he'll get stronger every day."

I nodded and looked down at the ground. "I pray that's the case."

"It's not only him though, is it?"

His voice was low and when I looked up, I met his gaze head-on.

"No," I said simply. I crossed the room and dropped onto the new couch. Fox sat down beside me, his weight creaking the springs beneath us.

"You're going to be okay," he said after some minutes. "I know you're in your head about Lee too."

I glanced at him, but he was focused on the hammer in his hand. He turned it over and over again. It still felt strange to talk about me and Lee with Fox. Maybe because he'd been there for my heartache over Lee and Willow, but he hadn't witnessed me and Lee in high school. To someone who didn't understand the history we had, it might seem I was naïve to take him back. Then again, Fox wasn't challenging my decision. Maybe it was really just me, staring down a future that looked a hell of a lot like where Lee and I had been before.

"He left me the last time, and I never got over it."

"And you don't think he's learned from his mistakes?" Fox laughed under his breath. "He was an eighteen-year-old idiot the last time."

Our eyes met and he smiled.

"I know. But he doesn't belong here anymore, Fox. Same as me."

He sighed. "I can't tell you that you and Lee are going to work out just because you love each other. That's some fairy tale bullshit that I believed for far too long. But I will tell you that stuff like recording contracts take time. My buddy used to work in legal for Sony, and sometimes agents and the company would go back and forth for months." He paused. "My point is, y'all will have time to talk it through."

"I keep telling myself to take it a day at a time, but I'm not great at that, I'm realizing."

"Yeah, me either. It's just not the way I'm made."

"What happened with your girl?" I asked.

His nose scrunched. "What?"

"The girl you loved, the girl you thought you'd sail off into the sunset with."

His jaw gripped, and then he shook his head. "I didn't really want to sail off into the sunset. I just wanted her to be there when I got home."

I thought for a second that he might elaborate, that he might say more about his life before Mountain View, but he stood.

"Sometime I'll tell you more," he said. The side of his mouth quirked up. "But that kind of conversation is going to require whisky and given your track record, I ain't sure you can handle it, Snow White." He started laughing and I did too. Word about my lengthy conversation with Slugger had spread through town like wildfire.

"Snow White didn't really talk to horses, though, I don't think. Mostly woodland animals. And besides, a study said horses can understand as much as a three-year-old human."

"Oh, okay," he said. "Then by that logic we should make Denton Herald the town therapist."

"Not unless you want a broken bone," I said. Denton Herald was a three-year-old menace.

"What were you talking to Slugger about anyway?" Fox walked over to the lighted mirror and flicked the switch on and off, then paced toward the wine cooler.

"I can't remember a thing," I said, laughing. "Probably lamenting my bad fortune." Tomorrow was the big Panthers benefit. I'd tried calling and texting and emailing Merry, but she wouldn't respond. I hoped that meant she was busy, that the event would go swimmingly after all, but I had a suspicion it was going the opposite way.

"You could've just stayed and talked to me. I am sort of the town bartender, you know, and that's what we do." He squatted down and jostled the cooler.

"You had Annie over," I said. "And she and I aren't exactly on good terms right now."

His hands stilled on the cooler, and he glanced at me. "Yeah, but she was leaving. Like she said, she was just over to talk about Mountain View's defense."

I thought to bite my tongue, but I couldn't for some reason. "You can't tell me she was with you, in your bedroom, to chat about Mountain View."

Fox stood. "Yeah, I can." He ran a hand down his beard. "She caught me in the store when I was coming in from a run and followed me upstairs when I told her I needed to change my shoes. I'm not going to say she doesn't flirt with me or kiss me on occasion, but that's as far as it goes. She's semi-involved with a guy she dated in college."

I held up my hands. "I shouldn't have said anything. What you do with Annie or anybody else isn't my business. I'm just explaining why I opted for Slugger."

I got up from the couch and glanced in the big mirror, at my black Lululemon running shorts streaked with white paint, at my makeup-less face, and my hair gathered into a sloppy bun.

"What a mess," I whispered. "I'm a mess. Everything is wrong," I said louder.

"No, it's not," Fox said. He stood next to me.

I looked at the two of us in the mirror. Him, hulking next to me in his dirty work clothes, me scowling at him.

"How do you figure? I had it all together—the pretty townhouse, the perfect job in the best city."

"Maybe you're just being broken down so you can be made into something better," Fox said.

"Where'd you get that? A Hallmark card?"

He grinned. "No, but I'm sure it's on one somewhere." He looked at me. "I took an art class one semester in college and really liked this mosaic artist, Isaiah Zagar. His work is made mostly with broken things—plates, bottles, wine glasses, bike wheels, stuff like that that he makes into something beautiful. When things got really bad in my life, I remembered that, and it gave me hope that although I felt broken, my life might turn out like one of his pieces in the end."

"I think it will," I said. "And I'll hope the same for me."

"You've got a lot of beauty in your life still. You've got your parents and somewhere to call home. You have friends and a man who loves you." His eyes met mine in the mirror.

"Miss Norwood?"

I whirled around to find Richard Brantley, the state representative who'd parked on our land to look at land configurations for the stadium. He was wearing the same pressed khakis and white button-down.

"Oh. Hi, Mr. Brantley," I said. "What brings you to Mountain View again?"

"The guys outside said you were up here and that I shouldn't disturb your parents. I'm sorry to hear about your daddy's heart attack." He shuffled his feet.

"Thank you," I said.

"I'm . . . afraid I've come with some news that will affect this town, possibly this farm," he said.

My heart started beating fast. Surely there wasn't something else. I couldn't take it.

Fox's face drained. "That can't be right," he said, interjecting. "The stadium is slated to go to Cardinal River. Our attorney said last night it was practically a done deal and that the announcement would come in the next day or two. This is a historic town, Mr. Brantley. You're standing in the founder's barn." I could tell he was forcing his voice to sound calm. But a vein bulged in his neck. He held out his hand and Mr. Brantley took it. "I'm Fox. I own the hardware store in town."

My body began to quake, a tremor-like shivering that I couldn't control. I stared at Mr. Brantley.

"I know. It's not on the register of historic places, though, I'm afraid," Mr. Brantley said. "I'll just come right out and say it because I know my boss spoke with your mayor this morning and she's aware—the stadium is going to be built here in Mountain View. We haven't had a chance to plan out the specifics of where it'll go yet, but—"

"Why?" Fox barked, his earlier steadiness suddenly gone.

I froze, and regret swept through me. I was stunned by my reaction. This was for the best, wasn't it? The stadium would only help Mountain View thrive.

"Why would the state choose this town?" Fox went on. "We made it perfectly clear none of us want this stadium and that we'll fight it."

Fox's gaze suddenly snapped to me, and I knew what he was thinking. All of this was my fault for not signing the petition. Maybe he was right.

"Mountain View wasn't our initial choice," Mr. Brantley said. "It's enough of a headache to find the right place to build. We didn't want to deal with the noise y'all are making, but the truth is that we'll have to deal with it—and y'all will too. No petition or lawsuit has the power to stop it." He sighed. "You're right about Cardinal River. We had a tract set there that wasn't currently being farmed and thought we were ready to go, but a couple days ago we realized that the soil samples were showing heavy clay buildup around the perimeter. We thought to push it east ten acres, but then we were butting into that housing development next to the Dollar General. There's just not enough room over there. We had to pivot."

Fox made a frustrated noise and jammed his hands in his pockets. "This whole county is filled with open land.

Can't y'all just go somewhere else? This stadium will kill everything this town is."

Ordinarily I'd say something about how the town would thrive with the stadium, but for some reason, I couldn't. I only stood there, my body still strangely shaking.

"I'm afraid not," Mr. Brantley said, his tone indicating that he truly regretted breaking this news. "These towns were selected after years of strategic deliberation."

I looked out the window toward the fields. The river curved in the distance, and Route 2 jutted across it toward Cardinal River. It had always been a pretty, unobstructed view. I imagined a parking lot instead, filled with Range Rovers and Porsches, BMWs and Teslas.

The room silenced. I could feel Fox's anger and, below us, Vern's rhythmic hammering sounded like a bomb ticking.

"I want you both to know I tried to dissuade them. I didn't like the idea of the stadium being here. I told my boss several times it was Ronald Robinson's town and a landmark—even if not officially. I've been a fan my whole life." Mr. Brantley said. "But when it comes down to it, I'm just a surveyor and I don't make the decisions."

"Then what the hell are you doing here? You're important enough that he sent you to break the news," Fox said finally, then shook his head. "I'm sorry for my tone, but you have to understand that what you're saying feels like a death sentence and it ain't welcome news." He took a breath and glanced out the windows.

"I'm here to collect soil samples, not to be the messenger," Mr. Brantley said to Fox. "I only came by personally because I hoped to park here again, and I thought it only right to tell Hattie what I was doing and why." He looked at me. "I'll try my best to spare your farm, Miss Norwood. I can't guarantee it, but I'll try. Everyone's land is on the line right now."

"I understand," I heard myself say, but I wondered if that was the truth right now, with the bulldozers potentially pointed at our land. My palms felt clammy.

"We're going to fight this. Tell your boss," Fox said.

Mr. Brantley reached out and put a hand on Fox's arm. Fox's body twitched, and at first I thought he might draw back and punch him. But he didn't.

"That's your right. But I'm going to tell you from experience, it'll be in vain." Mr. Brantley pushed his glasses up on the bridge of his nose. "In a couple weeks, the tract will be set in stone, and then my boss will come here for a town hall meeting to go over the footprint and the farms involved." He shifted his briefcase from one hand to the other.

I swallowed hard. Mama and Daddy would be on pins and needles until that hearing. Everybody else would be too.

"I'm not really supposed to say this," Brantley went on. "I could probably get fired. But the one thing you can demand is more money for the land they're taking. Don't let anybody take that first offer."

"No one gives a shit about money. It's not like the money will get anybody their homes back," Fox said, his earlier anger reemerging.

"You're right, but maybe it would buy them a new start." Brantley looked around the newly renovated room and then back at me. "I'm going to try my best to save this place," he said again.

"Thank you." My voice was monotone. I imagined the way Mama and Daddy would react if our farm was taken and suddenly felt as though every ounce of energy had been drained from me.

"I've got to be on the road, but I'll keep you apprised of any forward movement," Mr. Brantley said. "I'm sorry about the news."

Neither of us said anything as Mr. Brantley started down the stairs. I listened to him go, his loafers making light taps on the new floor.

"I don't want to be a broken piece of china anymore, Fox," I whispered, staring at the doorway. "All of this is my fault, and I don't think I can take much more."

"No, it ain't. You heard him. Cardinal River's shitty land was the reason the stadium's coming here."

I looked up at him. His face was drawn with concern, and I nodded.

"Maybe ours will be just as bad and they'll have to find another town after all. I'm not losing hope." He walked toward the door and I followed. "Come on. This room looks good and I think we're both done today." He'd given me grace. He could have blamed everything on me. But he didn't.

"Do you think Annie's told anyone yet?" I asked when we reached the stairwell.

"No," he said, his frame washed in the steps' shadows. "I'm sure she's in shock. I'll go by and check on her when I'm through here, help her figure out when to call the town meeting."

I followed him down the stairs, trying to calm myself by breathing in the sweet scent of the magnolia reed diffusers we'd put at the base of the stairwell. I couldn't go to the meeting. Even though Fox hadn't blamed the news on me, others would regardless of any facts to the contrary. Plus, I needed time to sort through whatever it was I was feeling. I hadn't felt the peace I'd expected to feel when Mr. Brantley delivered the news, yet I knew the truth—the stadium would give this town a fighting chance.

"My parents are going to be devastated," I said when we reached the bottom.

Just beyond where we were standing, the ceiling of the hayloft disappeared, giving way to the open barn floor.

Sunlight streamed in through the windows, illuminating the shine on the new hardwood dance floor and sparkling the crystals on the chandeliers.

"I know it ain't going to be welcome news, but it's going to be okay. We're going to find a way to stop it. I don't care what Brantley says." Fox didn't look at me when he said it, but I felt a strange sense of hope at the chance the stadium wouldn't happen.

"Vern, watch yourself!" Fox shouted. Vern was teetering on a ladder, affixing just-cleaned crystals to the final chandelier. Fox raced toward him. "You should tell your parents, Hattie," he said to me. "I'm going to go by and see Annie in a second, I've just got to—damn it, Vern."

Fox reached the ladder, just as Vern took a misstep on the top rung. Vern steadied himself and laughed.

I opened the side door that used to go into the tack room and stepped out into the heat. Mama and Daddy were sitting on the porch under a little umbrella Mama had picked up from Walmart a few years back. My phone rang in my back pocket. I took it out and my body rushed with nerves when I saw Lee's name.

"Hey," I said. "How'd it go?"

"Well, Hat, I'd say it went better than anybody expected." I could hear the excitement in his voice, but there was trepidation too.

"What do you mean?"

His voice made me feel unsteady. I walked toward Mr. Robinson's truck and sat in the driver's seat with the door open.

"Alan started out just telling us about the company, but then in the middle of the meeting, he got a call from the front man of this band called Porch Light. Turns out, he was calling to tell Alan he got some bad news from his doctor and that his band won't be able to go on Tommy Sutton's European tour in a couple weeks. Alan was out an act." Lee paused.

I gripped the leather steering wheel to keep from bursting into tears. Tommy Sutton was arguably the biggest name in country music right now. I could see where this was going, and it was away from me.

"Alan suggested that our band take their place, second opener. It's going to take a lot of expediting, but he basically owns the label and has connections everywhere, so he asked if we could stay and record a few songs now. I told him I needed to have my attorney look over the contract, of course, but Harden just got back to me with the okay. You still there?"

"Yeah," I said, forcing my voice to sound cheerful.

"So, we'll stay and record for the next week, and Alan's hoping he can release the first single as soon as possible. He says we really just need one song out there ahead of the first tour stop in Luxembourg. He can release the others while we're on the road." Lee cleared his throat. "We won't really have any fans or anything, but he's confident we'll become known fast because I'm already . . . well, I'm already . . ."

"Famous?" I asked. "*The* Leland Lockhardt?"

Lee laughed.

I remembered the way Alan had approached Lee at Founder's Day. He'd known exactly what he was doing, and he was smart. Lee was already pretty much a household name, and a semi-scandalous one at that—which was a bonus when it came to country stardom. Squeaky clean wouldn't stand a chance. Damaged men with hearts of gold and voices of angels had been the stars of country since Hank Williams and Johnny Cash.

"I guess," he said. "If the European tour goes well this fall, we'll be put in Tommy's stateside tour this spring too." He paused. "It's all happening so fast. I know it's not what we planned."

I glanced at the bench seat beside me and started to cry, quietly, so Lee wouldn't hear.

"I'm excited for you," I said as happily as I could muster.

"Hattie. Baby. I promised you we're going to be okay and we are. I ain't going anywhere," he said, hearing through my tone. "I love you."

"I love you too," I said. "And I'm thrilled for y'all. I really am. It's just that I thought you were coming back and we'd have time."

"So did I. But sometimes life throws you a curve. We'll figure things out. Is there any way you can come here this week? Alan's renting us a few penthouses downtown. We could talk things through and sleep in and I could book you a bunch of tickets to see us play in some of the coolest cities—Paris, Madrid, Berlin. It'll be an adventure."

Tears ran down my face. I tipped my head back against the old cracked leather headrest.

"I can't. We have the wedding this weekend, and Daddy's not doing as well as I thought. Dr. Gerard said he won't be fully recovered for two or three months, maybe longer. I can't leave."

"I forgot all about the wedding. I'm sorry, Hat. And I'm sorry about your daddy. He seemed like he was recovering quickly at the clinic, but you never know with these things."

"And the state's putting the stadium in Mountain View. We just found out a second ago. They haven't decided exactly where in town, but it's Mountain View for sure."

"Damn," he said under his breath. "I'm going to call Alan and tell him we're coming home tomorrow."

"You know you can't do that," I said. "Y'all being home won't change what happens with the stadium and we don't know any specifics besides. We'll be fine for the wedding too. I have a phone and a speaker. And Daddy just needs time."

I sniffed and we both fell silent. He'd be in Nashville and then in a few weeks he'd be in Europe for months. My heart suddenly felt like it was being strangled, and I knew why. We were falling apart again.

"I think you were right," I said finally. "We only work here."

"What are you talking about?"

"We both know what's going to happen next, Lee. You're going to be wildly famous again. You're going to travel all over and everybody's going to fall in love with you."

"I only care if you love me," he said.

"I can't leave my parents to follow you around the world. I will always love you, Lee, but I can't do this again." A sob punctuated the last word.

"I'm coming home. I'm going to tell Alan I'm leaving. Hattie. I can't breathe without you."

"Yes, you can," I said when I could find my voice. "You can't come back here for me. You said the same thing to me when I was going to leave for Charlotte, remember? The only way Mountain View works is if we both choose it, and neither of us wants it. I can't let you . . . I can't let you throw this opportunity away. You'd resent me for it. The guys would too."

"Then at least say you'll stay with me. Please, Hattie. We can Facetime and I'll come home when I can."

"You won't be here and I won't be there for months, maybe longer. It's not fair to either of us." I wiped my cheeks and laid back on the bench seat. "I'm never going to regret saying yes to you again. It was—"

"Don't, Hat." Lee's voice was rough, and I could tell he was crying. "You're ripping my heart out."

"I don't want to. I want you more than anything and I'll always love you." I sighed. "You promised me you wouldn't leave me, and I can't let you break your promise. So it's going to be me this time. You have to go, Lee. I have to set you free."

I heard him sniff, his breath catch.

"This is why I didn't want to take that call."

"I know. But you had to."

"We should have never left my room. Everything was perfect there. It was just me and you and our love. I can't let you leave me."

"You don't have a choice." I started crying again, my mind fixed on that night and what could have been. "I have to go."

"No. Hat. Please. Let's just sit with this a while longer."

"I love you, Lee. I'll always love you. And I'm so proud of you."

He started to reply, but I ended the call before I could hear it. I let go of my phone, and it dropped to the rusted floorboards with a clatter. Tears streamed down my face. My heart felt pulverized and numb at the same time.

In the distance, I could hear Mama calling my name. My phone started ringing. I knew it was Lee, but I couldn't answer. I wanted to curl into a ball, to close the door to the truck and never come out despite the stifling heat. But she would come for me. And I would still have to tell her about the stadium.

I sat up and looked at my reflection in the patinaed rear-view mirror. My eyes were red and puffy, my cheeks were blotchy.

I turned my phone off and tucked it in my back pocket. I started walking toward the house and past the barn at the same time Fox emerged from the entrance. He took one look at my face and pulled me into his arms. There was something about the bulk of him, the way he enveloped me, that made me feel safe, and I leaned into him and sobbed into his shirt.

He didn't ask me what happened. He only held me. And when I had cried all I could, I lifted my head from his chest.

"Thank you," I said.

Fox nodded, then let me go.

"Lee is staying in Nashville," I said. I was amazed at my calm tone, that I didn't break down when I said it. I swallowed. "We broke up."

Fox's brow furrowed. "I thought he promised you he wouldn't do that again."

"He didn't. It was me," I said. "I'm going to be here for a while." I gestured to where Mama and Daddy were sitting, waiting for me to deliver the news that our town, possibly even our farm, would be overtaken by concrete. "He's going to be the star he's always been. That's just who he is. And I can't follow along after him."

"I'm sorry," Fox said simply. He pushed his hands in his pockets and glanced at Mama and Daddy.

"We don't have a band for Saturday's wedding," I said. "I guess we could just play a playlist or I could ask Tosha, but I'm not sure 'Gave the Quarter Pounder a Quarter of My Heart' is really a wedding song."

Fox laughed. He pulled his lips in and out as though he was considering something and then shrugged. "I could play."

"Really?" I stared at him. "But when I told you that you should join up with Lee's band the other week, you said—"

"I said I didn't have star power. I don't. But I do know how to play some songs on the piano. My mama was a piano teacher. I can borrow the keyboard from the church."

"Okay, great," I said, mostly because he was our only choice. Even if he just played a decent "Heart and Soul" or "Twinkle, Twinkle Little Star," it would probably be just fine with Delinda. For the next wedding, we'd have to come up with something permanent, though.

"Let's go tell your parents about the stadium together, and then I'll go by Annie's and the church."

I glanced into the barn. It was absolutely stunning. I had Fox to thank for it. I had Fox to thank for a lot of things.

"Thank you," I said. "For all of this."

"You've got to stop thanking me," he said, then looped his arm over my shoulders and we started walking toward Mama and Daddy.

CHAPTER SIXTEEN

"May I have the next dance?" Dolly asked a taxidermy skunk who was still sitting in the pews we'd pushed out of the way for the reception. The place was filled with stuffed animals and not the kind you made at Build-A-Bear. Delinda and Timmy had started setting up at eight this morning, and it had taken them a full three hours to unload Delinda's taxidermy collection from their U-Haul. A full-sized alligator leaping from a fake pond with a gazelle in its mouth was the decoration beside the altar, and on the other side they'd placed the largest opossum I'd ever seen.

"Where even are we?" I asked her under my breath. The wedding was over, and we'd just finished setting up for the reception while Delinda ushered her guests outside—the random assortment of Mountain View residents Cricket had been able to force out of their houses amid their grief over the stadium, her mama, Timmy's daddy, her maid of honor, Peaches, who'd kept an unlit cigarette in the corner of her mouth for the entirety of the service.

I turned the cake plate boasting a Twinkie tower and stepped back. The snack table looked as good as it could.

Dolly moved a small vase holding two red carnations—the only flowers Delinda had brought with her—to the spot next to the vanilla moonshine.

The carnations made me think of the photos I'd seen of the Panther's Narnia benefit on Instagram. The event had turned out worse than I could've imagined. Merry would never speak to me again. The tables had been adorned with big carnation bouquets—I guess because of the rose allergy and in the wake of the last-minute change, that's all they could muster—and it was clear Subway had done the catering. Still, it seemed like a presidential event compared to this taxidermy wedding.

Dolly grabbed a clear plastic cup from the stack next to the moonshine and filled it to the brim with the vanilla variety. She took a sip.

"Pretty good," she said. "If we drink enough of this, we can pretend we're in a zoo instead of surrounded by hundreds of dead animals."

I glanced around at the squirrels, chipmunks, birds, foxes, and coyotes sitting on the chairs around the room. When Delinda and Timmy had first arrived, they'd proclaimed that they wanted these "friends" to take up the first three rows and that the people should sit behind them.

A loud boom rang out, rattling the old barn windows. Fox walked in from the entrance in his black suit, shaking his head.

Dolly whistled under her breath. "If I wasn't married to the most handsome man in town, I'd go for that one," she whispered.

"Yeah," I said simply. He'd looked so good when he'd walked in ahead of the wedding, he'd nearly taken my breath away. But I couldn't tell Dolly now. Not tonight when she was drinking and had absolutely no filter. I'd spent the morning crying over Lee. I'd spent the ceremony wondering what it would've been like to marry Lee, and my heart wasn't even close to free. Fox knew that. But there was always the chance, late at night, with the alcohol simmering in our chests, that if he knew I thought he was attractive, one of us could lean in.

"Nobody died," Fox said when he reached us.

Delinda's bouquet was made of spent shotgun shells affixed to plastic zip ties and she'd planned to do her bouquet toss out of a potato cannon. Fox had tried to talk her out of it. Rocky had too. But she swore up and down that the shells were all empty and that none would go off and kill someone when they were blasted into the air.

"Everybody ran except for Delinda's mama. She caught it and started making out with Timmy's daddy." His nose scrunched.

"That's interesting," I said. "But what I'd really like to discuss is why you undersold your piano playing."

Fox laughed.

"What do you mean? I didn't say much about it at all. Only that I could do it."

"Her processional was Mozart, 'Sonata in C,' to be exact, and you played it without sheet music."

Delinda had requested "Proud to Be an American" at the last minute, but Fox had convinced her to save it for her first dance.

"Everybody knows how to play one song by heart. And I told you, my mama was a piano teacher."

"He's right," Dolly said. "I know how to play 'Chopsticks.'"

I laughed. "You want to get up there next?"

"Hell no. The last five days were performance enough for me. You don't even want to know how many hot dogs we handed out. I had to talk to every one of those people too."

Rocky wandered into the barn in his tight Wranglers and flannel shirt. "The mother of the bride is asking for Hank Williams Jr.'s 'Family Traditions' for the dance with her new son-in-law."

"For real?" Fox said.

"Nothing should surprise you right now," I said. The wedding guests starting pouring back in. Delinda in her Mossy Oak wedding gown and Timmy in his tuxedo T-shirt appeared first, followed by the crush of Mountain View natives that I figured, at this point, were here for the spectacle and free alcohol. Everybody needed it after the veritable funeral that had happened at town hall last night. I hadn't attended, but Mama said Annie told them that the attorney advised nothing could be done until notices were sent to selected farms so everybody had just sat around for four hours and cried.

"Want a moonshine to loosen up your voice?" I nodded to the canisters.

Fox shook his head "Nah, alcohol has an anesthetic effect on vocal cords."

I stared at Fox, having a feeling that when he got back on that stage, his singing was going to surprise me just as much as his piano playing had. I'd been struck by his voice the one time I'd heard it before, and he'd only been singing along to the radio.

Fox turned around and walked toward the stage. When he got there, he leaned down and extracted a guitar case I hadn't noticed from behind the stage steps, took off his suit jacket, and rolled up his white sleeves. Then he sat down on the piano bench and flipped the microphone on.

"Now that we're all back from that bouquet toss to remember, let's settle in for the first dance. Timmy, Delinda, we sure are happy for y'all."

The guests lined the perimeter of the dance floor in front of the pews occupied by the taxidermy animals as the couple made their way to the middle. The dainty chandeliers glittered down on Delinda's orange hair covered in a fishing net veil as Timmy pulled her close, her hands knotting the back of his Kentucky waterfall mullet. Fox began to play the most moving rendition of "Proud to Be an American" I'd ever heard. His voice was deep and smooth, a melding of Chris Stapleton and Sam Cooke. People around me began to weep, and my own eyes welled at the final chorus.

"I think we should renew our vows so Fox can play this song for us," I heard Dolly say to Rocky.

"This wedding might not be so terrible after all," I said. Dolly laughed and filled her glass with moonshine one more time.

"I wouldn't go that far."

Dolly was right. By nine o'clock, three fights had broken out, the snack table had been overturned, and the bride and groom had long since left in their 1987 Ford Fiesta adorned with Dale Earnhardt stickers, saying they'd be back sometime to get their animal friends. I hoped that sometime was sooner rather than later.

"I done nabbed most of these," Timmy's dad said to me, taking his hand off of my back to gesture around the room at the animals. He'd asked me to dance several times throughout the evening, and I'd been able to avoid him by making myself busy. But now, with the crowd dwindling, he'd asked me again, and I'd felt like I had to agree. "Stuffed 'em too. If you got any critters you want preserved, you just come on down to Cardinal River and bring 'em into my barn." When I didn't say anything, he went on. "I'm sorry to hear about your town. Some of us was for the stadium in Cardinal River, but I wasn't one of them. I'm relieved we ain't getting it, but sad for y'all."

"Thanks," I said to both things.

"This singer's good. Not as good as George Jones or nothing, but he'll do for my little boy's day." He was talking loudly, nearly yelling.

I looked up at Fox and he grinned at me. I knew he wanted to laugh, but he couldn't.

Fox had been singing for two hours straight, seamlessly moving from piano to guitar, singing everything from George Strait to Taylor Swift to Ed Sheeran to the Avett Brothers. I'd grill him later about how he knew how to do all that. This kind of skill didn't just show up because your mama was a piano teacher.

He was singing a Morgan Wallen song now, "Spin You Around." Dolly and Rocky were behind me arguing like they normally did when they'd been drinking.

"You were looking at her. Yes, you were," Dolly insisted. Who she was talking about, I'd never know.

"You're ogling Fox like he's a damn ribeye steak," Rocky said. "You always said you liked your men on the smaller side, but I have a mind to say you've been lying this whole time."

"Excuse me," I said to Timmy's dad. "It's been nice dancing with you, but I need to handle something." I disentangled myself from his grasp and turned toward Dolly and Rocky, hoping to stop their argument in its tracks, just as Rocky leaned over their linked hands and threw up. The vomit splattered on Dolly's rhinestone shoes and she screamed, a bloodcurdling yell that tore through the barn.

Fox stopped singing and jumped from the stage as Rocky threw up again and sank to the floor. I lunged for Dolly's arms. She'd been terrified of vomit since second grade, since Linds threw up in her lap on the school bus on the way to the children's museum in Rock Hill. Dolly's lips paled, and she wobbled in her vomit-soaked heels.

"Don't pass out," I shouted. "Look at me."

I was vaguely aware of Fox at our feet, muttering something to Rocky, and of the party guests dispersing around me.

"I . . . can't," Dolly whispered.

I pulled all 110 pounds of Dolly a few feet out of the way to dry ground, but she still rocked in her heels and collapsed against my chest.

"Here. Let me take her to the truck." Fox appeared in front of me and scooped her into his arms before I could reply. Rocky was propped next to the refreshments table, his body lying across spilled pork rinds, crackers, and half-spent bottles of Cheez Whiz. "I'll come back to get him and then I'll take them home," he said over his shoulder as he walked toward the barn doors.

I ran to catch up.

"I'll come with you. I'll sit in the car with Dolly while you get Rocky."

We stepped out of the barn into the night. The air smelled like rain, and I glanced back at Mr. Robinson's truck. I was reminded that Lee and I got caught in that downpour only a few weeks ago. They'd been recording nearly nonstop the past few days. I knew because he'd been texting me. Calling me too. I'd only sent one text back: *Let me go. I love you.*

Fox unlocked his truck. I thought of the music he'd played tonight and wondered if he'd ever been scouted or anything. Surely he had. I thought Lee was talented—and he was—but Fox's music was different. It almost seemed easy to him.

"She ever do this before?" Fox nodded to Dolly in his arms. Her head hung like a ragdoll's away from his shoulder, but her eyes were open now and she was mumbling something I couldn't understand.

"Yeah. All the time. She's petrified of vomit," I said. "She usually bounces back quickly, but she's also pretty drunk tonight. I don't think I've ever seen her quite this bad."

Fox made a dismissive sound and then opened the back door with his free hand. He set Dolly on the seat and I climbed in beside her, expecting Fox to close the door, but he paused. His gaze settled on my face, then drifted over my blue chiffon mini dress I'd had since high school.

"I don't think I told you how beautiful you looked tonight."

I stared back at him, at the green eyes and full lips illuminated by moonlight and didn't quite know how to reply.

"I know this wedding wasn't the kickoff you'd hoped," he said in the wake of my silence. "And the taxidermy guest list ain't going to win this place a spot in *Brides* magazine." He grinned, his smile transforming his face into something truly magnificent. "But the couple was happy and you pulled it off."

"*We* pulled it off."

"Yeah. I'll be right back." He shut my door and walked away. Dolly stirred beside me and then started to snore. I watched Fox's back, the square of his shoulders, the strength of his steps. He carried himself with the confidence required a man of his size, and yet I knew that was only his shell. He'd been through a lot, and there was so much I didn't know. There was so much I wanted to know.

Fox emerged from the barn moments later, holding Rocky up as he stumbled toward the truck. When he opened the door to help Rocky onto the seat beside Dolly, I climbed up to the front and sat in the passenger seat.

"I'm sorry, Hattie," Rocky mumbled from the back as Fox settled behind the wheel. "Timmy's dad wanted to go toe to toe on shots of shine."

"It's alright," I said.

Fox started the engine and flipped on the radio. You could barely make out Dixie Lee and Bing Crosby singing "The Way You Look Tonight" through the static as we started up the drive and turned down Route 2. Behind us, Rocky's snores joined Dolly's.

"Are we going to talk about your music?" I asked. Fox's eyes remained trained on the road. "I know you said your mama was a piano teacher, but you just played and sang for hours. Everything from Mozart to Johnny Cash to Ed Sheeran without one sheet of music. You didn't just pick that up from your mama, and it wasn't some hobby you brought out for the night."

"No," he said.

"No what?"

"We're not going to talk about it."

His fingers gripped the steering wheel and his eyes narrowed at the road. "You were in a bind, so I did it."

Up ahead, the stoplight blinked red. This time it wasn't only a sign for Fox to stop the truck, it was a sign for me to let the subject drop. He wasn't in the habit of making me talk about my pain, and I couldn't force him to talk about his. I didn't know much about the memories that haunted him, but it had to involve his music. He'd put the pain aside to help me. The least I could do was let the topic lie.

"Everybody kept telling me how great the barn looked tonight," I said. "You transformed it."

"Doing stuff like that, fixing things, might be my greatest passion." He turned the truck down the dirt road. "You can't fix most things in life. It's gratifying to be able to repair something once in a while."

Mrs. Muffet had bought another ceramic figure in the days since I'd been to Dolly's. An enormous pig sat on the walk up to her door.

"How did you learn how to do all that stuff?" I asked. "You don't have to tell me, I mean, I just wondered."

"I told you my daddy was an alcoholic, right? Well, before he got sober, the older man who owned our local hardware store sort of took me under his wing. I guess he knew what was going on at home. Every time I'd come in his store, which was pretty much every Saturday, he'd show me how to do something—wire a fixture or use a table saw."

Fox pulled the truck around a sizeable pothole in the street used to launch bottle rockets on the Fourth of July.

"When I was eight or nine he started taking me to farm expos. He'd pretend to let me tell him what to buy for his store while pumping me full of about every snack they offered." He smiled. "I have really vivid memories of being at those. There were acres of tool displays, tractors, and irrigation systems on one side and on the other, bags of feed and fertilizer, flowers, shade trees and fruit trees." He looked at me, then laughed. "Sorry. I doubt you share my enthusiasm for farm expos."

"It actually sounds like a lot of fun."

"I'm going to one Friday down in Rock Hill. If you can get someone to watch over your parents for a bit, would you want to come with me?"

"Only if you buy me snacks and let me pick out some stuff for the store." I'd meant it to be funny, but the moment I said it, I realized I was making light of one of the most important moments in his life. "I didn't . . ."

"Alright." He smiled at me, and I relaxed. "But you're going to have to share the kettle corn."

Fox turned the truck into Dolly and Rocky's driveway and shut the engine off.

"You think they're going to be alright or should I stay?" he asked me. He leaned over the center console close to look in the backseat and his eyes steadied on mine. It was only after a few seconds that I realized he was waiting on me to answer his question.

"Oh, they'll be fine. Rocky's mama is babysitting overnight. She'll look in." I glanced back at my friends. "Deb's used to it anyway. Not sure if you can tell, but these two have always been wild."

"I don't think you've got much room to talk, Snow White." He stepped out of the cab and opened Dolly's door first. I started to get out too, but he stopped me. "I got this."

I swung my legs back in and closed the door. I watched the way he carried my friend, the way he bent low toward her head and whispered that he had her, that she was going to be okay. Some people were birds, freewheeling through life, while others were rocks, steady and strong. Fox was the latter.

He disappeared into the house, then emerged a second later and came around to my side to get Rocky.

"Will you hold this?" Fox whispered, giving me a mangled handful of yarn as he tried to wake Rocky.

"Ah, Deb's friendship bracelets." I set the yarn in his cupholder. "She's been passing these out to people for decades."

"Way to make me feel special." His voice barely faltered as he hoisted Rocky up and out of the truck. "She gave me two—one for you and one for me. They're matching." He laughed and started walking Rocky toward the house.

"Guess you're stuck with me now then," I called lightly from the window. "Once you put it on, you can't take it off or your hand will fall off. That's what happened to Jethro Cuthert."

"Pretty sure that was a lumberyard accident, but I'll throw the bracelets out the window on the way home just in case," he called out before he disappeared into the house again.

I laughed, leaned back in my seat, turned the staticky radio up and closed my eyes. "I Still Miss Someone" by Johnny Cash was playing, and I couldn't help but wonder what Lee was doing, if I'd made a mistake by breaking up with him.

I pulled my phone from the pocket of my dress. *I miss you.* I sent the text before I could think much about it, and a second later, he sent me a picture of us, propped up on a music stand. We'd taken it with an old Polaroid we'd found in his drawer the night I'd stayed over. I was smiling, leaning back against his bare chest. Lee also texted:

Change your mind.

"All good things come to an end." Fox's voice startled me as he got in the truck.

"What?" I locked my phone and put it back in my pocket, wondering if he'd somehow seen my texts or if maybe this spontaneous sentiment was meant to tell me I'd been right to leave Lee despite the brutal crush of pain every time I thought of him.

"Tonight. It's gotta end. I'm beat," he said. "Let's hope nobody's still hanging around when I get you home."

CHAPTER SEVENTEEN

At first glance, it looked like a county fair. The place was crushed with people—families and kids and serious farmers alike—and the air smelled like funnel cakes and fried Oreos. In the distance, live bluegrass music hurried along, while the local country radio station blasted from overhead speakers. A woman in a prairie dress held a program out to Fox and then to me.

"There's a hog calling contest at 1:30. Winner gets a pig. You want to try it?" Fox laughed, then stopped in front of a Kubota tractor display.

"Not unless your store wants a new mascot. My Maw-Maw always said I was the world's loudest squealer."

Fox glanced at me. "That ain't a hog call."

I spotted a kettle corn vendor beside the livestock tent and started walking toward it.

"Where are you going? I'm supposed to be looking at new stuff for the store," he said, following me.

"I told you I was here for the snacks," I said. "Plus, you can't fit tractors in your store." I dug in my purse for the crumpled ones Daddy had given me when I left the house, insisting that I have a good time. After yesterday's fiasco with Juniper, our next bride-to-be, who was also Miss Pine Summit 2022, I was glad to have a day spent wandering around a veritable fair with Fox. She'd spent the whole walk-through criticizing our choices from the chandeliers to the flooring.

"Guess you're right," Fox said. "Kettle corn first."

He edged me out of the way when we reached the kettle corn attendant, a friendly looking lady with freshly dyed red hair—I could tell because red streaked her fingers.

"We'll take a large bag, please." Fox handed her a twenty before I could gather enough ones.

"Thanks," I said.

He gave the bag to me, then told the woman she could keep the thirteen dollars in change.

"Well, that just made my day," the lady said, slipping the money in her apron. Then she looked from me to Fox and back again. I took a bite of the warm, buttery, sugary popcorn. It was like heaven in a bag. "You know, it's a breath of fresh air to see y'all today. Couples don't seem to match anymore nowadays. Me and my Jerry used to do it all the time. I'd buy those little iron-on patterns from the Walmart and make me a sweatshirt and him a T-shirt. I hope that when folks see y'all today, they'll be encouraged to keep that old tradition going."

Fox and I looked at each other and started laughing. We'd been sitting beside each other in the truck for over an hour, but neither of us had noticed that the blue T-shirt he had on under his overalls was the exact color of my sundress.

"Thank you, ma'am," Fox said politely. "And I'm sure the missus here will be excited to try out your iron-on idea the next chance she gets." He flung his arm around my shoulders and pulled me close. His chest shook with suppressed hilarity, but he didn't show it.

"You have a lovely day," I said.

We started to walk away, and the lady called out. "Don't forget to enter the necking contest at three sharp on the main stage. Couple who kisses the longest gets two dozen turkey necks," she yelled. "Y'all are a shoe-in. It takes passion to kiss for an hour or so, and y'all got that spark, I can see it. I'm a matchmaker on the side. J'Adore Love is my name."

I burst into laughter, and Fox, who seemed to be able to control himself, waved.

"Thank you kindly, J'Adore. I hope we'll make you proud," he called back. Then he turned around and started laughing so hard tears filled his eyes.

"Who came up with that prize?" I asked, still laughing. "Want to make out for an hour for a sack of turkey necks?"

Fox grinned, but then his face sobered and he reached for a handful of kettle corn.

"Fox! Hey!" A guy our age in a John Deere green polo and dirty jeans ran out from a permanent barn structure with a sign out front that said Mechanic's Shop. He extended his hand to Fox, and Fox took it, then clapped him on the back.

"Good to see you, man. I didn't know you'd be working out here," Fox said.

"Yeah, me either," the man said, rolling his eyes. "Marsha's got the fluttering eye syndrome again."

"Fluttering eye syndrome?" I asked.

"This is Hattie, she's my—"

"Lady. Yes, I can see that with your nifty matching get-ups," he said. "You know, Foxy, I didn't think of you as the matching type, but I guess since you got yourself a lady as fine as this one, anything goes, eh?"

"She's not my lady," Fox said. "Hattie's one of my good friends from Mountain View."

"Well, that's too bad." He stared at Fox as if he'd forgotten his train of thought, then he snapped. "Oh. That's why

I'm out here. I got that 1 Series Round Baler you were interested in here in the building if you want to see it?"

"Yeah, I would. Thanks for flagging me down," Fox said. "Do you mind?" he asked me. I shook my head and we followed the John Deere rep into the building.

The sound of screeching metal echoed in my ears as we passed tractors and balers and planters and irrigation systems and made our way to the far corner where John Deere occupied a quarter of the whole display space. A bench sat under one of the few windows next to the John Deere exhibition, and I started toward it.

"Go look at that baler. I'll wait here," I said to Fox.

"You sure you don't want to hear about the features?" he asked, grinning.

I shook my head and sat down, content to scarf down kettle corn and people watch. That was the best thing about going out anywhere, after all—the people watching. Especially for the mullets. You never realized how many mullet varieties there were until you gathered a bunch of country folk in one place.

An older couple in full denim danced past me to the Darius Rucker song on the radio. Fox wandered into the aisle right beyond them and stepped out of their way.

"Ready?" he asked when he reached me.

"What'd you think about the baler?"

"It's great technology. I went ahead and ordered one for Mr. Harold. He's getting older and could use the help."

"But what if he can't afford it? I know things are slowing on the farm."

"He's been good to me. It's a gift."

"How can you—" I wanted to ask him how he could keep giving out favors, first to us and then to the Harolds, but he changed the subject.

"There's a lecture on the teaching stage about hydroponic farming. I'd like to go to it if you're cool with that."

"For sure," I said.

We walked back toward the entrance and right as we passed the Bobcat display, a fiddle wailed from the speakers, its tune so haunting, so familiar, that it stopped me in my tracks.

"What is it?" Fox asked, but I barely heard him. It was as if all of my senses had stopped working except for my ears.

"Lee." I might have whispered his name, but then his voice came through the radio, echoing through the space and over me.

He knew where he was going when he got
in that Chevy,
with his dog and his lady beside.

It was my song, "I Borrowed His Truck." I pinched my eyes shut, vaguely aware of Fox's hand reaching for mine and pulling me into the corner of the room, barely aware of his arms around me.

I could hear the pain in Lee's voice, pain that clipped the end of each phrase and prodded into my soul. It hadn't been there the last time. The last time, I'd heard longing, I'd heard hope.

Tears filled my eyes, and as Cassidy's fiddle stepped in for Lee's voice, I pushed my face against Fox's chest and sobbed. His fingers stroked my hair, and his arms held me tight even after the song was over, through Alan Jackson's "Chattahoochee" and Sam Hunt's "Walmart."

"I didn't think it would happen that fast," I said, pulling back in Fox's arms. I wiped my cheeks.

"It is extraordinarily quick," Fox said, his voice low. "Almost unheard of. But I guess it makes sense ahead of their tour with Tommy. Lee didn't tell you what single they were thinking of releasing first?"

I shook my head. "I haven't been talking to him to find out. I want to, it's just . . . I can't. We're over. We could keep it up and pretend we're not, but our relationship would just die a slow death." I took a breath. "I shouldn't have reacted that way. He told me it would be a fast turn and I should've been prepared to hear one of their songs."

"Just because you broke up doesn't mean you don't love him anymore. And it caught you off guard." Fox leaned back. "Do you want to go home?"

I shook my head. Fox's arms dropped away, but as they did, his hand caught mine and squeezed it once.

"You're going to be okay."

His fingers loosened, intending to let me go, but for some reason, my hand tightened on his, holding it fast. When he held me, my heart steadied and my breathing calmed. I couldn't let him go. Fox looked at me.

"Can we just . . . will you just hold my hand?"

"Yeah." He grinned. "I promised you snacks. Let's get some fried Oreos and watch the kids chase some chickens. I think I saw that's coming up in five. Come on."

He led me out of the exhibition hall and into the sunlight. I squeezed his hand and he squeezed mine back, and I suddenly believed what he said—that I might be okay after all.

I dug my hand into the kettle corn bag. By now, it was only kernel hulls and sugar, but we'd been driving for forty minutes and I guess I needed something to keep my sugar levels spiked to an unnatural degree.

"You should've brought the rest of that funnel cake with you, Snow," Fox said over the radio blasting Lady A. Right here, driving through the cornfields between Clover and Mountain View, we could still pick up Charlotte's Kat

Country. You had to take advantage of the signal while you could because the minute we reached Pine Summit in five miles or so, we'd lose it, and back to the '40s we'd go.

"I see I'm never going to live my chat with Slugger down," I said. "And yeah. I bet you'd be thrilled to have powdered sugar all over your beautiful gray leather."

"That's what vacuums are for." He smiled.

He started to say something else but was interrupted by Cassidy's fiddle. He reached for the dial and switched the radio off.

"You didn't have to do that," I said.

"I don't care to hear that song."

"It's okay now." I turned the radio back on. "It took me by surprise the first time, but I've got to get used to it."

Lee was singing about me now, about us falling in love in Mr. Robinson's truck, but for some reason instead of overwhelming grief, this time I felt pride in the man I'd always love, a man who'd also always been an advocate for my dreams.

"I'm happy for him," I said when the song was over. The road curved around the base of Pine Summit, and the music cut in and out before surrendering to static. "Staying here would've ruined him eventually." I stared out the window at the farms at the base of the mountain dappled with moonlight and the mountain itself cloaked in darkness.

"If you stay here, will it ruin you?"

The question hung in the air, and I turned to look at Fox. His attention was fixed on the dark road, and I knew it was on purpose. It was one of those questions he didn't like to ask and didn't like to answer.

"I don't know." I crumpled the spent kettle corn bag in my palm. "I love my parents, but this life I'm left with isn't my own. It's my Mama's and my Daddy's. It's what they wanted. Not what I wanted." I laughed. "I sound like a two-year-old. I know a lot of life is doing what you don't want to, that you're supposed to be selfless and live for others and all of that."

"Do you think you could get your job back if you could leave?" He glanced at me.

"I don't know. I doubt it. The pictures I saw on socials of our gala looked pretty bad and it was all because of my mistakes. I know Merry was out tens of thousands and she won't talk to me. I've tried."

"I could hire somebody to help your parents while they recuperate and somebody else to run the events so you could go," he said.

I grinned, thinking he was joking, but his face was earnest.

"I'm only going to say this once, because it sounds arrogant, but I have a lot of money, more than anyone knows. If I can use it to help someone I care about be happy, I'd say that's a damn good use of money, wouldn't you?"

I was stunned, but now it all made sense—his buying the tractor for Mr. Harold, donating his time to us, covering the crew's salary. It was more than generous, no matter how much money he had.

"I . . . I can't let you do that."

"And I can't live in the same town as you, watching you dwindle away, knowing you feel like you're wasting your life when I could help you out of here." He looked at me, then fixed his eyes back on the road. "Now, do I think you could do something great right here in Mountain View? Hell, yes. But you have to want to be here."

His words echoed what Lee had said to me that day on the porch.

I thought about Fox's music. He hadn't only been performing that night. His soul was in each song. "And you don't feel like your talents are wasted here?"

"No," he said. "I mean, I might not be using all of them, but I don't really care. This place is my home. It's where I want to be."

It was hard to fathom yearning for Mountain View. But Fox wasn't the only one. Dolly and Rocky had made it clear they'd never leave either. And then there was the rest of the town, my parents included, who felt the same way. Something in me couldn't imagine settling for a small life when the world was so big, so full of opportunity.

"Will you just think it over? My offer?" Fox asked.

"Okay."

I wasn't going to take him up on it. I couldn't. Up ahead, on my side, the Amtrak train to Columbia blew its whistle. If you squinted, you could see the stoplight on Main Street past the train track in front of us and the construction equipment gathered beyond it in the distance.

"What do you think Pearl and Cyrus are going to do with that bag of turkey necks?" I asked. I did it to change the subject, but also because I couldn't get the image of the big bag of necks out of my mind. The winners of the necking competition had gone at it for two hours and five minutes. Fox and I had pretty much covered the entirety of the expo by the time Pearl and Cyrus—a couple in their sixties—stopped kissing and were handed a plastic bag filled with their winnings.

"I have no idea." Fox laughed. "I mean, maybe they own a restaurant and can use them for broth? Either way, that was about the most entertaining thing I've seen in months."

The lights blinked red on the railroad crossing and the gate swung over the road. Fox stopped the truck as the Amtrak lumbered by. I unbuckled and reached for the bottle of water rolling around by my feet. The train was never fast at first. It always took a solid five minutes for the track to clear when it came through.

"It was a great day," Fox said. Our eyes met, and I leaned over the center console and gave him a hug.

"Thank you for inviting me," I said. "It was just what I needed." I pulled back just slightly, but his gaze held mine and before I could really think what I was doing, I kissed him. His lips were soft, a contrast to his beard that prickled my skin, and his mouth surrendered to mine. His hands grazed through the hair at my nape, and when my tongue swept his, he suddenly pulled away and gently set me back in the passenger seat.

"I'm not Lee."

The last of the train passed. In the quiet, I could feel my heart beating. I could taste the sweetness of his mouth on mine.

"I know," I said as the gate rose. "I'm sorry. I don't know why I did it. You were there and I . . ."

"It's alright. You've had a hard day. But maybe . . . just don't do it again, okay?"

He glanced at me, then guided the truck over the tracks. I wanted to remind him that he'd kissed me back. He hadn't pushed me away, not initially anyway, but maybe he just felt sorry for me.

I closed my eyes and tipped my head back against the seat. I'd felt so sad when I'd heard that song over the radio. I'd been so down. And Fox had steadied me. He'd been doing that for quite some time now. Maybe that's why I'd kissed him. Being near him made me forget that I was in freefall.

I tried to steer my mind to Lee, to the way he made my whole body catch fire. I didn't feel the same consuming elation around Fox, and yet, there were moments over the past weeks that I'd felt things—warmth when he held me, a tingling in my stomach when we danced.

Fox's hand grasped mine. Just for a second.

"Stop thinking about it." He grinned, but there was a difference in his eyes, a knowing that wasn't there before. I wondered what it meant. "It's not a big deal. It was just a kiss."

We crossed over Main, and Fox groaned.

"I forgot it was Friday. I guess I've got to entertain the town after I drop you off. They're already in there, I bet. A couple weeks ago, Tosha set up at three to make sure Lee and his guys didn't get to play first."

"Next week, they'll be my problem." I laughed. Cars and trucks lined Route 2. "Is Bobby Jo having a party we didn't know about?"

"Damn," Fox said under his breath. "No. It looks like the town—and lots of others—have decided that they ain't waiting 'til next week and that your barn is the bar tonight."

"But we didn't tell anybody it was ready yet!" I babbled as Fox pulled onto our drive. The gravel was crushed with cars. There were so many that Fox could barely fit his truck through.

"Since when does Mountain View care?"

He was right. No one had consulted Mr. Fox about whether or not they could descend on the hardware store every Friday, and no one had asked us now. I guess because the town had pitched in to help us renovate it, they saw the barn as rightfully theirs.

I dug my phone out of my purse and dialed the house number. Mama answered on the first ring.

"Do you see all these people?"

"Yeah," she said. "I would've tried to stop them, but your daddy needed a shower and then he felt pretty weak, so I couldn't." She sighed. "Just let them have their fun. We were planning to let them come next week anyway."

I hung up, and Fox pulled his truck into the grass around the side of the barn.

"If I just made tire tracks, I'll fix it before the wedding," he said. He turned the ignition off, distractedly staring at the crowd of people pouring from the entrance. "There's only thirty or so, max, at the store each week. Who are all these people and where did they come from?"

I got out of the cab and he did too. We walked in the side door to find the barn crushed full and an older man I'd never seen playing bluegrass on the stage.

"Excuse me," I said to a girl that looked nearly identical to Megan Moroney, "Why are y'all here?"

She twirled a long blonde strand and laughed. "Well, the guitar player, Woody, from that new Leland Lockhardt Band everybody's been talking about posted a picture of this barn on their Insta today and said that this is where it all started—or where they got discovered, rather. He said that the barn would be open from here on out on Friday nights, so I guess word got around? I'm a singer and my boyfriend, Heath, and I have an act. I know there might not be any scouts here tonight, but on the other hand, it might be our lucky day."

"Oh, nice," I said, faking it. Inside, I was panicking. I wanted to punch Woody. We'd only planned on Mountain View. Hosting all these people every weekend hadn't been in the cards. "Can't wait to hear you."

I dug my phone out of my purse and switched my Instagram from my personal account to the Robinson's Events page. I had hundreds of notifications. Woody had posted about the barn earlier today, but of course, I hadn't seen it. The only pictures I had on the events account were the ones I'd taken for the introduction and for Founder's Day. The taxidermy wedding wasn't exactly on brand for us, so I hadn't posted any from that and hadn't been on the account in over a week.

I held the phone up to Fox.

"Shit. This is more than we bargained for. Let me go talk to Vern and see if he can bring the bus around for rides home." He nodded toward the far corner of the room where Sterling and Vern sat together, Sterling's unplugged disco lights sitting on his lap, a bottle of his peach jubilee in his hand. "Looks like everybody's brought their own poison, and I don't recognize half of these faces, meaning they're going to be heading home to Cardinal River or Pine Summit or further."

I looked around at the crowd as Fox went to talk with Vern. People were filming the guy on stage and taking selfies that I knew they'd post later. To an events coordinator keen to have a big blowout event, this viral word of mouth on socials was like winning the lottery. But no one was paying us, and I hadn't planned on this. And there was nothing worse than being unprepared. It usually meant disaster. This sort of thing, if it got out of control, could slash the metaphorical tires of Robinson's Events before it even got rolling.

"Sterling's pissed." Fox materialized beside me. "That guy took his spot. I guess somebody decided on a sign-up system. And he wanted me to tell you that he saw a guy throw up next to your dad's truck."

"Great." A symphony of curses sounded in my mind. The dance floor would be scratched and sticky with spilled drinks and with one swift push, our walls could be punched in. We were doomed.

CHAPTER EIGHTEEN

I took a sip of my coffee and scrolled through the posts and videos people had tagged us in over the last six days. They were endless. They showcased wannabe Chuck Berrys and Tim McGraws and Carrie Underwoods hoping to get discovered like Lee's band—though to my knowledge there hadn't been a legitimate music executive on our property since Founder's Day. Now and then, videos of the Leland Lockhardt Band from Founder's Day and videos of Lee from Europe were intermingled with the ones from our barn. I guess fans tagged us since they were discovered here. I hurried past those. It wasn't that I couldn't bear to watch them. I could manage just fine. But if I watched for too long, I started questioning myself and the questioning would ruin my day.

"Are you hanging in there okay?" Tammy called out from the Cut & Curl. She was lugging a huge sign onto the sidewalk that read *Save Mountain View—Home of Ronald Robinson and Leland Lockhardt.* Below the letters were big pictures of Mr. Robinson and Lee. Annie had organized a protest on the Cardinal River town line, where the state had deposited a bunch of construction equipment. I knew that's where Tammy was headed.

With the barn's popularity, Annie had introduced the hashtag *#savemountainview* to cling to the content, and it had started trending. She was hoping to broadcast the protest today and get a bunch of views. Even though the town's attorney and Mr. Brantley had said nothing could be done, Annie didn't believe them. She'd researched a bunch of cases like ours and decided that if the town could stir up a true public outcry, the state might back off after all.

Pretty much the whole town would be at the protest. Even Mama and Daddy. Daddy had seemed to regain some of himself in the last few days. He'd even asked Mama for an extra pancake this morning.

"I guess. Tired, though," I yelled across the street, watching Tammy try to shove the sign into the back of her Kia Soul.

"Fox says the crowds keep coming every night, even though it was just supposed to be Fridays," she called back. "I'm sorry. Wish I had some donuts ready to give you."

It was news to me that Fox had any idea about what was going on at the barn. I hadn't heard from him since the night we got back from the expo. I knew it had to do with the kiss. He'd acted like he'd been okay with it, but there was no other explanation for his absence, especially when I'd needed his help more than ever. What I couldn't figure was that Annie had kissed him before too—he'd told me she had—and he wasn't avoiding her.

"Yeah. It's becoming a problem. We've got the wedding tomorrow, you know, and I can't have hundreds of people scuffing up the dance floor and puking in the bushes right before. I had to sit out on the driveway last night and turn people away for six hours. They were all mad to hear that we're only open Fridays, and this week it'll be after the wedding reception is over at ten."

Tammy whistled.

"Where are they coming from?" She pushed the sign toward her trunk a different way, realized it wasn't going to fit, and stood back. "Oh! And I keep meaning to tell you about my niece, Susannah. She just got engaged and they're hoping to get married in December. The barn would be a perfect place."

"We're booked solid every weekend until next March." I'd been surprised too, when I'd checked our website's booking system last Sunday and found it full. "But if she wants to try for a weekday, we could squeeze her in. And I don't know where they're all coming from. One girl said she'd driven in from Greenville and a guy I spoke with said Columbia, but it's hard to tell, really. I'm mostly just trying to keep up with selling drinks and making sure nobody dies."

The second night the crowds came, Mama handed me a couple bottles of Jim Beam and said to put our new liquor license to use. Cletus had given the approved license to Mama at the town meeting. We'd made nearly a thousand extra dollars that night. The subsequent nights, after I'd gone into Cardinal River and stocked up on alcohol, we'd turned a profit of at least a couple thousand.

Tammy laughed. "You want a ride to the protest?"

I glanced up the street toward the hardware store. The parking spaces in front of Fox's Hardware were empty just like I'd hoped.

"No, thanks."

She folded the sign, pushed it into her trunk and shut the door. "Okay. See you there."

Tammy got in her car. She had no idea I hadn't signed the petition yet. When I'd stayed in Mountain View past the time everybody thought I would leave and when I'd stepped in to run the events business, I guess people assumed I'd abandoned my harebrained idea about the stadium being a good idea. I hadn't. Not entirely anyway. And that had ended up being a good thing. Because last night, right after I waved off a pickup truck full of shirtless teen boys in camo pants, Merry texted me. She said she'd been heading over to my townhouse to pack my things up to ship back to Mountain View when she heard from Eliott Walker that the events deal with the Panthers might still be on the table after all and wanted to talk. She asked if I had time at the beginning of next week, and we'd scheduled a call for Monday.

The thought of leaving Mama and Daddy made me anxious, but I didn't even know what Merry would say. And if for some reason CLE got the Panthers deal, maybe there was a way I could work part-time from Mountain View after the stadium was built and check in on Mama and Daddy more frequently—that is, if the stadium didn't end up on our farm. Thinking of the possibility made my heart drop to my stomach.

I took another sip of my coffee and threw the disposable cup in the trash can next to the old five and dime. I'd gone into the barn today to make sure it was ready for the team of people the bride, Juniper, had hired to transform it into a rose garden. She'd wanted to have the wedding outside but was concerned about rain. She'd also found that one of the little sconces beside the stairwell was askew. I'd been polishing crystals in the barn when Fox had hung the sconces up the first time, and I remembered he'd had to go back to the store to get a special type of wrench—a speed wrench he called it. Daddy had all kinds of tools, which Fox had used on site, but clearly he didn't own one of these. I figured I'd just go into the store and borrow one, then have Mama return it to Fox later. Nobody locked their doors around here—even business owners—and I figured now, when he and everybody else were at the protest, was the perfect time for me to grab it.

I walked up the two steps to the doors, pulled the photo of the wrench up on my phone, and stepped inside. I pushed the door shut while I examined the picture, zooming in on the right side where the inside of the ratchet had a star shape.

"Hey."

I startled at the sound of Fox's voice. He was toward the back of the store behind a counter, a sea of various nails spread out in front of him.

"Oh. I thought you might be at the protest."

His forehead crinkled. It was then that I realized the error of my statement. I was standing in his store, needing something.

"I mean, I thought you'd be, but I'm glad you're not." I walked toward him. I pulled at the straps of my white tank top, suddenly wishing I'd worn the yellow sundress I'd considered.

"What can I help you with?"

He looked down at the nails when I got close, pushing the little metal pieces into groups.

"I . . . I need a speed wrench, I guess. The sconce next to the stairwell came loose." I gripped the edge of the glass counter, and when he didn't reply, I held the phone toward him.

Fox's eyes met mine. The green was almost stunning today, brought out by his white shirt and tan skin.

"I know what a speed wrench is."

He turned his focus back to the nails.

"Did I do something wrong?" I asked. "You haven't been around and it's been a mess at the barn."

He ran a hand across his face.

"I said I was sorry after it happened . . . after I kissed you." I stumbled over my words. "If that's why you're angry. I've thought that might be the reason, but then again, you said Annie's kissed you before and you're not mad at her."

He didn't say anything, only stared at me. "And I promised you it wouldn't happen again."

Fox shook his head. "I ain't mad at you. But it is the reason I couldn't come around this week," he said. "Because even though I told you I didn't want you to kiss me, I did."

I froze. I could hear my heart in my ears.

"And I wanted to kiss you again," he went on, his voice low. "The one was like a drug, and I can't get it . . . I can't get you out of my head. But I was engaged once, to a woman who loved somebody else like you love Lee. I swore I'd never do that to myself again."

I didn't know if I was breathing. I couldn't look away. I couldn't move. I was shocked by his words, but my body wasn't. The familiar warmth I felt in his presence, the tingling in my stomach was there like before.

"So I'll play for that wedding tomorrow since the bride asked me to, and I'll help you out when you need a hand, but I can't pretend to be your friend when I want you this way." He swallowed. "Annie can kiss me all she damn well pleases and I don't feel a thing," he said. "But you just look at me and there's this insatiable ache for a love I can't have."

"Lee's gone." The words murmured from my lips, and I wondered if I'd even said them out loud.

"Yeah. But he's still here." Fox reached out and touched the top of my chest with his fingertips. My breath caught, and then his thumb arrested the edge of my chin, tilting my mouth toward his. I leaned in toward the counter, and his lips found mine. His kiss was slow; every movement of his mouth, every sweep of his tongue an intoxication I hadn't realized I'd been missing. I reached for him, deepening the kiss, and a small noise escaped my lips.

He pulled away, as though he'd just realized what he'd done. His body tensed. His jaw gripped and his shoulders squared. "I'm sorry," he said. "It won't happen again."

CHAPTER NINETEEN

I didn't realize I was allergic to flowers until tonight. I'd been around huge floral displays at nearly all of my events, but nothing like this. Every space of the barn that wasn't covered with people was covered with flowers. Thick swags of pink and white roses and hydrangeas and greenery were draped over the doors, and vases on tall stands were interspersed along the walls. During the ceremony, a real grass aisle had stretched from the barn doors to the altar where an archway of all white roses waited.

I sniffed and dabbed my itchy eyes gently, so I wouldn't smear my makeup.

"Got any more hooch?" An old guy in suspenders yelled above Fox's singing Florida Georgia Line's "Simple." He waved his empty wine glass in my face.

It had been difficult to look away from Fox tonight. It didn't matter what song he was playing.

"We only have wine." I smiled at the old man and stepped toward the bottles on the other end of the bar we'd set up at the back of the barn. Juniper had absolutely forbidden hard liquor at her reception, saying some of their guests couldn't behave on it. I was guessing this man was one of those people.

"Pookie must've given me some of the stuff from his own collection then."

"Would you like some wine?"

"Naw. I'm gonna see if Pookie's got another flask."

He wandered away, and I surveyed the room, wondering who Pookie was. Overall, this wedding looked like something you'd find featured on *The Knot*. Juniper had classy taste, and her new husband, Wyatt, seemed to be of the same mind. His dark blue Brooks Brothers suit that matched his groomsmen was refined and in style. The guests seemed to take note from the bride and groom—mostly, at least—but there were always renegade guests like the hooch man.

Yells rang out from the crowd of guests on the dance floor. Juniper and Wyatt were in the middle. Her perfect French twist had come free of its pins since the dancing started over two hours ago, and now her blonde hair cascaded down her back in waves. When Fox took a break from singing and let his guitar take over, Wyatt dipped her low and kissed her hard.

My cheeks flushed at the gesture, and my gaze drifted to Fox. I'd been acting like a girl with a middle school crush ever since he'd arrived today.

Outside, the sound of a muffler roared through the open barn doors and then another. They didn't silence as they usually did when they flew past my house down Route 2. I stepped out from behind the bar and pushed my way toward the exit, running into hooch man and a short little man with a rat tail in all leather—I guessed he was Pookie—taking turns with a rusty flask that looked like a relic from the Revolutionary War.

"Shit," I breathed when I glanced out at the drive. Trucks and cars were turning onto our property in droves, wedging between wedding guests' vehicles and driving through the grass. I'd stationed Daddy and Mama up at the top of our drive for this very reason, but I guess they'd abandoned their post. I pulled at the pink organza fit-and-flare dress I'd borrowed from Dolly, then kicked off my wedge heels and started toward the first truck I saw.

"Hey." I tapped on the window of a little Colorado parked behind the bride and groom's limousine and was met with a bedazzled cowboy hat and long Jimmy Page hair.

"What's up, darlin'?" the man said. "If you're coming over to get my autograph already, I'm sorry to say I only sign after I play."

I looked him over and laughed. "You won't be playing right now. There's a wedding going on. Barn's not open for another half hour."

"Whatever. You were sent over here by Ricky, weren't you?" The guy shook his head. "He's trying to get the glory before me, but I say go on, Ricky. Be my opening act."

"No," I said evenly. I glanced around, noticing groups of people walking toward the barn, some with instruments. "I own this place. I'm Hattie Norwood," I called out as I turned away from the truck and started running back to the barn to stop the musicians from crashing Juniper's wedding.

"Oh, wow. Leland Lockhardt's girl," the rhinestone cowboy called back.

I ignored him and tried to flag down a group of girls in matching chaps, but they acted like they couldn't hear me.

By the time I reached the barn at least two dozen uninvited guests were mingling with the wedding guests. Some were helping themselves to the wine. Thankfully, Juniper and Wyatt were fairly insulated in the middle of the dance floor, and time was almost up. Maybe they'd never know.

I paced toward the bar and snatched the empty wine bottles, then bent down to put them in the recycling bin and get new bottles from the wine cooler.

Fox started playing Kenny Chesney's "Back Where I Come From," the song Wyatt had requested for a sendoff. Relief settled over me.

When he reached the last line, the whole place erupted. Sure, it was the last song and a song that meant something, but the noise was less of an agreeable cheer and more of a startled screech.

I stood up, a Sauvignon Blanc and a Chardonnay in my hands. When my eyes met the stage, I nearly dropped the bottles. Lee, in a white T-shirt and jeans, stood beside Fox with his guitar. When it was time for the second verse, he leaned in to Fox's microphone and sang.

I couldn't move. The incessant screaming around me seemed to dull, and I watched people raise their phones to record Lee, whose gaze swept over the crowd and back again. He was supposed to be in Madrid. At least that's what it said on the band's Instagram.

Fox's voice joined Lee's at the chorus, as Lee continued to scan the room, it suddenly occurred to me that the man I loved and the man I'd kissed the day before were sharing a stage. I ducked down as Lee's eyes swept the back of the room, then made a beeline for the exit. Adrenaline surged through me as I ran through the grass, dodging a swarm of people coming from trucks parked where peanuts used to grow.

"Leland Lockhardt is here!" I heard a girl screech.

I couldn't figure why Lee would fly across the world tonight of all nights, and I had no idea what I'd say to him when he found me. Maybe he wouldn't. At least not for a while, until the crowds died down. There was no way he'd be able to get out of that barn without being swarmed.

When I reached Mr. Robinson's truck, I climbed inside. I sat in the silence and forced myself to breathe deep, to pick out the smell of leather and old polymers and the tinge of grass from below the holes rust had eaten in the floorboards.

Suddenly, all I could think about was that I'd betrayed Lee. I hadn't really. I knew that logically. We were broken up. But he'd left his tour to surprise me for a night, undoubtedly thinking I was as torn up about our breakup as I'd been the last time—and I was—but I'd also been kissing someone else.

The passenger door hinge screeched. I startled as Lee climbed inside the cab. My heart was racing, and I pushed my palm to my chest as he glanced out the window beside him. Finding he hadn't been followed by any fans, he turned to me.

"Lee, what are you doing—"

"Are you hiding from me?" He grinned, but his eyes were serious. I scooted toward him and wrapped my arms around him. I couldn't answer the question. I couldn't hurt him that way. Touching him was the only thing I knew to do. And then he drew my face to his and kissed me hard. His mouth possessed mine, and my fingers threaded his hair.

"I've missed you so much," he said against my ear. I closed my eyes, intoxicated by the feel of his lips on my skin. "I came as soon as I heard. I'm sorry if I took too long, if you're mad at me."

"Heard what?" I leaned away from him. He looked puzzled.

"About the stadium. I left Madrid in the middle of the night, the minute he told me."

"Who? What are you talking about? Nothing's been decided yet. I mean, I heard they might decide on a tract as early as next week, but that's it so far."

"I'm talking about the state saying they're situating the stadium's footprint to save the most productive farms."

I shook my head. "I haven't heard anything about that."

Lee's fingers stroked up and down my back. He only touched me like this when he was nervous.

"I hope to God I'm mistaken, Hat," he said softly. "But Woody's godmama, who lives in Columbia and serves as a recorder for meetings at the capital, told him she heard they're going to take the farms that produce the least. They pulled production numbers and everything." He paused. "She said it's your land down past the Simpsons' and the Whitackers', all the way to the edge of my property line."

My skin prickled with goosebumps and my chest felt tight.

"The surveyor said he'd do everything he could to save our farm."

"Woody's godmama said they didn't even care that this was the Robinsons' homeplace, that the only thing they took into account was the money they make off those farms," he went on as though he hadn't heard me.

My eyes welled. Nothing had been confirmed. This was information heard thirdhand, and yet, deep inside I could feel it. They were coming for us.

"I've got to go talk to Mama and Daddy." I pushed across the seat and opened the door, but Lee caught my arm.

"We're going to get to the bottom of this," he said. "If it's true, we'll get through it together, okay?"

His eyes searched mine.

"But we're not together."

He laughed under his breath. "You might have broken up with me, but we'll always be together, Hat. My heart's yours. It always has been."

At once, the echo of Fox's kiss pressed into my mind.

"I kissed Fox." The words blurted from my mouth. Lee leaned away from me. He looked shocked.

"What? Why? Do you love him?"

"No," I said quickly, immediately wondering if I was telling the truth. "Not the way I love you."

"Then I don't give a damn."

Lee pulled me deeper into the cab and cradled my face in his hands. His mouth dropped to mine, and he kissed me slowly, his teeth bearing softly on my bottom lip, his tongue seeking the warmth of mine. The familiar burn of desire washed through me.

"I'm going to say something and you're not going to argue with me, understand?" His voice was low, and I nodded. "I'm quitting music. Cassidy can take over on vocals for the rest of the tour. He's decent enough. But I ain't leaving you again. No amount of fame or success is worth losing you."

"Lee, you can't."

"It ain't up for discussion. I'm choosing Mountain View, or wherever you are," he said. "I love you."

"I love you too."

I leaned into him as he kissed me again. Yet I wondered, as my body flamed with his touch, if he still held my whole heart.

"Come on," he said. "Let's make a run for it up to your house. We can tell your parents what I heard."

CHAPTER TWENTY

The rumor was true. My hands were shaking as I gripped Mama's and inhaled the scent of town hall—the old coffee smell and the Murphy's oil soap and Mrs. Harold's White Diamonds perfume.

The stadium tract had been announced this morning, and a town meeting had been called to discuss the details.

After Lee told us what he'd heard from Woody's godmama, I'd tried to get in touch with Mr. Brantley for several days but heard nothing back. I'd forced myself to move on with my life, to view the rumor as a rumor until I heard otherwise.

Instead of dwelling on the possibilities, I'd engaged with the two hundred thousand followers that had started following Robinson's Events after a video of Lee and Fox's duet went viral, even being reposted by Kenny Chesney himself. I'd actually gone live with CMT earlier today. They'd reached out about highlighting Robinson's, calling it the next Bluebird Café. The interview had been great, and though I knew it would mean larger crowds on Fridays, I was excited about it. I could charge a cover and turn a nice profit on drink sales too.

But when the interview ended, and I'd exited the barn, I'd noticed Mr. Brantley's old Ford Taurus parked next to our house. I knew before I went inside to see him what I'd find. I could feel the truth of it like I had when Lee had mentioned it the first time.

When I walked through the front door, Mr. Brantley was sitting in the living room with my parents. My phone had started ringing before I could sit down—my scheduled call with Merry—but my job and the Panthers contract suddenly didn't matter anymore.

"I was just telling your mama," he'd said. "I told Alfred I needed to be the one to tell you, that it was only right." His voice had been shaking, and when Mama and Daddy turned to look at me from their position on the couch, I'd nearly thrown up. They were both crying.

He'd told us that the footprint required all of our land. He said he'd fought for us, but that at the end of the day, the state prioritized keeping productive working farms intact. He said construction would commence October 1, that they would pay us top dollar for our farm and our business losses—$800,000—and that the state would extract Mr. Robinson's truck from the ground and pieces of the barn and take both to a music museum in Nashville of our choosing.

At first, Daddy had wanted to fight it, but Mr. Brantley said it was no use. Mountain View's attorney had already negotiated the best rates for all the affected farms, and the state wouldn't budge otherwise. The quiet that fell over us after that was akin to that of a funeral home visitation.

"And what about our history? They're just going to plow over it?" Dolly's voice brought me back to town hall, to the crowd of neighbors who had taken the news of Mountain

View's demise soberly. When the attorney, Yolanda, had delivered the final plan in her red power suit, and Alfred Moore, the representative from the state, had confirmed it, I'd expected hysteria. I'd expected outrage. Instead, there were quiet tears and bowed heads as Annie cried through her questions asked on behalf of the town to Yolanda and Alfred at the front of the room.

"We promised Ronald and Elita that we'd be good stewards of their land," Mama whispered.

"I know, Helen Sue, but we don't have a choice," Daddy said from her other side.

My eyes teared as Dolly pushed her way out of the line of folding chairs and up to the front of the room where Alfred Moore stood in his cheap gray suit in front of the dusty red auditorium curtain. Mama and Daddy were right. We'd promised to take care of the Robinsons' beloved farm, and in a way that promise had extended to the town too. I guess I'd thought I was protecting the town's longevity by supporting the stadium—if you just looked at the facts, it was the truth—but now that the stadium was going to require the obliteration of the Robinsons' homestead, what would be left of the town's history to protect? The very founding of it would be forgotten. A town's history—the good and the bad—was its soul. Take that away, and its life went with it. It would become a sort of no man's land. Maybe that's what the town had been fighting against all along.

"Where do you live, Mr. Moore?" Dolly asked when she reached the front row.

"Columbia, of course," he said in his signature monotone. Mr. Brantley would have been a better person to deliver the news. He was at least compassionate.

"Imagine we came by and told you that we were taking your home," Vern said from the middle of the room. Sterling was crying next to him, and Vern clutched his hand.

Mr. Moore chuckled. "I guess I'd go find another one."

"And if the state took the whole city of Columbia? Not only your home and your livelihood, but every road you'd ever driven, every landmark that made it special—the state house, the horseshoe—and put in a nice mall, you'd be okay with that?" Cletus barked. I noticed he'd put extra gel in his sideburns for the occasion. They glistened like he'd glued two hairy slugs across his temples. I smiled in spite of myself.

Mr. Moore cleared his throat. I watched the way he looked at Vern and Cletus, even Dolly who was stunning in a leather dress. He thought he was better than them, better than all of us.

I wished Lee was here, that he hadn't left last night to clear out his apartment in Nashville. He hadn't known the news was officially coming today, but he'd know what to say to Mr. Moore, how to command his respect. Fox was another, but he wasn't here either. Surely he knew what was going on. I glanced out the window. You could barely make out Fox's storefront from where I sat. The old glass doors were bathed in golden hour light, as was a strange BMW. It was a vintage model, maybe something from the '40s. I was certain I'd seen Katherine Hepburn zipping around in a similar car in one of her movies.

"I wouldn't be okay with it," I heard Mr. Moore say, finally responding to Cletus. "But it wouldn't be my call. The taxpayers vote to pay for bonds that help fund things like stadiums. They voted to finance sixty percent of this build, with Eliott Walker financing the other forty."

One of the hardware store doors opened. It helped to stare out at Main Street and ignore the chatter, to pretend that the last lifeboat still intact in my life hadn't just sank with the pronouncement of the state's plan.

"You've fought against us this whole time," Annie said to Mr. Moore, her tone suddenly sharp and clipped and nothing like the mayoral calm I knew she'd hoped to maintain.

A man in a cowboy hat and a starched white shirt sauntered out of the hardware store. Everything in me froze. It was Alan, the executive who'd discovered Lee. I'd only seen him the one time, but I knew him instantly. Maybe he was here looking for Lee, to try and convince him his quitting had been a mistake.

I thought about the way I'd made up an excuse to stay in with my parents the night Lee came back and pretended to be too busy at the barn to go over and swim with him yesterday. I knew Lee wanted to talk about us, but I wasn't ready. Maybe this was why. Maybe I knew something like this would happen, that Alan would come poking around begging for Lee to think rationally, to come back, and Lee might take him up on it.

Mr. Moore chuckled.

"I don't mean to make light of this, Annie, but anyone with objective eyes can see that this town is failing. I would have thought after giving y'all all this time, you'd see the light and cling to the stadium like the winning lottery ticket it is."

I heard the gasps around me, but I kept my eyes fixed outside on Alan, who was circling his car, keys in hand. Fox burst from the doors. He was furious. His hands were balled in fists and his frame was hulking, his shoulders squared, as he pointed at Alan and started shouting. I couldn't hear what he was saying, of course, but Alan held up his hands, then got in his car as Fox gestured for him to leave.

I watched the little car go, fully expecting the cowboy hat to fly off and land at Fox's feet, but it didn't somehow. Fox stood in the road until the car disappeared. Then he ran a hand across his face and walked back inside the store. I wondered what Alan had said to upset Fox. It wasn't like they'd had any interaction before. There was a chance he'd come into the hardware store asking after Lee. Maybe Fox knew Lee and I had reconciled and he was driving Alan out of town to protect me. The thought made my heart ache, and suddenly I was brought back to the way he'd kissed me in the store that day.

"I'd hoped that one townie holdout would have spoken some sense into y'all by now," Mr. Moore said.

Mama's hand tightened on mine, and my attention snapped to the front of the room. I let go of her hand and stood before I really knew what I was doing.

"I'm the one you're talking about." I started crying. "Like you, I thought the town was dying anyway and that by supporting the build, I was helping Mountain View, a place founded by people I love dearly. But when you decided to take our farm, the Robinsons' homeplace, I realized what the rest of the town already knew—that a stadium might bring revenue into this town, but it wouldn't honor what the Robinsons started."

Everyone was looking at me. I wiped my tears with the back of my hand.

"If Mountain View dies, it should die as itself," I went on. "I know that's not going to happen, but it's what should have been. I'm sorry for not seeing what y'all have been trying to tell me."

My words lingered and nobody spoke or moved. I knew to some I seemed selfish, like I'd only come around because the state was taking our farm. That was true in part. But really, the change had just altered my view and helped me see what was important.

"You could've helped stop this," Mrs. Harold said, rising from her chair in the third row in her vintage Pooh Bear T-shirt. She pointed a finger at me. "We could have been a united front. Now it's too late."

At once, I couldn't take it anymore. I sobbed and shimmied out of the row and into the aisle. I practically ran toward the back doors, my face pouring snot and tears. I vaguely heard Mr. Moore laugh and say that my signature wouldn't have done a thing to stop the stadium, but this town would never believe that. I pushed out of the doors and onto Main Street, immediately turning toward Fox's. I knew he was having a hard day himself, but he was also the only one who'd shoot me straight about the town ever forgiving me.

My heels clapped against my leather flip-flops as I crossed Main Street. I wiped my eyes and tried to take deep breaths to calm myself. I didn't know what we'd do when they bulldozed our house and the barn. I couldn't bear to envision it. I didn't know if Mama and Daddy would want to find other land around here or if they'd find the proximity painful. A part of me hoped they'd want to go, that we could start over where nobody knew me as the traitor of Mountain View. I had a feeling it would take years, maybe forever, for the town to see past what I'd done.

I grasped the old metal knob and opened the door to the hardware store.

"What are you doing here, Hattie?"

Fox was sitting on his barstool behind the cash register. His face looked ashen, and he stared down at the old button keys. I wanted to come right out and ask him about Alan, but I didn't want him to think I'd been casing his store.

"Why weren't you at the meeting?"

His eyes met mine.

"I was on my way there when . . . I'm sorry about your farm." he said, not answering my question. He crossed his arms.

"I don't know what to do, and the whole town hates me." I swallowed a sob. "I thought I was doing the right thing, but now I know I was wrong. They're going to demolish everything—every trace of the Robinsons and everything the Robinsons worked so hard to build for us."

Ordinarily, he'd comfort me with a word or with a hug, but this time, he just sat there and shook his head.

"Yeah, well. I'm glad I won't be here to see it happen."

"What?"

I caught his gaze, and he shrugged.

"I'm moving to Nashville. That Alan Brownell saw the video of Lee and me from the other night and insisted I be properly compensated for my talent. He caught me on the way out the door to the meeting." He sounded as though it was an effort for him to avoid yelling, and his shoulders tensed as if he'd like nothing more than to shatter the glass case in front of him. He traced the round keys with his fingertips.

"I don't understand. You said Mountain View was where you belong, and it doesn't sound like you want to go besides." I stared at him, feeling like my heart was being strangled. "I saw you out the window of town hall. You were shouting at him. You were angry. Why are you going?"

"Well, shit, Hattie. Sometimes you get an offer you can't refuse," he said sharply. "Kind of like the one Lee offered you the other night, right?" His gaze bore into mine. Heat rushed through my body and tears prickled my eyes. "And I was mad because he told me I should sell my store for half the price it's worth. I might be making a deal with him, but he ain't going to stick his nose in my business."

"Fox." I whispered his name. The realization that he was leaving washed over me like a tidal wave. It felt like a part of my soul was drowning. In that moment, I knew why it had felt wrong to tell Lee I didn't love Fox. Lee wasn't the only one who held my heart anymore. "I still don't understand. I thought you meant to live here forever." He stayed silent. "When are you going?"

"Early tomorrow morning."

"Tomorrow morning?" I asked. "Why that soon?" It was too fast.

"I'm going to tie up some loose ends from the road and leave Vern and Sterling the keys in case anyone needs to grab a shipment—or anything else they need in here. Loraine will list it for sale in the next day or two."

"Okay," I said. He clearly wasn't going to answer my question. I thought to tell him that Lee and I weren't together again, that I had feelings for him too, but what good would it do? He'd made up his mind.

Fox didn't move, just sat there staring at the cash register as though it was the most interesting thing he'd ever seen. I studied his face—the deep green eyes, the trimmed beard, the soft lips.

"I'm going to miss you." I turned away before I could break down again and started to walk out the door, but he walked toward me and caught my arm.

"I'm sorry for what I said before—about Lee," he said. "It's none of my business." I was acutely aware of his fingers on my skin, of the way he looked at me. I could see the longing in his eyes, and I could feel mine in the pit of my stomach. "Getting to know you has been . . . I'll never forget it." He searched my face. "When Alan offered, my first thought was that maybe my leaving was meant to be. Otherwise," he paused, and his hand dropped to mine. "Otherwise, I would have fallen in love with you, Hattie, and I know at the end of the day, it ain't going to be me and you."

I wasn't breathing. For the second time in a matter of minutes I wanted to tell him that I was falling for him too. The words were on the tip of my tongue. But I couldn't. He was leaving, just like Lee had before. And if I told him I loved him, I'd have to tell him I loved Lee too. It was better left unsaid.

Instead, I wrapped my arms around him, and he pulled me against his chest. I burrowed into his plaid shirt, feeling the familiar comfort of his presence wash over me. I listened to his heart and breathed him in. He smelled like the store, like my favorite things.

"I hope I'll see you again, Snow," he whispered into my hair. "I'll always care for you."

"I'll always care for you too." I lifted my face to his. I let my tears fall, and he wiped one away with his thumb before I pulled away.

"I'll be cheering you on," I said, fighting back emotion. "But I wish you weren't going. We need you here."

"I'm sorry," he said.

I turned away then and walked out of the store before he could see me sob. At first, I thought he'd follow me onto Main Street, that he'd take me in his arms and kiss me one last time. But he didn't.

CHAPTER TWENTY-ONE

Mama and Daddy had left me. I stood in the parking space in front of the old ice cream parlor where Daddy's truck had been parked and dug my phone out of my purse. I startled when I saw the thirty-four calls I'd missed—thirty-three from Mama and one from Lee. By the looks of the nearly vacant Main Street and the time stamp on the first of Mama's calls, I'd been with Fox longer than I'd thought and the meeting had ended over half an hour ago.

I walked toward the stoplight and dialed Mama's number. As it rang, I thought about what the town would look like a year from now or two years from now when the stadium was finished. Up until today, I'd imagined the buildings fixed up and polished, the music notes etched into the limestone as pronounced and beautiful as the day they were created. I'd imagined the movie theater reopened and bars and restaurants and boutiques behind the old glass windows. But I guess I'd never really considered who would own those establishments. I suppose I was envisioning something like Phillip's Place in Charlotte. Thinking about it now, a store like the Cut & Curl or a diner like Paradise or Fox's Hardware wouldn't make the grade in such a place. Then again, Fox wouldn't be here anyway. He'd be off in Nashville making records and angry about it. I wanted to sit on the curb and cry.

Mama's voicemail picked up. I tried the house line. I couldn't figure why Fox was really going. It couldn't only be because he was afraid of falling in love with me. The echo of his words both warmed me through and speared my heart.

Maybe he was going because he knew what was coming. He knew that once the stadium came in, the condos would follow. If the Harolds and Turneys and Mainerts were honest, they wouldn't want to spend the rest of their lives staring at a concrete bowl. They'd eventually sell their farms to developers and leave. Everybody would. Because Mountain View wouldn't be the same anymore.

Mama answered on the second try and offered to pick me up, but I told her I wanted to walk home.

I turned left down Route 2, but not before taking a long glance at the sun starting to set over Pine Summit. I took a deep breath. Right now, the air was sweet. The smell of fresh cut grass and blooming wildflowers was heavy on the breeze. Someday soon, the air would smell like truck exhaust and Porta Potties and weed smoke and trash.

My eyes drifted over the wash of green stretching out on either side of Route 2 in front of me. It went as far as the eye could see. Even into Cardinal River. Just farms and little brick ranch houses dotting the landscape.

I wandered toward Slugger who was looking over the fence up ahead.

"I'm sorry," I whispered to the town, I guess, as I reached out and patted Slugger's nose. He tossed his head and stamped. "I know. You're mad at me too, aren't you?"

I remembered what Fox had said weeks ago, that family and community were what really mattered at the end of the day. I'd let ambition and selfishness and the desire to make something of myself eclipse what I'd been taught my whole life.

"You ain't drunk again, are you?" Lee pulled into his driveway in a black F-150 Raptor I didn't recognize.

"No, unfortunately. Did you get a new car?"

"Yeah. I got to Nashville and realized I couldn't fit all of my gear in that toy I was driving," he said. "Get in here, Hat." He gestured to the passenger seat and I climbed in. The new car smell was so strong, I rolled the window down. Lee turned the engine off and pulled me across the bench seat and into his arms. "I can't imagine the sort of day you had. I'm sorry I wasn't here when you officially got the news."

I looked up at him and started crying. He stroked my hair and whispered that it was going to be okay and when I couldn't cry anymore, he tipped my chin toward his face and kissed me. I leaned in to him, tasting the salt from my tears on my lips and the blue Gatorade in his cupholder on his tongue.

"I'm home forever now," he said. "If you want to leave, I'll leave, and if you want to stay, then this is our place. I just can't be away from you anymore, okay?"

His mouth met mine again and I closed my eyes, feeling desire pool in my stomach. His fingertips grazed my back, right at the hem of my shorts and then grasped my hips. I deepened the kiss, never wanting it to end. When it finally did, he looked at me and smiled.

"I love you," I said. I was reminded right then of Fox, of the way I'd wanted to tell him I was falling for him too. But I was right to keep it in. Because even if Fox had a part of my heart, I knew Lee still held the other.

"I can't believe they're going to take our house and dig up the Robinson's truck and take our barn apart," I said softly. "It doesn't seem real, that they're allowed to dissolve eighty years of history in a matter of a day or two."

"Maybe they won't." Lee grinned. "Maybe it's not too late. I might not be in Nashville anymore, but I got to know a bunch of people in the two weeks we recorded there—Miranda Lambert, Luke Combs, Thomas Rhett, Kenny Chesney, just to name a few."

"Oh, I see. Name dropping so I know how famous you could've been?" I smiled and he tickled my side. I howled and he laughed.

"No. But when I heard the news I decided to make a couple calls on my way home to see if some of them might be up for a benefit at the barn before the state bulldozes it. We got a lot of press the last time, and that was just me up there. If we got some big hitters to come and perform, maybe we could tell the Robinsons' story and create true public outrage to keep the town as-is. I know Annie's tried before too, but the reach hasn't been great."

"It's a good idea, but Yolanda and Alfred were clear that the state is done negotiating, that this is a done deal."

"We'll see about that. It's not over until it's over and so far, everyone I've called says they'll come and sing. I asked them if they could come next Thursday so it won't interfere with the weddings or the Friday night showcase. We're mostly doing Mr. Robinson's songs. I'll assign a few to each act. And in between, you'll tell the story of the town."

"Who will we get to broadcast it?"

"You can just use your Instagram and add the various acts as cocreators. It'll reach their followers that way."

"I could kiss you right now," I said. And I did.

"We might need to widen the stage a bit. I'll need to talk to Fox about that."

I shook my head and looked down at Lee's chest, studying the stitching on his Braves shirt.

"Fox is leaving tomorrow. I saw Alan in front of his store. At first, I figured he was here to find you. But I guess he was in town to offer Fox a deal. Fox said it was so good he couldn't refuse. I thought you knew."

Lee chuckled, took his hat off, and tossed it into the back seat.

"Damn. That's surprising. I could've sworn Fox was a lifer. He didn't seem interested in music. I didn't even know he played 'til the other night." Lee laughed. "But I'm not surprised Alan showed up here. He probably was trying to find me. I bailed and he needs someone to take my place. Guarantee he saw that video of the two of us online and thought Fox might work to fill in. I'm betting he also wants to lure me back by offering Fox some deal he thinks I want." Lee cupped my face in his hands. "But he doesn't know me. I already have everything I want right here."

I watched his expression for a sign that he didn't really want to give everything up, that in a way my breaking up with him was an ultimatum.

"If any part of you wants to get on stage and feel the magic of a crowd chanting your name and singing your songs, you need to go," I said. "I don't want to trap you here."

Lee laughed.

"It's not like I ain't ever going to play again. You'll let me up on stage at Robinson's, right?"

I nodded.

"Well, good. Because the only person I want to hear screaming my name is you."

CHAPTER TWENTY-TWO

The sun was barely up, but Mama's twenty-year-old Apple desktop monitor with the clear blue back blared yellow light into their bedroom. Mama and Daddy were gathered in front of it, silently scrolling in their matching plaid pajamas. Only a moment ago, they'd been arguing so loudly I'd originally thought Daddy had had another episode. Which is why I was also up at this ungodly hour.

"What are y'all doing?" I rubbed my eyes and pulled the sleeves of Lee's baseball sweatshirt into my palms.

They looked at me.

"We couldn't sleep, so—" Daddy started, but Mama cut him off.

"Looking at apartments." Mama sobbed the words, then turned back toward the computer.

I walked toward them, my feet threading the old carpet. They were looking at two-bedroom apartments in Charlotte. Gleaming white quartz countertops and polished hardwood floors gave way to floor-to-ceiling windows that looked out at the city skyline. My townhouse in Charlotte was nearly identical to this one, albeit a few blocks over. I used to love waking up to that view. Now, looking at it, I felt a sort of trepidation in my heart, the same feeling I'd had about returning Merry's call, so I'd texted her instead asking if we could talk later in the week, after Lee's benefit. I knew I couldn't close that door entirely—I might need the job—but working for CLE felt wrong somehow. Maybe it was because I'd been home for a month and had reacclimated to appreciate our small town, the coziness of carpet under my feet, the little kitchen with laminate countertops, coffees on the porch while breathing in country air.

"We figure you'll want to go back home when this is all over," Daddy said. "And we won't have anywhere to go, so we'll go with you."

"It's not over yet," I said. "Lee's putting together a benefit, a big one. He got a ton of great musicians to agree to come and sing a lineup of Mr. Robinson's old songs. I'll get online and showcase the whole thing while talking about Mountain View's history between the acts. He's confident we'll be able to get enough support to save the town."

Mama shook her head. "You've got to know when to quit sometimes, Hattie."

"This could work, Mama."

She turned back to her computer like she didn't hear me. "I don't like the tub in this one," she said to Daddy and closed the window.

"We could look for new land in Pine Summit or Cardinal River," I said. "Wasn't Bobby Jo telling you the other day that Loraine mentioned the Dillards might be selling their land down across from the Cardinal River Dollar General? It's not as much acreage as we have now, just ten, but we could buy it outright I bet with the payoff money."

"Yeah, but we'd still need something to do for work," Daddy said. "We still have to eat."

"Maybe there's some land out there with a barn. We could keep the events business going."

I yawned. I could smell the coffee from the kitchen and was suddenly desperate for a mug of it.

"Let me get dressed, and I'll drive into town and see if Loraine's at the Cut & Curl. She still has her appointment on Tuesdays, right?"

Mama nodded and sighed. As the town's realtor for going on four decades, Loraine would know if any properties were about to hit the market.

"I appreciate you doing that, Hattie, but we're happy to leave altogether. Cardinal River and Pine Summit aren't Mountain View."

"I know." I looked at my parents. They didn't belong in a city. And the longer I was here, the more I started to think maybe I didn't either.

Sure enough, Loraine was at the Cut & Curl, setting her hair, her head under one of the hooded dryers. I tried to ignore the giant photo of her with her signature floral scarf on the "for sale" sign in the window across the street at Fox's. I'd hoped I might catch him on his way out of town, but I supposed he'd left earlier than I thought he would. I'd tried calling him the night before, texting too, but he hadn't responded. It was peculiar. Most people would be over the moon to have their talents realized by someone like Alan, but I knew Fox wasn't. Yet he was taking the offer anyway.

"Well, hi there, Hattie," Tammy said. She smiled at me and tapped the top of a salon chair. "You here to let me do your hair? Finally?"

"Sure," I said, knowing I'd regret it. Maybe I'd agreed because I was desperate to show everybody in the town that I was sorry. Maybe I'd agreed because I knew in a month's time, Tammy wouldn't be setting anybody's hair—at least in this town.

I sat down in the chair, and Tammy twirled me around.

"Loraine, I was actually here to see you," I said, not sure if she could hear me with the dryer going.

"You're going to look like Marilyn Monroe when I'm done with you," Tammy said, running her hands through my hair. "It was a good thing you cut that extra length off. Your hair is perfect for a wash and set now."

"What, dear?" Loraine hollered from across the room.

"I wondered if you knew of any farms on the market in Pine Summit or Cardinal River?" I shouted as Tammy guided me out of my chair and toward the sinks at the back of her store. I eyed the cold mini donut machine longingly as I sat down on the stool and tipped my head into the warm water.

"Just the one little place near the Dollar General," Loraine said. "The others called me last night asking the same question. It's a shame it's come to this."

The shampoo smelled like coconut Suave. I wasn't expecting Aveda, but I guess I figured Tammy at least used Pantene.

"I will share something with you that I didn't share with the others, though, on account of you being a relation." We weren't really relations. Loraine's former husband was Daddy's third cousin once removed, but I'd gladly take any information she'd share with me.

"What?" I asked as Tammy slathered my hair with conditioner.

"You know Virgil McKinn? That cheat over in Pine Summit?"

I only vaguely recalled the name but nodded anyway.

"Well, Mira caught him over in Cardinal River gambling at the gas station with that young woman, Dasha, yesterday. He claims he just asked her to come with him because she was there when he won big last time."

Tammy ran the water over my hair, and Loraine rolled her eyes.

"I know a Dasha, but she ain't young. Maybe early sixties, my age," Tammy said.

"Like I said, she's young," Loraine said, grinning. "Mira, Virgil, and I are all in our eighties. Anyway, Mira told Virgil last year that if she ever caught him cheating again, she was going to divorce him and sell the farm. I'm not sure if she's counting this as cheating, but if she does, that nice big farm next to the foot of the mountain in Pine Summit is liable to come on the market."

Tammy wrapped a towel around my head, then walked me to the salon chair. I knew which farm she was talking about. It was almost at the town line, right before the railroad crossing. Right next to where I'd kissed Fox. I could feel his soft lips, the bristle of his beard. I shivered and Tammy laughed.

"You okay, honey?"

I nodded.

"Will you let me know as soon as you hear? I know Mama and Daddy would like to stay around if they can," I said to Loraine.

Her lips pursed. "I know everybody thinks you're a snake for holding out on the petition, and I have a mind to think the same, except I've been in the business of land for near forty years. This here land is some of the cheapest in the whole state. They would've taken it from us no matter what." Her dryer clicked off. "I suppose I just want you to know that I don't think it's your fault. And you've come around besides."

"Thank you." I looked over at the hardware store. "Did you see Fox this morning before he left?"

"No. He must've left before the sun came up because the keys were just sitting there on the counter with my contract when I came by at eight." She shook her head. "That man was one of a kind. I don't know why he's running away from us, but I do know he's running. Maybe he don't want to watch the town go up in smoke."

My scalp pinched as Tammy rolled my hair onto the curlers. I was halfway curled when the little bell chimed on the door and Annie appeared. Despite her normal polish—her smart linen pants and perfect white blouse, her carefully applied makeup—her eyes were bloodshot and bags inflated the skin beneath. I couldn't blame her. Nearly a year of her life had been dedicated to keeping Mountain View alive, and yesterday it had been sentenced to death.

"Hi, ladies," she said cheerfully. She looked at me and her eyes narrowed in confusion. "Getting your hair done, I see?"

I grinned and nodded.

"I'm making Hattie Norwood into Mountain View's Marilyn Monroe. Just you wait," Tammy said.

"Oh, she's been our Marilyn for the past month or so now I reckon," Annie said. She laughed under her breath and walked toward me. "Anyway. I ran into Lee on my way into town. He was mowing his grass. He told me about the benefit. I think it's a great idea."

"What benefit?" Loraine asked.

As Annie told Loraine, her face brightened. Unlike my parents, she clearly thought this could work. Or maybe it was just that she had more hope than they did.

"Speaking of musicians, though, I just popped in here because I saw your daddy's truck outside and I hoped it was you," Annie said to me. Her voice lowered on the last couple words.

Tammy walked to the back to get more curlers.

"I saw something on the way into my office just now on CMT's Instagram that nearly made me faint," she went on. "Look." She held her phone toward me. The screen displayed a photo of Fox in dark washed denim and a henley walking out of a glass building in Nashville, the sunrise washing the sky pink behind him. The caption read, *Breaking! Bond Hendricks of acclaimed country folk duo Dirt Road emerges from exile and inks new writing deal with Hot Rod Records after 2019's plagiarism scandal.*

I grabbed the phone from her hand and kept reading. The walls seemed to close in. I was barely aware of Annie standing beside me chattering about the photo.

Bond, formerly one of the most prolific writers in the industry, hasn't been seen since his brother, lead singer, Phoenix Hendricks, accused him of stealing his lyrics to craft some of his most famous songwriting credits, including hit songs for performers Tommy Sutton, Jason Aldean, Kenny Chesney, and Carrie Underwood. The rift caused the dissolving of the three-time Grammy award-winning duo and the fracturing of Bond's longtime engagement to actress Helena Phillips, who wed his brother Phoenix in 2022. In a statement issued this morning, Alan Brownell, CEO of Hot Rod records, said that despite the considerable fallout from Phoenix's accusations, there has never been evidence of Bond's alleged plagiarism and that Bond is ready to resume his rightful place at the songwriting table. Brownell also claims he has new evidence to solidify Bond's innocence and is planning to release that to the public in the next week. In addition to the hundreds of songs he's penned for others, Bond is credited with the majority of Dirt Road's hits including "Snake Creek," "On and On," "My Heart Forgot," and "Where the Statue Crumbled."

I stared at the title of the last song, recalling that day in the barn when we'd danced and he'd told me about his last job, that he'd been accused of something he didn't do. I remembered after, when we were polishing the crystal and "Where the Statue Crumbled" came on. I could still hear the tension in his voice. I couldn't get to the radio fast enough to turn the song off, and he'd left. He'd left at Founder's Day too. Suddenly, it was clear to me why—he'd been hiding from Alan. He'd clearly taken up residence in Mountain View because he figured this was the last place Alan would look. The video of Lee and Fox singing had blown his cover.

Still, I couldn't figure why he needed to hide from Alan or why he hadn't simply told him no when Alan asked him to come back to Nashville. I also didn't understand why he'd kept who he was from me this whole time. Surely I was trustworthy enough. He claimed he'd been falling in love with me.

I noticed there was another picture attached to the post and swiped left. It was a photo of Dirt Road on stage at the CMT awards. Fox was clean shaven, holding his guitar, leaning into a microphone, his piercing eyes fixed on his brother, a shorter, scrawnier guy with black hair who was clearly in the middle of a roar.

I swiped right. Beards were incredible masks. He'd fashioned himself an everyday country man here in Mountain View, and we'd all believed him. I wondered if he would have come clean to me if Lee wasn't in the picture, if he would have ever told me who he really was.

"Hattie." Annie jostled my shoulder. I jumped and Tammy cursed, dropping a curler on the ground.

"I'm sorry. I didn't hear you," I said. "This is . . . this is a lot."

Annie took the phone from my hand. "We should've known he was somebody. The music and even the way he—" She stopped midsentence and looked at me in the mirror. Her cheeks flushed, just slightly.

"Kisses," I said, finishing her sentence.

Tammy gasped. "Who are y'all talking about? Don't tell me Lee's been kissing you, Annie. Now that's not okay. First he's necking with Willow, then you?"

"Not Lee," Annie said quickly. "That's Hattie's man."

Our eyes met in the mirror and she smiled.

"Just like Jet, my man from college, is mine." Annie paused. "I've been so wrapped up in town business, I haven't told many people about us trying again." She patted my shoulder. "But I did tell our friend that day you lost it in his apartment. And right before I did, he told me that he had feelings for you. But I guess his feelings went unrequited since you're back with Lee. I thought for a minute that he might break y'all up."

I swallowed hard. I wanted to tell her it was complicated, that I thought I loved them both, and Lee and I weren't back together—not officially anyway—but there was no point. Fox was gone.

"Who are y'all talking about?" Tammy rolled a curler too tight and I winced.

"Fox," Loraine said from across the room. "They're just figuring out that the boy's famous." She chuckled.

Annie whirled toward her. "How did you know?"

"I have my ways. Mainly that he had to buy property under his legal name and although he paid in cash, he still had to have the deed switched over. He swore me to secrecy and I didn't let him down. I'm the only one in town that's known this whole time."

I grabbed Annie's hand. She glanced at me, surprised.

"I'm sorry for not signing the petition."

She grinned. "You can still sign it, you know." She tapped on her phone and then handed it to me. I scrolled down to the end of the petition and typed my name, then pressed submit. "Let it be known, ladies of the Cut & Curl, fine residents of Mountain View, that as of 11:38 AM on September 21st, our town is in agreement—we don't want the stadium," Annie said in her best mayoral voice.

"But it's coming anyway." Tammy affixed the last curler in my hair and gestured for me to go to the dryers.

"Don't count us out yet," I said. "Lee's pretty lucky and he's in charge of the benefit."

"I know that's right," Loraine said from the salon chair. Tammy smoothed the flyaways from Loraine's curled set and sprayed the whole thing with about a bottle of hairspray.

I pulled the dryer over my head and flipped the switch beside me. It roared to life.

"I'm excited to see your new look, Hattie, but I've got to be going," Annie said. She chuckled as she walked out the door.

I snatched my phone out of the pocket of my jeans shorts and opened my texts.

I know who you are now, I wrote to Fox. *I wish you would've told me.*

Tears filled my eyes as I stared at the words and then pressed send. Fox was a person of integrity. I knew he hadn't passed his brother's lyrics off as his own. But that didn't matter. Clearly he'd thought his past was something I wouldn't be able to get over, that the town would never get over. He'd worked hard to hide who he was. I wondered how Alan had convinced him to step back into the role he'd left behind.

"You're done," Tammy said when the dryer buzzed.

I went back to the salon chair and Tammy started taking the curlers out.

"Oh, these are perfect," she murmured as my hair emerged from the plastic and bounced tightly against my scalp. It took everything in me not to laugh. I looked nothing like Marilyn Monroe and everything like Sophia from *The Golden Girls*. I thought about the glamorous Helena Phillips, Fox's former fiancée. She was a timeless beauty with porcelain skin and silky black hair who had played badass spies, history's leading ladies, and rom-com love interests. I blinked at my reflection in the mirror, wondering how in the world he'd fallen for me.

"All you need now is a silky white dress and a strong wind." Tammy grinned, and I started laughing.

Tammy sobered and looked at me in the mirror. "It's been a long time coming, but you're finally home, ain't you?"

I fluffed my hair.

"Yeah, I suppose I am."

CHAPTER TWENTY-THREE

Luke Combs was on stage. I wasn't in the barn. In fact, I was about an acre away in my house, standing in my kitchen guzzling iced coffee while Lee, Johnny Law, Daisy Foley, and the latter two's bands were crammed in my living room hiding from the thousands on the lawn. The singing from the crowd was near deafening, even inside. I couldn't figure if it was because of the alcohol—I'd asked two breweries I'd worked with in Charlotte, Wooden Robot and Unknown, to serve drinks since I knew I'd be outnumbered and too busy today—or because at least half of the guests hailed from small towns around Mountain View and had never seen their country music heroes in real life.

I took a long drag of caffeine from my straw and sighed. It had been a long, wonderful day already, and it wasn't even half over. Miranda Lambert, who'd had to be back in Nashville by this evening, had been the first act on stage at eleven, but people had started pouring onto the farm at eight. By the time Miranda arrived at nine, a few hundred people had already crammed into the barn.

The news crews had started arriving at ten. I'd had WBTV from Charlotte and WYFF out of Greenville and WCSC from Columbia set up in various corners of the barn. They'd been broadcasting segments live all day. They'd also interviewed me several times about Mountain View's history and about the Robinsons. I'd been polished and articulate until the end of Kenny Chesney's set, when I happened to hear Miranda and Kenny singing a duet of Mr. Robinson's "Sing Me Home to Carolina." He'd written the song after he'd established Mountain View, when his fame was dwindling, and I didn't know anyone really knew it. I'd started crying in the middle of my interview with WBTV's Caroline Jordan, and to my surprise, she started crying too. The interview ended with a plea to viewers to help save Mountain View.

"Hat," Lee called from Daddy's La-Z-Boy. He was leaned back, his gray shirt still saturated from his singing backup for Thomas Rhett, his jeans just rumpled up enough by the recliner's footrest to display the custom Tecova boots Alan had gifted him for the Tommy Sutton tour. Daddy—who was selling tickets under a tent we'd set up by the road—would be none too happy to realize somebody other than him was sitting in his chair.

"Yeah?" I asked, setting my coffee down on the counter and walking over. Every inch of the living room floor was covered by somebody. Only the headlining artists got the furniture, apparently. Johnny and Daisy sat side by side on the couch.

"Excuse me," I said to a drummer. You could tell the drummers from the guitar players because they were typically more disheveled.

"We're out of here the minute we quit playing, right?" the drummer said to me. He pushed overgrown red bangs back from his eyes.

"Yep," I said. "Your driver will pull your bus around to the side of the barn like we've done with the others, and we've kept a path clear for y'all out to the road."

"Okay, thanks. I forgot a change of underwear."

I stared at him.

"I sweat when I play and if there was a lady or two..."

My nose scrunched, and I stepped over a few other musicians to get to Lee, who was laughing with Johnny and Daisy as though he'd known them forever. He'd only been in Nashville for a few weeks, a part of the country music community for less than a month total, and yet he'd made such an impression on country's biggest stars that they'd been willing to come to Mountain View at his request. His instant belonging wasn't lost on me. It was a part of the reason I hadn't been able to stay in the barn. Every time he got on stage, every time the music brightened his face, guilt arrested my mind.

"They don't believe me about Bond, that we had no idea who he was," Lee said, laughing. I forced a smile in an attempt to match their hilarity, but that's the best I could do. In the days since Fox left and we'd found out, I'd tried to reach out to him, but he hadn't returned a single text or call. I had so many questions in the wake of his absence. I'd wanted to google him to find out the answers about the plagiarism controversy, about his upbringing, about his rise to fame, about Helena, about why he'd left us, but couldn't. Despite him lying to me about who he was, going behind his back to find the answers felt like a betrayal. The truth was—I was having a hard time accepting he was really gone.

"We didn't," I said to Daisy. "Promise."

Lee pulled me onto his lap and wrapped his arms around me, enveloping me in sweat. I turned around and kissed him. I'd kissed him as often as I could today, hoping to dissolve the way I'd woken with the echo of Fox's mouth on mine in my dreams. Maybe I was dreaming about him because he hadn't left Mountain View happily and I wanted to know why he'd really gone. I suppose that sort of thing counted as the unfinished business psychologists always claimed visited your subconscious.

Lee had thought I was crazy when I mentioned that Fox seemed upset to go. He'd said that he was likely always planning on returning someday and was probably just irritated at how quickly Alan had asked him to step in. But he didn't know Fox like I did. To someone like Lee, someone meant for bright lights, not wanting to return to the stage at all seemed unfathomable. Lee might have decided to stay in Mountain View, but his mindset hadn't changed, not really anyway. I wondered if I could live with fame lying dormant in the bed with us.

"How? He's a legend," Johnny said. "I bet the guy couldn't even walk to his mailbox in Nashville without being hounded. Especially after the scandal." Johnny clearly took his name seriously, very obviously trying to mimic Johnny Cash. His hair was dyed black and his outfit matched his hair.

"I guess he didn't look like himself, and we don't get many celebrities in Mountain View . . . well, until recently," I said.

"You've always had Leland Lockhardt." Daisy gave a flirty little side smile at Lee. She looked like a hippie version of Carrie Underwood. Lee squeezed my thigh.

"Yeah, well, I'm different. Nobody's famous in their hometown," Lee said. "If I start acting the least bit conceited, somebody like Vern is going to remind me about something embarrassing like the Little League season where I got in my head about striking out and refused to swing. Or the time I got caught in the concession stand eating through a box of Fun Dips." Lee laughed. "That's why I love it here."

"Sorry to interrupt, Hattie." Johnny's guitar player materialized behind the La-Z-Boy, his guitar in hand. He had a Willie Nelson braid and a black leather vest on with nothing underneath to match the whole man-in-black theme of the band. "Is there any place I can go practice a second? This is a new guitar and the tuning sounds off."

"Sure." I rose from Lee's lap, but he pulled me back to him and kissed me again quickly, then let me go. "Right over here." I stepped around the group of Daisy's backup singers in matching Silkie flower dresses and opened the door to my parents' bedroom. Mama and Daddy weren't exactly keen on inviting guests into their room, but I didn't really have a choice. You could barely walk across the floor of my room. Extra extension cords and liquor bottles and heavy plastic cocktail glasses had been taken out of the barn and moved to my room for storage.

"You can play in here as long as you need to." I pulled my phone out of my pocket and looked at the time. "But I'll need to escort y'all down to the barn in half an hour or so. You'll hang out in the suite upstairs until Luke's done."

"Thanks," he said.

Out of the corner of my eye, I noticed a pile of laundry on the floor next to Mama's side of the bed and walked toward it while the guitar player set up on the couch at the foot of the bed. Mama would be horrified if somebody saw her underwear—or as she called them, her unmentionables.

"Bond was definitely blacklisted at first." Johnny's voice came from outside the door where I'd left Lee. "Phoenix was pretty convincing that Bond had stolen his lyrics. I guess it didn't really take much, though, when I think about it. Phoenix was always more of a celebrity, I guess. But his celebrity was really all Alan's doing. You know how he likes to make caricatures out of his musicians. Phoenix had that pizzazz he likes. Bond was sort of thought of as the support when it came to Dirt Road, but he was definitely better than Phoenix when it came to songwriting. Had about the best track record in town, actually. Everybody wanted his songs. Until the news broke and then nobody did." He paused.

My hand stilled on the pile of Mama's clothes as the guitar player tuned one string after another.

"I'm just glad Alan had the decency to release those videos of Bond in the writing studio and clear things up. I can't believe Phoenix just issued a public apology and went off to his house in the Bahamas. Changes how I feel about him, for sure."

I wondered what videos they were talking about. In my refusal to google Fox, I hadn't seen anything about it.

"Damn," Lee said.

"I mean, there were always whispers that Phoenix was full of crap. Some people said he might've accused Bond because he wanted to ruin his career so that he wouldn't have the net worth Helena required—which was supposedly equal to or more than hers. Apparently after Helena cheated on Bond with Phoenix, she tried to get Bond back and people thought maybe Phoenix accused him in retaliation," Johnny shrugged. "I thought that was too far-fetched to be true, but now I'm not so sure."

My heart seized. I could hear Fox's voice that day in the hardware store, the determination that he wouldn't love someone that couldn't love him back again. I leaned down to pick up the laundry, and my hair fell in my face, the overbearing scent of four washes of Pantene consuming me. It had taken that much to undo Tammy's Marilyn Monroe style.

"That doesn't seem far-fetched, actually. I met Helena once a few years back when Phoenix did a solo showcase at the Opry," Daisy said. "She's . . . how do I put this nicely? She's materialistic and shallow. I mean, I like nice things too, but the one time we talked she just kept going on and on about how Phoenix couldn't find the right canary diamond she wanted for her first anniversary ring and complained that he couldn't get them in to *Vanity Fair*'s Oscar party. I couldn't figure out why it was all on him. She has the sources to find the diamonds and the connections to get in to the fancy parties. She just wants her man to treat her like she's some ordinary girl he picked up in town."

"That doesn't sound like someone Fox, I mean Bond, would go for," Lee said.

Johnny laughed. "You haven't seen her in person. She's hot in movies, right? But she's even hotter in real life. She might actually be the hottest person walking on this earth."

Johnny kept going on and on about Helena's finer attributes as I stood in the doorway with Mama's dirty clothes. I looked down at my legs. I didn't work out, not really. I was skinny, sure, but I wasn't toned all over. And I didn't wear much makeup, and my breasts were small. I glanced at the back of Lee's head, suddenly questioning how I was perceived. Sure, I was pretty in a small-town way. But compared to the glamor of celebrity women, I doubted I could hold a candle. I forced the critical thoughts from my mind, closed the bedroom door, and started past the living room toward the laundry closet.

"Rumor has it Bond's slumming it at Tommy Sutton's while he looks for a place," Daisy said.

"He knows Tommy like that?" I heard Lee ask as I opened the closet door and jammed the clothes into the empty washing machine.

"Yeah. He's written at least seventy-five percent of his catalog."

"That blows my mind," Lee said as I walked back toward him. Behind the TV, Mama's bird clock chirped five. Luke's set would be over in twenty minutes.

"Johnny, y'all need to head down in fifteen minutes or so," I said, sitting down on the arm of the La-Z-Boy next to Lee.

"Yeah. I got it." Johnny looked at Lee and winked.

"What?" I asked. "What's that?"

Lee cleared his throat.

"Nothing really. I just asked Johnny if I could play a song by myself right before they go on." His eyes met mine, and then he looked away. Johnny kept grinning at him like he knew some secret I didn't. I didn't like surprises when it came to events. It disrupted the flow and could completely throw off a timeline. But I could hardly tell Lee no. His band wasn't here. They were off touring in Europe without him, so he hadn't wanted to do his own set. The least I could do was allow him the chance for one song.

"Which song?"

"It's a surprise," he said. "Come watch me?"

I nodded, and he grabbed my hand and pulled me toward his chest. His other hand looped around the back of my head, his fingers in my hair.

"I love you more than this whole world. You know that, right?" he whispered, his blue eyes on mine. His breath smelled like Dubble Bubble. He'd chewed the same gum since Little League.

"I love you too." I leaned in and kissed him.

Daisy whistled behind us. "I hope y'all keep that going when you get back to Nashville," she said. "Don't let the bright lights change you."

My lips broke from Lee's, but before I could ask what she was talking about, Lee responded.

"We ain't going back to Nashville." His gaze didn't break from mine. "I dissolved my contract last week. We're staying right here."

"What? You didn't tell me that," Johnny said. "I mean, I knew you were taking a break from the tour because of what's going on in Mountain View, but I didn't know you were done all together. Was Alan that angry about you bailing on Sutton?"

Lee glanced at Johnny. "He wasn't happy about it, but he wasn't going to cancel my contract either. That was all me. I just don't want it anymore."

Johnny shook his head. "Man, that's bullshit. I just watched you play with Miranda and Thomas. You love it."

Lee's face tightened. He only looked like that when he was called out by the truth. My heart dropped into my stomach. I hadn't asked him to stay here, to give up his dream for me.

Lee looked at the clock on the wall. "I've got to go down and play my song," he said to me. "Come on."

I suddenly felt like I was about to vomit.

"Johnny, I'll send my friend Rocky up to escort y'all to the barn in a few minutes," I said. Johnny nodded. "Don't forget your guitar player. He's in my parents' bedroom." I tipped my head back toward the door behind me.

We got up, and Lee kept hold of my hand as we wandered around the musicians on the living room floor and out the front door. The field was crammed with lawn chairs, and Luke's voice belting "Golden Sky" bellowed over the guests' singing. The air smelled like beer and kettle corn.

I glanced over at the vendors set up on the drive, their lines some two dozen deep, as we wove through the maze of people toward the barn.

Some people shrieked as Lee passed by and snatched at his free hand, at his jeans, at his T-shirt. Each time, he'd turn and smile but kept moving. Friendly but not familiar. He carried himself the way fame had taught him. It was like second nature.

By the time we reached the side entrance to the barn, Vern was directing Luke's tour bus our way, and the final notes of his set echoed over the crowd.

I followed Lee into the barn, immediately struck with the heat of four hundred bodies packed like sardines in front of the stage.

"Hey," I said to Rocky, who was standing beside the stairs to the stage in his reflector vest. He was taking his role as security guard very seriously and had their son Clay's fake pistol in a holster around his waist. Never mind that each act had brought their own security detail. Luke's actual bodyguard, a man who'd make Fox look like an ant, was standing behind the stairs looking bored.

Luke walked off the stage, and I turned to say thank you about the same time Lee did. Then he disappeared out the door. Lee thanked the rest of Luke's band as they departed, and I asked Rocky if he'd go up and get Johnny and his band from the house.

"I will as long as I can stay upstairs with them while they're up there with Dolly," he said. Dolly was helping keep snacks and drinks stocked in the bridal suite, aka our green room. "My baby's sexy and those men are liable to notice."

"Yeah, sure," I said. It was kind of cute, Rocky being jealous. To his credit, Dolly had been a loud fan of Johnny Law's since his debut album seven years ago, and although I knew she'd never cross the line, she might swoon a little in his presence.

Rocky left and Lee scaled the steps to the stage with his guitar. People whistled—girls screamed—and he pushed his hair back from his face, pulled the stool over from the side of the stage, and started to play. I knew the song immediately. It was one of Mr. Robinson's old ones.

I pushed my way into the crowd. It smelled awful, like B.O. and beer sweat, but I'd told Lee I'd watch him and wanted a better view than the side of the stage. His eyes followed me, and when I stopped in front of him, he smiled.

"This song has always been one of my favorites of Mr. Robinson's, and about a month ago I realized it had stayed with me for a reason," Lee said into the microphone.

He strummed the guitar, the gorgeous old simple melody silencing the chatter in the barn.

> I lost you
> The light of my life, I lost you
> To gather the stars, it cost you
> and I fell from the sky 'cause I lost me
> Without you I knew that I lost me
> I was alone and blue, and I lost me.

Goosebumps pricked my skin. Emotion strained his voice. The loneliness mentioned in the song made me think of Fox as Lee played the interlude. A dull ache washed through me. Fox was alone—at least I figured he was—in Tommy Sutton's big mansion, and something wasn't right.

Someone in the crowd yelled, "I love you, Lee!"

His gaze broke from mine for just a moment, and he grinned at the fan and waved. Then his eyes met mine once again.

> I love you
> The girl of my dreams, I love you
> Where you are is heaven, I love you
> and I know it because you love me
> You could have all of the world, but you love me
> Let us never part 'cause you love me.

The song wasn't over, but he put his guitar down, grabbed the microphone from its holder, and walked to the edge of the stage.

"Will you come up here?" he asked me.

I nodded, but I couldn't figure what he was wanting me to do. Maybe he wanted to dance. That's what the Robinsons did sometimes if Mr. Robinson needed a break from playing.

I pushed through the crush and scaled the steps to the stage. When I got there, the crowd started cheering. Lee took my hand. His fingers were shaking.

"What are we doing?" I whispered, but he smiled and dropped to his knee.

I gasped. His thumb brushed over my knuckles. Everything around me dulled—the noise, the smells, the song in my head. His free hand went to his pocket and he extracted an enormous emerald cut diamond.

I'd dreamed of this moment for over a decade, but in all of my dreams we'd been alone—in Mr. Robinson's truck, in Lee's pool, floating down Cardinal River.

"Hat. I should've done this years ago. But we're here now and . . . I've loved you forever and I'm going to keep loving you forever. Nothing in this world makes sense without you." He paused and for a moment, I thought he might stand up. "Will you marry me?"

The crowd was dead silent. Lee smiled at me and I grinned at him. My body surged with want, my heart surged with love, but my soul whispered no.

"Yes," I said, but the word landed wrong inside, like I'd spoken out of turn. "I love you." In less than a second, my voice was eclipsed by cheers and screams so loud I couldn't make sense of what had just happened. Lee pushed the ring on my finger, drew me close, and kissed me deeply.

"Come on," he said when his lips broke from mine. He waved to the crowd and clasped my hand with his other. "Johnny Law's up next," Lee shouted as I followed him down the stairs.

At the foot of the stairs, he turned right, into the shadow of the stairwell leading up to the loft, pulled me close, and kissed me again.

"You're going to be mine forever," he whispered against my lips. My whole body tingled with his touch and I closed my eyes. This. This right here was where he should have proposed. "I told Johnny a few days ago that I wanted to ask you and he gave me the idea to sing to you."

I stepped out of his hands, his words startling me awake. This was why saying yes had felt wrong. I placed my palm on his chest, and Lee grinned at me.

"I said yes up there because I love you, but I can't marry you."

I started crying, and Lee clutched my hand.

"What?"

"I've watched you all day and I've listened. You're trying your hardest to make us enough for you, to make this little town enough for you, but it's not and it won't ever be. I won't trap you here."

"Hat, you're not."

I was sobbing, my chest heaving, and he wrapped his arms around me and held me close. He touched me often, he hugged me plenty, but never like this. The last time I'd felt this kind of embrace, the sensation of being completely absorbed into someone else, I'd been in Fox's arms. His face that last day materialized in my mind. I'd thought it best to keep my feelings in, but standing here, it was clear how much of my heart I'd given away.

"You're not trapping me here," Lee whispered in my hair. "And you're always enough. If we decide that we want to move to Nashville someday, we can do that. And if this benefit doesn't work, we'll have to go somewhere, but I want to go with you."

"I don't know what will happen here." I tipped my chin against his chest to look at him. "But what I do know is that I'm going to stay. I won't leave Mama and Daddy, and I know I can do great things here." I swallowed hard, feeling the tears streaming down my cheeks. "But you . . . Lee, you come to life on that stage. You belong there. And you belong in Tennessee." I gestured toward the stage. The crowd roared as Johnny and his band started playing. "You were only in the industry for a month and look how quickly you built these relationships. These people were willing to travel to the middle of nowhere to play just because they knew you."

Lee squinted and sniffed before he looked away from me.

"Mountain View might be gone in a month," he said finally. "And you're telling me that even if it is, you won't consider Nashville with me?"

My mind reeled with his question. I didn't quite understand why I couldn't say that I would. He pulled away from me a little and lifted my chin to his face. His eyes bore into mine.

"You don't love me anymore."

I shook my head.

"That's not true. I'm always going to love you."

"No," he whispered. "That night before I left for Nashville, you still loved me. I know you, body and soul, Hat. Your heart was mine, all mine, and my heart was yours. We were so in love that we slept holding hands, remember?"

I started crying again and nodded.

"But the day I came back from Europe, the first thing you did when you saw me was hide." His voice broke. "I knew it. I knew deep down in my soul that I'd lost you, that something had happened while I was gone, but I wouldn't believe it."

"I didn't mean to." The idea that I was about to lose Lee over my love for a man who'd gone, a man who'd covered up who he really was, made my knees weak. "I thought you were leaving for good."

"I didn't say I blamed you," he said. "It's my fault. I left and you thought it was just like the last time. You gave up on me and I deserved it." He sniffed. "And now I've . . . I guess I've got to find a way to live without you."

Suddenly, it occurred to me that I could be making a huge mistake. I'd loved Lee my whole life.

"Could you wait? Could you just stay a while? I think I'm confused. I just need time, I . . ."

Lee grinned despite his tears.

"Aw, Hat. It ain't going to change. The love we had was the forever kind, the kind that endures time and distance and lust. I think the only way it can break is if something equally as strong comes along and snaps it in two. After that, I don't think it can ever be the same."

I tipped my head into his shoulder and cried.

"I'm always going to love you." I could feel his words in the rumble of his chest, and I looked at him.

"I love you, Lee."

He didn't tell me to take it back this time, but instead, leaned down and kissed me slow. I felt it all—every movement of his lips, the way his tongue brushed mine, the way he tasted, the way he knew how to make my body come alive.

"I'm going to go now," he whispered after.

"No." I panicked and clung to him like a toddler being left at preschool for the first time. He took a step, but I wrapped my arms around him and grabbed the back of his shirt.

"Hat. You're going to have to let me. It ain't fair and you know it."

I stepped away from him. I let my hands drop to my sides, and then, remembering, I reached to my left hand and started to pull the ring off. He stopped me.

"I don't want it," he said. "Keep it or sell it. But if you keep it, let it remind you that I love you more than you can imagine and that no matter what, to me, you'll always be my girl."

I swallowed a sob.

"Okay."

He hesitated. I thought he might kiss me again. But he just wiped his eyes, then walked out the back door of the barn, leaving me without him, turning the ring on my finger.

CHAPTER TWENTY-FOUR

Nothing deterred a South Carolina mosquito. Not citronella or lavender or eucalyptus. Not even DEET, my current chemical of choice. I slapped my arm, smooshing a cluster of the buzzing, blood-sucking insects.

I turned toward the cushions on the wicker couch, the sun's warmth on my back. I pushed the old outdoor pillow covered in the faded flamingo print under my head and tried to close my eyes again, ignoring the fact that the minute I did, at least fifty mosquitos would land on me. I was tired and grumpy, and nothing really helped that except for a nap on the porch in the sunshine.

It had been a long week. Lee was gone. He'd left to rejoin the tour the minute he walked off the farm. I'd tried my best to keep my mind off his proposal, the way he'd looked in the shadows, the way him leaving had crushed me as though I'd been the one doing the leaving. I didn't know if I'd made the right choice. A part of me would always love him. But I also felt the truth of what he'd said—that this time, things were different. This time, I was sad, but it wasn't all consuming. I'd even half-forgotten about the proposal until people showed up on Friday night and started asking about my ring. I hadn't been able to take it off. It wasn't that I'd changed my mind, but every time I thought to pull it off my finger and put it away, an image of our home being bulldozed popped into my mind. I didn't quite understand what that was about, but maybe now that I was about to lose my physical home, my mind was reminding me that I could get through it, that the place my heart had called home for so long had changed too.

That change had been obvious in the hour after Lee left. I'd rushed to the house as Daisy took the stage, locked myself in my room, and called Fox. Of course he didn't answer, but my heart had raced with each ring all the same. When Lee had said that something had shifted when he'd gone to Nashville, he was right. For the first time in my life I'd fallen in love with someone else. Someone who now refused to talk to me.

In the days after the benefit, I thought Fox might reach out, but he didn't. Coverage of the concert and of Mr. Robinson and of the state's plans to obliterate Robinson's historic town had spread far and wide, even prompting discussion on *The Today Show* and *GMA*. Everybody seemed to agree that the town should be spared. My phone hadn't stopped ringing since Daisy's tour bus took off down Route 2. Even Merry had called to congratulate me on a great event, and I'd had the courage to tell her, after she'd offered me my job back, that I'd only take her up on it if the worst happened, if the stadium was built. She said she'd wait to hire anyone new for another month and would keep my townhouse ready for my return until I said the word.

Annie was thrilled with the attention, and we'd all been pretty optimistic—until this morning. Mr. Brantley had paid us a visit just as the sun was coming up. Mama had seen him getting out of his car just as she was pouring her cup of Folger's. His pressed khakis were rumpled and his shirt was stained. When he finally made it to our front door, Daddy answered and asked him in, but he refused.

I'd pushed around Daddy and talked Mr. Brantley into sitting down for a cup of coffee. When we'd finally settled around our kitchen table, Mr. Brantley had taken a sip from Mama's prized Minnie Mouse mug and started talking.

"Y'all have whipped up quite a stir," he'd said. "I understand what you're doing, but I liked you better when you were for the build." He'd attempted a laugh, but it wasn't one really.

"That was before there were plans to knock down our home, the home of a legend," I said. "And when that happened, I realized I was wrong to side with y'all. This town is the Robinsons', and they would've wanted it to remain like it is. I thought all along that innovation required big change, but that's not true." I'd waved my hand toward the windows. "We've turned a barren farm into a thriving events venue. Mountain View can revive itself in a way that's organic to its origin."

"I'm sorry to say it's going to be reborn as the home of the Carolina Panthers whether y'all want it to be or not," he'd said.

Daddy had started to argue with him, but he'd interrupted.

"I've been sent up here to ask y'all to let things go," he'd said. "Because my hands are tied. So are my boss's. The state ruled on the build and it's going ahead now." He'd paused then. "Take these next couple weeks and say your goodbyes."

Mama had started crying like Mr. Brantley was talking about a person. In a way, he was. I'd pushed back from the table and walked outside. My hands had been shaking, my heart pounding, as I looked over the barn and the sunken truck and the field gleaming in the sunlight. It had no idea of its fate.

I'd called Annie immediately, and she'd said nothing as I told her the news. Then I'd texted Lee to tell him. He'd worked so hard to help and it was only fair. He'd responded the way he always had. He'd asked me if I wanted him to come home. The sentence shattered me. Lee knew it was hopeless now. He was asking me if he should come home for the town's funeral, for our love's funeral. I'd told him no.

I kept my eyes closed and slapped my thigh, hoping to dispel the prickle of a mosquito's snout. Inside, I could hear Mama and Daddy arguing. Most of the other families were planning to stay around, to buy whatever they could find in Pine Summit or Cardinal River, even as far as Clover. Daddy was of that mind and thought that even if the farm was gone, we needed to stay here with our community, that we needed to buy a farm with a barn so we could continue with Robinson's Events. Mama, on the other hand, wanted to leave entirely. She was concerned that without this particular land and barn our business wouldn't really prosper. She was worried about my future.

I didn't have an opinion. Maybe it was because I'd gotten used to my future being in limbo or maybe it was because I'd held to the wrong opinion for far too long but, right now, I couldn't think straight to figure out what was best.

A throat cleared behind me.

"Uh, Hattie? I hate to disturb you."

I sat up, knocking my phone off the cushion beside me. It landed with a thud on the wood porch slats in front of Grady Armstrong wearing the Leland Lockhardt uniform—jeans, a T-shirt, and a trucker hat. He picked my phone up.

"Here you go."

"Thanks. You sounded good at the barn the other week," I said.

Grady was the grandson of Kay and Bowen Armstrong, who owned the farm across the river from ours in Cardinal River. When I went off to college, he was in fourth grade. Now he was a college graduate and a musician too, apparently. He'd played four solo songs a few Fridays ago, alternating between singing, guitar, fiddle, and piano. It was impressive.

"Yeah, thanks. I've been working on it." He glanced behind him and his grandparents materialized around the corner of the house. I hadn't seen them in at least a decade, maybe two. I didn't realize they were that much older than my parents, but they were clearly in their later eighties. For as close as Cardinal River was, Cardinal River and Mountain View truly operated as separate communities. "About my playing—"

"Hi there, Hattie," Mr. Armstrong said. He was using a cane and wore a worn plaid shirt under his overalls. Mrs. Armstrong's arm was looped through his, and she smiled at me.

"We were driving past on our way into Clover for the Walmart and thought this was as good of a time as any to tell y'all what we've decided," Mrs. Armstrong said. She spoke loudly and her voice wobbled a little.

"She won't use hearing aids," Grady explained.

"I guess you tell her, Grady. We've decided, but it's right hard for me to say it out loud," Mr. Armstrong said. He gripped the edge of the bottom railing. I thought at first he might come up, but the two of them remained on the gravel walkway.

"Well, after I played that night at the barn, I got a call from a woman named Jackie Fowler who's a scout for a small label," he said. "After a lot of talking, I signed a contract to record with her, and I'm moving to Tennessee on the first."

"Congratulations," I said. "That's wonderful, Grady. I didn't have any idea anyone like that was in the crowd that night."

He shrugged. "That's the point of scouts, I guess. She said she didn't introduce herself because she didn't want to spoil the spirit of the night with business. Anyway."

He looked back at his grandparents.

"Since I'm going, and Mama and Daddy . . . well, my parents are gone, MawMaw and PawPaw think it's time for them to move down the road to Pine Summit to make good on that deposit they put down at the retirement home."

"I'm excited about it," Mrs. Armstrong warbled. "Maryanna and Bill are down there, Ruth and Lincoln too. They get three meals a day, all the dessert you want, happy hours and bingo and crafts and field trips."

"It's practically Dollywood," Mr. Armstrong said.

"We're getting a lot of target spot on the soybeans and the land's getting tired anyway," Grady said. "When we heard the news about the state bulldozing this place, we were mighty upset. And then over the course of last week, after my contract came in and we realized MawMaw and PawPaw were moving anyway, we thought maybe we could help."

Mama and Daddy's voices were rising inside, their disagreement reaching a fever pitch.

"You know we got five hundred and seventy acres, right?"

I nodded.

"Well, we read up on it, and the stadium and parking lots require five hundred even. So, this morning, we called down to Columbia and formally offered our land to the state for the stadium for free."

"What?"

I stared at Grady and then at the Armstrongs. They were beaming.

"But it's your land. Y'all have been farming it near as long as the Robinsons. And anyway, wouldn't the state have already checked your place out when they were looking for land in Cardinal River originally?"

"Not really. We're the largest producers in town right now. They passed over us pretty quickly not realizing what Grady knows about the crops," Mr. Armstrong said. "They'll figure out it's going down the tubes when they test the land, though."

"They won't run into the same issues they had with that other tract," Grady went on. "We ain't got an abundance of clay or anything."

"And as far as the land goes, we're ready to leave it. The foundation on the house is cracked and sinking and sooner or later it'll be torn down. And our land is just land. We were planning on leaving it anyway," Mrs. Armstrong said.

"I can't believe it." Tears filled my eyes, and I flung my arms around Grady and then walked down the stairs and hugged the Armstrongs too.

"Now, we don't know if they'll take our offer since there ain't much convenient land around ours for extra parking lots and it's a little further from the train station," Mrs. Armstrong said when I stepped out of her arms. "But we're praying the state will take it anyway. They'll save millions in payouts if they do. Plus, Cardinal River has changed much more than Mountain View over the years. It's got the Dollar General now and that Pizza Inn on the border that everybody seems to love. Mayor Lee was starting to get excited about the stadium before they pulled the plug."

"Y'all are angels on earth."

Generosity always took me off guard. The general belief seemed to be that people were good, but this good? It had been the same with Lee and with Fox, only the Armstrongs were offering their entire livelihoods to help us.

"No. We've come to understand that Mountain View is like our home too, and if we ain't going to use our land we might as well try to protect the neighbors we love," Mr. Armstrong said. "It was 'cause of y'all that Grady achieved his dream and then when I fell off the plow back in March and broke my hip, y'all's handyman came and helped Grady plow the last three hundred and seed too. Told me I couldn't give him a dime. That there's a neighbor."

Deep longing swept through me. Of course Fox had gone to help the Armstrongs. Of course he'd done it for free, expecting nothing in return. He gave love out the same way, even knowing he wouldn't receive it back.

I eyed Daddy's truck and then looked at Grady. "Do y'all have a second to go in and tell Mama and Daddy what you told me?"

"Yeah, sure," Grady said. "That okay with you, PawPaw?"

He nodded and so did Mrs. Armstrong.

I clutched Mr. Armstrong's hand. "We'll never be able to thank y'all enough. Even if it doesn't work."

I smiled at Grady and started toward the truck.

"Will you tell my parents I'll be home late tonight, maybe tomorrow morning? That I'll call them? I have to go somewhere."

CHAPTER TWENTY-FIVE

It was dark by the time I pulled on to his street. I pushed a Lifesaver mint into my mouth and glanced at my reflection in the rearview mirror. I didn't look my best. In fact, I looked like I'd been out working on the farm all day, but if I'd delayed at all, I wouldn't have come. I sniffed my sundress, hoping it didn't smell like the sour cream and chive gas station chips I'd bought somewhere around Knoxville.

It had occurred to me, when I'd pulled off the interstate to get gas, that I had no real idea where I was going. It wasn't like Tommy Sutton advertised where he lived. I couldn't text Lee. That wasn't fair. So I'd texted Daisy. Within a few minutes, she'd texted back with the address.

The road was completely dark and wove up a mountain, through a practical forest. Daddy's truck sighed as it shifted into a new gear.

"Sorry," I said as though it could hear me. Daddy would never forgive me if I killed his beloved truck.

There was a chance she'd sent me the wrong address. There hadn't been a light for miles and the road kept going up, my GPS indicating that the address was still a distance away.

Suddenly, the trees cleared a bit and the road dead-ended into a huge metal gate. My headlights shined beyond it, through the slats and over a manicured lawn with a fountain to a sprawling Mediterranean mansion. There were a few lights on, but most of the house was dark. He might not be home.

I noticed a call box on the side of the gate, so I rolled down the window and pushed the button.

"Yes?"

The sound of his voice nearly broke me. I hesitated. What if he wouldn't let me in? What if he was in there with another woman?

"Fox? It's me. It's Hattie. I . . . I need to see you." My tone was breathy and uncertain.

He didn't say anything for a few long seconds.

"Okay." A shrill note sounded in the night, disturbing the crickets and the intermittent owls, and the gate opened.

My heart was racing, my hands sweating, as I drove the truck around to the front of the house. When I was a few feet from the door, I caught the sparkle on my left hand, the ring I hadn't been able to remove. I stopped the truck, shut off the ignition, and looked at the ring one last time.

"Goodbye, Lee," I whispered, and then pulled the diamond off and put it in Daddy's glove box.

I climbed out of the truck and started toward the front doors. They were at least fifteen feet tall, made of thick beveled glass. It was dark behind the panes. I suddenly had an urge to turn back, to run toward the cab and leave before he could reject me. My body quaked with nerves.

I reached for the doorbell, a round ruby clutched in a gilded lion's mouth, but before I could press it, the door opened.

He had shaved—well, mostly, a little stubble had grown back—and he was wearing sweatpants and a T-shirt, something I'd never seen him wear in his whole time in Mountain View. But he was still Fox. His eyes found mine and stayed. I waited for them to soften, for him to take me into his arms, but he didn't.

"What are you doing here?"

"Can I come in?"

He nodded, then stepped aside to let me through. The place smelled like a luxury hotel, like gardenias, and the ceilings in the foyer towered over us, finished in dark wooden beams. It felt strange to see him in a place like this, unnatural almost, like a lion in a zoo. But then, I knew the hardware store owner, not the star.

He walked through an arched doorway, and I followed into an enormous living room with a huge limestone fireplace on one end and an arched colonnade down the length of the room. A black grand piano was situated next to the fireplace, and a glass of whisky sat on a side table next to one end of a gray couch that faced a matching one.

Fox gestured to the couch opposite the one he had clearly just been occupying, as if I was a business acquaintance and he was about to conduct a meeting. I sat down on the cushion, and he sat across from me, his fingers immediately seeking the glass.

The only lights on were two floor lamps on either end of the room and his face was washed in shadows. He took a small sip of whisky, then set it down.

"Do you want a drink?"

His voice was strange.

"No." The one word was all I could muster. Otherwise, I would cry. I thought of the last day I'd seen him in the hardware store, the way he'd looked at me, the way my heart had gone to him. That man wasn't the one sitting in front of me.

"Then what do you want?" He sat back.

I couldn't answer him. Everything my mind came up with refused to make its way out of my mouth.

"I saw the video. I know you and Lee are engaged, so I know you ain't here for me." He took another long drink. "And if you're here to ask me to come sing for Mountain View, Hattie, I can't."

"We're not engaged." Maybe it was the sound of my name on his lips that forced me to speak. I could hardly stand it, sitting here like this, feet away from him.

His gaze stayed on mine, but it didn't change with my news.

"I said yes for the cameras, but I couldn't. I couldn't because I love you, and I should have never let you leave." Emotion caught the end of my sentence, but he didn't get up or reply. "Why did you leave? I know you didn't want to."

He looked down. "Because I had to," he said. "Alan threatened to tell the town who I was and what I was accused of doing if I didn't come back and write Tommy's next album. I used to write all of his songs and his last album sort of tanked without me. Alan's lost a lot of money." Fox shrugged. "He said he had video of me in my studio at his office writing the songs Phoenix accused me of stealing and that in exchange for me coming back, he'd send the footage around and clear my name." He paused. "I asked him why he was just now coming forward with it if he'd had it the whole time, and he said he'd found it recently when he and the security guys were clearing out memory. I didn't buy it. I think the controversy with Phoenix made our album sales spike and made him richer. I don't think he thought I'd up and disappear on him, though. Anyway. I left because I didn't want Alan to ruin what I had in Mountain View."

He took another sip.

"I thought once I left town, nobody in Mountain View would be able to figure out who I really was. I was going to stop here and shave first, then head into the studio and sign the paperwork, but the minute I got to town, Alan said he needed me to come in and help this other songwriter on a bridge. So I did. The damn cameras were right there when I pulled up. The next day I was all over social media, and I knew y'all saw it. There was no way you didn't."

"Fox, I don't—"

I started to say that I didn't care about any of that, that Mountain View didn't care about any of that, but he kept talking.

"When Phoenix accused me of plagiarism, everybody believed him. People I'd known for twenty years believed him, Alan believed him, my—Helena—she believed him. My whole world disappeared. I couldn't let that happen this time. I told myself I'd come back to Mountain View when I was through writing for Alan. I meant what I told you—Mountain View is my home. But now, it's just like Nashville all over again, except this time it's the truth. I'm a liar."

"No one thinks that, Fox. Everyone saw the news. They know you didn't steal those lyrics." I started to get up, to move toward him, but something stopped me.

"That ain't what I'm talking about," he growled, his tone pushing me back into the cushion. "I let y'all believe I was a normal blue-collar guy, just like every other man in Mountain View, only I'm not, am I? I'm a wealthy musician who ran from a scandal, but that ain't the worst of it." He fisted his hands. "When everything happened here those years ago, I got in my truck and I drove south. I didn't know where the hell I was going, but I ended up in Mountain View to see Mr. Robinson's town. And then, on my way out, I was driving down Main when I saw Fox's Hardware Store for sale, and you know, it triggered a memory of when I was eleven years old. Mama was going through an old trunk of hers and handed me the one letter she had from my real daddy a few weeks after they met in Myrtle Beach. She never wrote him back."

I couldn't breathe.

"I read the letter once and tore it up because Phoenix kept calling me a bastard, saying our daddy wasn't really mine even though he'd adopted me. After that, I never gave my biological dad much thought. But when I saw Fox's Hardware for sale that day, I thought maybe it was fate, because the only things I remembered about that letter was that he told her he'd just bought a hardware store in his little town, and his name—Fox Ryan. I bought the store, thinking I could learn more about the father I'd never known and start fresh. He never knew about me."

I must have gasped, because Fox's face hardened.

"I lied to you. I lied to everyone. It's inexcusable," he said. "I told myself I couldn't say anything about me being Mr. Ryan's son. I thought it might change how the town thought of him and that wouldn't be fair. But I should've come clean about everything."

I couldn't look away from him. None of these things changed who he was. None of these things changed how I felt about him.

"The way you're looking at me right now," Fox said. I watched him swallow. "Is the same way Helena looked at me after Phoenix told her I'd stolen his lyrics." He downed the rest of his whisky. "I've missed you every second I've been gone. I've wanted you since you first walked into my store to meet Annie that night. And I've . . . I've loved you since we danced that day in the barn. But I lied to you, Snow."

I stood and walked toward him, then sat on his lap and took his head in my hands.

"I'm not Helena," I said. "No one—not me, not anyone else, thinks you're a liar." I ran my thumb across his face, and his hands pulled me close. I could feel his heart against mine, the way his embrace enveloped me and warmed me through. "Mr. Fox was just like you. He was kind, the heart of the town. He would have been proud to know you were his. Mountain View would be proud too."

Fox's eyes filled, but he blinked the emotion away.

"I've heard what you said, but I love you all the same," I said. "And I want you to come home. I don't know how long it'll be there, but—"

Fox's lips met mine before I could finish. He tasted like whisky and as I opened my mouth to his, I turned and wrapped my legs around him. He gripped my hips, and I deepened the kiss, his tongue sweeping mine. His hands palmed up my thighs, pushing the hem of my dress to my waist.

"I love you," he said, kissing my neck. I whispered his name, and he brought my mouth to his again. My body trembled. "I'll come home with you," he said, his tone raspy. "Just as soon as we're finished here."

CHAPTER TWENTY-SIX

"Snow."

Fox's voice nudged me awake. I breathed deep and stretched. Daddy's truck smelled like coffee. I reached across the center console to Fox's hand. He took it and smiled. I knew we were close to home. I'd fallen asleep only a half hour or so into the drive, but a while back I'd stirred when the whir of the interstate gave way to the hush of a two-lane and the bright highway lights faded to the moon.

"Look up there."

I sat up from my slouched position and squinted down the dim road. At first, all I could see was the old McDonald's arches and the shadow of the high school as we passed Main's dead end on Route 2. But then I saw what Fox did. Cars and trucks were parked along the side of the road as far as the eye could see.

"It's Friday," I said. "I completely forgot. I just left. It's past eleven. Mama and Daddy have got to be beside themselves. Then again, Daddy didn't say a word when I called to tell him I was almost to Nashville, and they know these nights are late."

"Then they've got it under control," Fox said. "I guess that means they were okay with you coming to get me?"

I squeezed his hand. "I told you everyone in this town loves you."

"I hope you're right." He sighed. "I know I've got to go back to Nashville to get my truck and all, and I'll have to go help Tommy lay down these tracks when he's off tour, but I don't ever want to call another place home again. I hope to God the Armstrongs can convince the state to take them up on their land."

Fox cranked the window down and breathed in the country air. I did too—the fresh cut grass, the wildflower blooms, the loamy undertone of river.

"Fox," I started, then stopped. "I mean . . . I've been calling you Fox, but I know it's not really your name. I know it's Bond, but . . ."

He laughed and pulled the truck onto our drive between a dually truck and a jacked-up El Camino.

"I don't really care what you call me as long as you love me," he said. "And I don't hate my real name. But I've grown fond of Fox."

"Okay." I leaned over and kissed his cheek. He stopped the truck in front of Daddy who was sitting behind the ticket table where the path leading to the house met the drive. The sound of Tosha's voice and loud cheering spilled from the barn. Something about all of this—Fox beside me, my daddy being well, Tosha being appreciated for her art—as quirky as it was—all of these people coming to Mountain View to play music like Mr. Robinson had always dreamed made my heart settle. Maybe tomorrow they'd plow down our house and the barn too, but they couldn't take this moment.

When Daddy saw his truck, he walked over.

"Well, look what the cat drug in." He clapped Fox on the back when he reached us. "How does it feel to drive a real truck?"

Daddy grinned, and Fox smiled back.

"Why are you asking? Are you giving me this one?"

Daddy chuckled. "Nope. But I probably owe it to you. If it wasn't for you helping us with all of this," he waved his hand toward the barn, "we'd be sunk." People spilled out of the doors and onto the lawn, their hands lifted high, enjoying the music. "And then there's the matter of you coming back with my little girl when I knew these last weeks that that's all she really wanted."

"Well, Mr. Norwood. She's all I've wanted for some time too."

Fox looked at me, and I smiled. "Thanks for letting me borrow your truck, Daddy."

"You're welcome. Drive it down into the field and park it next to Robinson's, won't you, Fox? An old Cobalt just left and that place should be open. There ain't any other spots." He surveyed the field. "And while you're down there, y'all might want to check in. Helen Sue's been peddling some new cocktail she came up with using Cletus's moonshine. You never know how that'll go."

"You can say that again," Fox said. "At least there ain't much glass down there."

"That's right," Daddy said as a car pulled up behind us. "Now get on."

Daddy tapped the front of the truck and Fox steered it down the drive, skirting girls in fringe jackets and jean skirts. When he pulled the truck beside Mr. Robinson's and stopped, he looked out the window at the rusted cab. My gaze followed his to the place where I'd first realized love and the place I'd realized I'd let my first love go. Fox turned to me.

"Are you sure?"

He didn't have to spell it out for me. I knew what he was asking. I stared at him, past the forest green eyes and soft lips and strong body to the soul of the man who held my heart.

"Yes," I said. "He taught me how to love, but I love you."
Fox leaned over the console and kissed me.

"When we get in there, do you mind if I get on stage and talk to the town for a second? I think I owe them that."

"Of course not," I said.

He got out of the truck and came around to open my door, then took my hand. We walked across the grass and into the barn.

It was hot, the place crushed with sweating bodies, most holding a clear cup filled with a blue liquid I was guessing was Mama's cocktail. A bluegrass band that must have followed Tosha was on stage.

"I'll hop up there when these guys are done," Fox said. He squeezed my hand, and I stood on my tiptoes and looked around for Mama. She wasn't behind the bar. Maybe she'd gone up to the house to whip up a new batch of her drink.

As I scanned the crowd, I noticed many strangers, but pretty much the whole town was there too. Dolly was in a pink sequin Barbie dress in the dead center of the crowd next to Annie, who had slipped out of her mayoral uniform to don a fitted black dress. A dozen teenagers stood next to them. At the very front of the crowd, Sterling held his disco lights up, casting green and blue and red beams on the ceiling while Vern bobbed his head to the music, his wispy mullet floating in the intermittent breeze. Toward the back of the barn, a group of the Melodies gathered—Bobby Jo in her fall applique vest, Belinda with her cowboy hat perched atop her beehive, Tammy wearing her George Strait concert T-shirt from the '90s. The picture of George Strait made me think about the first time I'd heard Fox sing.

"Sometime I want you to sing—" I started to tell him that I wanted him to sing me "I Can Still Make Cheyenne," but just then a guy in a slouchy button-down and distressed jeans pushed through the crowd to where we stood at the edge of the stage.

"Bond. Hey, man."

Fox's eyes brightened, and he let go of my hand to take this guy's. I recognized him from other weeks.

"Jason Conley? What are you doing here? I haven't seen you in forever."

"Since you won that Grammy for *Polaroids*."

"Sounds about right." Fox clapped the guy on the back. "How've you been?"

"Good, good. I've come down here a couple of times and found some great raw talent." Jason paused. "I thought you were back in Nashville."

"I was until a few hours ago, but Nashville ain't home anymore, man. I'm finishing the rest of Sutton's album from here." Fox glanced at me. "This is my . . . uh . . . my girlfriend, Hattie." He hesitated on the title, a question on his face. I smiled at Fox and held my hand toward Jason.

"Nice to meet you."

"You too," Jason said. "I heard you're the mastermind behind all of this."

"She is," Fox said. "And Jason's a talent scout for Mercury."

"I'm sorry to hear y'all are in limbo about this place's future," Jason said. "Everybody loved Mr. Robinson, and these open mics have been a gold mine for us scouts recently."

"Thanks," I said. "We're hoping by some miracle we'll get to keep it."

On stage, the bluegrass band said their farewells.

"Excuse me," Fox said to Jason. He nodded toward the stage. "I've got to say something real quick."

"Sounds great. I've got to catch this group anyway. Hey," Jason lunged for the lead singer of the bluegrass band as he pushed into the crowd, and I stayed where I was at the foot of the steps. I liked the view from here. I could see everyone I loved. I could see the joy this place, the music, painted on people's faces, and if I listened really hard, I could hear the sound of Mr. Robinson's voice. *"Well, isn't this fine, Hattie."*

Fox tapped the microphone and the crowd silenced. Some people gasped.

"I'm going to get right to it, folks. Y'all gave me a home, and I wasn't honest with you. I didn't talk about my past, but omitting the truth is the same as lying in my book. Y'all know now that my brother, Phoenix, lied about me plagiarizing those songs, but that ain't what I'm up here to clear up."

You could've heard a pin drop. I looked at the people looking at Fox. No one was red-faced or angry—in fact, most were smiling. That was the thing about a small town—in good ones, everybody was family.

"When I first visited Mountain View, I was looking for a fresh start, just like the Robinsons all those years ago. I didn't think that start was here, though, until I drove down Main and passed the hardware store." He cleared his throat. "My daddy wasn't my daddy by blood. I always knew that, but I'd only seen one letter from my biological father to my mama, and I knew he didn't know about me."

"You're Fox's boy," Sterling shouted. He was grinning ear to ear. "We all knowed it from the minute we saw you. You'd have to be blind as a bat not to see the resemblance. If there was such a thing as cloned humans, you'd be his."

Shock painted Fox's face.

"Fox may not have *known* known, but I think he did deep down," Bobby Jo hollered from the back. "Right before he got real bad sick, he said he'd had a dream about a boy that looked like him walking into his store. He told me I might think he was crazy, and I did until I saw you."

Goosebumps prickled my arms.

"Why didn't y'all ever say anything?" Fox asked.

"Us old folks kept it to ourselves," Vern said, wrapping his arm around Sterling. "Plus, it ain't our business. You said you had a daddy and it wasn't our place to say that maybe he wasn't the only one."

"You coming back home?" Tammy yelled.

Fox swallowed hard, and then he smiled. "Yeah."

My heart felt like it could burst. The crowd erupted then, and Fox started to walk off stage, but Sterling caught his ankle and said something that made him stop.

"Alright, so Sterling here has requested a song. And although I ain't got a guitar, maybe one of you will lend me yours?" Fox nodded toward a group of young guys in matching white cowboy hats.

The tallest of them, sporting micro dreads pulled back in a ponytail, pushed quickly through the crowd and handed his guitar to Fox.

"Thanks, man," Fox said, fitting the strap over his shoulders. He adjusted the microphone and then strummed the guitar once. "I think I'll play a new one tonight. I wrote it about a month ago up in my apartment downtown. It's about a girl that stole my heart, a Miss Hattie Norwood." He paused and looked at me. The crowd whistled and cheered.

Fox started to play. The tune was slow and simple, the sort that stirred you. I watched his fingers on the frets. They moved effortlessly. They'd moved over my body the same way, as though he'd been born knowing how to love me.

The crowd shifted, and I watched as Annie turned away, pushing through the crush toward the door. My spirits fell. I hoped she'd been honest with me about not having feelings for Fox. I hoped the song didn't break her heart, that it wasn't the reason she was leaving.

> I ain't used to sunshine
> Sons of hollers don't wash in light
> When I saw you glowing in that midnight
> I knew you'd never be mine.

My fingers balled into my palms as the deep timbre of his voice wavered over me.

But I'll settle for two hours of light, dear,
I'll settle for two hours of your face
You ain't mine, but I've got your shine
to carry me through the day.

Every word wrung my heart. I recalled the near misses—the touches, the kisses, the words we said. They were exactly what he said they were—glimmers of light.

When he was done playing, I walked up the steps and across the stage toward him as the guests clapped and cheered. Dolly whistled, the shrill come-home-for-dinner whistle her mama had always done.

"Guess you were wrong about me never being yours," I said when I reached him. I wrapped my arms around his shoulders and kissed him.

"Guess I was." He grinned.

"So next time—"

"Sorry to interrupt, lovebirds!" Annie's voice ricocheted over us, and she pushed through the crowd, holding up her phone. Her face looked like she'd just won the lottery, not like a person whose heart was broken by seeing me and Fox together.

She climbed on the stage. "Good to have you back, friend," she said to Fox, then clasped my hand and smiled.

Annie snatched the microphone from the stand and then, as though a light switch had been flipped, she started to sob. I walked toward her, but she waved me off. In the back of the room, I noticed Mama had returned to the bar with another enormous pitcher of her blue cocktail.

"It's over," Annie cried into the microphone.

The barn silenced. Fox's hand curled around mine. At once, I felt dizzy, like the walls might close in. I reached for Fox's arms to steady myself, and vaguely heard him tell me it was going to be okay.

"The Carolina Panthers," Annie said through her tears, "will be building their new home on the Armstrongs' farm in Cardinal River."

A collective gasp rang out through the crowd.

"What?" someone said loudly.

"Mountain View will not be touched." Annie sniffed, then suddenly reverted to her earlier merriment. She held up her phone. "Alfred Moore just called from Columbia."

Sterling let out a loud whoop, and the noise jarred everyone from their shock. People started kissing and screaming and crying like it was D-Day.

Fox pulled the guitar from his shoulders, tipped me back, and kissed me hard.

"I can hardly believe it," I said, a little breathless.

I looked out at the crowd of my neighbors, my family, and at once thought of how adamant I'd been that the stadium was the right choice, that I belonged somewhere far away from this backward little town.

"Remember when I told you that you could do remarkable things right here?" Fox's face was alight with the news. "Look what you've done. These events saved this place. I know I didn't know them, but I'd think the Robinsons would be proud."

"We did this together." I grinned at him, and he kissed my forehead.

Someone started chanting "Long live Mountain View!" And, as I joined in, as Fox pulled me close, I knew I was exactly where I was meant to be.

ACKNOWLEDGMENTS

First, foremost, and always, thank you, Jesus, for the gift of stories and for imagination. When I write, I get a little tiny glimpse of how you might write each of our stories and I'm grateful.

I got the idea for this book when I was on book tour in Wardensville, West Virginia, a few years ago. After my talk, my mom and I went to the most amazing barn party with a fantastic bluegrass band on a perfect late summer night, and after, I knew I wanted to write a book that captured that same dreamy energy. Thank you to Marlene and Tom England of WordPlay for inviting me to your beautiful town!

Thank you to my fantastic agent, Kate McKean, for the encouragement, the listening, the sharpening, the cheering on. You're the best!

I'm the luckiest author in the world because somehow I get to work with the most enthusiastic, fun team at Alcove Press! Jess Verdi—you are sunshine incarnate and have guided this book to becoming exactly what I dreamed it would be. Thankful for you! Thank you also to Rebecca

Nelson, Thai Fantauzzi Perez, Monica Manzo, Dulce Botello, Mikaela Bender, Cassidy Graham, Stephanie Manova, Megan Matti, Doug White, Matt Martz, and Heather VenHuizen for the countless things you've done to support this book. I'm so grateful!

Forever thankful to my author buddies who understand this beautiful, weird writing life. Couldn't do it without you, Kimberly Brock, Marybeth Whalen, Kim Wright, Erika Montgomery, Cheyenne Campbell, Kristy Woodson Harvey, Jenni Walsh, Meagan Church, Adele Myers, Vanessa Miller, Sarah McCoy, Leslie Hooten, Sarah Henning, Erika Robuck, Melissa Ferguson, Brooke Lea Foster, Annabel Monaghan, Michelle Gable, Rachel McMillan, Meredith Jaeger, Aimie Runyan, Wade Rouse, Yvette Corporon, Heather Webb, Eliza Knight, Lauren Edmondson, Camille Di Maio, Mary Kay Andrews, Madeline Martin, Heather Bell Adams, Amy Jo Burns, Lauren Denton, Kimmery Martin, Sarah Loudin Thomas, Kristy Cambron, and Taylor Brown.

Thanks to my best friends who are always there for me and make my life so much fun! Love you, Maggie Tardy, Mindy Ferguson, Christine Scott, Carolyn Lux, Jessica Shanks, Julie Cribb, Julie Barfield, Katie Gignac, Kristin Conway, Michelle Cowan, Arden McLaughlin, Ronni Bishop, Courtney Joyce, Jodie Bolowitz, Katie Burgess, Kasey Fisher, Krisha Chachra, Jamie Harrington, Joy Haser, Hollie Hogan, Laura McKnight, Sanghee Ku, Megan Fair, Kizzie Kincer, Gracemarie Bartle, Liz Moore Powell, Katie Pesta, Megan Maloney, Angie Quigley, Jen Price, Amelia McGirt, Amanda Shanks, Britt Stiling, Thuvan Cordero, Megan McCarthy, Elaine Ulery, Sarah Ward, Rudy Saunders, Stacy McLaughlin, Merriweather Franklin, Kitty Hurdle, Becky Chavaree, Janet Zylstra, Kay Houser, Loraine Tolliver, and Pat Brooks.

Authors and booksellers have a special bond. We wouldn't be able to exist without each other, and I'm thankful to have found bookseller friends that are like family! Thank you to Olivia Meletes-Morris and Wendy Meletes of Litchfield Books, Sally Brewster, Sherri Smith, Halli Gomez, Jamie Brewster of Park Road Books, Alison Sheridan of Cleary's Bookstore, Kimberly Daniels Taws of the Country Bookshop, Gary Parkes and Karen Schwettman of Foxtale Bookshoppe, Sharon Davis of Book Bound, Maggie Robe of Flyleaf Books, Lisa Lee Swope of Bookmarks, Jen Sherman of Bookish Cedar Creek, Stephanie Crowe of Page & Palette, Sue Lucey of Page 158, Shaye Gadomski, Micheline Johnson and David Craddock of New Chapter Books, Ashley Warlick, Alyssa Fikse, and Beth Johnson of M. Judson Books, Tina Greene-Bevington of Bay Books, Lady Vowell Smith of the Snail on the Wall, Andrea Jasmin and Adah Fitzgerald of Main Street Books, Keebee Fitch of McIntyre's Books, Jill Hendrix of Fiction Addiction, Justin Souther of Malaprop's Bookstore, Dawn Miller of Pelican Bookstore, Dawn Nolan and Dawn Hylbert of Cicada Books, Dan Carlisle of Taylor Books, Anne-Marie Johnson of Books-A-Million Beckley, Matt Browning and Brian Mann of Plot Twist Books, Ashley Skeen and Mandee Cunningham of Booktenders, Sedley Abercrombie of Pig City Books, Leslie Logeman of Highland Books, Marlene England of WordPlay, and Stephanie VanAlmen of So Much More to the Story.

I am absolutely, positively indebted to the editors, writers, book clubs, bookstagrammers, reviewers, and book lovers who read, champion, and love my stories! Thank you, Adam Rathe, Annissa Armstrong, Bubba Wilson, Laura Beth Vietor, Linda Burrell, Dawn Fowler, Cassie Bustamante, Ashley Hasty, Ron Block, Ashley Kaufman, Martha

Yesowitch, JJ Holshouser, Caroline Sanders Clements, Isabelle Eyman, Francene Katzen, Ashley Blank, Molly Neville, Lisa Harrison, Brenda Gardner, Lysette House, Cristina Reely, Krista Hall, Valerie Souders, Nicole Fincher, Reca Porter, Christine Mott, Tammi Tremblay, Andrea Lowry, Anna Kate, Melanie Highsmith, Nancy Betler, Samantha Gross, Laura Murray, Amanda Anson, Cindy Jones, Ashley Curran, Sarah Floyd, Alex Dudich, Renee Blankenship, Tamara Welch, Terilynn Knezek, Ana Raquel, Jayda Justus, Noelle Dunn, Nina Sumner, Dallas Strawn, Harris Murray, Phyllis Mahoney, Julie Chan, Betsy Asplund, Mary Hudome, Debby Cooperman Stone, Barbara Luffman, Lanie Wood, Angel Cinco, Barbara Khan, Beyond the Pages Book Club, Bookbonders Book Club, Friends & Fiction Book Club, the Queens University Friends of the Library, and many, many more I'm accidentally leaving out here.

Thank you to my family, who has always encouraged me to live my dreams—Lynn and Fred Wilkerson, Jed, Hannah, Reece and Davis Wilkerson, Gran Lee Ballard, Momma Sandra Wilkerson, Diannah, Johnny, and Jeremy Callaway, Josh, Bethany, Elise, and Mady Callaway, Cindy Hanna, Bill Sothern, Samantha Hanna, Jamie, Jancis, Porter, and Maeve Hanna, Jim Wilkerson, John Auge, Bill Ballard, Janine Hopkins, Blair and Zach Markell, Davis Ballard, Maggie, Drew, Ava, and Claire Tardy, Sarah and Richard Gotlieb, Lori and Randy Musil, Keith, Brittany, and Rhett Musil, Jeremy Musil, Ryan Musil, Becky Callaway, and Alice Jean Gauldin.

Finally, words can't express how thankful I am for my little family, John, Alevia, and John. You are my best story come true. Thanks for always cheering me on.